CW00487154

WINTER OVERRUN

LOST TIME: BOOK FOUR

DAMIEN BOYES

WINTER OVERRUN

Lost Time: Book Four

Copyright © 2018 by Damien Boyes.
All rights reserved. With the exception of excerpts for
review purposes, no part of this book may be reproduced,
stored in a retrieval system, or transmitted in any form or by
any means, electronic, mechanical, photocopying,
recording, or otherwise, without the prior written
permission of the copyright owner.

Proofreading by Tamara Blain.
Cover by Wadim Kashin.

PUBLICATION HISTORY
eBook 1ˢᵗ edition / July 2018
Print 1ˢᵗ edition / July 2018

This is a work of fiction. Any similarity between the
characters and situations within its pages and places or
persons, living or dead, is unintentional and coincidental.
Obviously.

ISBN: 978-0-9950464-4-3

THANKS_

Mom and Dad, for everything you do.
Alex Sayapov for talking through some rough spots.
Tamara Blain for finding plot holes and typos.
Wadim Kashin for bringing my world to life.
To Jacob and Josh for the constant distraction.
And to Maryellen, who makes this all possible.

To you reading this, and to everyone who reached out to me over the past years, I appreciate your interest, your feedback and kind words. I hope you'll continue to stick with me cause I have lots more stories to tell.
As always, if you have any questions or comments, you can email me at damien@damienboyes.com

PART ONE_

WINTER'S RISE

WINTER'S STOMACH IS TWISTED, his head fuzzy. His unfamiliar body leaks sweat in the thick night air. This is his third night hunting, the third night in a row without a prize —and the last night he can risk inhabiting this skyn.

It has to be tonight.

He tenses, tries to still thoughts that rattle around in his mind, that pound on the inside of his skull as though his Cortex has somehow come imbalanced. It's at these times he's almost thankful for his condition—for the cold void yawning in his head. For his *lack*. If he were the same as everyone else he'd have given up by now, broken by the weight of the incessant fear and crushing anxiety of what he's planning to do.

Most people would have deserted by now, but luckily for him, he doesn't feel fear. Doesn't feel anxiety. Doesn't feel anything at all. Which makes his job much easier, relatively speaking.

Tonight he's going to kill someone—if only he can find the right target.

He's chosen this waterfront path as his hunting

grounds, concluded it possesses the greatest potential for success. It's secluded, a strip of forested trails crisscrossing between the Docklands—a once future-city that's now mostly converted to body locker warehouses—and the lake to the south. The paths are dark, lit only by the blue light of the moon. They were designed as a refuge from the incessant glow of the city, and this time of night the only people who come here are reszo.

The digitally restored don't tend to wander far from the heart of Reszlieville, where their party never ends, but the Docklands have become a popular haunt for reszos too. There's always someone around, neglected skyns pulled from stasis and lumbered out for the recommended period of physical activity. Even people who've all but abandoned their bodies to live like gods on the virt mesh still need to the occasional exercise.

They emerge, logy from their virtual kingdoms, shuffling stiff-legged, to treat themselves to some chew time or simply remind themselves what it feels like to have blood pumping through their veins. They'll be weak, dazzled by the fog of reality, readjusting to a body they haven't worn in weeks or even months, and easy to subdue if his initial strike should somehow miss a killing blow. The resistance should be minimal. Ideal prey.

His plan is sound, his precautions exhaustive—why then can't he simply pick someone and be done with it?

A couple approaches, arm in arm. Winter's pulse rises, his hearing flattens to a high-pitched whine. They see him, but don't register him as a threat. His skyn is blandly handsome. Unremarkable. Just another reszo out for a stroll.

They won't be suspecting it. The male, maybe he's a bithead. It's hard to tell, even in the bright moonlight. They're both attractive, move with the casual grace of immortals, but there's two of them. His plan doesn't include multiple targets.

They pass, and he doesn't alter his stride. Soft footsteps on pavement fade into the darkness behind him.

Winter's body vibrates with tension. He might not feel fear, but he has no desire to be caught. An impulsive choice could set him back months. SecNet is everywhere, knows everything, can retrace people's movements back in time for weeks—where they went, who they talked to, how long they sat on the toilet, and what they ate based on what came out.

This means he needs to be careful. Very careful. He's about to cut a stranger's head off. Not just cut it off, but pry into the target's mind. Hack the skull, then the Cortex firewalls to get at the pure coded thought within. The rithm. Memories.

Emotions.

This is what he desires more than anything else: to feel something, *something real.* No more tainting his thoughts with crude, AI-generated simulacrums of pride or passion, or home-rolled code impersonating a fleeting moment of joy. He's tried them all. They're ephemeral, don't stick. Nothing will do but the real thing, and for that he needs a mind, an active rithm running on a Cortex.

And for that he needs a head. Just a simple head. Why is that so hard?

Another man approaches. This one?

He's alone, not too big, neck a good height for the swing. Winter checks around him with side to side flicks of his eyes, doesn't alter his gait.

No physical witnesses. A green glow in the corner of his eye shows he's clear of SecNet's unrelenting vision. SecNet is usually everywhere. A network of various police and city and military and Union sensors. Personal devices capturing

feeds in real time and DroneSense watching through a
million individual points in the sky. Normally there's
nothing in the city that goes unnoticed, but the system of
trails was designed as a haven from the constant hum of the
city, from the ubiquitous EM fields permeating everything.
SecNet has no presence here.

And even if an image of his biokin is caught—be it by a
stray drone or a target's personal feed device—he's wearing
an untraceable body, bought custom from a backdoor
fleshmith. It'll trigger a null result in SecNet. He's
completely anonymous.

That is itself a problem, and the reason he needs to act
tonight. He doesn't know how much longer he can rely on
the shield of anonymity. This is his third night out, he can't
escape the cameras indefinitely. Enough null hits and
SecNet will become interested in the unregistered skyn and
alert a lawbot or constable to investigate.

He doesn't have much time left.

He can't wait for the perfect moment anymore. This has
to be the one.

As the distance between them closes, he goes through
the rehearsed motions in his mind. Twitch his wrist to
release the collapsible blade concealed in his loose-fitting
jacket, call out a wordless shout, and when the target hesitates, slice through his neck with one swift, powerful swing.
He envisions the blade as it severs skin and bone, cuts the
diganic connection between flesh and machine, then passes
clean through the other side, severing the head.

He understands the irony. Knows his lack of fear and
revulsion and remorse makes it easier to use a surgical-sharp
tool to decapitate an unsuspecting victim and carve a slice
out of his thoughts. He knows it will be unpleasant for both
of them.

He doesn't want to, but there's no alternative.

With the Cortex exposed he'll have only moments to tie in, syphon out a snapshot of the target's mind, and pass the coded thought through a relay of rented drones running deep-encryption protocols. He'll take as much as he can, but he can't stay long. Even under the best of circumstances, with no nearby witnesses or passing bots, and if he's able to crack the target's cortical security, he'll only have a few moments to grab whatever he can.

He won't actually be copying the target's mind, as much as he'd like to. With a full rithm at his disposal he could analyze and unpack the coded engrams at his leisure, not just briefly graze through the target's moment-to-moment consciousness. But he doesn't have time for that. He's fairly certain he can hack the external firewalls, the ones that let the rithm in and out of the body through the combined senses and external link port, but it'd take hours to crack the second set of protection that secures the target's neural pattern. He'll have to settle for a tap of the active thoughts. A snapshot. Playback only.

He knows the target's thoughts will be distasteful. There'll be horror. Shock. Pain. After all, his head will have just been severed in a brutal random attack. But even terror is better than the numb buzz Winter feels now.

It won't be much, but it'll be enough.

It has to be.

Winter tenses, readies himself, and at the last second notices the light leaking from the target's eyes. Lenzs. He's live, transmitting his view of the world out to the link. There could be thousands of people watching, or no one at all, but still the risk is too great.

The chance passes and Winter nearly cries out as his body shakes with need.

He can't wait any longer. Now. *It has to be now.*

Winter's considering the risks of extending the hunt to a fourth night when he hears footsteps, light but rhythmic. A jogger. Ahead, around a bend in the path. He emerges a moment later, running up the path bare chested, dark skin glistening in the moonlight. He's wearing thin black shoes and skintight shorts that hug his hips. He's all muscle, probably revved, and not remotely virt-dulled. He's not an optimal target by any means, but Winter can't wait anymore.

They catch eyes in the gloom. Winter doesn't immediately look away, and they share a moment of unspoken connection. He knows this makes him appear trustworthy, two ordinary humans passing congenially in the night.

The target won't be suspecting. This is his chance. This is what he's been waiting for.

He's practiced, knows the strike. The footwork. The follow-through.

The target is only steps away.

There is no alternative.

With two seconds to contact Winter twitches his wrist, releasing the blade silently down his arm, depositing the grip in his palm.

One more step, and as the target passes Winter plants his left foot, reaches back with the blade jutting from his right hand, and swings as hard as he can, using the considerable power in his torso and shoulder to deliver maximum impact.

He's mid-swing when the target sees the blade and reacts, tries to twist away, lifts his arms up in protection.

The blade severs the target's arms mid-forearm, which slows the blow enough that the swing misses his throat, catches him instead under the chin and lodges itself in his jaw.

Not an ideal outcome.

The target screams something, a wet gurgle of pain and rage and confusion as Winter yanks the blade free. Blood pours down his torso, streams from his stumps, but he's still on his feet, and the confusion doesn't last long. He can't fight, but he can run.

He nearly gets away.

Why does the world make everything so hard?

The target stumbles and gives Winter the chance to swing the blade once more. The tip catches his Achilles tendon and the target flops head over heels with the next step, rolls, and somehow lands back up on his good leg and hops away, moaning and gurgling all the while.

This isn't how it was supposed to work.

The target will likely have sounded an alarm in his head. The drones will be coming, the police not far behind.

Winter spins and pursues the target as he bounces away on one leg. This needs to end. Now.

He grips the blade tighter and launches himself after the target. It isn't difficult to catch the hopping man, and Winter sprints right past and takes his head off from behind in a single, powerful swing. The body collapses and the head falls and rolls a short distance away. Helpless eyes glare at Winter as life quickly drains away.

The night grows eerily still. He doesn't hear sirens. The skyn was likely registered, and Second Skyn will already know about the trauma. But he has time.

Winter uses the blade's edge to scrape the bottom of the Cortex clean of viscera, rinses it with the flask of water he's carried with him, toggles the Cortex's interface seal open, inserts a probe, and initiates the connection. Then his specially trained AI goes to work.

Winter can only wait now. Wait for the encryption-cracking entity to either pierce the cortical firewalls or fail. The entity wasn't cheap, but it came with assurances. The best code this side of military, his supplier had claimed. If he's to be trusted—

The AI reports back green nearly instantly, and the unexpectedly efficient result convulses Winter's spine.

Success.

He's studied the human mind in great detail, he knows what he should be feeling now, if he could. If he *did*. He knows it would be excitement.

Relief.

Anticipation.

Winter initiates the transfer and begins streaming the jogger's still-racing thoughts over a series of rented drones to an encrypted file in an anonymous body locker where his primary skyn is waiting, free from any potential record of involvement.

His work is almost done.

His mouth floods with saliva. Reminds him that, even though he may have a prosthetic mind, deep down, he's still an animal.

He sets the probe to continue streaming for five minutes. He'll never get that much, of course. Second Skyn will perform a remote shut down long before then.

The head goes in the lake, probe and all. It'll keep transmitting from the bottom. Next he unstraps the blade from his arm, tosses it out as far as he can throw it. He goes in after it, takes a running dive, swims out two hundred meters and lets himself sink, like he's falling into a warm bath. He blows out the air from his lungs and falls into the blackness

WINTER   11

until the pressure in his ears becomes uncomfortable, then he cuts the connection. Eventually someone will find the skyns—the victim and an untraceable black market scafe job —but nothing will trace them back to him.

He's done it.

He's won.

When he opens his eyes he's back in his own skyn, nestled safely in the medpod, just as he left it. He thinks the pod open and it hisses quietly as the seals pop and the systems cycle. He rises and walks two shaky steps to the wall, where a notification is flashing. A file has been received.

A file one minute and seven seconds long.

Sixty-seven seconds of pure feeling.

He takes his cuff from its cradle on the single shelf in the room, sits himself down on the narrow bench, affixes it to the port on the back of his neck, and loads the file straight to the workshop in his headspace. He extracts the compressed thought, harnesses it with code lattice that'll remove the emotions from their context and help graft them into the holes in his mind. It takes a moment for the conversion, and he sits completely still until it's ready.

Once it's done, he doesn't hesitate.

There's a rush—

—then bright bursts behind his eyes so vivid he thinks he's dying. A side effect of the injection, a bad reaction corrupting his rhythm, unraveling his pattern...

But no. This isn't death. Not at all.

He feels alive. *Alive.* Maybe for the first time in his life.

His mind is aflame, a riot of pure emotion. This is what his target felt at the moment his head was removed.

First comes what must be fear, a stark, all-encompassing dread that fills his gut. Winter has never in his life imagined his mind capable of such depth. His head swims at the sudden breadth of awareness, at the scope of it, at the unfathomable void of potential experience he now knows is waiting for him.

A spiked undulation roils through his belly. His eyes well and he sobs, a sound he's never made before: guttural and raw, as if from a dying animal.

But there's more. Anger. Revulsion. Frustration. It's endless, and he wants to feel it all.

Even as tears spill down his cheeks, even as his chest heaves in misery, his lips spread in a rictus grin. He's so overcome with the power of his feeling he can't help but revel in it. In the pain. The suffering.

Does everyone feel like this? Is this what it means to be human?

He laughs. Another first: an honest, spontaneous laugh. A laugh that shudders through his body like an electric current, energizing him.

Laughter. How could he ever have lived without it?

He knows the grafted emotions will soon fade, that eventually his mind will return to the frozen expanse of cold rationality, and that it will take dozens, maybe hundreds, of injected rithms to make these emotions permanent, but still he's elated.

It worked.

He knows what he has to do now. He'll never go back to the way he was. It's only a matter of time: soon, he'll be whole.

Just like everyone else.

THE SUN's no more than a frozen ball in the sky, dusting the blue line of the horizon with a fine crystal mist. I'm perched next to a small black hole in the sheet ice that stretches out over the ocean farther than I can see. Behind me there's only endless rock and snow. White-topped mountains cut me off from the world.

Nothing lives here, nothing could. This is a dead place.

Luckily, this life's almost over, and soon I'll be dead too.

Actually, I'm looking forward to it.

Not that anyone's asked, but I don't know if I could explain why I need to keep coming back here. Maybe it's the austerity of the landscape, or the klicks of silence in every direction. The absolute solitude, just me and my thoughts...

Either way, right now, there's only one thing I know for sure: I refuse to spend my last hours slowly wasting away, not this time. Starving's miserable. It's painful and lasts forever.

I've spent time in the Arctic, the *real* Arctic. I was one of the soldiers caught up in the Incident at Alert during the war, or at least that's what they called it afterwards. But when we dropped in we had 100 kilos of gear supported by a cold weather exo-suit and the guarantee of regular resupply. Sure, we thought we were about to be invaded, but at least we had warm meals.

This is entirely different. I'm on my own out here, been living for weeks on what I scavenged from the wreckage of the plane—which wasn't much to begin with. I've been skirting the edge of death for days.

Thankfully I've finally stopped shivering, which means time is running low. My body's given up on trying to keep my extremities alive and is conserving its waning energy to keep my heart beating. It's one of death's small mercies I've come to appreciate: the less time you have, the more focused you become. This is when I feel the most still, the most at peace.

I've come to crave these last few hours before my body gives out, when the world narrows to a sharp point and there's nothing but my next breath—but the suffering it takes to get to these sweet moments of numbness got old a long time ago.

My arm quit trembling well before my body stopped shivering. I haven't felt anything past my shoulder for hours, but I can still see the tip of the rough spear in my peripheral vision. It still waits, motionless, poised over the black hole in the ice. Hopefully my muscles will be able to respond when I need them to or this will have all been for nothing. And even if they do still work I'll likely lose some fingers to frostbite. It's a shitty situation all around.

I'm not giving up, not yet. I've got an hour of sunlight left, maybe a little more, but if a seal doesn't poke its nose up through the hole in the sea ice before the sun goes down, I'm going to take two steps forward and drop through the ice and into the ocean and let the frigid water take me. I'll bask in the chill for a few seconds as my body succumbs to shock, and revel in those empty moments of pure nothingness when everything resets and I'm once again back at the crash site. I'll have a fresh supply of rations and plenty of fuel for a fire. It won't be paradise but it'll be better than this.

I could use the break.

Death definitely has its allure, but as much as I've come to appreciate teetering on the edge, I still prefer my hands warm and my belly full.

Either way, I'll be happy for a change. The wind is daggers today. It shears across the open ice, slicing through the cheap arctic survival gear I found among the plane's wreckage. The insulated nylon shells were meant to keep downed survivors warm for a few hours, days at the most, not last for weeks of hard living.

Nothing I have is meant for long-term use—that's why I need to catch a seal. With a seal I get meat. With the meat I can survive while the leather cures. With the leather I can make a proper pair of boots, and with my feet dry maybe I can come up with a way to survive out here. Except I've been at this for days—I don't even know how many at this point, dozens stretched out over seven or eight runs—and haven't seen signs of a single seal at the air hole.

Other than the fish I caught on the second day, I've had nothing to eat but the emergency rations I stretched as far as they'd go, some tea made from what little lichen I could scrape from a nearby scrub of rock, and melted snow.

Thinking about food causes my brain to send the signal for my empty stomach to rumble, but it dies somewhere down my throat. My body knows it's starving, no use wasting the energy complaining about it anymore.

I risk a glance back at the sun, hoping a seal won't pop

up in the seconds while my eyes aren't fixed on the black circle at my feet. It's already fallen since I last checked, now nearly touching the ice. Days are mostly night up here, and this one's nearly up.

Somewhere in the distance the ice cracks like a bomb going off, and it reverberates under my feet a moment later. I turn instinctively toward the sound and a notice a black speck approaching across the ice. I squint behind my snow goggles and can barely make out the shape. It's getting bigger. A person.

Someone's coming.

But no one's allowed in here. That's the whole point. And I know I sure as hell didn't ack any visitors.

What's she up to?

I reengage my raised arm and it screams at me, drops to my side, and refuses to cooperate further. The spear falls out of my slack fingers and thuds in the powder at my feet. I won't be picking that up again.

I'm done.

The figure solidifies as it approaches. It's hurrying now, arms crossed over its chest. Whoever it is probably wasn't prepared to walk into the Arctic. The virt won't let them freeze to death, but they won't be comfortable while they're here. Which is fine with me. No one asked them in for a visit.

Another second passes. Then another. The wind scours dunes of frozen snow around my feet. I'd be angry if I wasn't relieved. Into the water it is.

I take a step toward the hole, but before I can take the plunge I recognize the figure by the way it's striding through the snow, as if on a reluctant mission: Shelt.

I haven't seen him for months—though I haven't seen anyone for months. Shelt took over Elder's transition counseling sessions out in the real world and has been pestering me with messages to come to one. He thinks I need help.

Up until now I've ignored the suggestions that maybe it would help to talk to someone. Both he and Connie won't shut up about it. What makes him think coming here in person is going to be any different?

I don't need help, I don't need to talk, I need to be alone. Locked away from the world, where I can't hurt anyone else.

I'm dangerous. I don't know what I'm capable of, but I know one thing: keeping my broken mind busy dying is all that's keeping the dark thoughts from creeping in—from getting out.

I can't let him get out again.

Shelt finally shuffles up to me and stops on the other side of the hole. He stamps his feet, raises his arm to his nose, and drags a line of mucus across his sleeve. I sometimes can't believe how real these simulations are.

"Why the shit is it so cold in here?" Shelt mutters. He crosses his arms and immediately starts trembling.

"I don't want to encourage visitors," I answer. "I don't even feel it anymore."

"That's the whole point, isn't it?" he says, jumping straight into it. "That's why you're here... You think freezing yourself solid is some kind of solution."

"Then you understand," I say and steel myself to take the plunge. The initial burst of cold will burn, but just for a second. It's all good after that.

"I don't understand shit," he replies and steps closer. Close enough he can finally smell me. His nose wrinkles so hard it jerks his head back. "Is that *you*?"

I shrug. "No toilets at the North Pole."

"Why are you doing this?" Shelt asks, visibly fighting

back a gag. I knew I smelled, but didn't realize quite how bad it was. Wearing the same clothes for a month probably has something to do with it. "You were doing so well—"

"After fighting off a rampaging artificial superintelligence that wanted me erased?" I say, reluctantly sticking to the lie that a rogue SI killed all those people, not a twisted version of my own mind in a series of stolen bodies. "Things change."

"Let me help," Shelt offers. "You're not alone out there."

"That's why I'm in *here*," I reply. "It's better for everyone."

"But why?" Shelt asks, confused. "What happened?"

He's concerned, wants to help. But I can't tell him, not after what I did. *What I am.*

I can't tell anyone.

I take a long look at the man standing impatiently in front of me, hands on his hips, lips screwed up, waiting for his answer. The virt assigned him a random avatar, his face could be anyone's, but the expression is pure Shelt. He's waiting for me to break down and spill my pent-up suffering, but I'd never do that to him.

"I just want to be alone," I say instead.

Another crack snaps in the ice, this time closer, and Shelt drops to his knees and covers his head with his hands as if someone's shooting at him. "What the hell was that?" Shelt cries as the boom echoes off the distant mountains.

"Ice. We're standing on the ocean."

Shelt looks down at the snow under him and leaps back to his feet, cups his hands over his mouth, and blows steam through his exposed fingers. "Why does it have to be so cold?" he asks.

I shrug. "It suits me."

Shelt trembles through a whole-body shudder. "Fine,

chitchat's over. I'll get to why I'm here. You may not want my help, but I need yours."

His words spark something inside me and I do my best to douse it before it flares. "I don't want to hear about another—"

"A girl is missing," Shelt interrupts. "A grassr. Ran away to Reszlieville and disappeared. Her brother found me. He's desperate. No one will help him."

"Call a cop," I reply.

He cocks his head at me, exasperated, and for a moment I catch a glimpse of the stimmed-up tweaker he was when I first met him. "You think we didn't try? She's a grassr, lived her whole life on the fringe of civilization. She's got no rep, there's no evidence she's in any danger. Puts her at the bottom of everyone's list."

"What do you expect me to do?" I ask, and take another glance down at oblivion through the hole in the ice.

"How about give a shit about something other than yourself."

That cuts a little close. "You and I both know what I went through. What I did for Dub. For Miranda and Tala. I stopped a goddamn SI and saved your goddamn life in the process, then spent every dime I had to get everyone back to their skyns..." Except it's all a lie and the truth is way worse.

"Sure," Shelt says, and smiles through quivering lips. "But that was then. Besides, I know you. Whatever's happened that you think you need to lock yourself away in here, you can't help but help. It's who you are."

I stare at the hole at my feet. Just a step away from a hit of pure peace. Just plunge through and the virt resets, kicking Shelt out at the same time. I could end this conversation right now.

Shelt sees me hesitate and presses. "The brother's name

is Amos. I have a counseling meeting tonight and I told him to meet me afterwards. I told him you'd be there, and I keep my word, so don't make me a liar."

I shake my head. "Shelt, I—"

"He doesn't know anyone," Shelt continues. "He's lived his entire life on the Preserves. Never been to a city, let alone someplace like Reszlieville. He's out of his depth and insistent something's happened to her. You can help, so you must."

Oh, I must?

"No," I answer. I'm not going out there. Maybe I could help, but who knows what other harm I could do in the process.

"Tell him I'm sorry," I say, then call up my console and have the virt eject Shelt. "He's better off without me."

He starts to protest but his voice cuts off as he winks away.

I look down at the hole and ready myself to step through, but just as I'm about to move a slender brown head with a black nose and two small inquisitive eyes emerges from the water. The seal's nostrils flare, taking in a fresh breath. He sees me but doesn't retreat, just floats there, breathing. Guess I'm not much of a threat.

Looks like I can't use the hole now though, it's occupied.

Fine. I didn't want to spend my last moments wet anyway.

After the sun sets I'll strip and go lie in the snow, enjoy the hallucinogenic spasms making me feel hot as I freeze to death.

Besides, before I die I want to have a chat with Connie about letting visitors in without permission.

By the time I drag my worn-out body back to the cave I've been squatting in, the sun's casting long orange shadows across the snow. For a home it isn't much—just a hollow of rock overhung by ice—but I dragged part of the surviving fuselage to cover the entrance and packed the holes with bits of cloth and seat stuffing. It isn't pretty, but so far it's been enough to keep me alive.

On my first run I tried to stay at the crash site, thinking I could use the wreckage as a makeshift shelter, but the plane was too damaged and couldn't keep out the minus-thirty-degree air. I froze to death in my sleep when the fire went out in the middle of the night.

After resetting for my second run I bundled myself up as best I could and tried to find a new place to survive. A hungry polar bear chased me down not a half day into my search, and I bled out on the snow as it made me its lunch.

I found the cave on my third run and have used it since, rebuilding it a little better each time I start over.

After I slide the fiberglass cover away, I pull back the first-class curtain hanging across the entrance and climb through the small opening into the dark cave. The fire from this morning went out hours ago and only a dull orange light bleeds in through the fuselage windows. My smelly nest of bedding is tucked under a low shelf of ice. The remains of what wouldn't burn from the survival rations are in the garbage pile against the other wall. Eventually I'll have to start keeping this place cleaner, but until I learn to survive more than a few days at a time, hygiene is at the bottom of my list of concerns.

I have just enough fuel left for one fire—the remaining safety cards and some scraps of luggage that survived the initial fire after the crash. I was going to use it to cook up the seal meat, but now I'll enjoy one last stretch of warmth, then strip off my clothes, go lie in the snow, and wait to die. It shouldn't take long.

Connie materializes while I'm struggling to burn the laminated safety card with a lighter that refuses to spark into flame. She's radiant. The cave is nearly dark but I can see her just as clearly as if she were standing in a well-lit room. Her curly auburn hair's pulled up into a loose bun and she's wearing a light shirt and shorts, like she just came in from gardening on a warm summer day.

She looks at me, smirks, and says, "Still no dinner?"

"No," I mutter and toss the lighter into the fire pit. So much for warmth. I guess I'll skip straight to dying.

"How much longer do you have this time?" she asks, my impending death now a topic of casual conversation. After first accidentally freezing to death and then the polar bear, I ended the third run dying from sepsis after slicing my thigh open dragging the hunks of fuselage across the snow to the cave. Other than the one time I broke through a layer of thin ice and drowned, and the time I plunged into a hidden crevasse and cracked my head open, my deaths have all been slow and painful, mostly starving to death. I'm not doing that anymore.

"I'll start over tonight," I say, conserving my strength. Even talking has become exhausting. I'll just lie here another moment. Hopefully I'll be able to drag myself back outside. I don't want to waste time in here dying when I could get it over with quick and easy, but I need a minute to rest.

"You could at least let me get you a cup of coffee," she says, and as she holds out her hand a steaming mug appears in it. The smell of freshly brewed coffee fills the cave and makes my mouth water. I want to take it, but I can't. I have to do this myself.

"It's against the rules," I say.

She shakes her head. "They're your rules," she says as the coffee winks away. "No one's holding you to them but you."

It's true. I could make it easier on myself. Tweak the simulation to make more of the plane survive. To have better arctic gear aboard. To make food more plentiful or the weather more cooperative. But what would be the point? I need this. I need to keep my brain occupied. Hovering at the edge of death is the only thing keeping the desperate thoughts in my mind from taking over.

I can't risk him getting out. Not again.

There's something inside of me. Another me *I* never was, a twisted me, violent and cruel. He got inside my head, infested me with his memories. I know every sick thing I did trying to get back into my mind, experienced every sick decision he made.

For a few moments, when he was trying to snatch my body out from under me, we shared a mind, my thoughts were his, and I relived every horrible thing he'd done to find me.

Every person he hurt.

I still remember. Every one.

Eventually my rithm rejected his and kicked him back out to the body he'd mindjacked. I thought I was free, but soon enough I noticed the parts he left behind. It wasn't until weeks later that I began to notice them—the alien thoughts oozing through my mind. Spikes of rage and crushing guilt. They started small at first, absent nudges, like someone looking over my shoulder. Then the images came, memories I'd never lived, like someone else was in my head with me, sharing my brain. Then came the blackouts.

I don't know what happened during those dark times, I only know I always ended up back in my apartment, with no hint to tell me where I'd been or what I'd done—no matter how hard I tried to retrace my steps.

The other version of me is still inside me. Me, but not me. My own evil twin living inside my head. I call him Deacon, after my middle name.

I kept a lid on Deacon's presence as long as I could, until I'd cleaned up the mess he created and tried to fix all the pain we'd caused. Then I came here.

He wants out, I know it. That's why I can't trust myself, but as long as I'm trapped in here, so is he.

That's the truth, that's the reason I'm out here, and that's why I have to stay. I've seen what I've become. I *know* what I'm capable of. There's a monster inside me, a part of me that craves the freedom of pure self-interest, to simply take what I want—and I can't blame it all on Deacon, because he's *me*.

All those terrible things they blamed on Eka—the murders, the mind jacking...Dora—it had been *me*. Ankur covered it up, but that doesn't make me any less complicit. In fact, it only serves to prove my point: I went along with it.

I hid behind Ankur's lies, then bought myself absolution. I didn't argue when they called me a hero for defeating a rabid superintelligence, as Ankur made the story look, and even my guilt-filled attempt at fixing all the damage I'd caused by spending nearly every dollar of Connie's inheritance on lawyers and new skyns for the people I'd betrayed —my friends, the people closest to me, hell, people I didn't much care for in the first place—was to make myself feel better about the pain I'd caused.

I got my life back, *Finsbury's* life. Put the Gibson ID back in storage and believed it was over—and that's the worst part. I'm not only dangerous—I'm a hypocrite, self-interested to the end. And every second I'm in the world only makes the lies bigger.

Even after all this time, I don't know if I'm truly guilty of the things Deacon did. No, I didn't make the decisions to act, but we both started as the same person, so how can we not both be to blame?

The law is clear: crimes committed by a rithm are tied to any potential backups. Even backups created *before* the crime was committed.

It only makes sense. Skyns are becoming cheaper and cheaper. Suicide bombers are a lot more willing to blow themselves up when they can count on an almost immediate restoration into another secondhand body. And murder sprees still happen all the time—even after the courts came down hard on that initial spate of idle rich sickos who made a game out of virt-style murder missions through the real world, killing and robbing and causing general mayhem across the Union to see who could last the longest before someone shut them down.

They blew their Cortexes just before capture, then immediately restored from earlier versions of themselves and pled innocence, claimed to not be responsible, said they'd never do such things. The laws were amended real quick after that, and now people are more careful to remain anonymous when they go on their fits of cross-country mayhem for sport.

There aren't many who know the truth about me. Saabir, my sort of lawyer, knows some of it. Knows it was me inside Dora—or a version of me anyway—but even he doesn't know the whole truth. Doesn't know about the blackouts, and the sudden all-encompassing urges that try to snatch my thoughts away.

I was in the back of his office one time and asked him what would happen if the truth came out. He leaned in, put his hands together, and in the same calm voice he'd used to ask if I wanted tea, said, without a doubt, if it ever came to light that I'd killed and mindjacked people while under the influence of mind-enhancing shyfts, especially while working as a cop in the Psychorithm Crime Unit, then restored from a backup to get out from under it all, they'd toss my mind in a stock and forget about it forever. If I was lucky.

Time crawls at low resolution in the stocks. Forever actually lasts forever.

So I need to lie. Every day. To everyone. I'm not guilty— but I may as well be.

I'm not sure what makes me more dangerous: the dark impulses swirling around in my head or the fact that I'm no different than the self-interested, destructive liar that the other me was.

That's why I came here, and that's why I can't leave: this frozen cycle of death is keeping the monster that lives inside me in hibernation. The only person I can hurt in here is myself.

"About those rules," I say. "You're not supposed to let visitors in."

Connie feigns a puzzled look. "Someone was here? I didn't notice."

We both know she's lying and she isn't trying to hide it. I'd be mad if I weren't so tired. "Shelt."

"Oh really?" she says. "Funny that, him showing up here, out of the blue."

"Not so out of the blue," I answer.

"What did he want?" she asks, ignoring the bigger point.

"You already know what he wanted," I say.

"Tell me anyway," she answers with teasing smile, the one I can't resist. "Or are you in a hurry to go kill yourself some more?"

I've got nothing left in me to argue, not that I ever could. Sometimes it's hard to believe this Connie is just a simulation. Her sideways glances and winking inflection are so spot-on, I mostly forget the real Connie died almost two years ago. I suppose it's a little macabre, living with the ghost of my dead wife while I slowly and repeatedly commit suicide, but I don't know what else I'm supposed to do. I'm broken, and she's all I have left.

"A girl's missing," I say. "Her brother's come looking for her."

"And what are you going to do about it?" she asks, her tone not quite stern but sliding toward the professorial. She knows what she wants to hear me say, but today she's not going to get it.

"Nothing," I answer. "The cops don't care, why should I?"

She stops and looks at me. "Because you do care."

Do I though?

I remember. There was a point, way back when, that I believed I was doing good. I thought I knew what was right. But now I've seen the other side of myself, the side that hurts people without a second thought, all in the name of what's right.

How can I trust I even know what's right from wrong anymore?

"Maybe. Once. But that was another me."

"I don't believe that," she says, and waves her hand in the small cave. "You want to live the rest of eternity like this? This is no life at all. Why are you wasting away in here?"

I raise my feeble arm and tap my head with bone-white fingers. Frostbite for sure. They'll turn black if I stick around a few more hours. "I can't do anything out there until I fix what's in here."

"You're not going to fix anything by dying on a loop," she counters. "The only fix is out there, and you'll never find it if you don't start looking."

"Don't you understand?" I say, my voice rising. My frustration is strong enough to give me one last dying burst of energy, but I can't bring myself to look at her while I say it. "I can't go back out there. I'm dangerous."

Of all the people I've lied to, why continue to be cagey with Connie? I know exactly what's wrong with me, what's infested me. I even gave him a *name*.

I know what I'm capable of, but if I can't even admit it to Connie—*who isn't even real*—how am I ever supposed to admit it to anyone else?

"You can't hide in here forever," she says, quietly now. She's up to something. I can tell.

"I can try," I answer as I unzip my coat. My body's so frail my clothes are hanging off me. Time to get undressed, get this over with.

Connie doesn't say anything else, and for a moment I think I've won, but then I feel a tingle in my spine and a tug at the base of my skull. It takes a second before I realize what's happening—she pulled my plug.

"What did you do?" I blurt, not so much mad now as panicked.

"Your skyn's been in the pod too long," she answers, her voice clinical. "Medpods need to run a maintenance cycle every sixty days, and you've been in here twice that, so I started one."

"You're kicking me out of my head?" I say, and my stomach tenses. I look around for something to grab onto, for an anchor, but nothing here really exists. "I can't go out there..."

She shrugs. "It's for your own good," she says. "Your skyn needs the exercise. The cycle takes eight hours. Either you can stay in your locker and stare at the timer, or you can go find out about that missing girl."

"Stop this—" I say, but it's too late.

"Tell Shelt I said 'Hi,'" Connie says as the ejection sequence takes hold and something grabs me by the mind and sucks me out of the cave and back into the confines of a warm slab of meat.

Back in the real world again.

Shit.

THE MEDPOD thrums under my suddenly too-sensitive body. The world feels slippery, like friction's set too low. It's been a long time since I've been fleshed. I'm going to need a few minutes to get used to it.

I squeeze my fingers into a fist, catching myself up with the flow of realspace, adjusting to the skewed timings of thought after the smooth cause and effect of existing so long in a high-revving virt, living at four times the speed of normal.

There's a soft hiss as the pod powers down to standby and begins its maintenance cycle. I'm locked out of the Arctic until it finishes. Now I have eight hours to kill before I can get back to the deepfreeze.

What the hell am I supposed to do with myself?

I take it easy at first, reacquainting myself with my body, and for the first time in weeks remember what toes feel like. I take a breath and I'm filled with a surprising nostalgia, as though I've come home. It takes being disembodied for a while to appreciate being back in one

Virtual worlds seem real in every aspect, but they're not

flesh and bone. Nothing like being alive. Turns out I've missed it.

The pod tilts to vertical and I tell it to slow down, I'm in no hurry. I roll my shoulders and flex my calves, give my dormant muscles and nerves time to get back the idea of supporting me. The room's lights are up and a news digest of what's happened since I last saw the world displays on the livewall in front of me, next to a fake window showing a view of a shimmering lake through a forest of pine trees. When I left the Arctic the sun was going down, but here it's only mid-afternoon.

Even though I've only been gone a few short months, the wall tells me the world has continued its race forward. The hurricane season is in full force, with two Cat 5's already making landfall in the Gulf and another brewing. Thousands are displaced, but with the battering the islands and Gulf states have taken over the past few decades, most of the people who still live in the Hurricane Zones are battened down in their bunkers. Everyone else either fled or died a long time ago.

Fate has finally brought its Ancestor program to the Union, with clinics open in seven cities across North America, including one right here in Toronto. And as Fate helps more and more people convert to digital immortality, reszo rights continue to be threatened as more and more people obliterate millennia-long preconceptions of what it means to be human.

Which makes me wonder—how are Xiao and Ankur faring in their war against Fate? The last time I saw them they were intent on stopping Fate's spread across the world by any means possible, but with new clinics opening here, they must not have gotten very far. I consider for a moment trying to contact them, but I have no idea how. Or if they're even still alive.

Not much I could do for them now anyway. I have my own problems to deal with.

In lighter news, someone's managed to survive for more than eight-hundred straight hours in Decimation Island Live, the reszo battle royale game show where contestants fight to the death, and that puts her only a game and a half away from being the first to complete a full century—a thousand hours without dying. People seem taken by her story, but I skip past it. I've never been much for sports other than hockey, and not even that since they introduced the glowing sticks.

The feed continues, but I stop paying attention. All this change, and none of it matters. I should probably be pissed at Connie for dropping me back out here, have her sprite reprogrammed for ignoring my specific instructions to keep the outside world where it was. But slipping Shelt in against my wishes is exactly what the real Connie would have done, so it's really only following its programming. She can't help but be her.

If I didn't want that I could replace her sprite with something more compliant, one who barks "Yessir" like a 1950's British colonel and does exactly what it's told. But I haven't, so I guess this situation is on me. No one to blame but myself, as usual.

There has to be some kind of problem with me—other than the obvious—that I'm hung up on the digital ghost of my wife, but even knowing there's something creepy about my attachment to her, I can't let her go. Sure, deleting her would remove some friction from my existence, let me live the way I want to, but losing her again wouldn't make my life any better. Her being her is part of the deal.

She thinks she's doing what's best for me, but she doesn't know. Doesn't know what's inside me. I don't think she's capable of knowing. Which, again, is on me.

So fine, I'll have a little eight-hour staycation. Order some food and watch the wall and when the pod is ready I'll lie back down and return to the crash site. This time I think I can make it work. All I need is better luck seal hunting, I know it.

I can survive there.

The pod finishes rising, and I take a step forward and shiver at an unexpected twang from my hamstrings. My body's creaking like a cottage with a freshly stoked fire warming from the winter cold, but I don't mind it. It's comforting somehow. Familiar.

My conditioned urge to urinate when I wake up takes me into the closed-off toilet/shower stall, but nothing comes. The pod kept my urine recycling and my bladder is completely empty, which is somehow a complete letdown. I didn't expect I'd miss the feeling of emptying my bladder.

Since I'm already naked I slide the door shut behind me and throw the shower on and stay under it for a long time. Long enough I get over my missing whiz and then feel bad about how much water I'm wasting. When I'm done I let myself air dry while I scroll through the feeds on the wall, looking for a sitcom or something to distract me, but ever since Connie died I haven't had the appetite for casual entertainment.

After what's happened over the past few years—the accident, losing Connie, the repeated restorations and battles with enemies real, imagined, and homemade—I'm lucky I'm only play-acting at suicide in a virt. After the war plenty of guys went all the way with killing themselves. I didn't even get the chance to make that decision. After I died I woke up to someone else's life already in progress.

My whole life began and ended in the span of an instant. I didn't even have a chance to guide it one way or another. The other Finsbury—the one I call Deacon, the one who got to wake up at Second Skyn first—*he* got to decide. He still had his job. He still had his name. He had his entire future ahead of him, could have been something better. Instead he fucked that all up. He made those decisions. He stole those people's bodies, used them like puppets to get what he wanted, not me.

He became the monster, and I'm the one who has to run from the pitchforks and torches. The resentment makes my mouth itch—

Shit. This isn't working.

I can't sit here with nothing but my thoughts for eight hours.

I shut the wall off and sit on the pod's mattress as it vibrates under me. The subsonic whirr of the cleaning cycle is the only noise in the tiny room, and somehow it's quieter in here than out in the snow. Everyone sees the bright images of the snow-covered ice and imagines it silent, but the wind can roar as loud as a freight train, and the shifting of the ice erupts like mortar fire.

With the display off, the room is even smaller. Just four square walls with a bathroom behind a sliding door, a kitchenette behind another, a set of drawers and clothes washer behind a third, and the medpod installed at the center. It's a glorified storage unit for a virt-locked body. Most people don't even bother with a bathroom. Why pay the extra for a toilet when the pod takes care of that for you?

I sit another minute as the shivering bed numbs my ass.

Maybe I'll just go out for some food. Out, eat, and straight back.

I'll keep to myself, keep it under control.

Nothing will happen.

A prickle of doubt trills in my stomach as I pull my set of clothes from the washer, get dressed, and slide my tab into my pocket so I can read while I eat. The wall said the humidity was in the high forties, so I don't bother with the jacket. Years as a head of security and then as a detective trained me to wear a suit jacket whenever I left the house. With SecNet watching all the time you never know when a random camera snap will end up on the feeds. Being a cop is a public job, and I wanted to make sure I looked professional if I ever found myself at the narrow end of media scrutiny, but it's so hot out right now I don't give a shit about looking professional. As a matter of fact, I kinda wish I had a pair of shorts.

The unit door seals behind me as I step out into the narrow, door-lined hallway and head out for a burger and a beer at Francesco's up the street.

Nothing's going to happen. I can't get into any trouble by just walking up the street.

THE SUN IS BLAZING. Skyns run hot as it is, and the humidity's so high the air feels wet. I'm already sweating in my thin shirt.

Right now the Arctic chill doesn't seem so bad.

I hop in a Sküte and crank the AC while it ferries me three blocks up to the local burger shop. I stand in the window and watch the street as I eat. The meat in the burger's red and juicy and obviously artificial, but it tastes great just the same. After months on the ice, eating anything warm and greasy is a welcome reminder of my former life out here.

After lunch the warmth outside is oppressive, but still a novelty, so I decide to kill time with a walk, reacquaint myself with the city. It changes so quickly these days, entire neighborhoods transformed in the span of months, it's impossible to keep up with it all. Brutalist housing blocks rebuilt as vertical farms. Stretches of suburban wasteland razed and refashioned into tiny, self-sufficient enclaves. Back to the little towns this place once was.

No one will argue that as more and more people have

gone digital, the pace of life hasn't increased measurably. Although some people haven't accepted it yet, the argument is over whether all the change is a blessing or proof humanity is hurtling toward collapse. It's both. It's a cycle, death and rebirth, and no matter whether you're blessed or cursed, the other side is always approaching.

That's nothing new. We as a species have never been good at thinking much past our next meal.

I walk for hours, never quite ready to head back to the pod, and my feet take me up to the Danforth. I stop in front of a hard-angled brick church that looks more like a castle, lopsided parapets and narrow windows perfectly designed to conceal archers, and the big, curved stained-glass window between them could have once housed a drawbridge.

The church is multi-multi-multi denominational. The display out front shows a Bris tomorrow at nine followed by an Iranian Wedding and then a midnight Bright Ascendance ceremony for someone named Archie Goodwoman. A study group meets every Wednesday afternoon for a competitive selection of homemade treats and interfaith communion. And every Tuesday, Thursday, and Saturday at five, Shelt runs an open-door transition support group, offering a safe space where the newly restored can come and deal with the existential mindfuck that is going digital.

I duck through the front door, slide into a pew under the balcony overhang at the back, and bask in the AC. Shelt roams the aisles, pontificating, while almost everyone's turned around in their seats to watch. The rest stare at their hands or off into space. They must be the newbies. I know how they feel. I was once the guy with the dazed look on his face, opening myself up to a group of strangers, and the only commonality we had was the plastic in our heads. It's where I first met Shelt. Or Deacon did, anyway. Sometimes it's hard to remember which life was his and which is mine. I suppose the difference is negligible at this point. I'm both of us now.

Shelt flashes me a bemused look when he finally notices me. I don't think he expected me to show, which makes two of us. I didn't expect I'd be here either. I sure as hell didn't intend to come up here when I started walking, yet here I am.

"This is what I mean when I say 'We are not the faces we wear,'" Shelt says to a woman in the middle of the room, continuing the discussion I entered in the middle of. She's young and blonde and indistinguishable from all the other pretty reszos. "We are indoctrinated into our exteriority from birth—and how could we not be? Back then we were tied to our bodies, confined by them. You still hold onto that embodied mindset. I know it isn't easy, but you have to let that go. You are your mind, not the shell that contains it."

He sounds like Elder, the just-shy-of-zealot Bright who ran the transition counseling meeting Shelt and I first attended. Shelt was Elder's protégé, but whether Shelt knew it then or not I'm not sure. It sounds like Shelt's converted, gone all the way and opened his mind to the Bright Church.

I can't see ever wanting to do that. Two voices in my head is plenty. I don't need a whole congregation in there.

"But when I look in the mirror, I see me looking back from a stranger's face," the woman says, her voice small. "How can you say that's not who I am..."

"You need to look through the mirror to the eternity beyond," Shelt says, as if that means anything. The woman seems to get it though, because she takes a breath and nods and smiles back at Shelt's lopsided grin.

A group of teens are milling along the sides of the room,

holding props and costumes in such an odd array they could be for anything from an anarcho-punk retelling of the *Wizard of Oz* to *Twelfth Night* with robots.

Shelt gets the hint and finishes up with some closing thoughts before dismissing the group. He reminds them about the donuts in the kitchen as I slide out of the pew and wait beside the doors as everyone leaves. As Shelt approaches down the aisle he takes the cookie-cutter pretty girl he'd been talking to aside and asks if she could make sure the kitchen lights are off before everyone leaves.

She hesitates. I think she was planning on ghosting, but she says she will and follows the rest of the group as they file out the double doors. The kids are already erecting a glowing metal castle set as Shelt comes up to me with a huge grin across his face.

I don't like having to tell Shelt I'm not here to help, but he needs to understand my presence can only make things worse. He doesn't know everything, but he knows there's more to the truth. When I first met Shelt he was a skewed tweaker, paranoid someone was out to get him. But he wasn't wrong, someone *was* out to get him. *Me.*

He was always sharp, and he seems to have straightened his mind out some in the time I've been away. He isn't going to let me off easily.

"You tricky fucker," he says and comes in for a hug. "You came."

I'll use the truth against him. He doesn't know exactly what happened, but he knows enough, and he saw the fall-out. He knows something messed me up. He knows how everyone suffered because of what I started. I can lean on that. I'll get him to understand. I need to be alone. Being out here isn't a good idea for anyone. I'm toxic.

I'll tell him I'm sorry and head back. The pod will be done soon anyway.

"Just for a minute," I say. "I only came to say I can't help that kid, you and I both know that. I need to get my head right." I force a smile, really try to sell it. "I figured you'd be proud of me, letting go of my body. I basically live in a virt now."

"Let go of your body, but never reality," Shelt answers. "You are still woven into the fabric of this world. You must maintain your agency within it or you will stagnate."

"Stagnating's fine with me," I tell him and turn to leave. "I'm sorry, I am, but I can't help you."

Shelt steps around and puts himself between me and the door. My immediate reaction is to grab his wrist, spin him, and press him into the doorjamb with my forearm on the back of his neck, but I breathe through it, exhale, search my mind for any stray filaments of alien thought ready to snatch up the reins and take control, and let myself relax when none appear.

Shelt's eye twitches at something he sees flash across my face, but he doesn't mention it, saying instead, "Connie told me the pod won't be ready for another hour."

"Connie told you, did she?" *What am I going to do with her?* "I'll walk slow." I move to slide past him but he angles his body in my way again and I sigh. "Let me go, Shelt."

Shelt considers this, then says. "I'll make you a deal—"

"I'm not interested in—"

"Hear me out," Shelt says, then pulls his face into a devious grin. "Connie and I both want what's best for you—"

"It isn't really Connie's—"

Shelt cuts me off again. "You want to have *that* discussion now instead?"

I shake my head. I don't. Parsing out the tangled feelings I have for the simulation of my dead wife is not a conversation I'm ready to dive into. I just want to leave.

"In that case," Shelt says, "come with me now and talk to Amos—that's his name, Amos—and afterwards, after you've talked to him, after you've heard his story, you're free to go back and hide in your head and I won't bother you again. Or don't come, and you'll have a standing appointment with me every night while I come visit you in the virt and annoy the living shit out of you. Connie will let me, you know she will."

She will too. Both because she thinks I shouldn't be hiding away, and because she'd think it was funny. The momentary press of sweet memories flips to a dull ache as I remind myself of the truth. She's dead.

She died, and my attempt to find her killer led me to terrible places, led me to do terrible things. How do I know the same thing won't happen if I stay out here?

I don't. But remembering Connie, I do know one thing: she'd want me to do what I could. To help.

Fuck.

Besides, if I don't I'll have Shelt as my wacky next-door neighbor on the tundra.

"Fine," I say, but Shelt's already leaving.

"Let's go," he calls over his shoulder. "I told Amos to meet us at Yumi's, and we're late for the reservation. Yumi's gonna love sending me to the back of the line."

"How'd you know I'd even show up, let alone make a reservation for dinner?"

He stops and opens the heavy wooden door, and the dense city air billows in. "I know you think you're all complicated and tortured, Fin, but you're really not that hard to figure out. You know what your real problem is?"

"What's that?" I ask as I fall in beside him on the sidewalk.

"I knew you'd show up because you can't resist. You can't *not* help. I know that as much as I know, even after all this time, you still haven't learned to *accept* help, even when you need it."

He's half right. I'm not afraid of accepting someone's help—I'm afraid of what might happen to them if I do.

HE SHOULDN'T HAVE COME HERE. NOT like this.

Winter stops and holds his breath, peels back the layers of silence surrounding him. The night's hush has changed. The normal quiet buzz of the wooded waterfront trails is muffled, like someone's thrown a blanket over the trees.

His stomach clenches and his hands bead with sweat. Something is amiss, he can sense it.

Why did he try this tonight?

He crafted a routine, honed the variables to all but eliminate risk. It was working—*why did he choose tonight to change his routine?*

After that sloppy first attempt his missions became easier, rote exercises, the samples easily extracted from unsuspecting targets. Between then and now he's extracted eleven samples without so much as a whiff of opposition. The key, he discovered, is to trust his instincts, strike without thinking, and remove the head before either of them expects it.

Every few weeks he'd return in a burner skyn, quickly narrow in on a target from one of the recently decanted reszos out performing preventative exercise on their under-used bodies or searching for a brief release with a willing participant. Up until now he's encountered no problems, no resistance. The blade he concealed on his arm performed flawlessly, and he never needed to resort to his sidearm. He's seen barely a mention on the feeds of the mutilated skyns found scattered amongst the waterfront trails. It seemed no one much cared about disposable people and their lost minutes.

But it wasn't enough. *He wanted more.* He couldn't help himself, and now look at the trouble he's in.

Winter doesn't know why he is the way he is—whether it's a quirk of genetics or the result of an upbringing by helperbot caregivers as a ward of the state—but he learned early on he was broken. A defective model.

Eventually he came to realize his only choice was to rewire his brain, to start over and build himself back up from scratch, so when he was of age he went digital. He went to Second Skyn, and they mapped his brain connection by connection, measured the synaptic response and charted paths of brain chemicals as his neurons fired with thought.

They saw right away he was different. His pattern was unusually dark, misshapen. A storm of activity in the prefrontal cortex, and an emptiness in the amygdala, where his emotions should have been. They tried to fix him, and it seemed to work, for a few days at least, but the emotions quickly faded, and after three reattempts they gave up.

He anticipated going reszo would be the answer, that life in digital would be the solution to a lifetime of droning through the unyielding emptiness in his head, only able to temporarily vent the unbearable, unceasing, nameless frisson polluting his thoughts by binging and purging party-sized all-meat pizzas or abusing a fuckbot for a few hours, but he was wrong. It was only the beginning.

Before he resorted to collecting the samples, he tried everything to fill the yawning void in his head. Tried patches and grafts to bring his rithm in line with the rest of humanity, to make his mind work like everyone else's, but nothing ever worked for long. So he put his considerable intellect toward understanding himself. He studied. Learned everything there was to know about the rithm, discovered exactly how his mind was spun, then opened it up to figure out how he could plug in some feeling. He went as far as he could on his own—after that, he needed an external source of thought. Required feelings to graft onto the stumps in his brain.

He tried to find an alternative. Sucking memories out of a bloody skull wasn't his first choice, but after narrowing his options it became the only choice.

Memories are plentiful on the undernet, shyfts that replicate feeling and experiences. People mod themselves all the time, get braver or more compassionate or live through someone else's eyes. Fall off a cliff. Rob a bank. Give birth. Unfortunately, these shyfts are all built to hook into rithms complete with functional emotional engrams. People whose brains are already capable of processing emotion. They don't work on him. Not for longer than an instant, anyway.

He even tried to secure a full psychorithm, a real working mind he could dissect thought by thought. He sourced one, came close to accepting the seller's conditions, but ultimately decided against the transaction. Contraband minds are dangerous, highly illegal, with the potential to draw unwanted attention. With all the problems in his mind, he doesn't need the added complexity of dealing with a criminal investigation. Plus, there's no way to know if a secondhand mind is real just by looking at the pattern, and no way to be sure it isn't full of trojans or viruses or collapsible engrams. Or something even worse.

No, he needed a fresh sample. He needed to trust the source. Needed pure, unadulterated thought. For his own safety. There was no alternative.

That brought him here, to his missions at the waterfront. They've gone so well he relaxed his caution. Thought he could wring even more out of his hunts, decided he wanted to taste the sampled thought for himself, straight and warm and fresh from the target's still struggling mind, not relayed over a series of drones, like a meal that had spent too long in transit, offered stale and cold upon arrival.

He convinced himself the risk was minimal and abandoned his safeguards, for just one night, and went out to hunt in the skyn registered to his name, wearing the face connected to his rep. He decided the minimal increase in risk was worth drinking straight from the source.

How wrong he was.

The police have found him.

Winter spins to retrace his steps back along the path, to flee the unseen something he knows is waiting for him, and that's when he hears it: a deep whir, approaching.

A drone, and by the pitch of its rotors, a large one.

A Service drone.

He turns again, away from the approaching drone, and almost immediately hears another ahead of him.

He's caught.

Service drones come equipped with infrared vision, t-ray scanners. Once they're close enough they'll find him. They'll see the weapons he's carrying, even through his clothes.

There's no escape.

His body reacts to the stress—heart thudding against his ribs and knees quivering in anticipation—but he doesn't feel the jab of impending doom that should be forcing him to action. He takes a moment, acting against all self-interest, and reaches into his storehouse of memory to sieve through the various flavors of terror he's collected over the past months. He selects a particularly intense one, channels it to the surface, and imagines feeling it for himself.

Almost. He can *almost* sense what it would be like, the head-to-toe shock of adrenaline transmuted into unconsciousness action, fight or flight made visceral. But the sensation quickly dissolves, replaced by the knowledge of its inherent artificiality.

These feelings aren't his, they're echoes of someone else.

It's for the best, anyway. In this situation the blind panic of true fear would be a distraction. Instead he's able to immediately formulate a plan of action and set it in motion.

He hasn't come this far by accepting defeat so readily.

He cuts from the paved path into one of the many side trails leading into the brush, hunched over, moving quietly as he's able, and the enhanced vision of his skyn makes it easier to avoid fallen branches as he snakes through the trail toward the water's edge.

There is nothing inherently illegal in walking the trails at night—on the contrary, that's what they're here for. He can't be the only one out here. It's not his presence that poses a problem, it's his intentions: the weapons he's carrying, the sampling device in his pocket. Without these on his person, he's just another reszo out exercising his skyn in the night air. The police can't prove any different.

The drone's lights shine through the naked branches as

it hovers above the path a few hundred meters away. Its large rotors hum a note of shrill bass. A spotlight snaps on, and voices rise above the buzz. They're questioning someone.

At the water's edge he bends and slides the gun in first, watches it sink into the cold black water, does it quietly so the splash doesn't alert the drones. Next he releases the arm blade, takes a few steps along the shore, and lets it drop too. Finally he tosses the sampling gear, the probes and transfer cables, and they sink below the surface with a quiet plop.

Now he's no different than anyone else, but he has to hurry, get back up on the path before the drones spot him skulking near the water and take an interest in what he was up to.

He creeps away from the shore, picking his way along the winding trail back out toward where the police are waiting. Before he steps back onto the pavement he takes a brief second to compose himself, brushes a stray twig from his jacket, then steps casually out of the wooded darkness and sets into a stroll down the path toward the drone's light, just another innocent citizen out for a walk, curious to see what the fuss is all about.

Fifty meters later he rounds a bend in the path and puts himself square in the drone's sensors. Its spotlight blinks on his face and he raises his palm to shade his eyes from the glare. Two uniformed officers and a large man in an unflattering suit block the path.

"Hands where we can see them," the ill-suited man barks, and Winter raises his hands to chest height, palms out. He squints at the intense light from the drone. "What are you doing out here?"

"Simply taking the night air, Officer," he says. "Is there a problem?"

The suit shakes his head. "We'll see," the officer answers. "Scan 'im."

The drone's spotlight dims and various lights flash as it cycles through its complement of sensors. EM. Infrared. T-ray. Pattern match. In addition to running his biokin through SecNet, the police have the power to query his psychorithm through his retinas and match it to the person registered to operate his skyn. None of this poses a problem.

His initial burst of stress has dissipated—the drone won't detect elevated breathing or heart rate. His skyn is registered with Standards. His identity and rep are reboots, and relatively recent, but starting over with a new identity isn't a crime. Many reszos opt to shed the baggage of their previous lives when making the jump to digital. The process of changing one's identity and reinitializing a Social Faith reputation is lengthy but relatively uncomplicated. If the petition is granted—after a thorough criminal history and credit check—anyone can become someone else.

He barely remembers who he used to be as it is, sloughed off his old self so completely he sometimes forgets what his name once was, not that it matters anymore. He's known as Winter now, and as far as the police are concerned, he has the right to take a walk along the waterfront unmolested. The police have no reason to suspect him of anything.

"Winter—mononym only," the drone's simulated voice intones once the scan has completed. "Identity initiated one year, seven months, and thirteen days ago. No outstanding warrants, citations, or reprimands. Optical pattern scan identity returns as a match for registered skyn. No weapons or contraband detected."

"Rep's clean," one of the constables says, reading from

the data scrolling down the vizer over her face. "Doesn't look like he's our guy."

The suit squints and gives Winter an up-and-down look. He chose a simple outfit for his mission, loose black pants and a long-sleeved shirt, nothing that would arouse suspicion.

"Pat 'im down anyway," the suit says.

The other constable steps forward and frisks him, checking under his arms and paying attention to the inside of his thighs. After a moment he steps back and shrugs. "I don't think this is our guy."

"Who are you looking for?" Winter asks, his voice modulated to perturbed innocence.

"Someone's been out here hacking up bit-heads and scrambling their brains all to shit. Finally made enough of a mess now I'm out here in the middle of the night patting down you pervs, looking for him. So, how about it?" the suit sneers. "You our killer or you just out here to get your jollies in the bushes?"

He doesn't need to answer their questions. The police have no reason to hold him. No reason they know about, anyway.

Winter knows he should be respectful, or at least tactful, that a polite response will smooth the proceedings along, but he doesn't care. They can't hurt him.

"Your mandate is to uphold the law, not sit in judgement of my or anyone else's consensual acts within the bounds of that law." Winter would be enjoying this, if he could. "You have ascertained my identity and noted I am not a suspect in your investigation, and yet you continue to detain me and malign my character with implied judgement of a sexual nature. I could have your actions brought forward for review, were I to so choose. Now, am I free to go or shall we take this matter to the Citizen's Tribunal?" He digs into his mental archive and injects his thoughts with the one odd but well-worn sample of self-satisfaction he skimmed from a target who appeared eager for Winter to remove her head. He's unable to suppress the associated smirk.

The suit's face sags and tightens all at once. What alien combination of emotions must be playing through his head right now? Winter would give anything to taste them for himself.

"Fine," the suit grumbles with a roll of his eyes. "Beat it, freak."

"Good evening to you," Winter says as he passes, continuing along the path.

This place is ruined. He can never come back here.

They've taken this away from him, but no matter. He isn't worried or concerned. He accepts this setback as a matter of historical record. One way or another, he'll find a way to get his fix.

He always has.

SHELT LEADS me down the street to a busy Korean BBQ restaurant. We press through the line and an older woman with bright brown eyes and a thick head of dark hair greets Shelt with a stern look, but he slides past her mock scowl into a big hug and everything is forgiven. She shows us to a secluded table in the back where someone's already waiting —Amos, I assume. He's sitting with his hands flat on the table and an untouched glass of water in front of him. He recognizes Shelt from across the room and rises, keeping his hands at his sides.

Amos' youthful face is somehow already rugged, like he inherited it. A neat rust-brown beard angles down over his jaw and his dark copper hair's swept over his head in a hick wave—thick on top, shaved at the sides. I had one myself when I was his age.

He's wearing sturdy brown pants that sit high on his waist and a grey vest over a clean white dress shirt buttoned all the way to the throat with the sleeves rolled to tight donuts of fabric above the elbow. A well-worn, wide-brimmed black hat rests on the table in front of him.

Shelt said he's from the Preserves—a self-governed territory that stretches through the prairie provinces and down into the Midwest US—a grassr born and raised. Grassrs aren't a single people. It's a culture that transcends creeds and ethnicity—Old Order Mennonites and Aboriginals and off-the-grid survivalist homesteaders living side by side—but they all share a similar mindset: a desire to live off the land, simply and without reliance on modern technology. Most communities govern themselves, and welcome almost anyone who wants to join, as long as they keep the peace and pull their shared weight.

How much tech each community allows varies—some employ solar arrays and communal link terminals, while others consider anything up to and including a lightbulb as dangerous. The Union keeps them at arm's length when it comes to law enforcement. For the most part grassr communities keep to themselves and prefer to deal with problems quietly and internally.

It's not often a grassr leaves the Preserves, even rarer for one to brave the wilds of Reszlieville, ground zero for everything about modern life they've sworn to oppose. He looks calm enough, but I wonder how close to overwhelmed he is by this place.

Amos extends a dense-looking hand, nicked and stained from heavy use. "I appreciate you meeting with me again, Mr. Shelt," he says as they shake.

Shelt laughs. "I told you, leave the mister out of it, okay?"

Amos nods and his wary eyes shift to me as Shelt introduces us. "Amos Boldt, this is Finsbury Gage. He came to help you find your sister."

I shoot Shelt an irked glance before taking Amos'

offered hand. His grip is like carved stone. Life in the Preserves has built him sturdy.

"Pleased to meet you, sir," he says with a deference in his voice I haven't heard since boot camp.

"You too," I say. "But I should warn you—I only came to listen. I can't promise anything." Amos' eyes narrow, but he nods at my correction.

"You have my gratitude for whatever assistance you are able to provide," Amos assures me as we take our seats around the open BBQ stove at the center of the table.

A server drops off an assorted plate of thinly sliced meat, none of which I expect ever saw the inside of an actual animal, and Shelt starts cooking for everyone without asking. Amos seems content to let him. He's got his eyes low, keeping us in view but cutting off the commotion of the restaurant around us.

We sit for a long moment in silence. Amos doesn't offer anything, and I don't ask. I just want this over with so I can get back to life in the pod.

"Amos," Shelt eventually says as he flips the thin slices of veat on the grill, "why don't you tell Finsbury what you told me about Bee."

I stay quiet while the grassr takes a cleansing breath in and out, tugs on his beard, then launches into his story.

"My father named her Grace, but everyone calls her Bee on account of she's never still. Up before the sun, tending to the hens and the horses, and still has coffee ready by the time Father's at the table." He pauses and leans in as if afraid we might be overheard. "Father and I would never admit it, but she's become a better cook than Mother. There's nothing she can't do if she puts her mind to it. She's one of God's special creatures, that's plain to everyone who meets her."

"But something changed," I say. Something drastic, I'd imagine, to bring a girl like that to Reszlieville.

He cocks his head at me, but nods slightly. "Six weeks ago, give or take, I noticed a change in her. Smiles that used to come easily suddenly seemed forced. I'd find her sitting quiet, staring out the window at the fields. This was a girl who filled every room she entered, hiding in the kitchen in the middle of the day. It wasn't like her."

"Did you ask her what was wrong?" Shelt asks.

"Yes, sir, I did. Mother and Father did. But in all my twenty-two years I never heard her complain, not once. She waved off our concerns, cited lady problems. That was enough for Father. She convinced them, but I could tell she was acting. Weren't but a few days later she was gone. She left a note, said she loved everyone but not to come looking, that she'd finally heard her call."

"What does that mean?" I ask.

Amos' face sags and when he speaks his voice is quiet. "The only wistful thing I ever heard her say was that, in all her years of talking to the Lord, she'd never heard Him respond. As if His love isn't apparent in the bounty he provides. As much as she did, she always believed she was meant for more."

"You think she finally got some kind of response?"

"I think she wished one into being," he says, nostrils flaring. "She was talking to someone, sneaking in to use the village computer. After she left we had the sheriff pull up the records. He said it'd been going on for weeks."

"Do you know who she was talking to?" Shelt asks, then quickly flips the now smoking strips of meat Amos' story caused him to forget.

"We don't. We couldn't access the messages themselves, not without some kind of proof that Grace was in danger.

Even the local law figure she's just another runaway, that she'll be back eventually. It happens often enough, even with those you wouldn't expect. The lure of the big city is too much for some, but most of them return, and most of them broken in one way or another."

"So what makes you think she came to Reszlieville?" I say.

"No one would help, so the task fell to me. I made inquiries, tried to follow her trail. Talked to someone claimed to see her hop a ride on one of the automatic vehicles shipping out with the weekly harvest. I followed its trail to the yard in The Pas. A waitress in a restaurant nearby said a girl of Grace's description had come some weeks ago"—he runs his tongue over his teeth—"met with a man. But not any man," he says, and nods to Shelt and me, "one of *you*."

"One of *us*?" Shelt asks, straightening in his chair. I might not have to worry about getting out of this after all. Amos might piss Shelt off enough he'll walk both of us out of here. Either that or I'll have to pull him off the grassr kid, and by the way Amos' built, I'd rather not have to get between them.

"My apologies," Amos says, and gives Shelt a long contrite look. "I've had a draining stretch of days. I've always been taught to see the humanity in everyone, regardless of the form God gave them, and that should extend to your kind as well."

I can see Shelt deciding whether or not to make it an issue, but ultimately he decides to let it go.

"Apology accepted," Shelt says. "I know we restored can seem like monsters, and as much as we need to fight that opinion, we also need to understand that as we ourselves are the vanguard of change in the world, we must help guide others toward understanding as well. We need to live the change we seek, as I believe is in your heart."

I give Amos a look and he raises an eyebrow in confusion. I can't help him there. There's no explaining Shelt.

"You never said why you think your sister came *here*," I say instead, trying to diffuse the awkward tension. Shelt returns to the BBQ and dishes out the veat onto small plates and gives one to each of us. I'm not hungry but memories of starving to death goad me into eating anyway.

Amos ignores the food and continues. "I know you wouldn't expect it, living here in the center of it, but The Pas is not so cosmopolitan people don't take notice of a girl from the Preserves taking coffee with a beautiful white-haired angel."

"An angel?" Shelt asks.

"Yes, sir. That's how the waitress described him. Tall and broad shouldered with white hair swept back from a face that looked like a sculpture. Said he moved like a ghost and had a voice like perfumed honey." He looks around the restaurant at the picture-perfect patrons and I see them through his eyes. Even the dressed-down reszos are quietly striking. "One of *you*."

One of us, I get it. It's easy to understand why so many people in the world resent and fear reszos. Most of us do look an awful lot like we could have fallen from heaven. Guess that explains all the demons walking among us. "Fair enough. And you tried the police?"

His features grow dark. "I've slept the last three nights in the lobby of"—he thinks for a second—"the Fifty-Five Division Police Station. Not a single person came to talk to me. Just faces on screens. Every morning I made a complaint. Asked them what they had done to find my sister, and every morning we went through the same conversation like they'd never heard it before, then told me my concerns had been logged and were under review. By who? Under review by *who*? This morning I grew tired of talking to that damn voice, so I went to find a person." He pauses. Grits his teeth. "Lord as my witness, I tried to hold my temper."

He shakes his head, spears the slice of veat with his fork, brings it to his nose for a sniff, then returns it to his plate uneaten.

Of course they ignored him. A kid comes in out of the Preserves with a nonexistent rep and claims his sister is missing. There's no body, no proof of wrongdoing. No proof he even is who he says he is. If the Service chased after everyone who lost themselves to the hedonistic allure of Reszlieville, they'd need to triple in size and have everyone working on twenty-four-hour shifts. Until there's some kind of evidence a crime was committed, the police aren't going to do anything, least of all drop everything to start looking for a grown woman who escaped the Preserves for the freedom of modern civilization. They probably figure she's better off here as it is.

"Detective Yellowbird called me," Shelt says. "Said Amos tried to break past the security barrier, caused a bit of a disturbance. The lawbots tossed him out and she found him on the front walk, felt sorry him, and sent him to me."

That's Karin Yellowbird. If someone came into the station with a dying mouse she'd insist on working up a shoebox hospital bed and make you feel guilty for not donating your socks for blankets. "What's she expect you to do?"

He shrugs. "Something more than nothing?"

I'm not the person he thinks I am, not anymore. "I'm

sorry, Amos, I am, but I'm not a cop. I don't see how I can help you."

"Could you call someone?" Shelt asks. "Maybe a contact in the Service, urge them to look into Grace's whereabouts?"

"The only contact I have is the one who sent Amos to you in the first place. I'm not exactly the most loved person in the Service these days," I say. Getting kicked off the force for flagrantly disobeying orders doesn't leave a lot of goodwill. "I'm not in a position to start asking for favors. Besides, they'd tell me the same thing they told you: they need evidence of a crime before they can open a case."

"I see," Amos says. He pushes back in his chair, picks up his hat, and snugs it down over his eyes. "Then I shall thank you for agreeing to see me and be on my way."

"Where are you going?" Shelt asks, eyes darting between Amos and me. I know he wants me to do something to stop the kid from leaving, but I've got nothing to offer. My place is back in the freezer and it's time I returned.

"I came to this forsaken city to find my sister," Shelt says, "and I won't stop looking until I do. I will wander the streets until my shoes wear out and keep going until my feet are blistered and raw, and if my body fails before I've found her, my ghost will stalk this place until my work is done. One way or another I will find my sister, and I will bring her home. I never should have let her leave. If I return to my parents without her they will surely die from grief, and that will be my doing as well.

"Good day to you both," he says, and moves around the table to leave, but Shelt holds out an arm to stop him.

"Wait," he says, then to me: "Fin, there has to be something—*anything*—you can do."

I feel for the kid. I know what it's like to have something you cherish ripped away.

"Listen, Amos. I'm willing to help"—I flick a glance at Shelt and see his lips part in a wide, surprised smile—"but I can't do anything with what you've told me. You have to give me something to go on. Do you have a picture of her?"

He presses his lips together, nods, and pulls a folded photo from his pocket, a young girl on a spring day. She's standing in a field of knee-high grass, wearing a homemade blue dress the same color as her eyes. Her strawberry-blonde hair is pulled back under a bonnet, but renegade curls fly free in the wind. She's laughing like someone just told a joke.

"She's beautiful," I say.

"Yes, sir," Amos replies. "Inside and out."

I take out my tab and capture an image of the photo, and Amos narrows his eyes at me. "What are you doing?"

"I'm going to run her picture through SecNet," I answer.

"What's that?" Amos asks.

"You still have access to SecNet?" Shelt asks.

I answer Amos' question first. "It's a collection of inter-connected cameras and other sensors that keeps a running watch on the world. It sees almost everything."

His eyes dart around the restaurant, looking for the hidden cameras.

To Shelt I say, "And no, this is what I've been saying all along: I don't get to use SecNet anymore. They kicked me off the Service, remember. Access to the global surveillance network's all-seeing eye isn't just handed out to anyone who asks. That's why you're going to send Grace's image to Detective Yellowbird and have her run it."

"Is she allowed to do that?" Shelt asks.

"Oh, not at all," I answer. "But she started this. You tell her if she's going to be a busybody she has to deal with the consequences."

"Great idea," Shelt says, somehow vindicated, as if the potential of getting Yellowbird fired has no bearing on what we need her to do. "I knew you'd be able to help."

"We'll see," I respond, then flip Grace's image to him from my tab. He takes a moment to compose and send quick message to Yellowbird, then there's nothing to do but wait.

"How long will it take?" Amos asks.

"Who knows," I say, and scoop a forkful of kimchi from a dish on the table. "Knowing Yellowbird, we'll hear back before dinner's over."

Amos quickly got over his paranoia at the thought of being watched by an all-knowing security apparatus and discovered he loved Korean food. He didn't stop eating for twenty minutes, and practically scarfed down every scrap of food on the table. I don't imagine he's taken much time to eat since he left the Preserves.

He's finishing off my bowl of green tea ice cream when Shelt's tab chimes. It's Yellowbird with an answer. I knew she wouldn't be able to resist.

"Well?" I ask as Shelt reads the message. He doesn't reply. Instead he flips his screen toward me and shows me a video loop of a woman who looks a lot like Grace bouncing down the stairs out of what's probably a hotel lobby, then leaving the frame to the left of the screen. I don't recognize the building, but it's definitely in Reszlieville somewhere. I can't be sure it's her either, the woman's hair is shorter than in the picture Amos showed us, and she's wearing a barely-there party dress instead of her homespun clothing, but SecNet gives a 97.8% match, and SecNet isn't usually wrong.

"That's her," Amos says, his voice clenched, and nearly leaps from his seat to get a closer view.

"You're sure?" I ask.

"As I am of anything," he confirms. "I'd know my sister anywhere."

"Where was that taken?" I ask Shelt.

"At the Gaia, that new ultra-luxe hotel," he says. "The report Detective Yellowbird included says Grace shows up in and out of there a bunch of times in the past week."

"Sounds like an expensive place," I say.

"I couldn't afford to use their toilet," Shelt confirms.

"Right. So how does a girl from the Preserves rate staying at one of the fanciest hotels in town? Amos, how much money did your sister have when she left?"

"Some small savings perhaps," Amos says with a shrug. "I don't imagine much."

Then how's she able to afford the room? Maybe someone else is paying for it. Maybe that guy she met.

For the first time in months a desire that isn't based on the basic necessities of survival sparks in my chest. I'm curious. A grassr girl comes to Reszlieville with what amounts to change in her pockets and within two weeks she's staying at one of the most expensive hotels in the world.

Shit.

I take a deep breath and before the words leave my mouth I'm already regretting them. "Okay, I'll look into it."

Shelt actually whoops, drawing attention in the noisy restaurant, and smiles sheepishly. "Great, Fin. I knew you'd come through."

"Let's get started," Amos says. His body is tense, ready for action, but I'm going to let him down.

"Not so fast," I say, and as I do his face immediately clouds with distrust. "I have conditions."

"What conditions?" Amos asks, his voice on edge.

"I work alone."

He shakes his head, looks from me to Shelt. "She's my sister. I'm going to help find her whether you like it or—"

"No," I say before Shelt can get involved. It's for the kid's own good. I can probably spend a few more hours out in the world, but the fewer people around the better.

"I insist," Amos says, his voice as stern as he can make it.

"Look, no offense kid—" His back straightens in defiance but I continue. "Amos. You've got no rep, you don't know the city or anything about it, and most of all you don't know me." He squints at me but I keep going. "You want to find your sister and I'm willing to help, but we do it my way, and that means I work alone."

"Fin, if he wants—" Shelt starts, but I ignore him and keep my eyes locked on Amos.

"I work alone, or I don't work at all. That's the deal. You in or out?"

Amos looks like he wants to argue, but he's smart enough to see he's out of options. "I accept."

"Good," I say. "Where are you staying?"

"A capsule hotel by the airport," he says, and gives me the name of a sub-bargain hotel chain.

"Go there and wait. I'll be in touch when I know something."

Amos throws Shelt a questioning look, *do you trust this guy?* but Shelt waves away his concerns.

"Go do what you need to do, Fin," Shelt says. "Find

Grace. But if you need help, I want you to promise you'll ask."

"Of course," I lie. "And thanks for dinner. I'll be in touch." Amos takes a resigned breath but doesn't say anything else as I get up from the table.

I leave Shelt with the bill and leave the restaurant, hit the sidewalk and head south, toward the shimmering towers of Reszlieville.

Another hour. I can make it out here another hour.

At least I hope I can.

I hop a Sküte down into Reszlieville and before my ass has
even hit the seat it launches into an attempt to sell me a new
tab, tells me the one in my pocket is out of date, says the
problem with mine is you can still see it, the new one's
almost invisible, with screens that stick to anything and can
conjure the link in true-D. I immediately invoke my rep and
it's high enough to cut both the audio and the video, and the
bulbous interior of the AV goes silent.

This is a bad idea. I shouldn't be out here.

As much as I'm rediscovering the simple pleasures of
warmth and a full belly and human company, they're luxuries I can't afford. My head's in no place to be out looking
for a missing girl. I should be keeping myself under a frozen
lock and key. What good will I do if in trying to help one
person I hurt a bunch of others—

No, it'll be fine. I'll do what I can and then call it quits,
just another hour or two. I can manage that.

Besides, I feel good. My head's clear. I haven't felt that
malevolent shroud pass over my thoughts in weeks. Sure, I
was half-dead the entire time, but maybe my Cortex has

sorted itself out while I've kept it running on survival mode. Psychorithms supposedly have a self-correction mechanism built in—maybe a few weeks with my mind on ice was enough to reduce the swelling and repair the damage the other me left when he tried to invade it.

Maybe I'm better.

Maybe, but I wouldn't bet on it.

It's a short ride and the Sküte lets me out across the street from the Gaia. If anything, the night is getting hotter as the sun's going down. At least the heat-absorbing sidewalk's keeping my ankles cool.

The Gaia's on a corner lot, and must be brand new, because it definitely wasn't here the last time I was in Reszlieville. Its bottom floors are a boxy lattice of seamless wooden beams and jet-black phovo windows, and above that things get amazing. The rest of the hotel consists of individual open-air multi-level biospheres that stretch across forty-odd stories. Waterfalls cascade down past rustic cabins and trees that start on one terrace and end three stories up. Stories of misty rainforest span from luxury tents on the jungle floor up to a treehouse in the canopies. I don't know how they keep the snow on the mountaintop chalet floors from melting in the heat, but somehow the peaks above are still coated in white.

Rooms cost thousands a night. No way a girl fresh from the Preserves could afford to stay here. Either she had more money than Amos knew about or she made some fancy friends when she hit town.

I cross the street and enter the hotel lobby. Its burnished wooden walls scream of wealth. A sinewy humanoid housebot made to look like it too was meticulously carved from exotic lumber intercepts me by name, and my rep's high enough it even pretends I might be a paying customer.

"Good evening, Mr. Gage," it says. "Welcome to the Gaia. I don't have a reservation in your name. How may I help you this evening?"

I spread my tab and flick Grace's photo at the bot. "Do you have any record of this woman staying here? Or visiting?"

I'm not sure if the bot even bothers to scan the image. "I'm sorry, Mr. Gage, but the Gaia has a strict privacy policy for all of our guests, which includes guests of guests."

"Can you at least tell me if she's been here? You don't have to give me details, just a simple yes or no."

"Even a confirmation or denial would contravene our policy, sir," the bot explains with a practiced shrug of its rounded shoulders. "Thank you for visiting the Gaia and have a pleasant evening."

I figured as much. I'm not going to get anywhere without the Service Override to compel answers. This would have been a lot easier back when I was a cop. I could have put that bot in its place and made it tell me what I wanted to know. As it stands I've got no more clout than any other loser walking in off the street.

I don't like to admit it, because I know what the psychologists would say it means about my personality, but I miss feeling special. The badge gave me some small measure of power over the world. Sure, I tried to use that power to help people whenever I could, but that didn't mean I couldn't enjoy it at the same time.

When I last restored, my life was already a mess. I was off guard and running from the first hour, didn't have time to settle into my new life or notice the little ways it had changed. But once that was all over and my name was cleared and I'd done all I could to make up for the damage the other me had caused, that's when I really started to notice the differences.

Not being a cop anymore was bad enough, but then the dark thoughts started, then the blackouts, and when I retreated into that protective fantasy, a part of me was relieved. I didn't have to worry about what came next. I didn't have to move forward, figure out what my life was going to be.

But now that I'm out, once again immersed in the real world, it feels good to be doing something, to have a purpose. Even if it doesn't come with the perks it once did.

It's clear I'm not going to get anywhere with the hotel itself, but I've still got a little time before the pod's maintenance cycle finishes. I'll see if I can find someone who saw Grace hanging around, maybe another guest or a human staff member—if the hotel has any. I'll never get around a bot, but I might be able to convince someone not strictly bound by programming to talk to me.

I hang around outside for a half hour or so with Grace's photo up on my tab and my face set to nonthreatening. No one I talk to says they've seen her—those few who even bother to acknowledge my presence as they breeze through the lobby. At one point a housebot strides out and asks me to move along, but I ignore it. It can bar me from the hotel, but it can't keep me from asking questions on a public sidewalk. Even still, I feel the warning twinge in my head as the hotel dings my rep with a poor interaction.

A few minutes later I get a reminder notice that the pod maintenance cycle is finished. I've done all I can. Time to get back to dying.

I'm looking down the street to an approaching Sküte, ready to signal it to stop, when a pretty young woman exits the hotel lobby. Even from here she smells like money. She's wrapped in a skintight dress and has a sleek, silver-furred, dead animal draped around her neck and down over her chest. I'm not sure what kind of animal, exactly: I don't know of any that have ten legs.

Last shot, then I'm out of here. "Excuse me," I say as I step closer to her, holding Grace's photo up, "have you seen this woman?"

She barely glances at the photo before locking her shimmering purple eyes with mine. "Sure," she says.

I'm momentarily startled. I wasn't actually expecting to get anywhere with this. "You have?"

"You sound surprised," she coos.

"I just wasn't expecting..." I stammer, for some reason flustered by her intense gaze. "Where did you see her?"

She cocks her head at me and I can tell this isn't going to be quick. She's got all the time in the world. "Why should I tell a big piece of man like you where that little girl is?"

The way she talks, I can't tell if she's eighteen or eighty. She's definitely reszo—no one ends up this pretty without pulling some genetic levers—but anyone could be inside that skyn.

"She's missing," I say, playing the straight man to her one-woman show. "She was staying here."

"Oh really?" She looks up at the building, feigning disinterest. "What a coincidence."

"When did you last see her?"

"Who told you she was missing?" she counters. She knows something.

"Her brother. He came from the Preserves. They haven't heard from her in weeks."

She smiles to herself. "That doesn't surprise me."

"Tell me," I say, but I know it's not going to be that easy.

"Her brother," she says, looking past me up the sidewalk. "He as good-lookin' as she is?"

"He looks like a cowboy," I offer. "If you're into that kind of thing."

She swoons and fans herself with a practiced hand. "I always did have a weakness for cowboys. First time I fell in love was Michael Landon on the TV..." She looks up at me from under her thick eyelashes. "You remember him?"

I shake my head. "Before my time, I'd imagine."

"Too bad," she says with a little laugh, leaning forward and pressing her hand against my chest. Even though I know this is all a game and this woman is probably more than a hundred years old, my heart flutters with excitement and guilt. An attractive woman coming on to me while Connie's waiting at home...

No, *she isn't—*

I need to let my attachment to Connie's sprite go, it's unhealthy. Although I know I won't.

"So, you were telling me about this brother..." the woman continues when I don't immediately follow up on her come-on.

"He's off feeding his horse," I say, but I can't keep up the game much longer, I've never been much for subtlety. "Why don't you tell me where you saw his sister, and I'll introduce you?"

"Stop flirting," she declares, but lets her fingers linger on my chest as she pushes away.

"Grace," I say. Serious now. "Her name is Grace. Her brother just wants to know she's okay."

Her mask slips and she hesitates a moment, squinting her eyes at me as if searching for something on my face. "Sometimes it's hard to remember this isn't old and boring for everyone." She sighs. "I remember when I first came here, my family was scared too. Grace...I didn't know that was her name, she's just another one of those faces, you know. But I assure you, she's fine."

I'm all at once relieved she's okay and vindicated for not wanting to bother with all this in the first place, but I suppose it wasn't a complete waste of time. It was nice to get out into the world for a while.

"You know where she is?"

"Right now? No, but I've been slumming at the Zack Lazer every night this week, and she's been in there hanging with her crew." She cranks her personality back up to eleven and brushes past me. "Don't judge. I may be a goer, but the way that girl parties? She'd wear me out."

I watch her shimmy away from me, butt swinging side to side like she's throwing hip checks. She tosses the animal skin up over her shoulder and it watches me as she disappears into the busy sidewalk.

The Zack Lazer. I don't know the place, but I already know I'm going to hate it there.

A QUICK LINK check reveals the Zack Lazer is a notorious reszo fetish club, catering exclusively to the digitally immortal and those who worship them. It's in an old factory building tucked in on a slope beside the Valley Parkway. The building's original red-brick exterior is hidden under bright blue plastic, glowing neon orange and shimmering chrome—an eighty-year-old aesthetic vision of the future made real.

The line isn't long, probably only exists to present the allure of exclusivity, but I skip it anyway. A pair of very young-looking guys waiting at the front of the small queue grumble as I step past them and up to a tiny woman with a half-shaved head and an imposing bot minding the door. The bot doesn't move as the woman looks me up and down with distaste. Her expression is clear: I don't belong.

The reszos in line chirp insults at me, throwing weight around no one can feel but them. The bouncer is on their side, about to tell me to get to the back of the line, when her rep-check flashes its result onto her tab and tells her I can go where I please. Her back straightens and she gives me another look up and down, her distaste transformed to intrigue. She probably doesn't see people with a rep like mine around here very often, and I don't figure I much resemble the ones she does.

Some way or another I've managed to string together a point-nine-two rep score—probably artificially inflated by the approval I'd garnered after reports got out I'd taken down a rogue SI and then spent my dead wife's inheritance on lawyers and new skyns for its victims. Yeah, my life is in shambles, I have barely any savings left, I'm in love with a sprite of my dead wife, and a vengeful memory of my past self is stalking around my head, but at least my rep is strong. At this point I'll take what I can get.

The bot steps aside, putting itself between me and the chattering pair at the head of the line, and the woman waves me in with a sly glance and a bright, "Have a good evening, Mr. Gage."

I enter to a score of synthesized drums and low organ. Inside is a large circular room with the orange and blue lights low enough to hide how dingy the formerly white vacuformed walls are. It's not busy, maybe a quarter of capacity, the kind of place the twenty-four seven party crew end up when they've ground their rep down to a nub. Everyone here would rather be somewhere better.

Reszos occupy a raised ring of secluded booths circling the main dance floor, all designer outfits and bodies to match, but even in the dim light it's obvious they've seen better days. Their minds may be eternal but their skyns are still flesh and blood. Nonstop partying takes its toll.

The immortals sit on their perch, judging the evening's offerings, while the people on the dance floor peacock for attention. Here the crowd's mostly young morties in wild makeup—bright green and pink and gold eyes abound—for both the men and women, with a few way downmarket reszos thrown in for good measure. Every so often an invitation is offered, and a lowly human boy or girl is offered the chance to run with the gods—either for the night, or from the haggard looks of some of the people here, until their bodies give out from all the stimulants or their minds from lack of sleep.

Directly across from me, opposite the entrance, a bar sells all manner of intoxicants—alcohol and hard drugs for the organics, shyfts for the reszos. Most of those who aren't dancing or in one of the booths are hanging there. The bar has the biggest crowd, but the second biggest is congregated around one of the booths off to my right. I check who they're all gathered to impress and notice Grace right away. She's heavily made up, with glittering blue-black eye shadow and deep copper-red lips, and wearing silver poncho that wraps the back of her head and shoulders and leaves her midriff and the lower half of her breasts exposed.

She's easy enough to spot because she isn't in the crowd —she's sitting in a raised both with six other people, four male and two female, all of them young and pretty. From here I can only tell two of the males are obviously reszo. They aren't just handsome, they're human works of art, chiseled chins and high cheekbones and thick dark hair swept back from their broad foreheads—but their skin's so yellow and sunken, and their eyes so scrunched, they look like party zombies.

The two morty women are clearly paired up with the two male reszos. The couples are draped over each other, side by side on one end of the booth, the reszo males next to each other, haggard but relaxed, while the girls cling to their sides, eyes jittery from stim overload.

Surprisingly, Grace isn't a groupie. She's the center of

attention for the two male morties. A good-looking blond guy on her right seems put out while another, even better looking redhead on her other side is whispering something in her ear that makes her eyes narrow and her copper lips spread in a lewd grin.

The Zack Lazer is supposed to be a place where reszos can pick and choose, not the other way around. So why are those two guys so interested in Grace?

I wind through the sparse crowd and make directly for Grace's booth. She doesn't notice me as I step up onto the dais, but one of the blonde beside her does. He takes a look at me, glances over at Grace, and rolls his eyes. He figures I'm more competition.

The two male reszos are deep in a conversation about which one of their girls will give out first, and who they've got their eyes on as replacements. Up close their bodies look even worse. Their skyns radiate a sickly green color under the blue lights, probably jaundiced from pushing their livers too hard or from some kind of rampant STD. If they were human they'd be in the hospital, on the verge of death. Instead they'll likely party until their skyns give out, dump them, and buy new ones. The fun never has to end.

They don't acknowledge me either. I knock on the table, and the bouncing glasses finally get their attention.

"Grace?" I say, leaning over the table and ignoring everyone else. "Are you okay? Amos came to find you, he's worried."

Grace is still locked in a tense flirtation with the guy beside her. I know she heard me, but she draws the moment out before she swings her eyes around and lets her head follow slowly behind.

"Who. The fuck. Are you?" she asks, her words slurring out in a lazy drawl.

"My name's Fin," I say, trying to keep the surprise off my face. Grace isn't what I was expecting. "I'd like you to come with me and talk to your brother."

She doesn't look drugged, or like she's here against her will.

"Fuck. Off," she says, turns to the redhead beside her, traces her finger down his cheek and leans in for a wet kiss.

What am I supposed to do now? Here I thought I was on a rescue mission for a missing girl. I didn't consider she might not want to be saved.

I stand back, knowing I should leave this alone and walk away but still hesitant to leave her here, except I guess I'm not moving fast enough for her. She flicks her eyes at the two reszos on the other side of the booth and they spring up and over the table, their ebbing skyns concealing speed I wasn't expecting, and I jump back instinctively.

They land and I continue my retreat, get my hands up in defense. Back when I was shyfting, when I was super-charging my head with the revv code that made me think at the speed of light, they'd already be on the floor—wouldn't have made it over the table—but since I'm stuck with the world moving at regular speed, I'll keep it simple. I may not be revved, but my skyn is still top-of-the-line, nestled right up against the Human Standard limits. These guys are no match for me, physically at least, especially not in the shape they're in, but who knows what cocktail of stims and code they've got swirling around in their skyns. Best make it quick. I'll hit the first one that gets close as hard as I can and figure my next move from there.

I tense my legs, shift my weight to my back foot, and wait, but before either of them can press the attack the security lawbots are between us. The club's IMP must have predicted the fight and had the bots move to intercept us before we even knew it was about to happen.

One bot extends its arms as a barrier and walks me backwards off the dais, while the other keeps Grace's two reszo goons in place. It escorts me across the dance floor and out the exit and dumps me in front of the small woman at the door.

She once again looks me up and down and shakes her head. "I knew you didn't belong in there," she says.

Can't argue with that. My brain twitches again as I feel the Zack Lazer ding my rep with another negative interaction. At the rate I'm going it won't be long before I'm back down to mid-rep like everyone else.

I pick myself up and dust myself off and walk a few paces away from the catcalls of the crowd outside, the schadenfreude of watching the guy who skipped the line get kicked out ten minutes later too delicious to contain.

Now I have to call Amos. The good news is, his sister's fine, but I might leave out the part where I tell him she's turned into an asshole.

WINTER ISN'T BORED. Not exactly.

The physical sensations are pleasurable and the woman objectively beautiful.

The torrent of feeling flowing from her mind—a high gloss of erotic stimulation over nuances of simmering fear, self-loathing, and humiliation—still manages to blunt the edges of his yawning need, but the novelty has worn off.

As much as these feelings—as this ritual—fulfills him, it's no longer enough.

He needs more, already needs more.

He tightens her collar and slaps her once again, and her mindstream froths with a fresh burst of panic underlain by a sinuous wave of pleasure.

Winter is well-versed in the language of pain, was even before he found this place. He took so many samples, experienced so much vicarious horror and fear—he became an expert in it. The police interruption of his last mission along the waterfront was, in retrospect, fortuitous. He gave up the hunts immediately and without regret. But for the outside trigger forcing him to abandon his missions he might be haunting there still, bounded by the limited palette of sudden violence.

Not to discount the grandeur of fear—the terrified emotional responses he'd collected were exquisite. He lived and relived them, bathing in their majesty while he concocted a new method to obtain samples. By the time he finally worked out his next plan he knew each sickening beat of his targets' terror in intimate detail. He wrung dry every moment of existential torture from their final thoughts, replayed them until the concentrated shots of emotion lost their power and he needed something new, something more substantial than the trembling terror of the hunted.

He knew this because of Shireen, his fifth sampled mind. She had resisted. Even as her body lay severed from her head, her skull in the hands of a malicious stranger, she conjured a refuge of happy memories in her mind, protected herself behind a thought that shone with a singular ferocity—a loving embrace in the proud arms of her mother as she graduated from some deeply challenging educational pursuit—and it was glorious. Even tainted by the immediacy of her recent decapitation, the bloom of this concoction—a warm, positive, uplifting emotion—slammed into his mind and broke through to show him modes of being he didn't know could be so potent.

He immediately understood what drives the junkies who plug themselves in, day after day, repeatedly pressing their chosen button for doses of rewarding biochemical soup.

He needed more, needed all of it. Needed to experience every possible morsel of emotion he could.

Afterward, back in the safety of his home, he stripped out the negative taint of violence from Shireen's final thoughts and immersed himself in it, went back to it, over and over, until that button too lost its power. Once spent, he filed it away with the others. By then he knew what to do next.

It's an irony, he knows. His lack, the emptiness that defines him, is also what keeps him alive.

If, like everyone else, he'd been born with a sense of loneliness or loss, with the ability to feel depression or defeat, he might not have survived his childhood. An orphan in a drowned city—he isn't sure which, could have been Laos, could have been New Orleans—but he remembers the sterile government shelters, the hollow shelled refugees he lived with, and the nannybots who raised him. Many of the other children couldn't cope, would cry and wail for their parents as they were brought in, would rock, comatose in their beds, or soon died chasing the demons in their heads.

But not him. His lack allowed him to thrive.

He felt no remorse. No fear.

Winter did what he had to, to who he had to, to get what he wanted.

Back then, more than anything else, he wanted out of the refugee center. Six years later he bought his way out, an almost impossible act. Moreover, he left wealthy, flush with cred and the underground connections he'd made supplying the refugee camp with the luxuries unavailable inside.

He wanted a new body, a new face and a new mind he could make his own. Soon enough he'd gone reszo, and was examining his mind from the outside. Probing the gaps, searching for ways they could be filled.

He wanted to taste what it is to be fully human, and sampled deeply of fear.

In all this he succeeded, and in doing so he learned

something, something he never could have understood otherwise: fear is not only a defensive response to stimuli. It's a destination, something to be sought out.

Fear attracts.

He soon learned something else: fear can be pleasure.

And that's what led him here, to the underground sex clubs and the bounty of willing minds they proffered. If only he'd known, he could have avoided the messiness of the hunt altogether. Saved himself days of agitation and the cred for burner skyns. The shyfts provided by the reszo pleasure clubs were easy enough to simulate—his thought-psyphoning code integrated with them seamlessly. He used a fresh skyn when visiting, of course, but he didn't have to abandon it afterwards. The targets were willing, and they acked his offered shyft as a matter of course, without hesitation, unknowingly allowing him into their heads. These were places where shyfting was part of the experience, ones that, for a modest deposit, even supplied the SenShare cables intended for sharing sensation.

There were no uncooperative victims, no violence, no risk of discovery. They offered a far broader spectrum of minds to sample, and far, far more pleasure.

If only he'd known.

Places like this—dark, warm, smoky, and thick with an air of licentiousness—have existed since the time humans first lit fires in caves. Sex is primal, he now understands. And not only understands, he *feels*, rooted at the base of his spine, thick in his groin as the woman writhes over him.

The cable connecting them transmits this physical sensation up to her, while in return he feels himself inside her. They're sharing a single physicality, but he alone is receiving the stream of thoughts that run behind those sensations, sampling what mental images the sensations induce. For her it's mournful love of a past relationship gone sour, with the occasional irritant of stray thought about some co-worker.

He raises his hand and savors the prick of self-loathing as she lets him slap her once again. The perversity and the alienation, emotions delicate and sublime.

But even this has lost its potency.

He's caught glimpses of unexplored avenues of being. Emotions he understands but has still never felt.

Amazement.

Selflessness.

Contentment.

But he knows there is still more. So much more.

These quick glances, tangential collisions with real life, have only made the thirst more intense.

It can't be quick, or cursory. He needs to go deeper. To make it last. He can no longer simply skim thoughts. He needs to inhabit someone, to become them.

Finally, the woman straddling him climaxes, hits him with one last emotional burst of disappointed satisfaction, detaches the cable, rolls off without a word, and pads away.

She got what she needed.

And so did he.

He understands what he needs to do next. No more skimming along the immediate surface of his targets' thoughts. He needs to submerge, and consume their minds from within.

He needs to become someone else entirely.

THE NIGHT IS FINALLY BEGINNING to cool, but the air is still soggy with humidity and I shiver in the warmth. I'm down the street from the club but I can still hear the synth-beats leaking from the open door. The Zack Lazer is out of the way, on a side street directly overlooking six lanes of highway running through the city, and the sidewalk is empty. The moon is just a sliver in the sky but between the glowing building and the hovering floatlamps and the parade of traffic and Reszlieville's constant blaze, the city never goes dark.

A low whine comes at me from behind and I spin as a cloud of drones whizzes overhead. The flying bots pass and leave me staring at the whitewashed sky. The thumbnail moon and feeble stars can't compete with the megawatts burning around me.

I don't belong out here. Even surrounded by people, standing in the center of a city-sized spotlight, I feel detached from the world. Like I'm somehow less solid than everyone else.

I found the girl, time to go home.

This time though, when I reset the virt, I won't make my life so hard. I'll let more of the plane survive the crash, notch up the food supply, tone down the blizzards. I've been out in reality for eight hours and my head hasn't given me a problem. There's been no sign of those alien thoughts. I'll give myself a break and ease up on the virt's difficulty level. No need to torture myself if I don't have to.

I'm ready to get back. But more than anything I want to see Connie.

I'm pulling out my tab to call Amos when someone yells at me from down the street. I turn and see Grace stalking toward me—jaw locked tight but eyes hidden under her short silver poncho's hood—flanked by her two reszo pals. They're on edge, eyes wild, shyfted and gunning for a fight.

She stops a few meters from me and stares with a blistering hate that forces me back a step. "You think. Because I'm a wearing a girl. I won't light you up?" she snarls in her staccato purr.

Wearing a girl? *Wait--*

I put my hands up between us. I don't want a fight. "I'm not looking for—"

"You don't. Tell me. What to do."

I take another step back just as she springs, whirls in midair, and throws her heel around at my head. The dissonance of this wholesome grassr girl in party gear snapping a precise spin kick at me is shocking enough I almost don't get my guard up in time. Her foot slams into my forearm and grazes the side of my head, sends me skittering backwards, scrambling to put distance between us.

That's not—

She feints left then jukes and tries to catch me with another kick but I'm ready this time and knock that one aside, though not easily. She's stronger than she looks.

"You prov me. Then you scattle? Nu-uh." She casts her eyes to the side. The guys she was flirting with and the two other girls have arrived. This is a show for them now. "Bust my game. I bust yours."

She comes at me again, even faster this time, and I dance away, avoid engaging with her. *How can Grace be moving like this?*

I shuffle to the left and too late realize I've fallen for her trap.

One of her reszo buddies was anticipating my move and drops into a leg sweep, takes my feet out from under me. I hit the sidewalk hard, roll aside to dodge a boot heel to the nose, then pop back up to my feet before they can pile on.

Traffic buzz bleeds up from the highway, makes my brain itch. I don't want to fight, need to keep myself under control, figure out what's going on with Grace, but I can't help it, this is how it starts...

Unbidden, insidious, the black thoughts come, violent tendrils aching to take control. My resolve to stay out of the fight crumbles and I want to let loose on them. These fuckers think they can take me on? They don't know the shit they've stirred up. I know I can hurt them, know ten ways off the top of my head to break them into a thousand little pieces.

I flash back the revv's joyful thrust sharpening my thoughts, the pleasure I got from indulging in it. I could do it again. It would be so easy, let Grace come at me one more time and catch her off guard with a counter, break her arm in two places, and while she's wailing in pain ruin her knee with a side kick. Then I could get creative with the other two, take them apart one at a time.

I want to.

Yes.

NO—

It's happening again. My heart's thrumming, my vision's narrowed, and my head's seething with fury.

It's Deacon, filling my head with rage. He hasn't gone anywhere. I was stupid to come out here, shouldn't have let Shelt and Connie talk me out of what I knew was best.

I need to get out of this before he overwhelms me again, but there's nowhere to go. I'm trapped. Grace and her two reszo buddies circle, keeping their distance with their hands raised, rigid torsos balanced over flexed knees, cutting off my ability to escape, waiting for their chance to pounce. The only way I'm getting out of here is fighting, and once I start, no way I'll be able to keep my head.

A beating or a blackout, which is the better option?

They're moving in unison, rotating around me, keeping me guessing. They're practiced, like they've done this before. I take a breath, try to keep them all in sight at once, but they're too far apart and I'm forced to keep my head on a swivel.

No way a naïve grassr girl learned all this martial arts shit in less than a month, which means that can't be Grace. I don't know what's going on, but I've seen enough to know it won't end well.

Can't worry about it now. One of the male reszos lunges at me, and even while I know it's a distraction I twist to protect myself and feel a sharp jab in the kidney from the other side.

It's all I can do to keep the bloom of pain from over-whelming me as I toss a wide elbow backwards that sails over Grace's head. She ducks and circles back out of reach.

My vision ripples and I almost lose my grip on consciousness as Deacon tries to overwhelm me, fight my thoughts back to the surface to keep control.

He's coming. I can't stop him.

The other reszo repeats his lunge trick, but I don't take the bait, bracing for Grace to come at me from behind. Except this time he continues with his attack, drives at me with a raised knee. I get turned just enough so he skids past, but by then both Grace and the other guy are on me. Grace leaps up my back, constricts her arms around my throat, and pulls while her friend goes to work on my sides.

Pain explodes in my torso. I can't breathe. My narrowed vision fades even further. Once it goes, Deacon takes over. Who knows what he'll do once he's free again—

I force shake my head, suck a strangled breath, and tense to swing forward and throw Grace off me without hurting her too much, but she's already gone, backed off on her own, reacting to something over my shoulder.

I swing around and see what she's reacting to—

Amos.

What the hell's he doing here?

He's got his fists raised like a bar fight pro. The reszo who tried to catch me with his knee is already on the concrete, struggling to rise, while his friend is scrambling backwards, fending off Amos' repeated jabs.

Grace stands, watching, confused. There isn't a hint of recognition on her face. She has no idea who Amos is.

The reszo Amos is chasing suddenly stops his retreat, sets, and throws a hard kick at Amos' chest, but the grassr kid doesn't even pretend to dodge—he juggernauts right through it, catches the oncoming leg under his arm, drives the reszo off his feet, and slams the back of his stunned head off the sidewalk. He doesn't get up.

Grace still hasn't moved. "The fuck are you?" she yells.

Amos' chest is heaving. His adrenaline-narrowed eyes widen to confusion.

"Grace, it's me," he says as he treads toward his sister, his hand raised but the violence gone from his body. "Amos. Your brother. What has happened to you, blessed sister?"

"I'm no one's sister," she says and drops her hands to her sides, tensed, ready to fight.

Amos glares at me, mouth tight, like I had something to do with his sister's behavior, with why she's wearing a tiny skirt and poncho that barely covers her breasts.

I shrug and shake my head at him. "She was like this when I found her," I say. "She could be hurt. Maybe a blow to the head..." Except I know that's not true. Brain damage can cause extreme changes in personality, but it doesn't usually leave the victim with martial arts training. "Was she a fighter back home?"

Amos takes a second to toss me a glower. "Never," he says. "Grace embraced our doctrine of nonviolence."

I nod at the two reszos still incapacitated on the ground. "That didn't look nonviolent to me."

"I'm not as temperate as she is," Amos answers as he continues to advance on his sister, his voice calm, his words measured. "Please, Grace," he says. "You must recognize me."

Finally, Grace has had enough. "Fuck. You," she snaps. "And fuck Grace. Whoever she is."

Amos' face falls. "*You* are Grace," he pleads. His eyes grow liquid as he extends his hand. "You're not yourself. Let me help you."

Grace backs away, rolls her shoulders, and hops side to side on the balls of her feet, encouraging Amos to make the first move.

My mind's racing, struggling to find some reason that could account for what's happening. "Are you *sure* this is your sister?" I ask Amos.

He tugs his beard in frustration. "As certain as I've ever been of anything," he says. "I've known her from the day she was born. I watched her grow."

"You don't know the world," I say. "Someone could have made a copy of her body..."

That might explain it. A bioSkyn in Grace's image. But skyns take months to complete, unless whoever made it started before she left the Preserves...

Thin, but possible. I guess.

"The scar on your abdomen," he says to Grace. "Remember how you tried to climb that fence to get closer to the horses? I carried you back to Father. Doc gave you eleven stitches while I held your hand and told you the story of Daniel and the lions."

Grace slows and runs her fingers along the faint scar, laughs, and resumes bouncing from foot to foot.

"Grace..." Amos says, raw emotion tearing at his voice.

"*Grace*..." the girl whines in a mocking reply. She raises her hands and pulls the hood back from her head. If Amos won't come to her, she'll take the fight to him—

I see it before Amos does. The cuff riding the back of her neck. It was hidden by the poncho...

She's reszo.

Grace bursts past me, flying toward Amos. He backs off, hands raised, face contorted in shock. What must this kid be thinking right now?

He blocks her blows as she backs him into the fence between us and the steep wooded slope down to the highway.

How could Grace be a reszo?

The answer's simple and obvious: she couldn't.

Which means that isn't Grace.

It's Grace's *body*, but someone's replaced her brain with a Cortex. I didn't know that was possible.

Only four months away and already the world has skipped ahead on me.

Whatever's going on, whoever's inside her mind—it still could be Grace in there for all I know—that's still Grace's body. I don't want to hurt her if I don't have to.

Luckily, we've got the numbers advantage now. We should be able to take her down without too much trouble. If Amos can recover enough to co-operate. I'll just have to hope he can pull himself together in time to follow my lead.

While Amos has Grace distracted, I swing around and get behind her. She flies toward him, a flurry of fists, forcing Amos to once again raise his hands and retreat. That's when I make my move.

I rush forward and get my hands up under Grace's arms, knock the cuff off her neck, and lock my fingers over the sub-dermal port at the base of her skull.

She cries out and tries to swing her head back to catch my nose but I'm stronger than she is and keep her face pressed toward the ground. She's kicking and swinging her hands but I've got her. She isn't going anywhere.

Amos rushes in and takes her in his arms. "Grace," he says, "you're safe now. I'm going to take you home and you'll get better."

He doesn't know. Didn't see the cuff, or doesn't understand what it means.

"Amos—" I start, trying to warn him. His sister isn't who he thinks she is.

Grace squirms again and then all at once stops struggling and laughs. "I don't know who this Grace bitch is," she says, smug. "Bought this skyn weeks ago. Won the bid fair. You can't take it."

Amos blinks, confused. "You are my sister...".

"Whoever your sister was," the person in Grace's body says, "she ain't here. This skyn's mine now. You can't have it. Now fuck the fuck off before I get physical."

That's not Grace.

We may have found her body, but she's no longer in it.

PART TWO_

WINTER'S EMBRACE

GLENN STRIDES up the walkway to his house, bounds up the short flight of wooden stairs onto the front porch. He's been looking forward to tonight all week—date night. The one night he and Marcos can unplug and spend a few hours together, no distractions. They'll sit on the couch, sample some of that bourbon they had shipped up from the Dixie Bloc. They'll talk, make out a bit. End up in the bedroom.

His anticipation of reconnecting with his husband is mingling with the lingering high from his afternoon session at the club, naked, indulging in every form of hedonistic physical pleasure the human body is capable of. He wore that rented skyn raw. He doesn't even mind forfeiting his damage deposit—it was worth every cred he paid them.

The chairs on the porch are squared neatly off, fresh flowers in a clear blue vase arranged on a small table in between. He flushes with an uncharacteristic pride for the job he and Marcos did building it, for all the work they put into making this place a home. They restored the porch to its original specifications last summer, ripped out the tired plastic and replaced it with a period-appropriate wooden deck built from timbers shipped from a lumber yard up north, and finished it with a simple pergola. They sanded and stained until they had it just right. So much work, but in the end, so worth it. He still loves how it complements the front yard of trim green hostas in white mulch and the small patch of emerald lawn. The sense of accomplishment is buoyant.

He takes a breath, savors the night air in his lungs. Who would have thought he'd end up here? He spent most of his life merely scraping by, another genitect making incremental improvements to pharmaceutical-generating yeast cells in a rented bathroom lab, but nothing that had ever gained a foothold in the reengineering market. He hit it big with a fluke: an accidental transposition of two unrelated gene sequences that created a secretory pathway with an order of magnitude improvement in protein synthesis. The licensing rights bought him this body, handsome and healthy. This home, a *house* of his own, on the edge of Reszlieville of all places. And it brought him Marcos.

He really does have everything. The flush of gratitude nearly buckles his knees, and he laughs at the surprising intensity of it. *What's gotten into him?* He knows the post-club high usually lasts for a few days, but never has he experienced it with such strength.

He shakes his head. He's being silly. It was only sex.

The door opens as he steps up to it. He hangs his jacket on a hook in the front hall, pokes his head around the corner, and there's Marcos, perched sideways on the couch. Two glasses wait on the low table in front of him, and next to them sit the unopened bottle of bourbon with the waterfall on the label and a box of ice rocks.

Marcos. His hair is thick and dark and full, cut rough

and brushed to the side. His brown eyes sparkle. He's perfect. Perfect lips. Perfect heart. Perfect taut little body.

And still human. A perfect specimen of the form.

He first met Marcos on the link, both of them looking for something and neither of them quite sure what. They talked, connected. They spent days of virt-time together. Adventuring. Exploring. Soon, they fell in love.

Eventually he popped the question and had Marcos shipped up from Brazil. They were married a week later. A year ago last month now, and things still as good as ever.

"How was your afternoon?" Marcos asks. His accent glances off vowels just obliquely enough to make even the most everyday sentences somehow seductive. Marcos drops a frozen rock into one of the glasses and pours a healthy splash of amber liquid over it.

"Spectacular," he says, and brushes Marcos' fingers as he takes the glass.

Marcos flinches at his touch. Almost imperceptibly, but no mistaking it. His eyes flicker, distracted by some escaped thought, before reverting to their usual devoted shine.

But he can see it now. The smile just a little too firm. The sparkle now obviously practiced.

Glenn's previous good mood shrivels, sours to paranoia and frustration and bubbles up to anger. His lips pull back from his teeth as he narrows his eyes.

Who does Marcos think he is? To judge me?

His whole body is trembling. It's all he can do to keep from smashing his glass straight into Marcos' face.

Marcos immediately recoils, sliding away on the couch, obviously afraid.

He sees the fear in Marcos' eyes and snaps out of it. The anger dwindles as suddenly as it appeared.

Get it together, Glenn!

What is going on? Where is this anger coming from? It isn't like him, Marcos doesn't deserve it.

No, Marcos doesn't like it when Glenn visits the club. But he's a kid, still human. They've had this conversation over and over. He still doesn't understand that it's no different than a virt, the things he does there are with a rented body, an artificial slab of flesh and blood and over-stimulated neurons. There's no emotional attachment to any of the people he encounters at the club, it's purely visceral. Sex for the artistry of it. Erogenous zones played like instruments.

His feelings are for Marcos alone, and the body Glenn's wearing is reserved only for their bed. Isn't that what matters? Bodies are temporary shells, his mind is what's important, and no one gets to have that but Marcos.

Hot tears of remorse spill down his cheeks. *Why did I react so horribly?*

"I'm sorry," Glenn says, frantic now to make Marcos see his regret. He pushes in close, takes Marcos' hands. "I'm so sorry, I don't know what came over me."

Marcos is nodding, confused. He doesn't know what's going on either. "It's OK, honey," Marcos says, and pulls him into an embrace. "I know you are."

Marcos' arms are like a warm blanket over his jangled thoughts, and right now there's no place he'd rather be. His contentment is absolute. He never wants to move, wants to live in this cocoon of tenderness forever, can't believe he's gone his whole life never feeling something as simple as this—

But then he wants more. He feels himself grow hard. If a gentle embrace feels this amazing, he can only imagine how good the sex will be.

He pushes back and takes Marcos by the neck, presses his lips to his husband's.

Marcos responds, but tentatively. Which only makes Glenn want it more. This is his husband and they're going to kiss. They're in love and this is what it feels like to kiss someone you love.

It's only now he realizes Marcos is resisting, trying to pull away, and he stops, unsure for a moment where he is or what he's doing.

For a moment, he wasn't in control.

Like someone else's ideas were in his mind.

Maybe something's gone wrong. A glitch during the transfer at the club—

He dismisses the thought. Not possible. His Cortex would have reported an error if there'd been one...but the sensation was so intense—

"What is wrong with you tonight?" Marcos demands. He's standing now, backed away in the hall, his brown eyes strained.

"I don't know," Glenn says, and shakes his head. "Just a bit out of sorts for a second there but I'm fine now." He pats the seat beside him. "Come back."

Marcos considers this for a moment. "Fine, but I want you to take your cuff off."

This again. Marcos thinks the cuff is a distraction. Thinks the constant connection makes Glenn less present. But most of the time he's not even using it, barely pays any attention to the notices and feed alerts. What more does Marcos want?

"I'll put it on DND," he says.

"Take it off," Marcos replies.

He doesn't want to, but what's the harm? He could go without the link for a few hours—

NO!

The thought erupts from some recess of his mind he's never felt before, a supernova in a previously quiet corner of his brain. He doesn't know where it came from, but he can't ignore it.

"No," Glenn says, his voice quiet.

Marcos swallows whatever it was he was about to say. He's mad. Furious.

What has he done?

"Marcos, wait—"

Marcos holds up his hand. "Not a chance," he says and grabs his coat from the wall. "I'll see you in the morning."

"Marcos, baby, don't—"

Marcos leaves and the door shuts behind him. The house echoes with silence.

Glenn slumps to the couch, reveling in the exquisite misery. Then, once the initial gut punch has dissipated, he empties the glass down his throat in one long swallow and spends the rest of the night drinking his way through the rest of the bottle, getting drunk on the delicious ache of his broken heart.

No one moves.

Amos' face is all twisted up in fear and confusion and revulsion as he stares in silence at what used to be his sister's body, now possessed.

I'm breathing hard, realize I'm sweating in the close air. I've still got NotGrace's body secured, elbows under her armpits and hands clasped around her neck, stopping her from launching another attack or running, but the exertion of keeping myself tense, anticipating what she's going to do next, is wearing me out.

The two reszos Amos laid out groan on the ground. One of them slammed the back of his head on the concrete, likely fractured his skull. The other one seems okay but is content to stay out of the fight. His body doesn't look like it'd hold together for many more beatings as it is.

"I don't understand," Amos finally says, looking at his sister but talking to me. "Surely she must be sick, a disease of the mind—"

She isn't sick, someone removed her brain and replaced

it with a cortical prosthetic. "She's not lying," I tell him. "I've got my thumbs on her Cortex's IO port."

"Her—"

"It anchors her cuff to her neck, allows her to access the link directly with her mind."

"What is a cuff? I don't understand..." His nostrils flare and his face reddens and he strides up to his sister's body, gets nose to nose. "Grace, for the love of our mother, tell me you're sick. We can help you—"

His face twists up as he sees something he hadn't noticed before.

"Your eyes..." he says as NotGrace brings up her knee and catches him square between the legs. He drops with a strangled cry, clutching his groin. There's nothing I can do but watch him writhe on the asphalt and struggle to contain Grace's renewed attempts to escape.

"You fucks," she yells at the two reszos who have dragged themselves back to where their human companions are waiting. "Get. The fuck. Back here... Help me!"

She wiggles and kicks into my shins but I endure the pain and increase the pressure on her neck, pressing her chin hard into her chest until she finally cries out in frustration but stops resisting.

Amos is on his hands and knees, breathing through the pain. I can feel it from here. She nailed him.

"Those aren't," he says through clenched teeth, "your eyes."

The person inside Grace's body laughs again, taunting. "I told you. Your sister's gone," she says. I feel her cheeks spread in a wide grin. "Thoughts sucked out when they vacuumed her skull clean. This body's mine. Now let. Me go. Before I break. Your ass."

Amos rushes to his feet and comes at NotGrace with his

fists raised, but all of us know he won't follow through. Whether it's his sister's mind inside her body or not, no way he'll be able to bring himself to hit her.

He doesn't understand. He grew up in the Preserves, he hasn't seen the world changing hour by hour, hasn't seen then things I have. Just because Grace isn't in her body, that doesn't mean she's dead. Her mind could still be alive, stored somewhere, captured as a psychorithm. The question is whether the person I've got in my arms had anything to do with taking Grace's mind from her body.

"What's your name?" I ask.

"Fuck you. That's my name," NotGrace answers.

I jam my knee into the back of hers, buckle her leg, and press her down to kneeling.

"Let's get comfortable," I say. "Have a little chat about who you stole this body from."

"No way," NotGrace says and tries to struggle but she's got no leverage. "I got this skyn legit. Signed waiver and all." She looks up at Amos. "Voluntary disembodiment."

Amos wrinkles a look at me but I don't know any more than he does. People are selling their bodies now?

Come to think of it, that's nothing new at all. They've just finally made it literal.

"You're saying Grace gave up her body willingly?" I ask, and briefly increase the pressure on the back of her head. Keep the talking motivated. "For what...money?"

"Never," Amos says, horrified. "She would never—"

"Where'd you get the skyn?" I ask, changing tack. It doesn't matter who's inside Grace's body now. He or she probably doesn't know any more about the former owner than someone buying a stolen car would. But she bought it from someone. That someone might know what happened to Grace.

"Amos. Get my tab and call the cops. We may not be able to get her to talk, but Rithm Crime can. If we're wrong, we'll say our sorrys and everyone can go about their evenings." As Amos shuffles around and pulls my tab out, I lean in and put my mouth next to NotGrace's ear. I can't physically make her tell me anything—she isn't afraid of pain, probably has the receptors cranked down anyway. No, there's only one place I can hurt whoever's riding Grace's body—in the rep.

"No one gets to be as big an asshole as you are without pissing a bunch of people off," I whisper. "Why are you slumming in a shithole like the Zack Lazer? I bet it's because you don't have the rep for anywhere else, I bet you're pretty much unwelcome most places. How much lower will a ding by the cops take it? You want to risk bussing to the suburbs to find a party that will have you?"

NotGrace's chest rises and falls under me as Amos flips the tab over and over, trying to figure out how to work the thin strip of plastic.

"Hold it at the bottom, between your thumb and fingers. When it turns on ask it to send the police."

"Okay, okay. I'll talk. No cops," Grace finally says, her words stumbling out in a halting rush. "I'll talk."

"Where?" I ask. Amos stops fumbling with the tab.

NotGrace takes a breath. "Nandez."

"What?" I ask. "That a name?"

"Loo Nandez. The skyn merchant."

"You know this person?" Amos asks me.

I shake my head. "Never heard of him," I say. "But I don't get out much."

"How do we find him?" Amos says to NotGrace.

"Ain't a him," NotGrace sneers.

"How do we find *her*?" It's obvious Amos wants to let

loose on NotGrace, but the cognitive dissonance between the body he's talking to and the person wearing it is messing with him, making him jumpy.

NotGrace huffs a sigh. "Ask. Your fucking. IMP," she says. "She ain't hiding."

"Help me find this Nandez," Amos says to me.

I thought I was trying to find a missing girl. Hunting down a black market skyn dealer could take days. I can't be out here for days, shouldn't be out here *now*.

Months on the ice made me careless, tricked me into thinking maybe my mind had fixed itself. But this isn't something that'll spontaneously resolve. I have a monster living in my head, and he wants out.

I'm too dangerous out here.

I can't help anymore anyway. There's enough here to get the Service interested. If Amos is right, and Grace didn't sign her body away, then she was murdered and the police won't have a choice but to get involved. But there's always a chance she did, and if that's legal now, then I don't know what we can do—either way, I've done all I can.

"Call the police," I tell Amos. "Tell them your story again. They have a body, they'll listen to you now."

"*What?*" NotGrace says, resuming a struggle I shut down with a press of my thumbs into the back of her skull. "You said—"

"I don't owe you shit," I say. "You're wearing this guy's sister, no way I'm gonna let you walk away in it."

"Then we'll go find this Nandez?" Amos asks.

I shake my head. "No. We'll tell the police. They'll handle it."

Amos' eyes narrow. "You won't help me?" he asks.

"I'm helping," I say, the words bitter in my mouth. "But I've done all I can." There was a time doing all I can wouldn't have included walking away in the middle of an investigation, but those days are long gone.

"Shelt said you wouldn't stop until you found my sister."

"We found her."

"Someone *killed* her," Amos says, his back rod-straight, the tendons in his neck taut. "Don't you care who?"

"I've done all I can," I repeat, and settle in to wait for the police to arrive. "I just want to go home."

GAGE, FINSBURY_
22:55:21 // 07-JUN-2059

NOTGRACE'S BUDDIES are long gone by the time the
Service drones swoop in, neuralizers primed to stun
anything that moves, and lock down the scene. None of us
are going anywhere for a while but at least I get to drop
NotGrace from the headlock. She moves away from us—but
not far enough to draw any added attention from the
hovering drones. She knows she can't run.

The Uniforms arrive next, immediately separate us,
then rithmscan NotGrace and me while they try to figure
out who Amos is. Turns out the person inside NotGrace is a
low-life named Malcom Welwyn, an all-round asshole with
ties to a reszo collective known for all sorts of shady shit—
rep-theft, dealing unregistered skyns, plus assorted other
Standards violations. He's been hiding from a stack of
warrants inside various skyns for months, the anonymous
grassr girl he's wearing only the latest. He tries to talk his
way out of it then hints at resisting when they pull out the
binders. A long neuralizer blast from one of the drones puts
an immediate stop to anything he was about to do, and he

freezes and topples over onto the street, convulsing so hard he bounces.

Amos is watching all of this, hat crushed in his hands, and all he can see is his sister hitting the pavement face-first and he stops himself from running to catch her as she falls. He turns away as the lawbot picks NotGrace up under the arms and drags her twitching body to a cruiser to send it off for processing.

The constables turn to us next, and once they get our statements and figure out Amos is just a tourist, they park us on the curb while we wait for the detectives to arrive to go through the whole process again.

I spend the next hour chilling my ass on the concrete beside a devastated and increasingly irate Amos. One by one the investigation teams arrive and go over the details of the scene. Eventually Homicide, the Psychorithm Crime Unit, and the Ministry of Human Standards are all present and up to date, and arguing over who's in charge of cleaning up.

Amos' talking to anyone who will listen, continuing to insist Grace has been murdered, her body stolen from her, but the person behind NotGrace's perfectly functioning eyes is obviously alive enough, so Homicide packs up and bails—they have real murderers to catch.

That leaves Karin Yellowbird from the PCU and Olliver Brewer from Standards to fight over what to do about Grace's body.

I've worked with them both before—well, parts of me have. Deacon was posted to Rithm Crime back when he was first restored. Yellowbird was one of the first people he talked to in those early days after the accident, when he was still trying to decide whether he should resume his life without Connie or toss it all in and put a bullet through the glowing plastic masquerading as his brain.

Then, when I returned the second time, with my name in disgrace and my rep trashed, she was the only one who didn't immediately reject me. She isn't one to hide what she thinks, but she's solid. I can trust her.

Olliver Brewer—Special Agent Brewer, he reminded me when he arrived—not so much. I don't know how he's managed to keep his job, let alone make Special Agent in the Ministry of Human Standards. I don't believe he could pass the basic entrance exam.

His career's been like that magnetic hill in New Brunswick: his engine's stuck in neutral but somehow he's still accelerating upwards, coasting from constable to detective and now to federal agent, and right now, *he's* in charge of learning what happened to Grace.

Technically, Standards can pull rank on just about anything that fits their mandate of keeping humanity human, and one of their highest priorities is keeping sketchy, unknown rithms from running around causing trouble in unregistered skyns, and that's all Brewer can see here: a potentially dangerous unknown rithm—a cypher—inhabiting a disposable skyn. He doesn't care where Grace's skyn came from, and with the Cortex in her head gone that's what her body is now, a skyn—he only cares it's not registered with Standards. Once it's off the streets, his job is done.

If Standards takes charge of the case, I don't expect Amos will ever find out what happened to his sister.

We sit and watch while Brewer and Yellowbird have it out. They're about the same height but Brewer's three of her wide. His imposing bulk isn't enough to back her down though. She's claiming jurisdiction, but Brewer isn't buying it.

"This isn't the first missing body we've found with the wrong mind inside it," Yellowbird says. "It's become something of a trend lately."

"Standards is dealing with it," Brewer snaps back.

"Not from where I'm standing." Yellowbird replies, looking at NotGrace pulling away in the cruiser.

"That skyn isn't registered," Brewer states. "Standards violation, plain and simple. We'll pull the dude out, revoke the hardware, and send the rest back with the kid." He turns to Amos, mumbles, "Sorry about your loss," then swivels his head and yells, "Yo, pain in my ass," to a nearby lawbot.

The bot turns and its smooth white face glows green. The AMP's voice responds, "Detective Brewer, may I again remind you of the TSB Article on the use of proper names—"

"Nope," Brewer says. "Take the scrub for processing. Pull the rithm and Cortex and any other tech you find, and run the serials and all that, then package the meat for travel. Investigation closed, pending further review."

Amos can't take this anymore. He drops his hat and leaps to his feet, fists clenched at his sides, and gets right in Brewer's face. "'*Pending further review?*'" he hisses, jaw twitching in restrained anger. "Is that akin to '*my concerns have been noted*'?"

"Back the shit up," Brewer says as he takes a step back. His hand falls to his weapon. The lawbot stiffens, ready. As much as I'd like to see Amos work his frustration out on Brewer, if the kid so much as breathes wrong the bot will drop him with a shot from its neuralizer. Neuralizers lock up every muscle, and the pain can linger for hours. He's lucky the response drones have left, they've got even looser tolerances for potential violence. Amos would be spasming at Brewer's feet.

I glance at Yellowbird, pick up Amos' hat off the concrete, and rise slowly. "Disengage, kid," I say to Amos. "This isn't helping you. Or Grace."

Amos doesn't back down, but I hear the pain in his voice as he says, "They don't care about Grace. He called her '*meat*'—"

He just found out his sister's dead—or something worse than dead. I'm surprised he's held himself together this long. And Brewer deserves it, but if Amos goes off he's going to get himself hurt.

"Special Agent Brewer," I say as I creep toward them, angling to get to Amos before he does something he'll regret. Brewer will like me using his full title—it'll buff his pride a little, soften him up. "I know this looks like a typical cypher in an unregistered skyn, but there's something else going on here. A month ago, that skyn was a homespun grassr girl raising chickens in the Preserves. How'd an asshole like Maclom Welwyn end up inside her head? A case like this... A young, innocent victim, her body stolen and a Cortex hacked into it. That'd make all the top feeds."

This seems to catch Brewer off guard and he hesitates, maybe wondering why he's arguing about this. He drops his shoulders and throws Amos an amused sneer. He's being cocky, knows there's nothing the kid can do anyway.

"People go missing every day in this town," Brewer says, waving his hand like *what can you do?* "You got a missing person? There's a department for that. You think it's a murder, there's a department for that too. My job is to get unregistered flesh off the street, so that's what I'm doing."

I press Amos' hat into his chest and move him away from the line of fire. "Don't you care where the bodies are coming from?" I ask once Amos is safely behind me.

"Of course I do," Brewer says. "But at this point it doesn't matter who was in it before, or how it ended up with Welwyn riding it—a rogue skyn is dangerous. Which makes it my job it doesn't end up back in circulation. This isn't the first flesh we've found used to belong to a missing morty. We'll run the body through the sniffers, see what comes up, but unless you've got something for us to go on...?"

"Welwyn said he got the skyn from a fleshmith called Loo Nandez," I offer. "You could start with her."

Brewer rolls his eyes and turns away. I don't think he was expecting an answer.

"We know about Nandez," Yellowbird says. "One of the big skyn peddlers in town. Rithm Crime has been after her for months but we've never gotten close. She's got burner skyns everywhere, hops from one to another. She's hard to pin down."

"See," Brewer says, clearly frustrated he's even discussing this, "we're on it. Reszo Squad finds her, they can ask and we'll let you know. Okay? Everyone happy here? Not that I much—"

"The man with the white hair," Amos suddenly says.

Brewer grumbles in his throat. "Who now?"

"From the report I made..."

I can tell by the look on his face Brewer has no idea what Amos' talking about. He cocks his head and holds up his hand as the AMP relays the answers through the comm in his ear.

"Oh, right. Yeah, *him*. We checked out your story," he says, like he hadn't just heard about it a second ago.

"SecNet has no record of this guy. But thanks so much." He waves his finger in the air, signaling the roundup. "Let's clear out, people. We're done."

Amos is trembling, but I don't know if it's from fear or panic. "You can't—" he pleads.

"I already did," Brewer says, and turns to leave. "Go home, kid. Someone will be in touch about claiming your sister."

"Wait, Brewer," Yellowbird calls out, throwing me an exasperated glare. "Let me look into it. Give me forty-eight hours, anything we find, we hand it over to Standards and you can take the credit. What have you got to lose?"

He hesitates, considering. "You could lose that body, then that's on *me*."

Yellowbird sighs. "Olliver, we're not going to lose the girl's body."

"You used to be police before you moved up to the Feds," I say to Brewer. "What could it hurt to let her run with the case? You don't have enough to do already?"

Brewer shifts back and forth on his short legs before he says to Yellowbird, "You and I both know what's coming, maybe this girl got her body stolen, *maybe*"—he glances at Amos, lowers his voice—"but who knows she didn't sell it to Nandez? She could have gone bit-head and not told anyone, wouldn't be the first time. Maybe her body was sold. Maybe it was stolen. Maybe it was given away. Right now, it's Welwyn's word against nobody's. We got him. Job done. There's nothing here for you to investigate."

"We won't know if we don't look," Yellowbird counters.

"I know enough to close this case and save the taxpayers some money."

"A girl is missing, Brewer," Yellowbird says, her voice

stern, the usual half-joking edge sanded clean. "Don't you care? What does it matter to Standards if the Service investigates it as a missing person? You've got what you want: the body's off the streets. It doesn't have to be an either/or. You know we could work together occasionally. We share an office building, for Chrissake, why always the territorial dick-swinging bullshit with you? What could it hurt?"

Brewer looks from Amos to Yellowbird then huffs, defeated, and throws up his hands. "Fine, you want this case, you can have it. I don't have time for this shit."

He turns to leave, but stupidly, I can't leave well enough alone. "Where's Agent Wiser?" I ask. "Shouldn't he be out here with you?" Last I heard Special Agent Galvan Wiser was Brewer's partner—and acting Head Fed at the Ministry of Human Standards. Wiser was *my* partner when I first restored, when I was Deacon, and he just a rookie detective. The next time I came back he was bristling with prosthetics and had it out for me, blamed me for the accident that took his arms and legs. I think I blunted that somewhat when we were forced back together to fight what he believed was a rogue superintelligence, and he saw I wasn't the monster Deacon made him believe I was. But I know he still has his doubts. I'd have liked to see him, if only to see if he still suspects there's more to the superintelligence story than everyone believes.

Brewer's back stiffens, and he slowly spins to face me. "What's that got to do with anything, fuckbreath?"

Shit. Should have kept my mouth shut.

"Nothing," I say, backtracking as hard as I can. "I just thought if he were here we could work together—"

"You think I can't make my own decisions?"

Yellowbird suppresses a scowl that boils up and leaks

out through her eyes. I can feel her invisible frustration burning through her cheeks. "That's not what he meant, Special Agent," Yellowbird says, her tone like she's trying to talk a lion out of a tree. "I think he was trying to say we've worked together before, we could collaborate—"

"Standards doesn't need your help," Brewer says to me. "I don't even know why I'm talking to you, and for that matter"—he turns to Yellowbird—"why you've let a civilian into an active crime scene. This is just what I was saying about Standards and your sloppy fucking operation." He points to me. "You've got no standing here, get your ass back behind the tape." He waves over to one of the lawbots on crowd control, then says to Yellowbird, "This is our case. We'll run it."

"You'll try to find my sister?" Amos asks, relief clear on his face

"What?" Brewer looks at Amos like he forgot the grassr kid was still there. "No. This is an unlicensed skyn. We're done here."

"She's not an unlicensed anything, she's my *sister!*" Amos says through clenched teeth.

"I'm done with you," Brewer says to him as the bot arrives. He jerks his thumb at us. "Get them behind the tape."

"Please move behind the cordoned-off area," the bot intones as it raises its arms to move us back.

"*Brewer—*" Yellowbird starts, but Brewer doesn't let her finish.

"We've got a potentially murderous cypher off the streets," he says as we're ushered away. "This is a win. Now I have a report to finish, maybe I can get to bed before the sun comes up for a change."

The bot deposits us back behind the show tape where a small crowd has formed. Snoop drones hover at the edge of the invisible Service dronesense barrier, streaming the action to the link.

"You said to call the police," Amos says, his voice flat.

"The Union is going to let people sell their bodies now?" I ask Yellowbird as she approaches us.

She cocks her head at me and her usual smirk is gone, replaced by a thin-lipped grimace. She lifts the tape and points away from the crowd to where the snooping drones can't see us. I scurry under and Amos follows along behind.

"I didn't need your help," she snaps when we're far enough away. "You want to hide away from the world, that's fine with me, you do what you want." She walks up to me, her chin barely at my collarbone, and stares me back a step. "But don't think for a second I'm going to let you fuck up my job while you're at it. You may not care anymore, but I still do."

"I'm sorry," I offer, and I mean it. "I shouldn't have said anything."

"Damn right you shouldn't," she says, then sighs. "Brewer isn't wrong though." She looks at Amos—who's got his face scrunched up under his beard like he's listening to a low-cycle translator in his ear poorly explaining what we're talking about—then back at me. She reaches out and puts a hand on his bicep. "Don't worry, I'm not going to give up quite yet."

He doesn't react, as if momentarily unsure how to process what's happening, then his chest sags. "Thank you," he says. "I'm don't know how to believe she could be alive, but if there's a chance—"

"These days, there's always a chance," Yellowbird says, and I know exactly what she means. Death isn't what it used to be. "I'd have preferred if we'd been able to examine Grace's body, but I'll get access to whatever Standards finds, it'll just take some time. Until then I'll have the AMP run a more thorough SecNet search for Grace's biokin, extend it back further in time. Maybe we'll get lucky."

"What about Nandez?" I say. "She really that slippery?"

Yellowbird closes her eyes and shakes her head. When she opens them some of the optimism has drained. "We've nearly had her half a dozen times. She's got unlimited burner skyns, a different face every day. Any time we get close she drops her rithmcast and eats the cost of the body. She's like a ghost that shits corpses when it's scared."

"So how do you plan to find Grace?" I say.

"Jesus, Fin, what do you want from me?" Yellowbird throws up her hands. "This kind of thing clears maybe ten percent of the time. We just don't have the resources to chase down every unregistered skyn that lands in our laps. Yeah, she's a human, and a grassr, that'll gain some feed, we'll have some attention to spend on it, but Brewer wasn't just being lazy, the odds we find anything are slim. Maybe the AMP finds something in the data. Or Standards comes up with a lead from Grace's body, *maybe*—but I wouldn't hold my breath."

Yellowbird's words drag on Amos' face, but he isn't ready to give up. "Put me to work," he says.

She gives him a weak smile. "I appreciate the offer, but we've got it from here." She steps forward, putting her finger an inch from his chest. "As I'm sure Mr. Gage will agree, he and the Toronto Police Service appreciate your assistance tonight. You helped us apprehend a dangerous individual. But from now on, you'll stay out of it. Let us do our job. You could end up hurting your case, or worse, getting yourself hurt." She lowers her voice. "Do we understand each other?"

It takes a moment of consideration, but he nods. "Yes, ma'am."

"Good," she says. "I assume you're going home? Give the bot your address or a way to contact you and we'll be in touch when we know something."

Amos blinks, confused. He's been trying to get someone to take him seriously for so long now, he probably hasn't thought much about what happens next. The weeks and months that an investigation could take. The years of court time. He'll be a different person by the time this wraps up.

"Home?" Amos shakes his head and says, "No, ma'am. I'll stay until I can tell Mother for certain where her daughter's gone."

Yellowbird throws me a questioning glance. *Is he going to be trouble?*

I look at the young man standing between us, his plain but now dirtied white shirt rolled at the cuffs, his hat in his hands. I can almost see the sprig of hay hanging from his lip. He's just found out his sister's dead, or worse. I know about trauma, how it echoes. There's no one back home that's going to understand what he's going through.

"I'll take him to Shelt," I say. "Kid's been through a lot, maybe straight back to the Preserves isn't the best idea. Shelt's a counsellor, dealing with stuff like this is his thing."

"Fine," she says to Amos. "But remember what I said, let us do our job. And you," she says to me, "don't be a stranger."

I give her a noncommittal nod as she turns to close down the crime scene.

Get Amos to Shelt's, then it's back to the pod—I've been gone too long as it is. Deacon's doing summersaults in my head. My palms are itchy with excitement and my stomach is sour knowing his mind is rattling around in my brain.

He's getting stronger, almost got out. I can't give him another opportunity.

I need to get back to the cold and put him back to sleep.

THE FIRST TIME I was at *In the Flesh*, Shelt's back-then floundering skyn-rental shop, he tried to have his security drones kill me. I haven't been back since. Hopefully my visit goes better this time.

I show Amos to a plain brown metal door in the back alley of a nondescript commercial building at the edge of Reszlieville. It opens as we approach, and inside a man is waiting for us. Short blond hair, handsome, and completely naked.

"I'm so sorry about Grace," the man says, and when Amos starts at the man's flopping penis, the naked figure seems to remember he isn't wearing any clothes. He looks down at himself and twists his mouth up in a sheepish grin. Even if I didn't already know who was wearing the body, the expression is pure Shelt. "Sorry—I've been in so many bodies I don't even notice anymore," Shelt says, and covers his hairless groin with his hands. "I saw you coming and thought I'd show you in. I should have thrown a robe on first though."

Shelt steps aside to let us pass and Amos' eyes bug out.

If he was bothered by Shelt's nudity I can only imagine what he must be feeling about what he's seeing now.

In the Flesh isn't meant to be visited in person, or even by regular mortals. The only people who come here are reszo, and only with their minds. Some cast in direct from the Hereafter—unbodied rithms spending their basic on a few minutes or hours in the physic, feeling the pulse of blood through real veins and analogue nerves rather than the digital simulations they're confined to—while others momentarily slip out of their everyday skyns to hook up for an anonymous quickie with a stranger in a rented body, then drop out when it's all over and leave the mess for someone else to deal with.

The first floor is like a lobby of sorts, mirrored walls concealing the medpods new visitors emerge from. The room is bristling with people enjoying being back in reality, if even for a short time. Some of them wear robes or simple loose clothes, but most are just as naked as Shelt. No one cares. There's no modesty when the connection to your body is counted in minutes.

The simulated mirror walls display a shifting reflection of reality. One moment the patrons see themselves in a Roman bath, the next in a vast converted warehouse, lights pumping. The skyns parade around the room, dancing, mingling, enjoying the novelty of flesh and blood. A few flex in front of the mirrors, admiring the feel of spiking nerves and the response of real muscles. Others race in circles or jump in place. There's a small bot serving simple food, individual bites meant to spike specific taste receptors.

None of this fazes me, I've seen worse. Hell, I still have flashes of memory from Deacon's time inside Dora's body. The way the weight was distributed differently, the heightened sensitivity. I know what it feels like to be someone else.

Luckily, Amos pulls his hat over his eyes before he notices the small orgy in the corner.

I raise my hand to my forehead to shield my eyes, and the mirrors surrounding us disappear, turn back into rows of medpods and smooth white walls. None of this is real. Even the artificiality is artificial. The scenery around us is just TeleViz, images beamed directly onto our retinas by the projectors studded around the room. It's a top-of-the-line setup, and a huge step up from the moldy drywall this building had last time I visited. Shelt's doing well for himself.

"Yellowbird is taking the case," I tell Shelt. "But Amos wants to stay."

Shelt glances at Amos' downcast head with concern. "Come up to my office," he says. "We can chat about our next move."

Next move? There's no next move. Yellowbird's on it, told us specifically to stay away. I've done what I can. I'll leave the kid in Shelt's hands, make my excuses, and leave.

I nudge Amos forward and he keeps his head down, follows Shelt's naked heels across the open room and up a wide set of stairs to the second floor.

The stairs lead to a hallway that branches off into variously themed rooms, complete with period-appropriate food and overdone costumes—a cliché Old West brothel, a cliché Chinese massage parlor, a cliché Middle Eastern sultan's palace, and a bunch more. As we're walking down the hall toward the staircase at the other end, a door opens and a sweaty, red-haired skyn emerges from one of the rooms wearing nothing but high heels and a bunch of bruises. She sees Shelt and stops, brushes the damp hair out of her eyes. Amos keeps his eyes locked to the floor.

"Anything broken?" Shelt asks.

Without acknowledging us, the woman shakes her head at Shelt. "Nah. Exuberant, but mostly harmless."

"Good," Shelt says, and peers around her to survey the room. It's decorated like a seedy motel room from the last century: a small bed, a single lamp on a desk next to a heavy-looking black telephone complete with a rotary dial, sink in the corner of the room. Red neon seeps under the partially pulled blind. Two more skyns lie motionless on a disheveled, orange-flowered comforter. "Wash Anna and Winston out and prep them for the next booking. Put Anna in bandit gear and leave her in twelve. Winston needs the gimp outfit, then put him back in the harem." He inclines his head at the skyn she's wearing. "Get Mei cleaned up, then she can go in her pod for a few hours, let the swelling come down."

"Got it, boss," the woman says and clicks past us on stilettos to rinse her skyn and hang it up until the next customer needs it.

"How many bodies you have registered here?" I ask Shelt as we ascend the next set of stairs and through a thick door to the secured third floor.

"Seventy-eight in current rotation," Shelt answers without having to think about it. "I have a new batch coming next week."

"That's a lot of skin," I say.

"Immortality is boring," Shelt says as he leads us up to the third floor. "Variety is the spice of death."

We pass through a storage area full of medpods. About half of them are full, housing one of the organic costumes people come here for, skyns of every size, shape, and color.

A selection to satisfy even the most obscure physical tastes.

It's one thing to see them walking and talking downstairs, but up here they're still, with the quiet industrial shush of the medpods enhancing the inhumanity of it all. They're unsettling, these inert, empty shells. It's like we're walking through God's waiting room, passing hollow bodies all lined up just waiting for a soul to animate them.

Shelt points past the gallery of pods to the corner office and tells us he'll meet us inside. He opens one of the pods, climbs in, lays back, and after a moment his skyn goes slack.

Amos and I continue to the office and when we get there Shelt's already inside, back in his usual body—or at least the one I've seen him wear the most. Male, average height, ambiguously multi-racial, generically handsome. He could be anyone, and I think that's how he likes it. Another medpod stands empty in a corner. All this jumping from body to body makes my head spin. Amos' must be whirling like a tornado.

Shelt has the Tz in his office set to appear as if the walls are floor-to-ceiling windows looking out from the penthouse of a high skyscraper with a view out at the jarring expanse of the Hereafter. The Hereafter is the biggest virt in the mesh, a digital wonderland bolted onto a virtual recreation of the real world. It still kind of looks like Reszlieville outside, except, off in the distance, two buildings are slugging it out in a martial arts battle. Amos sucks in a breath and his legs wobble.

Shelt gets the hint and the windows fade to black while I lead Amos to a long couch and sit him down. He falls to the cushion and stays still, his head bowed. This is all too much for the kid. He's been through a lot in the past few days.

"Standards is going to release Grace's body once they're done with it," I tell Shelt. "Can you help Amos arrange to have it shipped home?"

"Sure," Shelt says, his voice hesitant. "How are you going to find out what happened to her?"

"Yellowbird is on it," I say.

"And...?" Shelt asks.

And I'm done with this. Grace is gone. If she isn't dead she's a rithm somewhere in the mesh. We'll never find her. What more does he want from me? I should have been back in the pod hours ago.

"Brewer says people are quitting their bodies now," I say, a frustrated anger starting to build in my gut. "Selling them to fund their conversion to digital. Who knows— maybe she did go willingly." I look at Amos. He's staring at me from under his hat, eyes tight. "What do you know about this guy anyway?" I ask, suddenly suspicious of this stranger sitting in Shelt's office. Amos doesn't move. "He shows up, claiming his sister went AWOL from the Preserves... How do you know he's telling you the truth? He could be anyone. I'm sure you've heard the stories. Forced marriages. Sister-wives. That stuff still happens. Maybe she was trying to escape. She could have been running from him..." He doesn't blink, his face settling to weathered stone.

I shift my gaze to Shelt. His eyeballs are squirreling around in his head, flicking between me and Amos' utter stillness, but I can't tell if he's suddenly realized I'm right and neither of us know who this Amos guy really is, or he's horrified because I'm being a huge asshole to this poor, devastated kid.

"Fin!" Shelt says, horrified. "The fuck!? Amos just lost

his sister." He steps toward the kid, his arms raised. "I'm so sorry, he's not usually such a fucking cock—"

Amos stands. Doesn't look at me. "Loo Nandez." His voice is so reasoned it sounds like a simulation. "How do I find her?"

"The Service is looking into it," I offer. My cheeks are starting to burn. Why did I lash out like that? I don't feel Deacon's corrupting presence, but that doesn't mean he isn't near. "They are far better equipped to—"

"Yeah, I know him," Shelt says, then turns to me. "You think he's so stupid he'd come without proof? Just because his head isn't linked doesn't mean he's a moron. He brought a complete record of their lives—photographs, birth certificates, videos from their mother and father, from people in his town pleading for someone to find her, to bring her home. You think I come to you with every sob story that falls at my feet? Do you think *I'm* a moron?"

"Shelt..." I start, but don't know how to finish.

"I don't for a second believe he isn't exactly who he says he is," Shelt says.

"I'm sorry," I say to Shelt, then to Amos, "I shouldn't have snapped at you like that."

I can feel it, just like earlier tonight, like before I put myself on ice. Deacon may not be here now, but this is how it starts: mood swings and foreign thoughts. Then the blackouts come.

"How do I find her?" Amos asks Shelt, ignoring me. Not that I blame him. If I was him, I probably would have taken a swing at me.

"I'll get in touch with her," Shelt says. "She won't talk to the police, but I'll get her to meet you."

"She could have killed Grace," I say. "Let Yellowbird handle it."

"No," Shelt says, and gives me a disappointed shake of his head. "Loo wouldn't have hurt Grace. She sells skyns, not people."

"Then get her to tell you where she got Grace's body and *you* tell Yellowbird."

"That's exactly what I intend to do," Shelt answers.

"I..." That throws me. Shelt isn't usually so ambitious. "You're going to go meet a notorious fleshmith by yourself? If she's selling stolen bodies you might not know her as well as you think. What if she's dangerous?"

Shelt turns to me, a look on his face I've never seen before. He's mad. I seem to have that effect on people lately. "Don't worry about it, Finsbury. It's obvious you don't want to be here. Go. I'm sorry I got you involved."

Shit.

Now I feel guilty. Have I been so wrapped up in my own head? "Let me come with you," I offer. "Just in case."

"I thought I could count on you," Shelt says. "The first time we met, I wasn't so sure. There was something off about you, that first version of you. Something cold. We all put it down to your restoration, to you losing your wife—but we didn't understand then the true depths of what you were dealing with. When you came back the second time—the *you* you are now—you were different. You're a good man. You risked your life to stop that superintelligence, and afterwards you fought to get Miranda and Tala out of the stocks."

While it's true, and I did do everything I could to put things right, he doesn't know my motives weren't even close to altruistic. Yes, before I confined myself to the Arctic I spent almost every dollar I had to clear Miranda's and Tala's names, then paid for new bodies once they were free, but I wasn't doing it for them—I was doing it for *me*. It was my fault they were stuck in reszo jail in the first place. Deacon had ruined their lives, and the least I could do was try to set them right again. Everyone had heaped praise on me, called me a hero, but I'm the only one who knows I didn't deserve any of it.

"I thought I could count on you," Shelt finishes. "Now I see I was wrong."

"Shelt," I say, wanting to tell him about the screwed-up thoughts in my screwed-up head, but not knowing where to begin I say instead, "you don't understand."

"No, I don't," Shelt says. "I wish I did."

"Let me come with you," I say again. "Just to make sure nothing goes wrong, and then you can take what you find to Yellowbird."

"I don't want to put you out," Shelt says, his disappointment clear.

"You're not," I say. "I was out of line."

"Well, okay then, if you're willing—"

"I don't want your help, Mr. Gage," Amos says, cutting Shelt off.

"Amos, look—"

"No, you look," Amos says, his voice low. "Mr. Shelt may believe you are a good man, and you may even be, but deep down, you city people are all the same. I know how you think. How you see me. How you see Grace. What you think of where we come from. You believe we are backwards, that we live in grass huts and fuck our cousins. You think we are less than you are." I try to object but he keeps talking. "You're right about one thing: we're not like you. We aren't hobbled by the crutch of technology. When your world comes crashing down, ours will survive."

"I'm sorry. I was—" I can't admit I was bubbling with alien anger so instead I say, "—frustrated about something else—and I took it out on you. I don't feel right sending you two off to hunt down a skyn dealer on your own. This city's dangerous."

"I can take care of myself," Amos says, his voice tempered.

"I've seen that," I say. "And I don't think you're backwards, not at all. I grew up in the country too—nothing like the Preserves, but I was far from a city boy for most of my life. I didn't mean what I said...I haven't been myself lately."

Shelt's face softens. "He really isn't an asshole," he says to Amos. "A few months ago he was a certified hero. If you want to find what happened to Grace, as shitty as he's being, he's still our best hope."

Amos chews on this, then finally nods, but I know he doesn't like it.

"It's almost two in the morning," I say to Shelt. "Is this Nandez woman going to see us tonight?"

"She'll be online," Shelt replies. "I'll set up a meeting. I have business with her anyway." He drops down onto the couch and his eyes twitch while he composes a message in his head.

Amos sits beside him, doesn't look at me.

I think at Connie to have the pod start warming up for me, that I'll be back in an hour, two at the most.

Two more hours, I can do that.

I hope.

NANDEZ REFUSES to talk over the link, but seems willing enough to meet us at a body locker retrofitted into one of the floors of an old office building downtown. We step out of the elevator onto a small frosted glass lobby on the forty-fifth floor that could have once been an entrance to a corporate law office, except it smells like a hospital and the floor is vibrating.

A security gate stops us from going any further than the empty lobby, but a few seconds later a woman emerges. She's small, with delicate features, a Southeast Asian complexion, large brown eyes, and stealth-jet straight hair cut at an angle over her shoulders. She's wearing a thin grey robe cinched at the waist, and a big white smile on her face As she looks past Shelt to Amos her smile wavers, and it momentarily disappears as her eyes shift briefly to mine.

"Good morning, Mr. Shelt," Nandez says, then regards Amos with heavy eyes. "You're the brother?"

"Amos, ma'am" he answers.

"Ma'am?" Nandez says with a curious smirk. "Works for me. This way, I have something for you."

She leads us through the gate into a large open room lined with rows of medpods, storage space for people to hang their bodies while they're jacked into the mesh. The only difference between the transparent pods is the color of the glowing bands along their tops—blue for human, purple for reszo. The reszos get to plug their brains directly into the mesh, while the humans only get to visit through crude hacks to their nervous system.

The floor is entirely automated. Bots maintain the medpods and the medpods keep the residents' bodies clean and comfortable, inside and out. For some, this is paradise. The idea that the Union keeps the basic income level at the same price as a twenty-five-year defrayed cost of the neural implants plus rented monthly podspace is a well-known, if unstated, policy.

Whether a utopia or a digital prison, virt life is one many choose for themselves: live the life they want, where they can be whoever want, in a world where they control the rules.

Who wouldn't want to rent Godhood for five bucks an hour?

Hell, I've been doing the same thing for months. Except my god hates me.

I've been reszo a while now, a few different times. When I first restored, when I was Deacon, I thought I'd lost my humanity somewhere in the process, that I was something less than human. It wasn't until afterwards, after I'd done everything I could to track down the man who killed Connie, that I learned I hadn't lost my humanity after all. What's more human than hurting people who get in your way?

We are what we do, not what we're made of. Human or reszo, one way or another, we're all fucked.

While I don't still have that reflexive attachment to the body I was born in, that doesn't mean I don't envy the people who still possess their birthed skyns, even if they don't appreciate what they haven't lost yet. Why reszos would bother paying to keep their skyn in storage while they live on the mesh is another thing, but I get it. Even though they could shed their flesh and live on a shared server somewhere for basically nothing, it's still a good idea to have one foot in the real world. In case the power ever goes out.

We move through the rows of medpods to the glassed-lined rooms lining the exterior walls, with windows overlooking the city. The rooms contain couches or tables and chairs. There's a couple small kitchenettes. Everything's simple and functional and clean and bright. A few of the glass walls are opaque white, probably in use by someone out of their pod taking a dose of reality.

Nandez walks into a room with low red imitation leather chairs. We sit and she blanks the glass.

"I don't trade in stolen goods," Nandez says, looking mostly at me. "That's policy. I'm not one to say what people choose to do with their bodies, but I insist on a verbal declaration of their voluntary disembodiment."

"*Voluntary disembodiment?*" Amos says, his genial disposition crumbling. "You sell corpses to monsters..."

Nandez doesn't change her tone. "People make choices, I don't tell anyone what to do. Some people don't want their bodies anymore, that's on them. But just because they don't want their bodies, doesn't mean they have no value. Plenty of people still want to be in the world, and custom scafes are expensive. Too expensive for most. I merely facilitate trade between consenting parties."

Amos rises, slowly. Nandez stays seated, doesn't move

to protect herself. "Grace would never sell herself," he says, voice threatening.

Nandez narrows her eyes at him, amused. "You have no idea what secrets people hide," she says, and flicks a little look in my direction. Shelt's watching Amos, so it's only shared between us. What's that mean? Does she know something about me? It's possible, I've done a lot of shit. More than even *I* know.

Another reason why my Arctic virt is better than the real world: the ice doesn't care about the lies I've told.

"No," Amos says, and his chest heaves. Whatever's been keeping him calm looks like it's worn off. "She would never—"

"This came with her body," Nandez says, and as she does a rectangle of video appears on the white wall. It's Grace. She's sitting...where?

"You're lying," Amos growls, and he launches himself at Nandez, letting loose with the fury he's been holding in since we first found Grace's body. I've seen him fight. He's quick and strong and in the prime of his life, but he's an old model. Human version 1.0. Next to the upgrade it looks like he's moving at half speed.

By the time Amos lands where Nandez had been sitting, she's already long gone—on her feet and spinning behind him. He crashes into the couch and scrambles to his feet, his face red and disheveled.

"You helped kill her," Amos yells, and makes another move to attack, but before he can the video starts.

"Amos," Grace says. His dead sister's voice stuns Amos better than a neuralizer could. He stops cold, and keeps his head low as his sister tells him why she gave up her body. "I knew you'd come, even though I told you not to." Her pretty face is sunken, dark circles under her eyes. "I'm only sorry I didn't tell you in person before I left. You'd have tried to stop me, and I couldn't risk Mother and Father knowing the truth." Grace pauses, the only movement the shallow rise and fall of her chest, then she takes a deep breath and continues. "I'm dying—cancer. I'm completely riddled with it, head to toe." She manages a rueful smile. "Doc Yuul said I had a month, maybe less. You know if I told Father he'd sell the farm to pay for treatment. That would ruin them, ruin the whole family, and I'd be dead anyway. I couldn't let him do that."

"We could have fought—" Amos cries at the screen, but Grace keeps right on talking.

"I've met someone. He's helping me—or, we're helping each other. I've sold my body, it's useless to me. I've left you the money. I know Father won't accept it, so give it to the church, for the Children's Ministry. Winter said he'd find you." *Who's Winter?* I glance at Shelt, but his eyes are locked on the screen. "Tell everyone you couldn't find me. That I disappeared. It will comfort Mother to believe I could still be alive somewhere—which I will be, but she couldn't understand." Amos is frozen to the spot, listening to his sister's last words. "I love you. Take care of yourself, big brother."

The video stops on a freeze-frame of Grace's smiling face, then cuts completely. Amos doesn't say anything, continues staring at the wall.

"She said she'd still be alive somewhere," I say tentatively to Nandez, guarding against Amos' pending eruption. "Does that mean digital, or in heaven?"

"I'd say her mind probably survived," Nandez says. "Her body was in good shape when I took possession—except for the cancer, which took some doing to eradicate I must say. No signs of external violence other than the trauma consistent with a neural pattern recovery. I had to graft in new eyes, replace the auditory canals. Her brain stem and white matter were Swiss cheese. It looked to me like she went through the rithm capture process."

"So she could still be somewhere, living on the mesh?" Shelt asks. He's trying to comfort Amos, but it isn't helping. He doesn't want to hear his sister's living some kind of undead half-life on a computer, trapped inside the very thing she avoided her entire life.

"It's possible," Nandez says without much certainty. "But you know as well as I do: if she doesn't want to be found, she won't be."

"Who is Winter?" Amos asks, his voice leaden. I'm wondering the same thing.

Nandez shuffles her bare feet on the polished concrete floor. "He's a supplier. Sends me bodies occasionally."

"All morties?" I ask.

She considers the answer, as though she hadn't before. "No, she was the first. All bioSkyns up until then, and nothing since."

"How do I find him?" Amos asks.

"You don't," Nandez says. "Not through me, anyway. I have the money she left for you." She waves at the wall and a banking transaction appears. "Where should I send it?"

"Fuck your money," Amos says. "I don't want it. I want to talk to this Winter. He's the last person who saw her alive, and he's going to tell me what happened to her."

"You already know what happened," Shelt says, his words soothing. "She wanted to spare you. She thought she was doing the right thing."

Shelt puts his hand out to comfort Amos but he swats it away and turns back to Nandez. "Where is Winter?" he demands.

"I don't know," Nandez replies. "No one's seen him for a while. And even if I did, I wouldn't tell you."

Amos strides forward, and this time Nandez doesn't try to get out of his way. She lets him grab her by the neck and slam her small body against the glass.

"Tell me or I'll wring it out of you," Amos hisses.

Nandez doesn't struggle. She simply looks past Amos and gives Shelt a displeased look. A second later Nandez's eyes go blank and her body sags, limp.

Amos' face grows horrified and he gently lowers Nandez's empty skin to the floor. "I didn't..." he starts, and his face contorts in grief. "I only wanted..."

Shelt shakes his head. "You didn't hurt her," he says. "She dropped the cast."

"She what?" Amos asks, his eyes darting back and forth between Shelt and the body lying on the floor. His hands are shaking.

"She was never really here," I say to Amos. "That body is no more Nandez than you are the clothes you wear."

A bot enters and we all stand back as it gathers up Nandez's body and carries it out of the room. As he watches it leave Amos changes. His posture deflates like the life has drained from him.

"Now what?" Shelt asks.

"You tell me," I answer. "Do you know who this Winter guy is?"

Shelt squidges his face up. "*Maybe*, but I'm not sure it's the same guy. The Winter I know is a rithmist, more of an artist, really. He creates these shyfts, they're like, emotional symphonies. Feeling without context. He's kind of a genius."

"He look like an angel?" I ask.

"Sometimes, I think," Shelt answers.

"Sounds like the guy to me."

"Yeah, but, how does a dying grassr end up with someone like Winter acting as a middleman to selling her body?"

"She said they were helping each other. Any idea what that means?" I ask.

Shelt bunches up his cheeks in thought, then blows out a long breath. "Could be anything."

"Can you contact him?" I suggest. "If he really was helping her he might talk to us."

"I could try," he says, and his eyes twitch as he pulls back into his head to arrange the message.

"No," Amos says, his voice small. "Grace is gone. I have to accept that."

"You don't know that," Shelt says. "What can it hurt to ask? Her rithm might still be active somewhere."

Amos doesn't look up. "Her soul has left her body," he says. "I didn't want to believe it, but I see it now. Grace is dead. Even if a machine copied her thoughts, that's all it'd be—a copy, not *her*. I can only hope she's in a better place."

I see Shelt wants to argue. Hell, I want to argue. My thoughts are in a machine and I'm far from dead, but I don't think this is an argument we can win.

"I've done all I can," Amos says after a moment. He straightens and regards us, tears welling in his eyes. "Now we must accept her loss and find a way to move forward with our lives. Grace was right, I'll tell Mother I couldn't find her. It will be easier than the truth."

Shelt tries again. "There's still a chance—"

"Thank you, Mr. Shelt," Amos says. "And you, Mr. Gage. I appreciate all you did, but it's time I went home."

Just then the glass surrounding us returns to transparent

and reveals two bots waiting outside. Security come to show us out.

"Come on," I say to Amos. "I'll take you back to your hotel."

"You're sure?" Shelt asks me. "I thought you wanted to get back to hiding."

I resist a smart-assed comeback. "Kid's been through enough. The least I can do is make sure he gets home safely."

Shelt manages a defeated smile but nods, and we let ourselves be escorted to the waiting elevator.

One last stop to make, then I'm done. I'm already anticipating the numbed relief of my pod.

Amos doesn't say much as we Sküte back to his hotel out near the airport. He mostly stares out the window, watching the lights of the endless city roll by. I can only imagine what he's thinking. He left the Preserves to find his runaway sister and found instead an existential paradox, one in which his sister is both dead and alive. Dead in a way that has her body still running around, and alive but only in the most technical sense. I live with this shit every day, and sometimes I have trouble reconciling my prosthetic brain and manufactured body with the fact that I'm still me on the inside.

Or at least I think I am, and apparently, that's all that matters.

The Sküte drops us outside the hotel and we climb out of the pod into the hum of the night. The air is cooling quickly, the city lights washing the low clouds a stark grey. Hoppers streak through the misty skylanes, cargo drones rise and fall from the loading docks surrounding the airport, and city service vehicles trundle through the streets collecting garbage and keeping the roadways clean. This is as quiet as the city ever gets, the closest it ever gets to a resting state.

I stand with Amos outside his lobby. Neither of us says anything, but he doesn't seem eager to go back to his room.

"Want to go find a coffee?" I ask. "We can talk..."

Amos shakes his head. He's broken but he'd never admit it. "There's nothing to be said. What's done is done."

"I'm sorry about Grace," I offer, and glance past Amos into the hotel lobby. Someone's coming out. He's tall, lithe, built for speed—and pretty, like an elf-prince rock star. His regal features are high and sharp, his silver hair pulled back from his face. He's wearing a tight-fitting blue vest, a slim white shirt, and leatherlook tights. A thick braid of white storage pucks hangs from the cuff secured to his neck.

Wait—is that?

Winter?

I reach out to grab Amos but he's already noticed my expression change and is twisting his back toward me. The elf stops a few paces from us.

What's he doing here? Shelt must have contacted him anyway, but how'd he beat us here? And why'd he come racing to meet us in the middle of the night?

He doesn't look particularly dangerous. His clothes are too tight to be concealing much more than a slender knife. Doesn't mean anything though—people don't need weapons to kill. In these days of carbon-reinforced skeletons and nanofiber-enhanced musculature, people *are* weapons.

Amos tenses beside me. "Winter—" he blurts.

The elf's face quivers. His ice-blue eyes widen and his thin lips draw into a tight grimace, like he just tasted something terrible.

For a second I'm sure he's about to attack Amos, and I

shift my weight to lunge, but the elf's expression isn't menacing. If anything, he looks relieved.

"*Mozzy...*" the elf says, his voice a hesitant drawl, and even as the word is leaving his mouth he seems confused he's saying it.

Amos' face flares with a suspicion that turns immediately into alarm. He leaps forward, gets Winter by the vest. "No one calls me that but—" He snaps a look at me and then back to Winter's startled face. "*Grace?*"

Winter follows Amos' gaze to me and we lock eyes. Time slows like I just acked a revv, and for a moment we're the only people in the world. The elf's breath catches. His eyes widen further, then narrow to slits. His face hardens. Before I can move to stop him, he shatters the illusion and shoves past us into a run.

Amos doesn't hesitate. He bolts toward the street in pursuit. I react a half-second later.

The kid's quick but the elf's faster. Winter's already across the four-lane road and racing for the doors of the extended stay hotel across the street. Amos is following but he won't be able to keep up. I put on a burst of speed and by the time we're on the other side I'm right behind the grassr and following him into the lobby.

It's empty save for a cleaning bot mopping the floor. The elf doesn't slow, streaking past the plastic chairs and out the rear emergency exit into the back parking lot. Amos and I burst out just behind, but Winter is already well ahead of us.

The parking lot is wide open, nearly empty. Winter is putting distance between us, but he's got nowhere to go. There's nothing ahead of him but a low fence, then eight lanes of highway and the airport beyond. I can catch him.

I fix my sights on Winter's back, give it everything I

have, pull past Amos, and start to close the distance. I'm halfway across the open lot when Winter reaches the fence. He doesn't hesitate. Doesn't look back. Just leaps over and scrambles up the slight grassy incline to the highway.

He isn't planning on crossing eight lanes of traffic on foot? He can't be—

But he does.

Traffic is light, which helps, but even light traffic in this city is dangerous. This time of night the highways are full of autosemi caravans, not to mention the other cars and AVs. He's going to get himself killed.

But that doesn't faze him. He doesn't stop, doesn't wait for a break in vehicles. He just runs, assuming the mostly automated vehicles will swerve to miss, and they do. He makes it easily across then darts through the manual lanes and slides down the incline on the other side, out of sight.

A familiar haze of anger comes over me as I jump the fence after him. My thoughts become brittle.

No—it's happening again.

Not now. I need to stop, to calm down.

But I can't let him get away.

I take Winter's lead and don't so much as slow down as I reach the highway. Air rushes past me as the speeding vehicles swerve to miss running me down, but I don't change my pace, put my trust in the vehicles to avoid me—and then I'm across.

My chest is heaving as I hop over the guardrail and spot Winter ahead, his braid of storage pucks flopping behind him as he sprints to catch an automated hauler rolling down the service road between the highway and the high airport fence. If he's able to climb aboard, no way I'll catch him.

I give my legs everything they have and try to reach him first. I don't know if Amos followed me across the highway.

Hopefully he wasn't so foolish, but I don't imagine he'd have thought twice about it.

Winter's too far away. He's just as fast as I am. Faster maybe.

I'm going to lose him.

The haze of anger thickens, clouds my vision. Deacon's coming.

I need to stop, before it's too late and I lose myself again.

I keep running.

Winter is only meters from the AV now. I'm not going to catch him.

I'm torn by a sudden overwhelming despair and hear myself cry out. A raw, angry howl of frustration that I don't recognize.

He's getting away.

I won't get my hands around his throat. I won't get the chance to pound on him until everything he knows comes spilling out—

As he leaps up and grabs the safety railing on the vehicle's rear end and spins to look at me, a bemused smirk on his face, my mind collapses in on itself.

No, not again.

Not after everything I suffered, months on the ice... It's happening again.

Deacon's taking over.

My legs falter, and I tumble into blackness before I even hit the ground.

MARCOS SAYS HE'S LEAVING.

Says in the past week Glenn has become a different person. Unpredictable.

That he no longer feels safe.

The worst part is, Glenn doesn't disagree. He feels it too. They've been fighting nonstop, had a monster blowup two days ago, and Marcos hasn't been back since.

He doesn't know what to think anymore. They never used to fight—they've been together eighteen months and he can count the number of real disagreements they've had on one hand. And they've always made up, always found a way to come to a mutual understanding, accepted responsibility and done what was required to get past whatever had come between them.

But in the past week his emotions have been out of control. He's been lashing out, his impulses swerving from tender to murderous in a heartbeat.

Something is wrong with him—*in his head.*

It fills him with revulsion, this sinister presence inhabiting him, a virus or malicious engram that snuck into his mind, running around loose in his thoughts. Who knows what it's doing in there, what damage it's causing. He needs to get it out of him, but he can't do it alone. He knows the ghoul in his head will resist. Only Marcos can save him.

He's brought this on them both. Best he can figure it started that last time he went to the club. Must have been one of the shyfts he used. It got into his pattern, slipped past the cortical firewalls, made him crazy. That's the only thing it can be. He invited a demon into his head.

Marcos has finally agreed to come back for one final talk, one last shot for Glenn to explain what's going on. He has to make Marcos understand: he needs help. He needs Marcos.

If Marcos will stay, he'll go back to Second Skyn and get restored to an earlier backup. One from right before his visit to the club. That'll fix everything.

Marcos has to see that, has to help him get there Glenn can't do it alone.

Glenn paces, through the living room, around the kitchen and back down the hall to where he started, circling for twenty minutes until he hears Marcos on the porch.

The man he loves comes in, the darkness in his eyes unable to conceal what must be hope as well. Glenn wants nothing more than to rush over and hold him, to tell him everything will be okay, but resists. He smiles instead, demure, grateful.

"Thanks for giving me one last chance. This is all my fault—you were right, I shouldn't be going to the club, should have been more careful. Something's wrong. Horribly, horribly wrong." His eyes flood and he can't stem the tears. He's never been so scared in his life. Never so deliciously scared.

Marcos' eyes narrow with concern, but his guard doesn't drop completely. "A virus?"

Glenn doesn't know, shakes his head in twitches. "Maybe. I... I just know something isn't right. I need to go for a restoration."

Marcos takes a breath but nods. He can see—*has to see* —this is the only explanation that makes sense. "Okay," he says, already taking charge. One of the many things Glenn loves about Marcos is he always seems to know what to do. "Take off your cuff. If you are infected with something, it could be transmitting right now. After all this why do you even still have it on?"

That's a good question.

Why *does* he still have it on?

He's thought to take it off twenty times over the past two days—his refusal to remove it the final straw that drove Marcos away—but whenever he made a move to detach it, he became distracted, or changed his mind at the last instant. For some reason, he hasn't been able to take it off.

Glenn raises his hand to his neck, determined this time. Marcos is here, there won't be any distractions, no reason not to remove it.

But he can't. His fingers stop, frozen over the piece of dull white plastic oblong on his neck.

He gathers his strength and forces his hand into motion, but it's like he's pushing against an invisible wall, a transparent impenetrable field protecting the cuff.

He can't do it.

Marcos' face grows dark. "You really want to play it like this?" The anger fractures when he realizes Glenn isn't playing. He's terrified.

There's someone inside him. This isn't just a virus, not just some malicious engram stealing his thoughts—*someone*

is in his head with him. Glenn can sense the foreign intention, feel the satisfaction it's drawing from his anguish.

Glenn shudders, can't catch his breath, his heart's
quaking.

He's been mindjacked. Infested with someone else's
thoughts.

He falls to his knees, a cry of existential despair
wrenched from his lips.

Someone's in his head.

"Help me," he pleads and Marcos rushes over, tries to
grab the cuff himself.

*—Winter can't have that. Without the cuff his connection
will drop. He'll lose his host, and he isn't ready to give it up.
Not yet, he's enjoying it far too much—*

Glenn slaps Marcos' hand away, follows with a jab to the
throat that sends the young man staggering. He trips, unable
to breathe, his windpipe likely collapsed, and topples head-
first into the fireplace, smashing his beautiful face against
the brick.

*—He's had fun. Loved, yes, loved this past week. He's never
loved anything before in his life. Was never able to. The
things he's experienced have torn the scales from his eyes. He
had no idea. The emotional ups and downs an exquisite ride.
He doesn't want it to end, but still he knows this run is
nearing its conclusion—*

. . .

Marcos lurches back up to his feet, moaning in shock and pain. He staggers, trying to flee. Blood streams down his face, darkening his shirt and the carpet under him. He tries to push past Glenn, but Glenn hits him. Just once, a full-throttle shot to the orbital bone that caves in his husband's eye socket and drops him to the floor.

No, he screams in his head. But only in his head. The word doesn't reach his lips.

He wants to go to Marcos, to help him—

Marcos isn't moving, must be unconscious—*maybe dead*. Blood pools in the worn creases in the hardwood. That punch was so hard—

Glenn tries to move, but no matter what he does, no matter how hard he struggles, nothing happens. He's been disconnected from his nervous system. He can still feel his body, but it's no longer accepting orders.

He's a prisoner. Trapped, an observer while someone else works the controls.

He screams again but the sound is just a void in his head, a hiss of wasted neural energy only he can hear, and he can only watch as the person inside his head leaves Marcos to die on the floor, lines his pockets with knives from the kitchen, and heads out into the night, looking to indulge in some mayhem before he releases Glenn's skyn back to him.

I SNAP on to an overwhelming thrash of screeching noise and dazzling light. My throat tightens and I can barely breathe through the surge of panic. I clamp my eyes shut and try to ignore the deafening sound while I pull myself together.

My world lurches sideways and pain flares up and down my body and I realize two things: I'm moving and I've taken a beating.

I don't know how long I was out this time, where I went or what I did, but whatever Deacon was up to didn't end well. None of that matters now, though. First I need to kill this noise.

I take a breath, brace myself, and open my eyes. The right one opens fine but I can barely get the left farther than a squint. The light is coming from a large curved screen flickering a mosaic of feed ads, and once the screaming starts I realize the noise is supposed to be music, Rake and Scrape metal or some shit like that.

The cacophony dulls my wits, but then it all snaps together and I recognize where I am. The hard plastic bench under my ass, the swaying motion—I'm in a Sküte with the window set to opaque, the internal speakers on high, and every ad in the world playing at once.

"Turn this shit off," I yell, and my jaw flares in agony when I open it. The music cuts and the ads switch off, leaving me in the Sküte's ambient internal light with my ears ringing over the whine of the motor, but at least it's quiet. I can think.

My whole head is pounding. I probe my face with tentative fingers and find the left side is swollen. My shoulder's on fire. My back feels like I've torn something.

What the hell did he do to me?

"Where am I?" I ask the Sküte.

"We are currently traveling south along Broadview Avenue, approaching Gerrard," it replies in the singsong voice of a cartoon mouse.

"Lift the screens," I say, and once again shield my eyes as the windshield clears and shows me the sparking lights of Reszlieville ahead and to the left. "What's my destination?" I ask.

"The intersection of Queen Street East and Logan Avenue," the Sküte informs me.

Why there?

"Where did you pick me up?"

"You hailed me outside 1810 Markham Road."

"What was I doing up there?" I ask out loud.

"I am unaware of your previous activity," the Sküte replies. "I suggested medical attention when you boarded, but you declined."

Was Deacon running from someone? Or something he'd done? What if he hurt someone again? My body shudders with an unsettling tremor.

I never should have left the ice. This is what I was afraid of—losing control. Losing *myself*.

I didn't take the threat seriously. I thought I could keep it in check, but I should have known better. Now, who knows what I've done.

Maybe I can pull a history from my tab, it should contain a record of where I went. I pat my pockets but can't find it. It's not on me or the seat or the floor. It's gone. Maybe I dropped it. Maybe I threw it away. Who the fuck knows anymore...

I drop my head into my hands and fight against the urge to freak out. I can't stand this feeling, not knowing where I've been or what I've been doing. It's terrifying.

Last thing I remember I was chasing Winter, he was getting away...

Oh, no— Amos.

He should be okay. He can take care of himself.

But what if...?

He was right behind me. *What if I hurt him?*

Shelt's club is nearby. I need to stop and check in, see if he's heard from Amos. Then I'm going to shut myself back in my head where it's safe. Where I can't hurt anyone ever again.

"I want to change my destination," I tell the Sküte. "Take me to In the Flesh instead."

"Absolutely," the Sküte answers. "We're now two minutes and seventeen seconds away."

I shift on the seat, trying to find a position that minimizes the pain, but I can't find one. Instead I concentrate on it, use it as a focal point to hold my broken mind together until I can get it locked away again.

"What the hell happened to you?" Shelt asks as I enter his office. He's waiting there with Amos, who seems fine, if a little perturbed. The annoyance on his face falters when he sees me come in. I must look worse than I feel.

"Do you need a doctor, Mr. Gage?" Amos asks and gets to his feet, eager to help.

I wave his concern away. "I'll be fine," I say. "I'm just glad to see you're in one piece."

His eyes narrow to somewhere between confusion and suspicion. "Why wouldn't I be? You chased him across the highway and I lost you."

"Yeah," I say, relieved I hadn't somehow turned on Amos. "I thought you might be foolish enough to follow me."

"What happened?" Amos presses. "When you didn't come back I was worried and contacted Shelt but he couldn't reach you. Did Winter do that?"

I reach up and probe my face. How am I going to explain the blackout?

"Lost my tab," I say to Shelt. "And I'm not wearing a cuff."

Shelt doesn't say anything.

"But you caught Winter. He must have put up a hell of a fight," Amos says, almost giddy. Scarily giddy. He's not dealing with this well. "What was he doing there? Why did he call me *Mozzy*? Grace used to call me that when I was a boy, how could he—"

"He got away," I say, and watch Amos' face fall. "He was too fast."

I hate the idea of giving up now—no question about it, Winter knew Grace, intimately, if she got to sharing child-hood names for her brother. Unless that *was* Grace inside Winter's skyn. There was something odd about him—he was confused at his own behavior there for a moment. My every instinct wants to keep up the hunt, but I have no other choice. I'll have to trust Yellowbird to find Winter.

"But your face..." Amos says.

"Oh, this?" I answer and put a chagrined look on my face. "I tripped, took a pretty hard fall. That's how I lost him. I just came to check to make sure you're okay, and you are, so I'm going to take off—"

"Wait, *what?*" Shelt says, and moves to intercept me. "You're going to walk in here with your head half bashed in and tell us some bullshit story about falling and then announce you're giving up? Did Winter do this to you? Fin, you have to talk to me."

Who knows what happened, but I'm almost positive Winter had nothing to do with it.

"No," I say.

"*Fin...?*" Shelt prods.

"I tripped," I say, the pain in my face and fear at knowing I'm still lying to everyone blending together and rising as anger. "I'm done. I can't help anymore."

Shelt looks back and forth between Amos and me. "Let me get this straight—you find the guy who last saw Grace alive, who might have had something to do with her death, who then calls Amos by a name only Grace would know— *and you're going to walk away?*"

"Call Yellowbird," I say. "Give her Winter's description. He should be easy enough to find. I'm no good to you anymore."

"What are you talking about?" Shelt says, his anger surging to meet mine. "There's something going on with you. Something changed after the SI. You hide yourself away, keep saying you're dangerous. What's going on with you? Let me help."

"You can help by letting me deal with it in my own way," I say, the closest thing to an admission of guilt he's going to get.

"Is this how you're dealing with it?" Shelt says, pointing to my swollen face. "By getting yourself beat to shit?"

"I have to do this my way," I say.

Shelt throws up his hands. "Your way is fucked, you know that. You're hurting and won't let anyone in. You've been hiding from whatever's going on for months now—how's that working out for you?"

"It was working out fine until you dragged me out here."

"You were killing yourself in slow motion."

"It was working," I shoot back.

"Bullshit," Shelt says. "Whatever's going on with you, it's clear you can't do it on your own."

I know Shelt, he's not going to give up until I give him something. I take a breath and it comes out in a sigh. "I'm having blackouts," I admit.

This stops Shelt dead. His brow furrows. "What do you mean, 'blackouts'?"

"Blackouts. Gaps in my memory. I snap off and when I wake up I'm somewhere else."

Shelt steps close. "When did they start? The SI?"

I'm not sure how much to tell him. What's enough to satisfy him without giving him the truth that the SI was really Deacon me in Dora's body? I just nod, keeping it vague. Let his imagination fill in the details.

"Jesus, Fin," Shelt says, his voice quiet. "Did it get in?"

I answer with another nod.

"I knew something had happened, but I thought maybe it was the trauma. An SI got into your rithm...fuck," he says, then looks quickly at Amos and realizes he's still here, watching. "You'll be okay, we just need to get you help. I'll call Vaelyn. Maybe she'll be able to—"

"Vaelyn?" I say, unable to hide the shock from my voice. "No fucking way I'm letting her mess around in my brain. It's crowded enough in there as it is." Vaelyn's a rithmist and an asshole. I had a run-in with her back when I thought I was hunting the SI. She didn't like me from the start, wanted to kick my ass the second she laid eyes on me. No way I'm letting her poke around my mind.

"Someone else then," Shelt insists. "You can't deal with on your own. Who knows what damage the SI did to your pattern, what it might have left behind."

"No," I say to Shelt. "End of conversation. I'm going back to the ice. I was fine for months, I'll be fine there again."

"You can't spend the rest of your life dying," Shelt says.

"Why not?" I answer. "It's what everyone else does."

"It's an avoidance, not a solution. What if the SI left a piece of itself in your head? What if it figures out how to take control?"

"Then at least it'll be locked away somewhere it can't hurt anyone," I answer.

"Except you," Shelt says.

"I can live with that," I say to Shelt, then I turn to Amos. "Call Detective Yellowbird. Tell her everything. She'll do her best to help."

"You're really giving up?" Shelt's looking at me, disappointment in his eyes. Like my mom that time in high school when I came home with another C in Science. She'd always wanted me to be a doctor, like her, but that was the day she finally realized I wasn't going to follow in her footsteps.

"I will," Amos says, but I can tell he doesn't understand

what we've been talking about. "Please take care of yourself, Mr. Gage."

"That's the plan," I say, and leave Shelt's office before he can try to convince me to stay, or tell me what an asshole I am.

He doesn't need to remind me, I live with me every second of the day.

The only choice I have left now is to lock myself away, once and for all.

I GET BACK to my pod, arrange my body inside and cast back into the arctic virt, braced to go through another crash landing and running scenarios in my head—strategies to make my chances of survival more likely—and instead find myself standing on the snowpack with the Northern Lights glowing in the sky like someone spilled a radioactive liquid over the stars. The wind is blowing around me but I don't feel the cold at all. Directly ahead of me a house, all clean lines and massive tinted windows and long boxy rooms of smooth grey concrete, has been built into the rocky mountainside. It looks like a super-villain's lair.

Connie's standing in the expansive front window, looking down on me. She gives me a little shrug, as if to say, *what do you think?* and I give her a thumbs-up. I was ready for another cycle of crash and burn out—but now that the house is here anyway, if I am going to hide myself away forever, I'd rather do it in there than in a stinking hole in a rock.

I see Connie smile, then she snaps her fingers and I'm inside next to her, looking out the window over a romantic depiction of the Arctic Sea, one where the ice hasn't all melted. A blue fire roars behind me, hot and cold at once, giving off an unexpectedly cool warmth, like spearmint in the air. The rooms are big and the furniture simple. A wide-open kitchen is off behind me. Hallways lead deeper into the rock.

"Well?" she asks, and even that proud syllable is enough to grab me by the throat and squeeze, choking me at the relief of being back with her. "Better than a cave?"

So much I have no words. I didn't realize until this second how much I didn't want to wake up once again and start clinging to the edge of survival. I can hide here. Keep myself locked away without the need to torture myself in the process.

Connie got it just right, again.

I can't believe how much I've missed her, it hasn't even been a day. I come back and she's created a sanctuary for me. Minimal and austere. Stripped down but not barren. I can stay here forever. Safe knowing I'll never hurt anyone else. The perfect tomb.

"It's great," I say, and as I do my surge of emotion at seeing her crashes into the memory of her death, calcifies, then shatters.

She's only a simulation—

A magical simulation, granted, better than any sprite I've ever come across. Better even than she was before Ankur—one of the smartest beings on the planet—dug her out of the link for me. I imagine he buffed her somehow, enhanced her personality routine.

But still, a simulation.

I'm in love with a *simulation*.

My chest sags and Connie narrows her eyes at me. "Want to talk about it?" she asks.

She's talking about what happened out there. She'll know some of it—have seen the report from the pod about the trauma to my skyn, maybe even know about the fight outside the Zack Lazer or chasing Winter. Maybe assume I had another episode—but she has no idea what I'm struggling with right now. She doesn't know that I'm in a constant battle with myself: should I delete her sprite and try to move on without her, or keep pretending she's not merely a copy, a ghost of the woman I love?

"Another blackout," I say, and move toward the kitchen. "Do we have coffee?"

"We have whatever you want," she says and points to a cupboard. A tin of freshly ground beans is waiting when I open the door. Out in the real world that little tin would be worth fifty bucks. But in here, like everything else, it's not worth any more than the electrons it's made of. Doesn't make the beans smell any less great, though, and isn't that what matters? As I stick my nose in and take a deep breath, Connie asks, "How'd you get hurt?"

I shrug, fill a kettle with crystal cold water, and set it heating on the gas burner.

She nods. Likely expected that. "You need help," she says. "There's something wrong with your rithm. I'm worried."

Everyone wants me to submit my head for examination. To let someone dig through my mind, rifle through my thoughts—expose myself to them, completely and utterly. Everything I am, every secret, opened up and vulnerable.

I can't do that.

I don't need help, I only need to be alone.

"This'll make everything better," I say. The kettle whistles a cloud of steam and I pour it over the grounds, let the aroma fill the kitchen. "Being here."

Simulation or not, being in here with Connie, with my mind safe from all the harm it could do out there, is the best thing for me.

Besides, my mind's already shattered. Maybe if I stay here long enough I'll lose the piece that remembers none of this is real.

WINTER HAS GROWN SO MUCH, in so little time.

These lives he's haunted—he's experienced beleaguered workdays and raucous second birthday parties. Endured both relationships and desperate loneliness. Been male and female and everything in between.

He's female now, and quite comfortable inside. He's come to appreciate the female physique, and the tendency of their thoughts to be simultaneously nuanced and intense. All his life he's been aware of his limitations due to his lack, but it wasn't until he played parasite with a few dozen lives that he realized he was also limited by his gender-driven lack. And his ethnic lack. And his cultural lack. And his lack of language. That in particular— discovering new concepts and shades of meaning through language—has been a revelation.

Humanity. We rise from a shared blueprint for neurons and synapses and elicit a universe of thought. The human experience is far more than any single person can ever dream to contain.

If they only knew.

Until recently, people seemed so foreign to him. He didn't understand their physical language, the way they reacted, these impulses they had. They seemed so sad. Conflicted and fearful. If they had any idea how so absolutely unique they are in their similarities, maybe life would be easier.

Everyone's the same, each in their own horrible way.

Fear, for instance, is in everyone. At some level, everyone is afraid of something. No one he's ever encountered but him is free from its embrace.

Love as well—it appears in everyone he's sampled. But while terror reverberates similarly for everyone, love's flavors are endless. Selfless. Begrudging. Possessive. Self-destructive. No wonder people chase it. Spend their lives worshiping it through song and deed, nurturing it, keeping it alive by any means necessary, no matter the cost.

He knew he was missing something, that the grey hum of his brain wasn't normal, but he had no idea what his lack had truly deprived him of for all these years.

Especially how much simple fun life can provide.

Winter sucks in a deep cleansing breath, gazing out across the sinewy towers and glimmering spires of Reszlieville. The summer air is delicious, heady with life. It's a beautiful night, one meant to savor.

Or it would be, if he wasn't trapped on a rooftop, holding a primed proximity charge in each hand, with Special Agent Galvan Wiser of the Ministry of Human Standards and squadron of his heavily armed officers behind him, primed to pounce, snipers ready to put Winter down should he so much as twitch his head an inch to either side of the narrow brick chimney he's taken cover behind.

"Enough's enough, Raylean, or whoever you are in there," Agent Wiser yells, his voice cracking. Even from behind the blast shield of his helmet it's obvious the child's nervous. Afraid, but trying not to show it. "You have until the count of three, and then I set the bots on you."

Winter has an alternative suggestion. "Agent Wiser, I should warn you if anything larger than your voice moves in my direction, I'll release the switch I'm holding and remove the top three floors from this building. You're already mostly plastic, but do you wish that on your colleagues as well? The ones who survive, that is. The outfit I'm wearing is quite densely packed with explosive material."

"The count of three, Raylean," Agent Wiser says.

Standards isn't backing down, just as Winter hoped.

It's funny. They still have no idea who he is. They keep calling him Raylean—as if she's anything but a passive observer in this. Sure, it's her skyn he's wearing, but he took over long ago. Raylean is a simpleton. She couldn't have conceived a spree like this, let alone planned, executed, and paid for it...

The research alone. The practice sessions. The weapon caches. He had decoy bots and a swarm of interceptor drones at the ready. These children they've sent after him have no idea who they're dealing with.

He's made this run last nine days. In Reszlieville. Nine days. Most people on spree don't get past day two, and that's on the move. He stayed within five square kilometers. Standards has SecNet and an unlimited budget for bullets and bots, and it took them nine days to get him. *Nine days.* Raylean down there wouldn't have lasted nine minutes.

He can feel her, squirming around in his subconscious, trying to exert some influence over her body—and he has to give her credit, the tenacity he drew from her likely has a lot to do with him lasting as long as he has. Raylean does not give up, and he loves her for it, but she's in no danger of overturning his control.

How could she? She may have a computer for a brain, but she's only human.

"*One—*" Agent Wiser yells.

The only question now is how to end it. Time has run out, but he can make his exit spectacular. If this is going to be his last spree, he's going to make it memorable.

His runs have already made him famous. The police think his sprees were perpetrated by different people, individual reszos glitched out and gone violently psychopathic, or another in the growing trend of bit-heads using the world as their live-action virt, seeing how long they can last, getting off on the carnage or notoriety or both.

No one knows who Winter is, but there's a small but vocal group on the undernet who believe his sprees are the work of a single person. He's famous, in a way—if anonymously—and this too is an unexpectedly novel source of emotional variance. Pride in the job he's done, vanity in knowing people noticed, and, as always, the twinge of potential sorrow in knowing it too will soon all go away.

The runs are becoming harder. The required planning more and more elaborate. He can't do it by himself anymore.

Standards has devoted a whole squad to quashing the trend of reszos gone murderous, with armed tactical teams stationed around the city, ready to spin up at a second's notice. SecNet is narrowed in on detecting aberrant behavior before it can become lethal. And all the while Second Skyn has been increasing the density of their Cortical security, making penetrating the neural firewalls to take control of his victims all the more time-consuming.

Second Skyn and the whole reszo world is doing its best

to keep the sprees quiet, to pass the rising violent outbursts off as isolated incidents committed by irresponsible discontents who tampered with their hardware and grew dangerous, just as anyone could if they injected a psychoactive substance—but the collateral damage from running gunfights is hard to brush aside.

But what they're truly hiding is more insidious: ultimately, even immortality grows tedious. Life loses its thrill and boredom breeds extremists—people more than willing to abandon societal norms if it means they'll get a spark of joy from it.

No matter how hard Standards makes it, the sprees will continue. They must: they're a natural outlet. A necessary side effect of conquering death.

"—*two*—"

All these thoughts and feelings in all these minds, they've taught him so much, opened so many doors, but once again, the effort has exceeded its return. The authorities tracked the hosts back to the clubs. They're looking for him—Agent Wiser together with that clown of a man who stopped him so many months ago by the lake. Though he's in no more danger of them finding him now than he was then, best to quit while he's ahead.

In any case, this line of sampling has lost its novelty. He's sampled a robust spectrum of minds, knows now what to expect.

He'll miss the sprees—but then, even murder becomes tedious.

"—*three*."

Winter hears the bots spring toward him and he flings the two proximity charges backwards, one on each side of him, and in the same motion dives off the roof.

The first sniper shot snaps past his head like the biggest

bee he's ever heard moving faster than the speed of sound. The second one hits him through the abdomen and his legs disappear as the bullet explodes through his spinal cord, but by this point even a paralyzed skin can't stop him. It only needs to last a few seconds more.

Twin fireball flares light the night for a good long moment as he falls, but he won't know until later how many people he caught with the blasts. Had to have taken out the bots at least. That'll look good on the virt replays. His fans will appreciate it.

He waits until the last instant to bid a final goodbye to his host and snaps the cuff from his neck, hoping the explosives wrapped around Raylean's skyn will trigger close enough to the ground that maybe the building will collapse.

Winter opens his eyes in his apartment's medpod, ignores the stiffness in his joints, and strides to the big window just in time for a rocket explosion downtown to flashbulb on his retinas. The flames billow up probably twenty stories.

Even here, kilometers away, the shockwave trembles through the floor. None of the buildings collapse though.

No matter. It was a long shot anyway.

Today was amazing. The best day of his life.

His brain is quiet, his lack satiated.

He feels whole, like a new man.

He feels human.

But he knows it won't last. It never does.

Soon enough, he'll need something new.

GAGE, FINSBURY_
13:42:54 // 09-JUN-2059

IT WAS dark when I first arrived back in the virt but the sun came up this morning and now it won't set for months. Connie said she wanted the drama of the aurora as a backdrop when I saw the place she'd designed for me, and brought the night on artificially, but since then she's let the calendar sync with real time. Just like the real world it's now June here, and living on the edge of the Arctic Circle, I won't see another night for seventy-two days.

I've barely been back in the cooler for twelve hours when Special Agent Galvan Wiser appears in my living room, unannounced. Connie isn't around and one second I'm alone, sitting on the couch, ruminating over the sorry state of my life while staring out over the sea ice and then he's standing in front of me in a suit and tie.

He's just a sim cast, but the projection seems real enough—it captures his displeased scowl perfectly. His head is shaved bald and a neat black beard starts just above his ears and runs down over his face. Both his arms and legs are prosthetics, but only the matte-black hands are visible poking out from his suit sleeves.

Normally I'd be mad, him abusing the Service override to barge into my head like this, but I'm still shaken by that last blackout and don't have the strength to work up a huff. I've been half expecting to see him anyway. I figured he'd try to drag me down to the station for an interview, so him coming here instead works just fine for me.

"I was out of town for a few days," he says by way of greeting. "Heard you were back out in the world causing trouble."

Galvan and I, we're past pleasantries at this point.

"Just doing my civic duty," I say.

"That what you call it?" he says, then takes a second to glance around. "What is this place, anyway?"

"My fortress of solitude," I tell him.

He smirks at me and whines the servos in his fingers. I'm not sure if the subtle reminder that he could punch a hole through a car door is meant to be threatening, or whether he's already frustrated with having to talk to me. Doesn't matter either way, there's nothing he can do to me in here, jacked-up prosthetics or no.

"Looks more like James Bond should be crashing through the skylight at any second," he says.

"That you in this scenario?" I reply, getting up off the couch and walking past him toward the open kitchen. The lights come up as I enter, and I grab a blue bottle of water from the fridge.

"Hardly," he says. "*I* have to play by the rules."

"I'm assuming you found him then," I say around the fridge door.

Galvan sighs and follows me into the kitchen. "Who?"

"Winter," I say, and take a long swallow from the water bottle. "Isn't that why you're here, to show me how much better you are at this than I was?"

He squints at me, presses his lips together. "We found his multimillion-dollar compound on the lake east of the city, but he wasn't in it. Bots were keeping the place clean, but no clothes or personal effects. He may well have never stepped foot there. He's in the wind, for now. But the AMP's on it, Winter can't hide from SecNet. We'll find him."

"What's Amos doing?"

Galvan gives me a quizzical look. "How the hell should I know? He's been told to go home and we'd contact him if we found any trace of his sister. So far he's refused to leave."

"Is he still with Shelt?"

"Again, how the hell should I know?" Galvan says with a roll of his eyes. He looks inward then says, "SecNet last puts him at his hotel room, safe and sound."

That's good. At least he isn't out wandering the streets looking for trouble. "What about that body merchant. Did you talk to her?"

"Nandez?" He shakes his head, begrudges a smirk. "You got closer to her than we have. She sent us Ms. Boldt's confessional though, the one where she relinquished claim to her body. Thanks for that. Little good it does—it's still against the law to sell your body, voluntarily or not."

"So then what can I do for you?" I ask.

"Can't a guy check in on his old partner?" Galvan asks, mock indignantly.

"Sure, a guy could," I respond. "But you wouldn't. So what is it?"

He cuts right to it. "After you chased Winter, where did you go?"

Ah, so that's it. I've been avoiding the question myself, hoping if I didn't think about it the person hiding in my head he'd just go away on his own and I wouldn't have to deal with whatever it is he does with my body while I'm not around.

"Nowhere," I lie. "Back to Shelt's." I can't tell him the truth is I don't know, and don't want to know. That I'd rather just lock myself away in here and not have to deal with someone hijacking my mind out from under me ever again.

"That how you got your face bashed in?" Galvan asks.

"My face is fine," I say, and pat my cheeks.

Galvan thumbs over his shoulder. "Not the one out there," he says, meaning the real world.

"It a crime to get beat up?"

"Depends on who's doing the beating," Galvan says. "Where were you yesterday morning between five fifteen and seven thirty-nine a.m.?"

He knows. I don't know how much, but he knows something isn't right with me.

"Do I have to tell you?"

"I'd appreciate it if you would."

"Are we both going to stand here and pretend you don't already have an answer?"

"Neither of us are really standing here," Galvan says. "Besides, I want to hear it from you. Maybe you have an explanation that's better than mine."

"I don't know what you're talking about, and I'm not obligated to tell you anything."

I wait for him to go official on me, force me into the Service virt for questioning, but instead he nods, raises his eyebrows. "For now."

I like that answer even less. "What's that supposed to mean?"

He asks instead, "What happened to you, Finsbury, with that superintelligence?"

I don't like where this is going. If he wanted to he could force me to submit to a deep rithm scan, pry my secrets out of my head and not have to play at asking. "Nothing you don't already know," I say.

He hums a bit in his throat. "It was a remarkable story, that. You taking out a malicious SI all by yourself. You're a modern-day god slayer, like something out of a myth."

The story is solid, I just have to stick to it. "What can I say. I'm a hero."

"*For now,*" he repeats, but I don't like his tone. He's onto something, and knowing him he isn't going to let it go until he finds out where it leads. He's been on my ass since my last restoration, and as hard as I've been trying to keep off his radar, Deacon isn't making it easy.

Galvan takes one last look around. "Don't go anywhere," he says and blinks away, leaving me to wonder exactly what he knows and how long before I've got my head opened up on a Standards examination table.

I SPEND the next few endless sunny days outside in a light winter jacket, exploring the base of the glacier, picking along the rocks at the ocean's edge, watching the green-blue icebergs drifting in the black water off the coast.

Thinking I might try a swim, I stripped down and jumped in, but even in June the water is only just above freezing and I don't last more than a few seconds before scampering back up to the house.

By all appearances this is a sterile place. Frozen, inhospitable to life. But yesterday as I was walking a pod of whales breached just offshore. I stood and watched as a calf leapt out of the water, playing with its much larger mother.

Turns out there's life if you know where to look.

Today Connie had a surprise. She told me the mountain range the house is built on sits on the edge of the tundra, and only a few kilometers away a massive herd of caribou is feeding on the spring cottongrass. She showed me down to the water where she'd placed a kayak packed with supplies, and gave me a wetsuit. Said I should follow the shore until I find the herd. It might be worth a trip, get out of the house, have a bit of an adventure. Give myself something to think about other than what's happening out in the real world.

It's like she knows what I'm thinking before I do.

I climb into the wetsuit and start off in the kayak. The landscape is stark and beautiful, the mountains rising into the brilliant blue sky. But you see one arctic mountain, you've seen them all. While I've been content here these past few days, my mind calm and clear like the ocean waters surrounding me, I'm already starting to get antsy. Connie must have sensed it, probably why she suggested this trip. She's tried to hide it, but I think she's getting tired of the endless games of cribbage.

Living like this, with warm meals and hot water and a solid roof over my head, is far better than the grim cycle of death, but playing survivor was never boring. Stressful and exhausting sure, but not boring.

I suppose I could plug myself into the open link, lose myself in another virt. A game, something with a bit more structure, or simply sit back and let it entertain me with an endless stream of exactly what I feel like watching, but I've resisted until now, been avoiding any contact with the outside world, and that means keeping the link off limits. I've managed so far, but I'm just about done with sitting in silence and staring out at the waves.

I guess it's true what they say: you can hide from everyone but yourself. I've never been good at sitting around doing nothing. Even though that drive has led me into trouble more than once.

The problem is, I can't stop thinking about Amos and Winter. About Grace. I want to know what happened. Now that I'm in no danger of losing myself to the intruder living in my head, all I want to do is get involved in the investigation. I resisted before because I was scared, but there's nothing to fear in here and my curiosity won't shut up. Every morning I've considered calling Yellowbird to ask her if she's made any progress on the case, but I haven't.

Not yet, anyway. Though the urge is getting harder to deny.

The more I've replayed helping Amos try to find his sister over in my head, the more I'm sure there's more to it than Grace simply giving her body to Winter to sell in some final act of altruism—or maybe that's what she thought she was doing, but that's not how it ended up.

I can't forget the look on Winter's face, his features livid in shock as he saw Amos, blurted the pet name his sister had for him, and then collapsed into confusion as the word left his mouth.

Winter wasn't the one who said Amos' name. Sure, it came out of his mouth, but he wasn't the one who said it. I've had enough experience by now to know that there's something odd about Winter. His reaction surprised him as much as it did Amos. I think that Grace is still alive, her mind at least, somehow inside Winter, trapped in his body. I don't know how, but it's hardly impossible. I'm living proof of that.

There's a chance Grace's mind is still intact somewhere, maybe even trapped in Winter's head. Maybe she gave up her body willingly—the video she left seemed genuine, but anything can be faked. Even if Amos believes she's dead because her body is, he doesn't know enough to even consider the alternatives. He comes from a world where dead is dead. He doesn't know the rules don't apply anymore.

I rest the paddle across the kayak and let myself drift while I call Shelt. Just quick, to see what's going on. He doesn't respond to my hail and I leave him a message, asking him to get back to me when he gets a chance. I could call Yellowbird, see if she has any news, but that would get back to Galvan and I don't want to cause her any more trouble than I already have. I could have Connie look into it, see if there's any public information about the case, but that'd be breaking my no-link policy.

Back to paddling, I suppose.

It takes a couple of hours, but eventually the mountains taper off and I round a bend in the shoreline to find a sea of caribou massed along the water's edge. They stretch out to the horizon, must be thousands of them. I lay the paddle across the kayak, dig a thermos of coffee from the storage compartment behind me, and drink it while I watch the herd.

I'm barely into my first cup when Connie puts a call through. It's Shelt, voice only.

"You called," he says, his voice hollow in my head.

"I wanted to check in," I say. "See if Yellowbird or Wiser made any headway on the case."

"They didn't do a damn thing," Shelt deadpans. "But I thought you weren't interested."

"You know that's not it. I couldn't stay out there, but maybe I can help from in here."

"*In there?*"

"Yeah," I say. When he doesn't respond, I ask, "Is Amos still around?"

He laughs. A short, sharp breath that's devoid of humor. I don't like the sound of it.

"What'd he do?" I say.

Shelt's quiet for a second, then he answers in a monotone. "I don't know if he found Winter, or if Winter found him, but Detective Yellowbird told me a Parks and Rec drone tagged his body this morning in the Don Valley. They figure Winter must have tried to harvest Amos' mind. Amos fought—even with the transfer cap on, with the probes jammed through his eyes and a spike in his brain—he fought. Still had the cap on when they found him at the bottom of a ravine."

I can't speak, can barely breathe. My throat's closed up.

"Amos is dead, Fin," Shelt says. "Still think you can help from in there?"

PART THREE_

WINTER'S BITE

WINTER REVERSES through his latest emotional concerto, rides the burst of humor from a crescendo that implodes back to the punch of revulsion that provokes it. No, that's still not right. The transition flawed, the cause-and-effect balance lopsided.

He's known it for hours, has been obsessing with this half-second of emotional about-face until the feelings have become empty of all meaning. The instantaneous transubstantiation of gut-wrenching disgust into levity still too jarring, too abrupt to resonate as authentic...

Then he has it: he's been trying to create a balance, but it doesn't need balance—it needs *greater* disproportion. He tweaks the cross-fade, pumping up the revulsion, then adds a touch of nervous anticipation to help bridge the two, and keys back up to the beginning.

He lives through it once more, five-odd minutes of pure emotion strung together like a theme park ride, and can't help but smile when it's over, then dives back in to live through it again. This is his best vibe yet. A hectic swirl of love and distrust that collapses in on itself as a serene apprehension that seems to last an eternity, but then slowly and meticulously swells back up through a swirling arc of loathing and lust and self-hatred until it finally crescendos into a surprised joy. The release at the end makes him laugh, every time.

He's done. It's ready for the people.

He packages the track up and distributes it to the feeds. Soon enough his fans all over Reszlieville—all over the world—will be living the new Winter vibe, running it through their minds like a living poem. Letting his thoughts into their heads.

They can't get enough.

Once again, Winter is famous. Though this time there's a deeper satisfaction to it. Or he knows there would be, anyway. He considers juicing the thought with a hit of the emotion from his archive, even knows the perfect engram for the occasion—a delicate vintage of proud achievement he captured on one of his sprees. But what's the point? Channeling secondhand satisfaction no longer brings the satisfaction it once did.

Back when he was running his sprees he thought the notoriety it garnered was enough, the minds it provided him sufficient to appease the lack, but even before the risks became too great the easy lures of voyeurism and violent spectacle wore thin.

Killing is easy. Destruction is easy. Sure, they attract attention, but the adulation they bring is ultimately a sour concoction.

Creation, however. Creation is *hard*. And the love generated all the deeper for it.

He's become something of an artist. Considers himself an impresario of human feeling. He knows the emotional scales intimately, has tens of thousands of sampled engrams, all neatly dissected, catalogued, and labelled.

He sees himself now as a collector of sorts. A curator who isn't allowed to appreciate the exhibits. A librarian who doesn't know how to read.

When he goes out, it's in his own body. He can pass now. More than that, he can attract. His command of emotions has made him magnetic, charming, desirable. There is nothing he doesn't want, no one he can't have.

But it's still not enough.

Ultimately, he now understands, the sprees disillusioned him, tainted his very understanding of emotion. He's felt everything, but still feels nothing.

It's taken a while, but he's come to realize that only through creation was he finally able to understand.

Yes, he's had plenty of experiences, but that's all they were —observations. A yard sale of feeling. A piggyback ride on someone else's flickering synapses. None of it was truly *him*.

If there's anything he's learned, it's that no two people's heads are the same. The push and pull of desire and repulsion is unique to each and every human from birth—as genetic hardwiring and environmental stressors intertwine to generate a range of emotional responses that, at times, are astonishing in their inconsistencies.

For instance, who would have thought that sexual gratification could be so vividly connected to death? It's obvious, now that he's experienced it. But before, when he could only rationalize emotion intellectually, he never would have truly understood it could feel so right.

He could steal minds for the rest of his days, live like a god among men. But it's become rote.

Worse, it's become easy. And nothing easy is valuable.

He's learned to interpret the scratches and nudges in his pattern and instantly respond with the correct emotional setting. And while he feels these emotions as they pass over him, he knows they're not his, not truly. They're toggles he's been conditioned to throw. They come from him, not through him.

He's no better than a bot.

Even after all this time, after all these lives he's amassed, they're still prosthetics, and rarely trigger on their own. Neural stencils, nothing more. Nothing resembling true innate feelings. It's all been playback.

He doesn't want to feel what other people are feeling. He wants to feel what he feels. Better to live as his emotion-less self than allow himself to be dragged in the wake of someone else's flux of conflicting impulses.

He's come to understand—it's not enough to feel on demand, *he* needs to be the one generating his desires. Sampled emotions won't do, he must go deeper, find a healthy rithm, dig into the code, pry the emotional engrams out, and graft them onto his at the root.

Hard as he's tried, he can't create emotions himself. As skilled as he is with the psychorithm, as much as he's learned, he isn't nearly skilled enough to engineer emotional engrams from scratch. The code is far too dense, and his many attempts never held together long enough to integrate.

No, he can't create the engrams, but he's capable enough to dissect them. To manipulate them...

He started by collecting samples, brief thoughts skimmed from the dying minds of his victims. That wasn't enough.

He graduated to prolonged parasitic exposure to emotion. Wasn't enough.

Even the adulation garnered through the mastery of the semantic art of emotional expression wasn't enough.

He needs to go deeper.

But not through violence or deception. No, not anymore.

He needs a complete rithm to complement his—one he can move into, reorganize, and repurpose as his own.

A union. Two minds become one. A lasting commitment built on mutual benefit.

Complete integration.

He just needs to find the right person to open himself up to.

Amos is dead, and it's all my fault.

I drop out of the virt immediately, abandon the kayak to float empty in the sea, and land in my body back in its pod. It's healed a bit from the beating I took, and after a dose of painkiller I'm able to move around without too much discomfort. While I'm dressing, I get Connie to call Yellowbird, but Yellowbird's either busy or ignoring me. Doesn't matter, I'll find her. I have to.

This is on me. I fucked up, ran away thinking I was protecting everyone from the evils inside me, and let Amos die because of it. I should have stayed out here, should have helped, blackouts or no.

It's what Connie's been saying all this time. Yellowbird wanted the same thing. Shelt all but begged me to stay and get help for my broken brain, but no. I was scared. I had to run and hide myself away.

Asking for help has never been easy for me. I learned to fend for myself at an early age. Mom and Dad loved me but they treated me more like a roommate than a kid, and I hated feeling like a burden. I thought maybe I'd managed to get past that, but I was deluding myself. Sure, back when it was me against the SI, yeah, I asked for help. But then I had no choice. I was up against a superintelligence, how the hell was I supposed to fight that by myself?

Then, after, when it mattered, I ran. Tried to deal with my problems myself, and look how it turned out.

I thought Yellowbird and Wiser could handle finding Winter. After all, they had SecNet and the combined resources of Standards and the Service to draw on, but while I probably should have, I never considered Amos would go after Winter himself. In retrospect, it's obvious. Of course Amos tried to find Winter. After he heard Grace's voice coming out of someone else's body, no way he'd ever give up trying to find her.

If I'd stuck around, if I'd gotten help with my broken brain, maybe he'd still be alive.

I thought with everything I'd gone through with Dora and the SI and the other version of me, that maybe I'd changed. Grown a little wiser. Learned something about myself. But doing something different once doesn't matter if you just go back to exactly the person you were afterwards.

I didn't learn anything. I can't let myself make the same mistake again.

After dressing, I go down and hail a Sküte and tell it to take me to Fifty-Seven Division on Eastern Ave, the set of buildings the Psychorithm Crime Unit and the Ministry of Human Standards share. Inspector Chaddah oversees the PCU, Galvan's running Standards, and neither of them will be terribly happy to see me, but that doesn't matter anymore. I'm going to help them whether they want it or not.

Galvan said Winter disappeared, his mansion empty, no

trace of him on SecNet. Either he's left the city or he's hiding—and I don't think he's left the city.

He's here, I know it. I'm going to find Winter before he kills someone else. I just need somewhere to start, and that means I need to talk to Yellowbird.

I'm nearly to Fifty-Seven when she finally gets back to me through the Sküte's screen. She's calling from outside, walking with the station in the background, her tab in her hand so I can see the disapproval on her face. I keep my end voice only. I don't want to have to explain the bruises.

"What the hell are you doing?" Yellowbird snaps. "Galvan told you to stay away."

"You can't find Winter," I answer. "So I'm going to."

"Now you want to come play detective?" she says.

"Looks like someone needs to. With all the tools at your disposal, I thought you could handle tracking down a single reszo."

Her eyes flare, then narrow. Her voice stiffens. "Don't you give me that shit, Gage. You don't know anything about it."

"I know you let Amos get himself killed," I snark back. I see pain flicker in her eyes and realize I've pushed too far. She's doing her best. But not everyone's best is always good enough.

"What exactly do you think you can do that we can't?" Yellowbird asks, her voice on edge. "Do you think you're really that much better than the rest of us? You think you're going to waltz in here and SecNet will magically spit out Winter's location for you? That the entire security apparatus of the Union is holding information back, waiting for you to come ask personally?"

This pauses me. What exactly do I think I'm going to do that she or Galvan hasn't?

Then I get over it. I don't know what, but it's going to be something. "It doesn't matter. I'm coming to the station now. Chaddah will listen to me. Or Galvan will."

Yellowbird sighs. I can see her willing herself calm, hoping it'll rub off on me. I imagine she's had a lot of practice at talking people down. Even these days, a native female cop doesn't make it this far in the Service without learning how to deal with friction. She speaks, her voice soothing. "Listen to what, Fin? You have nothing to add. Plus, if you recall, you left a bad taste in everyone's mouth the last time you were here. They've been happy with you keeping a low profile. You won't do yourself any favors busting in here and stirring up shit. Brewer got his ass bored out by Galvan for not taking Grace's supposed voluntary termination more seriously. Whatever the laws are going to end up being, as of right now it's still illegal to sell your organs. Doesn't matter if you do them one by one or as a skin-wrapped set. I know you want to help, but coming here isn't the way."

"I'm coming anyway," I say, but the urgency that filled me when I dropped out of the virt is waning. Yellowbird's relentless practicality is sinking in.

Yellowbird shakes her head. "You never quit, do you?"

"Only sometimes," I say, and try not to smile. "But I'm trying to change that."

"Jesus, Fin," Yellowbird says. "We've got everything under control here." She hesitates, brushes a thick lock of dark purple hair back from her wide forehead, and tucks it behind her ear. "But I'd like to catch up— I'm about to grab a coffee. Remember that diner near the station?"

Yellowbird and Samuel Omondi, the PCU's forensic tech, met me there back when I first restored into this skyn and had no idea what was going on around me. After everything that had happened, it was the place I learned I still had friends in the world.

"Yeah, I met you there with Sam," I answer. "How's he doing, by the way?"

"Sam is Sam." She chuckles. "He was married for a few weeks last month, did you know that?"

I shake my head.

"Some kind of a bet, apparently," she says with a smirk.

"What?"

She laughs and waves the question away, her irritation seemingly vanished. "It's a long story, I'll let him tell it." When I first met her, Yellowbird's aggressively cheery disposition was off-putting, but in the months I was gone I came to miss it. "Look, I'll be at the diner in ten minutes. If you decide not to bash your head against the Standards wall, maybe I'll see you there?"

I take a moment to consider and realize she's right. Will all the technology they have at their disposal, they still haven't been able to find Winter. What's storming in there going to help? Maybe there is another way.

"Yeah, okay," I say. "See you in ten."

She cuts the call and I amend the Sküte's destination. I don't know what Yellowbird knows, or if I'll be able to help at all, but I can't go back into my head and hide from the world, not anymore.

No more half measures. I'm going to find out who killed Amos and what happened to Grace. Then I'm going to deal with what's trying to get out of my head, or end us both once and for all.

Either way, no more hiding. If I'm just going to spend the rest of my life locked away, I might as well confess and let the state pay for my imprisonment. Eventually life trapped in my head will become just as empty and meaningless as a stock sentence anyway. If I'm out here I can try to offset the lies. Do enough good to dull them, at least a little.

All I can do is try.

Yellowbird arrives at the diner shortly after I do. I have coffee waiting for her. She slides into the booth across from me and shakes her head when she notices my swollen face.

"Jesus, Fin. Who'd you piss off this time?" she asks.

"Didn't get their names," I say. I don't add that I don't remember any of it happening. I got all the pain but none of the reasons why.

"Bet you had it coming," she says with a smirk.

I try to scowl in mock indignation, but contorting my face sends a fresh throb of pain through the side of my head and I wince instead.

"Shit, Fin," Yellowbird says. "Did you get yourself checked out?"

"The pod says I'm fine," I say with a tentative shake of my head. "Nothing permanent, just some bruising. It's already better than it was."

She points at my mottled face. "*This* is better?"

I nod. At least I can see properly out of both eyes.

She cocks her head at me, waiting for me to say something, but shrugs her shoulders when I don't. "Suit yourself," she says. "I'm not your mother."

"Still, I appreciate the concern," I say.

Yellowbird takes a sip of coffee, watching me over the rim of the mug.

"So," I say, "Winter..." She lowers the coffee, but doesn't take her eyes off mine. "What can you tell me?"

"Not much," she replies after a moment. "Not that I should be telling you anything at all."

"I can help," I offer. "Let me help."

She takes a breath and lets it out slowly. "Chaddah will have me on scut patrol if she finds out I'm talking to you." Yellowbird hesitates, twitches like she wants to look over her shoulder, but leans across the table instead. "The case is turning into a story. It doesn't make us look good—the PCU or Standards. Rumors are swirling about another reszo killer on the loose in Reszlieville and how we're doing nothing to stop him."

"'Another' one?"

"Murderers are a lot harder to catch when they're wearing anonymous, disposable bodies, and they know it. Without the possibility of getting caught to deter them..."

"Right," I say. "So, what *do* you have?"

She looks around, then leans in. "We tagged him once. Someone was skimming minds in the forested area south of the Docklands, down by the lake. It was grisly work. He removed his victims' heads, cracked their Cortexes, and psyphoned off as much as he dared. This went on for weeks before anyone bothered to check it out. It was just reszos losing a skyn and a bit of memory, no one died or anything, right? Wasn't high on the Service priority list. Eventually the feeds caught hold of it and drew a bit too much attention, and the Service sent someone to check it out."

"Let me guess," I say. "Brewer."

She shrugs and rolls her eyes. "He caught Winter up in one of the sweeps. To be fair, Winter didn't have any weapons, no priors. His rep was young but clean. Brewer had to let him go. The psyphonings stopped after that and no one bothered to follow up. That was more than two years ago."

"And nothing at all since then?" How's someone live in this city for two years and not leave a trail?

"A few SecNet tags—a handful of rep hits and open transactions. He must have been using scramblers to hide his biokin. There's nothing for months until he approached you and Amos."

"So why now?"

She considers this for a moment. "There are plenty of ways to skim memories that don't require decapitation. Who knows what he's been up to, but I don't for a second believe he quit hunting. We believe he killed Grace, captured her mind, and at least part of her still exists inside Winter's Cortex."

"That happen a lot?" I ask, thinking about Deacon rattling around in my head. "Minds joining themselves together?"

"More and more every day," she says and shakes her head. "People combining their patterns, seeing what happens when their minds are mixed in different ways. Most of the attempts end up schitzo and have to be put down, but we've just had the first reszo come forward and demand polyneural rights—you must have heard about that?"

I shake my head.

"Jesus, get your head in the world, Fin," Yellowbird chides. "This is reality now. Luckily for us it's still difficult to keep two patterns integrated and stable, but Standards is having a hell of a time keeping a lid on it. What can they do, they're using their fingers to plug a leaky seawall. It's only a matter of time."

"Do you think Winter and Grace integrated?"

"If I had to guess..."

"So why did they show up at Amos' hotel?"

She shrugs. "He appears in public for the first time in months and when he does it's someone else's words coming out of his mouth?"

"Grace was in control."

She nods, but she doesn't seem sure. "That's what we're thinking."

"So what's Winter's game, why's he mindjacking people, and why Grace?"

"We have no idea. Kicks? Curiosity? A perverse collector's mindset? We don't know anything about him."

I sit back and take it all in. Chew it over in my mind. "His rep," I say after a moment. "Did it change between when you checked at the Docklands and the other night at the hotel?"

"No," she says. "High eighties, both times."

"He's been inflating it, paying to keep it high. He's got money. Probably means he can afford burner skyns. He could have been out in a new skyn every night and no one would ever know."

"Now you see what we're dealing with. SecNet registers new cyphers every day. Anonymous minds running around in unregistered skyns—could be anyone inside those bodies."

"So what now?"

She takes a moment to answer, like she isn't sure she wants to. "We know two things: if Winter doesn't want to be found, we won't find him. He has the knowledge and the resources to stay hidden forever."

"Right," I say. "And the other thing."

"He knows his way around the psychorithm. If he's psyphoning minds—and carrying Grace around in his Cortex—he's got to be a rithmist of some skill." A smile is slowly forming on her face.

"What?" I ask, not sure I want to hear her answer.

"You found Nandez," she says. "We never came close."

"Yeah, so..." *Oh no.*

"You know people. People we'd never get to talk to us."

Now I know why she wanted to see me, know exactly who she wants me to talk to. *No way in hell.* "I was a cop, and to most people, once a cop always a cop. No one's going to talk to me."

Yellowbird reaches for her mug and brings it to her lips but holds it there without taking a sip. Finally she lowers the mug and slides out of the booth. "I'd never ask you to do something you're not comfortable with," she says and turns to leave, "but we get anonymous tips every day. You were never meant to be police, Fin. But maybe that's a good thing. You can do things we can't. If someone were to bring us information on the whereabouts of a potential suspect, well, we'd have no choice but to follow up."

"Let's do this again soon," she says over her shoulder, then heads down the aisle without a look back. The bell over the door chimes as she exits.

I need to call Shelt. I know I need help, and I can't do this on my own, but one thing's for sure: no way I'm letting him take me to Vaelyn.

Anyone but Vaelyn.

WINTER LIKES TO BE OUTSIDE.

Today he's seated on a park bench in Reszlieville. Children are playing with their nannybots on the grass nearby. The clear blue sky and soft spring breeze indicate it's a beautiful morning. The sun on his face suggests seven or eight different emotional responses, all but one of them pleasant. He chooses one at random, and remembers the time he and the family he never had took a picnic on a beach, remembers bodysurfing in the waves, eating meat and cheese between crusty bread. He doesn't know what beach, or even the people's names, but the memory is a comforting placebo all the same.

He lets it linger in his mind while he talks to his supplicants. The revv shyft he loaded into his Cortex earlier accelerates his rithm, lets him concentrate on seven conversations at once.

People constantly seek him out, vie for his attention. In some circles, the name Winter is spoken in breathless tones. Whispered like a sacrament.

He enjoys talking to people. Even when they don't opt

to open themselves to him. The simple act of communication does something for him. Makes him feel like he's a part of something larger than himself.

Maybe all the minds he's merged with are enacting some small influence on him after all. Though he's considered every one of the twenty-seven rithm mergers he's conducted successes on one level or another, he's never joined with a mind that's managed to stick around for long. Still can't find the One: the person whose mind is strong enough to fill the chasm in his head. The person who can help him become someone else.

Right now, he's talking to five people voice-only. At least two of them, he thinks—with the right nudging—will become integration attempts twenty-eight and -nine. He also assumes their patterns will join the others, subsumed by the depths of his lack, lost somewhere in the recesses of his ever-expanding mind. He doesn't hear from them much after that, though occasionally one of their stray thoughts will bubble to the surface of his attention and remind him they're still there, a part of him forever.

He has so many people in him now he's had to extend his rithm into the segmented datastrip braid hanging down his back. A bot whirrs past, walking a dog, and he readjusts the ribbon over his shoulder to watch the animal bounce up to a tree, sniff it thoroughly, and choose the perfect location to defecate.

Touching the braid's cool white plastic surface elicits conflicting responses. The need for extra storage is the only drawback he's encountered with the mergers. After only the third integration he reached his Cortex's onboard neural storage limits, and had to extend himself out onto his first datastrip. It isn't heavy, but it can be cumbersome at times, with the tendency to whip out if he moves his head too quickly.

He supposes he could remove it, but first he'd have to untangle his mind from those people who have given themselves to him, and he can't do that to them. They're part of him now, each and every one of them. Also, removing it would, at this point, likely corrupt his pattern entirely and they'd all cease to be.

Mostly, he couldn't bear to lose the minds he's collected; somehow it wouldn't be right to be without them. The ribbon, like the minds he's joined, is part of him now. Part of who he's becoming. One of the many trials he must suffer to achieve his humanity.

In addition to the ongoing conversations, he's also participating virtually in two simultaneous transition counseling sessions, one in a virt designed to look like a tranquil forest, and the other in what looks like might be a re-creation of the inside of a real church somewhere. Counseling, he's discovered, is a fertile source for potential integrates.

The programs are meant to help reszos adjust to their new lives and provide support for the initial days after the jump to digital. For some, swapping brainmeat for plastic can be unsettling. Many find themselves missing something they didn't know they had. Find they now have a lack of their own—almost like his, in a way.

Winter knows how they feel. Knows their pain. He strikes up conversations. Suggests meetings. He's gentle. Understanding. Charming. He offers to share their burden to ease their suffering. These integrates often come to *him*, with very little encouragement necessary. Others occasionally require more persuasive tactics, but eventually they too willingly come to join him.

These current meetings' crop of broken bit-heads, however, doesn't seem particularly worthy. As unmoored as they are, none of them seem the type to offer up their minds to him. He isn't concerned though. Every day Second Skyn sends out another batch of fresh reszos. More willing minds will be along eventually.

Besides, he isn't one to wait for what he wants to come to him. And he's come to suspect that he isn't going to find what he's looking for amongst his own kind. Reszo minds have already passed through translation routines, had their edges sanded down. They'll slip right through him every time.

There's only one other option: he needs to join with a mind that hasn't been dulled by the AI conversion to light-based code, bulked up with artificial pattern stabilizers and stitched-in operating engrams. He needs to merge with an organic mind, one gathered straight from a living, bleeding brain.

If he can control the capture himself, feed its pattern directly into his head through a basic translator of his own design instead of relying on some heavy-throttled AI, maybe the natural disorder of organic neural patterns will adhere more strongly to his, and become an emotional scaffold he can grow himself onto.

At this point, he sees no other option.

Locating a willing participant has as of yet been fruitless. Morties aren't as quick to give up their minds as reszos are.

The first time is always hardest. No one who chooses to go digital will trust the process to some stranger from the link. Winter's fame doesn't extend to the normal world. His name holds no power there.

Still, he has feelers out. His IMP watches a few

hundred feeds and forums and message boards, all over the link, places where people seek solace in strangers when they find themselves helpless or hurting or terrified as they watch the end of themselves approach. Places where feelings are raw and blistered. People worn thin and easy to manipulate.

There's no shortage of men and women, all over the world, looking for a respite from their impending death or absolution for some terrible thing they've done now that the end is in sight. It only takes one.

The One.

And then, suddenly, he finds her.

It's here, sitting on a bench in Reszlieville, the sun kissing his face, that Winter first meets Grace.

He doesn't know what it is that catches his attention, but something about her cry into the dark shines like a newborn sun. A text-only message, posted to a Christian support feed:

My name is Grace and I'll be dead soon. Does anyone want to talk?

"*FUCK OFF*," Vaelyn snarls when she notices me over Shelt's shoulder. Her nostrils flare and the tendons in her neck bunch up. She squares her broad shoulders and crosses her tattooed arms across a chest that's wider than mine. "Uh, uh. Not him. I got nothing to say to him."

"Vae," Shelt says, a leading lilt in his voice. "What have we talked about?"

Vaelyn scowls at me and mashes her lips together. Standing there, with her arms crossed, she doesn't so much look threatening as like a two-meter-tall, musclebound, tatted-up toddler. That her scarlet hair's pulled into short twin ponytails doesn't help. Last time we met she had the impulse control of a two-year-old as well. She didn't immediately launch herself at me when she answered the door, so maybe Shelt has managed to mellow her out some.

I've only met Vaelyn once before, but once was enough. One time too many. I came to her and Petra, her girlfriend, looking for information about my first restoration. She got her back up like it was her job and we almost had it out, then almost immediately after I left she was hard-locked with a bullet by Deacon wearing a stolen skyn. She lost some time, I'm not sure how much, and her skyn. She wasn't happy about it.

So I don't blame her for her reaction—the last time she saw me she ended up dead.

I'm still not sure if killing Vae and Petra and all those other people in that club was part of Deacon's plan, or if it was just collateral damage. I've got the memories of every awful thing he did in my head, but I can't for the life of me understand the reasoning behind some of them. As far as I can tell it was just another convoluted, inscrutable part of his desperate scheme to get himself back into my mind.

Of course, Vae doesn't know it was the other version of me who killed her—if she did, nothing Shelt could say to her would silence *that* rage—but she knows I had something to do with it, even if it was just dragging trouble around behind me, so as far as she's concerned, I'm just as guilty.

And that's not the only reason Vae's pissed at me. Shelt mentioned she hasn't seen Petra since. Petra's mother—who also happens to be the mayor—has her under lock and key.

The feed bonanza that followed when the mayor's reszo child was revealed to have been one of the people mowed down in a mass shooting in an illicit club almost broke her PR team. They were lucky they capped her drop in the polls to ten points, so she's keeping her kid out of sight for a while. Vae's broken heart is my fault too.

She must have figured I was the one to anonymously spring for her subsequent restoration and that replacement skyn she's wearing. Probably considers not coming through the door at me is her way of saying *thank you* for bringing her back to life.

"I haven't ripped his throat out," Vaelyn says, and her face stiffens. From frustrated child to prizefight stare-down

—there's the Vae I remember. My vision sharpens and my legs twitch, ready to fire. "And I'm going to let him walk away intact."

"Let's go, Shelt," I say, but don't take my eyes off her. I don't think she'll come at me through him, but who knows. "There has to be someone else—"

"There isn't," Shelt insists. He doesn't seem concerned Vaelyn might trample him to get to me, but I don't for a second believe he doesn't know a dozen other rithmists who could help us. He's got some ulterior motive in insisting it be Vaelyn. It wouldn't surprise me if he's working on some scheme to mend the rift between Vaelyn and me, not that I know why. I barely know her. We don't all have to be friends. "We need her," he says.

I put everything I have behind not giving in to the desire to snap something smart-assed. Vaelyn's kept it together so far, and knowing what I do of her, that can't have been easy. No way I'm gonna give her the chance to say I started it.

"Better for everyone if we find someone else," I say.

"Shelt, you know I've got no problems with you," Vaelyn says, and straightens to her full height. "But if you don't get him off my front steps I'ma tune up the other side of his face, even if I have to go over you."

"Knock it off, the both of you," Shelt says, and pushes past Vaelyn into her front hall.

"What'd *I* say?" I ask Shelt as he disappears inside. There's nothing standing between Vae and me now. If she wants to have it out, here's her chance.

She stares at me for a long moment. Long enough I have the chance to think about how long we've been staring at each other, before she twitches a squint and turns on her heel to join Shelt.

My heart is racing. I was fifty-fifty on whether we'd be

tearing the front yard apart with each other. I give her a second and then follow the inverted triangle of her upper body into her time-warp of a house.

I don't know what I was expecting when Shelt told me we were going to Vae's place, but it wasn't this. If ten minutes ago someone had forced me to guess how Vaelyn lived I'd have suggested some mixture of cardboard, spray paint, and shitty music.

Instead, she's got her own place in one of the nice pockets of houses left in the southeast of the city, a neighborhood that, except for the bots and driverless cars and phovo roofs, hasn't much changed in 150 years.

A private house in the city, has to be worth upwards of four mil. Nice place for a bruiser with a hair trigger.

Inside it's what I can only describe as...cozy. The house of a single, successful, slightly bohemian young woman. One with enough money to live like she doesn't have any. The yellow-tinged streetlights are on outside and through the front window I can see into the living room of the house across the street. There's a low light on and someone's reading with her back to the window.

Vaelyn's front room is laid out around a small, white-bricked fireplace. Pictures of what I assume are her family line the walls. Beyond, a dining room with a worn old table connects to an open kitchen. Narrow stairs beside us lead to a dark second story. The air smells like old wood with an underlying hint of fresh paint.

"You want tea?" Vae asks, and for a second I don't understand the question. The ordinary words and her scowling, hulking form just won't reconcile in my head.

"Tea?" I ask.

Vaelyn's frown deepens. She looks at Shelt, who's arranged himself on the couch like he's done it before. "You see what he's doing?" she asks. "You see that look he's giving me?"

Shelt blinks encouragingly at me, and I flash back to Elder, our first restoration counsellor, doing the same thing. Trying to get us to talk. To accept the changes we were going through as newly reszo.

Shelt's doing the same thing now: playing counsellor.

I knew it. I preferred him when he was paranoid out of his senses on shyfts.

"I'm just..." I start, but all I can think of is: "You have a nice house."

She inches her jaw forward. "Why wouldn't I have a nice house?"

"It's not what I was expecting," I offer. "I haven't exactly seen your sensitive side—I was imagining meat hooks and floor drains."

A smile glitches her stern lips, but she gives it a moment before asking, "Milk? Sugar?"

"Just black," I say, and she stalks off into the kitchen and sets the kettle boiling.

I sink down onto the white couch next to Shelt and he gives me a comforting smile.

I almost wish she'd have come at me. I'd have preferred to fight, because now I have to bend over, close my eyes, and ask her for help.

WINTER OCCUPIES a booth in an old but well-maintained
diner, watching through the window, inspecting AVs as
they pull in and out of the depot on the other side of the
busy highway. The hard plastic he's been perched on for the
past two hours has pinched his legs numb, but he doesn't
mind the physical discomfort. The usual grinding in his
stomach is absent today. Since he met Grace, the twitches
and pains have all but disappeared. Even leaving the famil-
iarity of Reszlieville for a harrowing trip to the edge of civilization wasn't enough to ignite them.

Soon, he'll be a new man. All because of Grace.

She's going to agree, he knows it.

He shifts on his buttocks to regain circulation, then
takes a sip of the sweet beige coffee he's been nursing since
he arrived two hours ago. Grace said to meet him here. Said
she had an answer for him but it had to be in person, that
she'd try to slip away from her parents and find a ride into
town.

She was supposed to be here an hour ago. *What if something happened?*

Winter can nearly sense the concern, the unease at not knowing if maybe she changed her mind, or her parents forbade her to come, or she fell from her hiding place in the AV and now lies mangled on the road, like some dumb animal who didn't possess the sense to avoid the wheels of a speeding vehicle.

He's only known Grace for a few short weeks, but in those weeks she's offered something to him that—in all the thoughts he's sampled, and all the minds he's integrated—he's rarely come across: she offered him hope.

Perhaps not true hope, but he's sampled enough to know hope when he almost feels it.

He's closer than ever to completing his life's goal. Completing *himself*. He hopes, yes, *hopes*—he can truly feel it; whether it's the true emotion spontaneously generated by his rithm or a sympathetic echo in his head he can't tell, but it feels real. Buoyant. Lending structural support to his willpower—he *hopes* that she hasn't ended up as roadkill.

What a wonderful feeling.

He can't help but smile. They're not even joined, and she's already brought him so much joy.

Another AV convoy rumbles past, a road-train of twenty-odd shipping cars driving only centimeters apart, likely ferrying goods from one of the northern ports, and when the dust clears Grace is hurrying across the pedestrian bridge over the highway, her simple blue dress hiked with one hand, bonnet crushed in the other.

She's radiant. Her voluminous yellow hair is unkempt, streaming from her head like the corona of a star. She sees him watching her through the window and her face splits in two with a grin that shows relief and gratitude and triumph all at once. She made it. She kept her word.

Maybe she does want to give herself to him.

A morty.

A virgin mind.

As she walks through the door, brushing the travel from her dress, the hope becomes so strong it verges on overwhelming.

She steps up to him, locks eyes, and says one word, "*Yes.*"

The urge to hold her is automatic, instinctive. There is no guile in his arms as they wrap around her torso, the trembling in his hands not a performance. She presses into him, her small frame unexpectedly lithe, and he savors the connection.

He learned early on in their conversations how strong she is. Maybe the strongest person he's ever met—apart from himself.

She told him how she hid her symptoms when they first began, passed them off as a cold, swore her doctor to secrecy when the tremors grew worse and the tests came back positive. She knew her parents would want to fight, but her condition was inevitable, and winning back a few weeks wasn't worth a lifetime of debt.

Instead, she decided to live her last months as the daughter and sister and teacher she'd been all her life—the girl who worked her parents' farm, who led family service every Sunday, who made the best chocolate chip cookies in the Preserves—not as the pitiable soul about to die of some horrible, crippling disease.

She snuck into the community terminal as often as she could when they were first getting to know each other, and after opening themselves up—her with fears of death and feeling as though somehow she still had work to do, and him confessing about his lack, and the constant empty ache of it —she was the one to suggest that she could be his anchor.

Said she finally understood what her God's plan was, why He'd taken her down this path. She'd offer up her own mind to save his.

Winter had been laying the groundwork, preparing to ask her to submit to the integration process, but he never for a moment believed she'd be the one to suggest it.

He knows how strong she is, but until now she was only potential, a voice whispering promises in the dark. Now that he can feel the strength in her, now that she's in his arms, he can truly believe it: this is real. What he's feeling now is real, and it's only the beginning.

Soon they'll be together, forever.

She's going to make him real too.

They separate, but somehow come away holding hands, and slide into their benches across from one another without letting go.

"You made it," Winter says.

"I did," Grace answers. "And soon, we'll never be apart."

We sit in Vae's living room, holding our mugs of tea and not talking for what grows to be an uncomfortable amount of time. Vaelyn's not going to say anything. I'm sure as hell not. That leaves Shelt to get the conversation started.

He finishes his tea in one long, awkward series of swallows, wipes his mouth with the back of his hand, and sets the mug on the neat coffee table between us.

"Don't you want to know why we're here?" he asks once he catches his breath.

"Why would I ask you a question I don't want the answer to?" she replies.

"Someone killed a grassr girl," Shelt says, then leans forward. "A sweet kid by all accounts. Came here to the city and ended up selling her body to the street. We think someone captured her mind first though and—well, we're not sure. Her brother came looking for her and we tracked her to this guy. We didn't know about him stealing her rithm then—but Fin and the brother found him and he recognized the brother. Called him by a nickname only the sister knew. We think he might have integrated her."

Vae's eyes narrow at me. "I knew it from the start. You're infected, Fin. Trouble follows you around like a disease." She takes another second then asks, "Where's the brother?"

"Dead," Shelt says, and gives me a rueful glance. We had it out on the way over, and he doesn't really blame me for Amos' death, but he's still not happy I wasn't around to prevent it either. "Same guy, we think."

Vae rolls her tongue around her cheek. "What does this have to do with me? You figure this killer must be a rithmist? What, you think we all know each other?"

"No, I—" Shelt stops, resets, nods at me to take over.

"I talked to Yellowbird about him," I say, "this Winter guy, and she thinks he's been psyphoning people for years maybe."

Vaelyn blinks twice and as I'm talking her gaze slides over to Shelt. *"Winter?"* she asks.

"Yeah. That's his name, as far as we can tell," Shelt answers.

"Skyn like a Scandinavian vampire?" she asks.

Shelt looks at me, unsure.

"I've been thinking elf," I offer, "but vampire works too."

"Why the fuck didn't you say so?" she says, leaning forward and setting her mug on the table with a clatter. "Gotta make everything so difficult—"

"You know him?" I ask.

She scowls at me. "You say one thing about rithmists all knowing each other, and I put your head through a wall."

"But you do know him?" Shelt prods.

Vaelyn sighs. "Yeah, I know him. He's hard to forget— the perfect blend of creepy and fuckable."

"Did you—" Shelt starts.

"No!" Vaelyn says, cutting him off. "Gross. I only met him once. I got myself invited to his latest vibe release party a month or so ago. We were introduced but he barely paid me any attention. He was all over some fresh-faced morty."

"When was this?" I ask as I'm fishing my tab out of my pocket.

Vaelyn's eyes flick to the left. "May second," she says.

I call up Grace's image on my tab and show it to Vaelyn. "This the girl?"

"That's her," she confirms. "Winter killed her?"

"That's the theory. Then took her mind."

"Shit," Vae says, staring at Grace's image, her jaw set. "I knew the way he was stroking that girl's hair. The way she let him parade her around. I knew what he was up to."

"What do you know?" Shelt asks. He's sitting up straight now.

Vaelyn looks like she doesn't want to answer, but Shelt doesn't back down.

"*Vae,*" he says, his voice rising.

"Winter showed up last year," Vaelyn says, all at once. "He was releasing these vibe shyfts, these emotional roller-coasters, plug one in and take a ride through a wood chipper of pure feeling. They were incredible, intense and visceral, swinging through euphoria and terror and rage and everything in between, emotions searching for context." She stares off into the distance like she's remembering a lost love. "They dredged up things I hadn't thought of in *years*. Hit me like nothing I'd ever felt. I know my way around a rithm —I've torn FRED apart strand by strand, rolled my own shyfts to tweak my rithm just the way I like—but this was like nothing I'd ever come close to producing. Made me jealous, tell you the truth."

"He's that good?"

She shifts her eyes to me and a satisfied grin eclipses her open longing. "I thought so at first—but once I started looking closer at his work, I pretty much figured there was only one way he could get such depth and detail in the engrams: the memories were real. Fucker was plagiarizing."

"As it happens, the Service agrees with you," I offer.

"First time for everything," she quips, but then her mouth grows serious.

Shelt notices the change as well. "What is it?" he asks.

"I know you're not going to like this"—she slips me a sidelong glance, as if she doesn't want to admit this with me in the room—"but I want you to know I am not involved and I don't approve. Okay?"

"Out with it, Vaelyn," Shelt commands.

"Fine," Vae says and slumps down onto her chair. "You know us, rithmists are fascinated by the mind, in all its forms. Deleting emotions, enhancing them, creating new ones. Playing with the signaling pathways, or attempting to come up with alternatives to the underlying structure..."

"*And?*" Shelt growls.

"There are a group of rithmists who have been...experimenting...with assimilating different rithms into a single pattern, merging multiple minds into one."

"Integrations," I say. "Polyneurals."

Vaelyn considers me with an exasperated glare. "You already know?"

I shrug. No point in telling her I heard about it for the first time a few hours ago.

"So what's this have to do with Winter?" Shelt pushes.

"Once I found out he was a hack I wanted to find out more about him, did a bit of poking around." She motions to me. "When you saw him, he have a storage braid hanging off his cuff?"

That white cord dangling from his neck. "Yeah," I say.

"Most likely he's integrated a bunch of rithms, that's what the extra storage is for: with all those extra people in there, his mind is too big for his brain."

"How many minds we talking?" I ask.

"Who knows. Dozens?"

Jesus. "So people just up and give their minds to this guy?"

"I saw him working that party. He's a charming mother-fucker, he gets what he wants. I bet he makes people think it's their idea to give their minds to him." Vae shrugs. "Thoughts are cheap. I've got backups frozen in a cascading revive order in a half dozen different data mines. Gets to the point, some people think—what does it matter what happens to me? So what if I die? I'm still going to live forever."

Even with all the shit I've seen it's hard to understand why someone would voluntarily opt to lose agency over their own thoughts, but at the same time I'm hardly surprised. I know what she means. Two years ago the idea that someone would be amassing minds in his head would have sounded like nonsense. Now there's a study group devoted to the idea.

"He's skipping the middleman and taking minds straight from the source," I say. "Grace must be in there too."

"First time I ever heard of a morty having their mind integrated though," Vae offers.

"So how do we find him?" Shelt asks.

She lets slip a lopsided grin and her chest puffs up. "I know people, heard more than enough rumors. I can ask around."

"Discreetly," I say.

She screws up her face at me, but she isn't mad. She might even be flirting.

Oh, no.

"Who do you think you're dealing with?" she asks and flashes me a sly smile. I don't answer and she doesn't press, but her eyes search mine and then she nods her head like she's filing something away for later. "Give me a couple hours and I'll see what I can come up with," she says. As she pads up the stairs she adds, "Wait here, I'll be right down."

She returns ten minutes later wearing a skintight silver mesh dress over an even tighter black bodysuit. She was already tall, but her heels are high enough she needs to duck her head through the doorway as she steps into the room. Her hair rages around her head, her eyes are smoky, and her lips are painted, battle ready.

"I won't be long," she says. "There's a carrot loaf in the fridge." She turns to leave but narrows her eyes at me and adds, "Shelt already knows this, but stay out of my room."

She spins on the balls of her feet and leaves us with her scent the air, something floral and musky that has me feeling a little heady.

"Shit," I mutter.

"Yeah," Shelt agrees. He stands and stretches and breaks into a wide grin. "I'm gonna hit Vae's shyft cabinet, she rolls a mean Bliss. You want anything?"

I shake my head. "Maybe some of that carrot loaf."

This morning, when I started out in the kayak, I never would have guessed I'd end the day eating carrot loaf on Vaelyn's couch while she's out hunting for a killer.

Strange as it is, somehow, I think things are about to get even stranger.

FIVE MINUTES after Vae leaves Shelt is already blissed-out on the couch. He's got a cuff on his neck and a burned-out shyft cradled in his slack fingers.

"You wan' one?" he slurs through loose lips. "Vae's got a whole shed load of 'em, help you-self...the pink ones are especially..." The sentence trails off as his eyes roll up into his head and he loses connection with reality. That's the Shelt I remember.

I leave Vaelyn's shyfts alone but open her well-stocked fridge and cut myself a slice of her carrot loaf. It smells good and tastes even better. Who would have thought Vae, on top of being a six-and-a-half-foot slab of angry muscle and aggressive sexuality, would be a surprisingly talented baker as well?

I grab another slice, leave Shelt to drool on the couch, and head upstairs looking for a cuff and a bit of privacy. When I pass Vaelyn's closed bedroom door I'm twinged by curiosity. She's turning out to be a woman of hidden talents. I wonder what she's so concerned with keeping from everyone?

With Vae out drumming up leads on Winter, I have a few hours of downtime. I suppose I could be out there with her. Pounding the pavement is the surest way of tripping over a nugget of information that could lead to him, but I figure I'd just be in her way. She has the connections, I'll let her work them.

Besides, I can use this time to see if I can learn anything about what happened while I was blacked out the other night. I can't run from it anymore. I need to know what Deacon's doing with my body while I'm not around to see it.

I keep Vae's bedroom door shut—wouldn't surprise me if she booby-trapped it somehow—but one of the other rooms is set up like an office—a couple of chairs, a desk, a few actual books. Neat and efficient. A couple cuffs rest on charging stands on the desk.

I step in and grab one and notice a grid of pulsating spheres hovering on the back wall, each a slightly different blazing ball of shimmering color frozen in eruption. I recognize them immediately as rithms, visual representations of minds. Or snippets of minds at least—they don't look like complete patterns. Flickering snapshots of thought traced and highlighted, glowing like ball lightning in mist.

Hand-painted labels name each pattern. "Lust" is dead center in the grid. The center of the sphere is a hot ochre blaze spewing two thick columns of orange light out that collapse against the pattern's invisible edge, while smaller pulsing streamers of light dance from the bottom, leaping in and out like dolphins at play. "Mirth" describes a fuzzy neon-green knot of light, while undulating rainbow contrails circle it like electrons, popping in and out of existence like fireworks in reverse. "Acrimony" is a bright core of burned-in blue, pockmarked and smoldering, while two explosions billow endlessly in front, like two eyes, churning with a cold fire. They're beautiful. Instants of emotion, frozen in time.

There's definitely more to Vae than she lets on.

I sit down on her hard, wooden desk chair and snap her cuff against the magnetic port at the base of my skull. I acknowledge the connection to my Cortex and think up my headspace back in the Arctic. Connie's waiting for me as I materialize in the open living room. She's got a fire roaring in the massive fireplace and an inscrutable look on her face. There's a bar cart next to her. Two glasses, a bucket of ice, and a crystal decanter of what I'm guessing is rye, probably a replica of some local producer. My throat twinges, caught between longing and revulsion.

"You back?" she asks as she fixes me a glass without asking. Two ice cubes, two fingers of amber liquid.

Connie used to bring me a rye now and then, sure. We'd take road trips, hit the small-town distilleries. It was something we enjoyed together, but she never once greeted me at the door like a woman from an ad in one of the magazines Grandpa used to keep in a cardboard box in his shed. And we sure as hell never drank from crystal decanters.

Suddenly I feel like an impostor in my own mind. "Just passing through," I answer quickly.

She holds out the rye but I decline it with a shake of my head and she returns it to the cart, pursing her lips. "Good. Need help with anything?"

"Yeah, that's why I'm here. The night I chased Winter, when I blacked out—"

Connie's sprite squints at me, but she knows what I'm up to. "You finally want me to retrace your steps."

"He's up to something," I say, not using his name, but

we both know who I'm talking about, or at least I think she does. "I need to know what."

"I wondered when you'd get around to asking. It seems to me this is a question you've been avoiding."

She got it wrong with the rye, but that sounds exactly like Connie. "I didn't want to know before. Now I do."

Connie's quiet for a second, then says, "I've already traced your skyn's actions as far as I could. Somehow you have two hours and twenty-four minutes unaccounted for. Not a single rep-hit, nothing to indicate where you went or what you did. Just after the time you say you blacked out, you hailed a Sküte, drove to an address a few kilometers away, and when it arrived at the destination you stepped out the door and disappeared. I can't see into SecNet of course, but as far as the public record is concerned you ceased to exist. Two hours and twenty-four minutes later you materialize on the street on the other side of the city and once more hail a Sküte. You know the rest."

"That's it?"

She gives me a one-shoulder shrug. "That's it."

It wasn't magic. So how'd he pull off the disappearing trick?

Should be easy enough to figure out. How would *I* hide my tracks if I needed to?

I need to put myself in his place—I'm exposed, don't have a privhood to obscure my identity, but I know I can't travel without SecNet watching my every move.

SecNet doesn't miss much, but everyone knows it's about as secure as a church picnic. It's made up of a haphazard amalgam of cameras and sensors and people with wide-open tabs sharing every move they make, forgoing privacy for a bump in rep. It works because it's multiply redundant, every part of the system has a hundred backups.

But it's still a system. A network. It handles hundreds of millions of requests every second from hundreds of millions of individual nodes all around the Union. And each node is a way in. It's a target-rich environment for people who make their living off SecNet's back—either selling access to the data, or offering protection from its vision. A few minutes' unrestricted access to the network can go for thousands. For twice that you can hire a tame AI to follow along behind you and scour the record of your presence clean.

I'd have had to contact a broker, set up the entry and exit points. Deacon disappears from the SecNet record at one place and reemerges in another. But he'd need to pay for it.

"I make any transactions?"

"Only two," she says. "The Sküte charge and an encrypted text."

"What was the text?"

"I don't know," Connie says, apologetic. "Reports only through an anonymizing service. There's no record of content or destination."

Tampering with SecNet is a federal offense. Galvan would have seen all this himself, yet he didn't mention any of it.

Why?

"No financial transactions at all?"

"None that I can find."

My forehead tingles. I don't know whether I'm relieved I'm not about to be arrested for breaching SecNet, or terrified to know Deacon has access to an account I don't know anything about. Probably crypto with the hash committed to memory.

This is why Galvan didn't mention the text or push me too hard about disappearing: without a payment trail, he can't prove I did anything illegal at all. It just makes me *look* incredibly guilty.

Okay, what now? I'm mobile, covered my tracks, where do I go? That's the question. It's obvious Deacon's operating with intent. He knew I'd try to see where he went, figure out what he's up to. He had a destination in mind and didn't want me knowing about it. What's he planning?

If it were me, probably a way to escape my head.

"Connie, give me a view of the city, centered on the airport."

The room dims and the dull concrete floor becomes an isometric view of the living city. We're looking south to the lake, which cuts off at the living room window.

"Based on the entry and exit points, can you give me a rough idea of how much ground I could have covered, say with twenty minutes spent doing whatever it was I did."

The map shades with an orange area that encompasses two domes, one green and one red, marking the start and finish of my potential trip: one in the west end near the airport when I left SecNet coverage, and one on the other side of the city where I popped back up. The orange spreads out from the highways, shows all the places I had time to reach when I wasn't being watched, and by the time it stops most of the map is orange.

I could have gone almost anywhere in the city. Or who knows, I could have made multiple stops. Or maybe I just sat somewhere and ate a sandwich. That's the problem. *I don't know.*

I don't like these holes in my memory. Feels like someone stealing my life away, bits at a time.

Well he can't have it. It's mine.

Connie zooms in on the city so the orange shading fills the view. "Based on the time you had available and the place you reappeared, and given traffic patterns at the time, you could have gone to anywhere in the highlighted area. Give or take."

"That's a big area."

"About fifteen hundred square kilometers," Connie agrees.

"Can you overlap any Service calls at the time. I got beat up somehow, maybe it was as part of something that got reported."

A splash of red icons spread across the city like pockmarks. "There were one hundred and seventy-six incidents, according to the Service feed. Mostly minor, a few assaults. A fire. There was one thing though." The map zooms in to a street view of a warehouse northeast of the airport. "Something big happened here last night. Reports of gunfire. Found five inert reszos, all of them with destroyed Cortexes, and a truckload of skyns, still fresh and cool in their medpods. Service feed has it down as a gang fight."

The map shows the warehouse still cordoned off with Service show tape, hovering drones streaming the scene live. Two cruisers and the FIS truck are parked in the adjoining lot. I wonder if Sam's in there now.

"There any coverage of the time we're looking at?"

"Not much public. Two cameras, no sound."

"Anything interesting?"

She pauses a moment while she runs through the history, then says, "Nothing." Then her eyes twitch. "Well, almost nothing. I nearly missed it."

The street view shifts to a camera from across the street.

The warehouse looks deserted, the only activity a drone streaking across the sky, but then it happens. A side door opens, for just a split second, then it's closed again.

"No one comes out," I say.

"I'd suggest the feed was scrubbed," Connie clarifies.

"What was I doing out there?" I wonder out loud. "What time were the shots reported?"

"Around six. But the inert skyns weren't discovered until a delivery bot found the bodies an hour later and alerted the Service."

They found a truckload of skyns...I wonder if I was meeting with fleshmiths, had a disagreement. Something that got me tuned up in the process.

I wonder if I put those reszos down?

Shit. No wonder Galvan thinks I'm up to something.

I am.

I can't let Deacon take control again.

"Looks like Vaelyn's back," Connie says. She's been watching the world for me. Seeing through my eyes for me while I've been in my head.

It's like she's part of me. We were never this close in real life. *Could* never have been.

I don't like it.

"Command action," I say.

Connie stiffens, her face switches to attentive, and she says, "How can I help?"

I don't know what to say. Stop pretending to be my wife? Stop being *you*?

I should swap out her sprite. Wouldn't it be easier, not seeing her every day?

But I know I won't.

"Amend behavior: no more bar carts, I don't want to be welcomed by a '50s housewife. Confirm."

"Command acknowledged," Connie says, and her robot face springs back to life.

There, now she won't do it again.

I know she isn't real, but it's better than not having her at all.

THEY STAND HAND IN HAND, gazing out Winter's floor-to-ceiling window, watching the churning city below. Grace's slender hand trembles in his. It's only natural, she's about to give up her body and join him in his mind. In *their* mind.

The bot is clearing the dinner dishes from the dining table, moving smoothly across the marble floor, whisking away the remnants of the Ethiopian feast they shared. Growing up in the Preserves, Grace didn't have the opportunity to experience the spectrum of ethnic and cultural foods in the world. They ate their way across the city, from Vietnamese street food to a traditional Icelandic buffet to Argentinian barbecue. Winter wanted her last days to be memorable, and indulged her with every luxury he could think of: he took her to restaurants, composed a new emotional concerto just for her, and showed her off at an exclusive party in its honor. He didn't once feel the urgency to see the process begin. He knew from the start how this all would end, and he's content to let it play out at her speed. Besides, he's enjoying living vicariously through her.

He knows this is new for him, this uncharacteristic

patience. He's already felt himself change since he met her, those short weeks ago. Her presence has affected him, imbued him with sensations he's never felt outside one of his samples. Through her eyes he's seen the city in startling new ways. He's always thought of the Reszlieville in mechanical terms—input and output with the people and bots and goods interchangeable components of its unceasing operation—while Grace sees it like an animal with an unquenchable hunger, like the cancer consuming her body: so blindly voracious it'll feed until it kills its host.

He squeezes her hand, knows that physical touch can be calming, and her weakened fingers close around his in return. Only moments left now. The time has almost come.

The neural transfer equipment is ready. Winter considered keeping the details of the procedure a secret, thinking Grace would be unconscious and wouldn't feel any pain, but Grace wanted the process explained to her, every step, every detail. Even the knowledge that capturing a mind requires direct connection with the brain wasn't enough to prepare her for the sight of the headgear and array of spikes that would plunge through her eyes and mouth and into her brain stem, tap into her synapses, and collect her thoughts. She was unsettled by the apparatus, that much was obvious, but she took it in stride—her death was imminent, either way.

The capture process is fatal, as the sensor wash injection destroys the brain cells. To live she must die, and even though the cancer makes that eventuality inevitable, knowing death is imminent will upset anyone, even someone as strong as Grace.

He hears her take a breath that bubbles in her lungs. She's spent nearly two weeks here with him—preparing herself, relishing her last moments, sparing her family the sight of her wasting away.

They walked through the city as Grace marveled at the everyday miracles he takes for granted, and as they walked they talked, Winter's gentle silence giving her license to open herself up to him.

She spoke of her guilt about her decision to run away, about the pain and confusion her disappearance would cause, but ultimately concluded it was the right choice. It would give her mother cause for faint hope that her daughter could be alive, somewhere. And even faint hope was preferable to the certainty of her mother's eternal grief if forced to watch her daughter shrivel and die.

She spoke of her brother, the proud, gentle man he'd grown into, and mourned that she'd never get to meet his wife, or her nieces and nephews.

Grace spoke of her dreams, of her family that wouldn't be. She laughed and she cried and she wailed until exhausted in Winter's arms.

She spoke, and Winter listened greedily.

Soon all this would be his.

He's been patient, and now his reward has come.

"I'm ready," she says, and straightens her shoulders as she takes her last steps. She has poise, even in the face of death.

She lies down in the cradle, rests her head in the clamp, reaches around and fastens the top of the headpiece. They practiced this a few days ago, as she wanted to participate as fully as she could.

Once she's secured herself in she catches Winter's eye and raises her hand. He takes it and is fascinated by how cool it is. How still. He anticipated she would be a riot of emotion now, but if she is, her body isn't betraying it. It's quite possible her serenity is real. That her impending death has calmed her. How wonderfully mysterious the human brain is.

Mysteries he'll soon understand for himself.

"Thank you for this," she says, and gives him a smile that even he can feel.

"No," Winter says. "You're the one who's saving me."

Head locked in place, she shakes her eyes instead. "I get to die knowing it wasn't for nothing. God sent me to you, and knowing I'm fulfilling his plan is comforting. I'd be dying either way, but meeting you gave it meaning."

Winter feels the corners of his mouth tug to the sides, and a sudden, unexpected surge of emotion squeezes his lungs until his eyes water. How is she doing this? Not even merged yet and already she's somehow conjuring feelings in him.

Could this be...*love*?

He knows he isn't capable of it, but he *has* felt it in others. Even if the feeling didn't originate in him, even if it's the simulated replica of someone else's longing stenciled over him, the feeling still exists. And aren't feelings, regardless of their provenance, whether stimulated through a painting or a song or a human connection or a drug or even a coded simulation, aren't all those experiences equally valid? Isn't feeling someone else's love still *love*?

If this is what she can bring out in him with her words, by her mere presence, what will integrating her thoughts bring?

He's made the same promise to her he's made to everyone, about this he wasn't lying—he'll open his mind to hers, their thoughts co-mingled. It's the best chance to ensure that her emotional capacity will take root in his rithm, will provide a scaffold for his feelings to grow onto.

Grace, he believes, will be different. She has to be. If she can't make him human, no one can. This is why he's sacrificing everything for the chance to be normal. Integrating minds, especially one fresh from the skull, can be dangerous. The integrated patterns could become unstable and collapse, or one mind could become dominant and eclipse the other. All the other attempted mergers didn't hold, they slipped through his thoughts without taking purchase and sunk to the bottom of his mind. His pattern overwhelmed theirs and they now reside in his subconscious as stray thoughts. He remained dominant, but what if it happened in reverse?

What if, instead of a co-mingling, it's *his* mind pushed below the surface, *his* thoughts eclipsed by Grace's dominant personality—it's possible, but he doesn't believe it will happen. He's too strong for that.

And besides, if something does go wrong he has contingencies in place. He's never had to use them, but should his mind be subsumed by Grace's he has an insurance plan to ensure his thoughts are returned to dominance. He isn't worried. Either he ends up with a complete mind, one with a fully integrated emotional psyche, or he restores to the backup he has waiting at the Orchid.

He squeezes Grace's hand as he initiates the procedure.

"See you soon," Grace says, and the auto-doc engages an IV that administers the anesthesia. Seconds later her eyes lose focus, then flutter, and her hand grows limp in his.

Winter stands at her side as the capture process begins. The doc inserts a breathing tube and regulates her heartbeat. Then the capture helmet is lowered, covering her face. He hears the spikes penetrate her skull, and the whirr as they deploy the nano-wire blossoms into her brain. He watches her sunken chest rise and fall in a slow, steady rhythm, watches for hours as her mind is catalogued and charted and extracted into a psychorithm, and when the process is complete, the auto-doc disengages the life support, and Winter watches Grace die.

But only temporarily. Her mind is still alive, and the body to be preserved in stasis and sent to Nandez.

Then it's all over. There's no point in keeping Grace waiting.

He's eager to join her, to be together with her forever. Hopefully they'll complete each other.

But if they don't, if something does go wrong, well, he can always have her erased.

Vae returns with a lead: she's found one of Winter's former victims. He's called Swade, and he gave himself over to Winter, body and rithm, voluntarily. He must have regretted the choice because he had that identity declared lost and restored from a backup. But this time he didn't have the cred for a new skyn, so he's been living virt-locked in the Hereafter.

Vaelyn promised him flesh time to talk to us, and we're meeting in one of Shelt's themed rooms. Shelt being Shelt, he installed us in a room designed to look like a scene from a '40s' detective movie.

"For real?" I ask as he leads us in.

There's a beat-up green leather chair behind a worn desk, two metal chairs for clients, and a long grey couch that looks like it often doubles as a bed. A dead plant sits on the windowsill that overlooks what I think is supposed to be L.A at night. Beetle-like cars chortle along the street outside, occasionally honking for atmosphere. It's good Tz. Shelt's even got a sensoria installed, has the air smelling like someone just put out a cigarette.

A skyn sits uninhabited in one of the metal chairs, a young white male with short brown hair, dressed in a slightly worn t-shirt, black jeans, and dusty black boots.

"You needed a skyn and a place to ask questions. How was I supposed to resist?" he says with complete sincerity. "You're the burly detective," he says to me, then looks at Vae, "she's the femme fatale with a secret, and Swade here will play the good-looking but troubled drifter who might have your only clue."

"Works for me," Vae says and installs herself in the leather chair, leans back, props her feet up on the desk, and puts her hands behind her head to wait for Swade to cast in. I drop onto the couch and Shelt parks himself beside the window, admires the virtual moon rising over the virtual hills.

"We're looking for a serial mindjacker here," I remind everyone. "He's killed people. Who knows how many."

"Yeah, exactly," Shelt answers. "This is some intensely dark shit we're dealing with, might as well have some fun with it."

"Yeah, Finsbury," Vae says, her voice low and trouble glinting in her eyes. "Loosen up a little why doncha?"

I can only shake my head. "Seems like we have our roles," I say to Shelt. "So what part are you playing in all this high drama?"

Shelt grins, eyes wide. "I get to be the camera."

Vae punctuates her laugh with a clap of her hands just as the skyn in the chair snaps to attention and sucks in a slow deep breath.

"Damn," Swade murmurs. "That first breath gets me every time." He looks around the room and nods in appreciation, sniffs the air. "Cool. Anyone got a cigarette?"

"Desk drawer," Shelt says, and the guy's face lights up like he won the lottery.

Vae slides the drawer open, grabs a red-and-white pack of cigarettes and a box of wooden matches, pops a white stick out of the pack, taps it three times against the pack, sticks it to her glossy copper lips and lights the tip with a flick of a match. She sucks in a breath, cocks her head, and blows a plume of smoke at the ceiling.

"Nice," she says before leaning across the desk and handing it to Swade, who's watching her with such naked lust it's making me uncomfortable.

"You're Vaelyn," he says, taking the cigarette from her and drawing a deep breath. When he continues, smoke leaks out from his mouth and nostrils. "I checked you out before I cast in, but who are these two goons?"

"They're with me," she says. "We have questions."

"About Winter," he confirms, and takes another long drag on the cigarette. "Yeah, I know. Sixty minutes of flesh time for anyone who knows anything about Winter, that's why *I'm* here. But who are *they*?"

"I'm Fin," I say. "I used to be a cop. Over there's Shelt, this is his place. That work for you?" He shrugs, blows a cloud of smoke at me. "Good. Now that we're all acquainted, tell us about Winter."

"First, I want some free time," he says, looking around the room. "I've been cooped up in the Hereafter for months, not a taste of flesh in all that time. I just got out here, I want to"—he rolls his shoulders—"explore my surroundings."

"After we hear what you have to say," I tell him.

"How about one quick fuck, then I'll tell you whatever you want."

Vaelyn stands, walks around the desk, puts her hands

on the arms of his chair, and leans into him, revealing the bulge between her legs she's been somehow hiding in the skintight skirt. "How about I take you for a run?"

His eyes widen and he swallows hard. "I'm all yours."

"*Ew*," she says, pushes away and scurries back behind the desk. "I hate it when they're into it."

"I'm up for anything," he says and ashes on the floor, "it's only skyn."

"That's not why we're paying for your flesh time, Swade," I say. "You're here to talk, so talk or we dump you back in the bits."

"Okay, okay," Shade says. "But afterwards—I get to take this skyn for a spin, right?" He looks at Shelt. "Right."

Shelt seems hesitant, but shrugs a nod.

"You knew Winter?" I ask.

"Why do you want to know about him?" Swade isn't done his first cigarette and he's already motioning to Vae for another one. She tosses him the pack and he lights a fresh one from the glowing embers.

"He's killing people," Shelt explains. "A young man from the Preserves, his sister too, but we think he snatched her mind first."

Swade sucks one last puff from his first cigarette before crushing it out on the desk and leaning back in his chair, already sucking away on the fresh butt. "No shit. I thought he was my best friend, you know. We used to talk about everything. I was out of my mind—literally. I felt like my whole life had been taken from me, that I wasn't real. He knew just what to say, how to make it seem like everything would be okay. I trusted him."

"How'd you meet?" I ask.

"Virtual counseling. We were just voices at first, but he knew me immediately. He knew what was broken, what I was scared of. Seemed to know my thoughts before I did. Eventually he suggested he could help—wanted to integrate with me, said only together could we be whole."

"So you went through with it?"

He shrugs and purses his lips, takes another long drag. "Even up to the last thing I remember, I wasn't sure what I was going to do. I only knew the thought of losing myself was terrifying, but not as terrifying as staying the way I was." Smoke pours out his nose, billows up around his face. "I came back a year later. Second Skyn hadn't heard from my Cortex in long enough it triggered an automatic restoration. But I didn't have the money for another skyn and I was stuck gaming the Hereafter, my mind still fresh from Winter's offer to integrate, but not knowing what choice I made."

"I'd bet you integrated," Shelt says.

Swade nods. "Yeah. I still think about him sometimes. I was freaked out when I first came back, stranded in the Hereafter, obsessed with what happened to my other self, whether he ever found what he was looking for."

"I can guarantee you he didn't," Vae says, and I shoot her a look. "What?" she says, defensive. "He's the lucky one. At least he's still in his own head."

That confirms what we know about Winter integrating rithms into his, but it still doesn't get us any closer to finding him. "When you'd talk, did he ever say anything about himself?"

"Sure," Swade says. "He loved to talk. Told me about his childhood. Told me how he watched his mother drown. How he was rescued from some flooded city and dropped into the refugee system. Lived moving camp to camp for years, just another unwanted or abandoned or orphaned child raised in squalor by government bots. He used to say that's what made him the way he was."

"Which was?" Vae asks.

"He claimed he didn't have emotions. Never a feeling in his life. That he'd never laughed or been in love or had his heart broken or anything."

"And that spoke to you," Shelt pipes in.

Swade looks across the room at him. "The way I was then, yeah. But I got better. I'm over him now." He puts out his second cigarette. "So, that it, we done?"

"Not yet," I say. "There has to be something else. Did he ever mention anyone? A place—what city was he rescued in?

"He never said. I don't know if he knew."

"What about a person? Family? A friend?"

"No, there isn't"—he hesitates—"wait, no. Yeah, there was a doctor. Someone he talked to. He mentioned her a couple of times."

"You know her name?"

He snaps his fingers, searching back through his memory. "Gard-Gardner? No, *Gartner*. Dr. Gartner."

"How about a first name?"

He shakes his head. "Only that she made him feel calm and that his stomach ached for days after she stopped coming to see him."

"It's not much," I say.

"It's something," Vae offers. More than we had a few moments ago.

Swade's watching us. "So," he says, expectant, like a puppy on a leash. "Can I take this skyn out for a ride or what?"

Shelt checks in with me and I nod. We're not likely to get anything else out of him.

"Go nuts," Shelt says. "Plenty of action on the main floor. I'll have a bot show you down."

Swade leaps up and races for the door, eager to be free and fleshed once again, even if for a short time.

Now to find this doctor, if she even exists.

WINTER NEVER IMAGINED life could be like this.

Up until now, each step he took toward reclaiming his humanity was incremental, advancing him only far enough to reveal how much further he had still to travel. Now that he's reached his destination, now that he truly feels the world for the first time, he's dazzled nearly senseless by what he's discovered—but at the back of his mind he can sense the cost of his bargain to integrate with Grace: he's traded a depth of some feelings for the breadth to feel everything. Even still, it was worth it.

Grace has settled into his mind like she was born there. He can feel her, glowing, the radiating force of her mind infiltrating and illuminating parts of his rithm that have never seen more than shadow. His mind has come unmoored, as though his thoughts have slipped the bonds of gravity and floated up into space. Every so often he catches himself smiling, for no reason at all, overjoyed at being overjoyed.

Emotions come to him now, unbidden, spontaneous.

Contentment. Gratitude. Awe. But most of all, relief. In knowing his trials are over, that his torment is behind him.

Now his life can truly begin.

Grace comes back to herself in pieces, floating in and out of consciousness, sort of like the time she got the flu real bad and was bedridden for a week. She feels movement, heat, and light, but can't hold on to the sensations. They're slick, as though through a dream.

Time spasms, lurching through hours. Her thoughts drag, misshapen, stretched out, like someone's jammed their fingers in her head and is working it like bread dough.

She doesn't know where she is or how she got here—reckons she must be dying—or dead. What other explanation could there be? There's no pain. Maybe this is Heaven.

Winter put Grace's flesh in deep stasis and shipped it to Nandez, along with the recording of her last wishes, and told the fleshmith to hold the payment and the message for six months, then release it to Grace's family. Her passing will be less painful by then, and the money sure to help the struggling farm. It's the least he can do.

His biggest problem now is he doesn't have a plan for what comes next. He no longer needs to secure more minds for integration. Has no urge to create. All he wants to do is roam the world and bask in experience. He goes to dinner, tastes each bite with newfound anticipation—delicious or disgusting it doesn't matter, the food itself only important because of the emotional punch it provides. He wanders the streets, letting the sensory overload of daily life in

Reszlieville work his mind like a puppet. With Grace in his head, everything is new, everything an adventure.

Then, all at once, he decides—he knows what he needs. A trip. A vacation. The first he's ever had. He'll take Grace around the world, and together they can savor all that life has to offer.

Her senses string together, memories come whole, showing her scenes like she's snuck in to watch them on one of the community terminals in town. She's feeling things she doesn't, as though they're being plucked from her, like raspberries from a bush. Like she's an instrument, and someone is wringing music from her.

Try as she might, she can't wrestle control. Her life is no longer hers, she's a passenger in her own thoughts, a voyeur in her own mind.

How has she come to this? She remembers her home. Mother and Father. Amos.

She remembers the doctor, telling her she only had months to live. Some vague memories of a city. Of a man guiding her. Of hope. Then nothing.

This isn't Heaven. Of that she's sure, but then does that mean—

He sits in his apartment, the city spread out before him, his mind racing with choices. The opportunities are endless. They could start with Europe, visit the ancient cities and sample the refined cuisines. Or maybe a safari, sleep on the savannah under the stars. Or eat themselves around the Pacific Rim. Money is no object. His only concern is avoiding the places in the world where reszos are still seen as less than human.

He browses the travel feeds, finds endless lists of exciting destinations, and just as many reasons another choice is preferable. He can't lock his excitement down, can't focus on one thing long enough to make up his mercurial mind. Grace is so thoroughly imbedded in him, has overrun his thoughts so completely, he's no longer able to control his impulses.

His mind is adrift in her. He feels unmoored, like he's in danger of losing himself completely.

For the first time in his life he's overcome by an existential dread—this is no sample, no foreign thought from somewhere deep in his rithm. This is him, his mind, sending him a warning.

He must be cautious. For now the promise of a functional mind is still too delicious to give up, but if it becomes too much, if he feels her strength rising, he'll need to enact his backup plan.

He hopes it doesn't come to that.

Suddenly she remembers. After who knows how many days or years have passed, she knows where she is: she's inside someone's head.

A word comes to her—Winter.

Then it all comes flooding back. Yes, Winter. She gave herself to a him, thought she could save him, that her inevitable death could redeem him, plug the holes in his brain. She knew very little about him, only that he was broken and in pain, but she truly believed she could bring the light of the Lord to him from the inside.

How wrong she was.

*It's only now—now that she can't undo her decision—
that she realizes how wrong she was, how arrogant. To think
she believed she could fix him, that she could presume to
understand God's plan for her.*

*This isn't what she imagined, not what Winter promised
at all. This isn't a coexistence, she's buried in him, her
thoughts a foundation he's built himself atop, but she isn't
completely powerless.*

*Her thoughts are slow, hard to solidify, but she has access
to Winter's every memory, his every impulse, and it doesn't
take long for Grace to understand Winter isn't nearly the
person he said he was.*

He's evil.

A monster.

Oh Lord, what have I done?

Winter's back on his park bench in Reszlieville, but unlike
before he feels no sense of contentment. Today the sky is
grey. It presses down on him, makes him feel small and
alone. The children playing nearby offer no sense of joy—
their cries are shrill, the unceasing noise grating in his ears.

He's overcome by a resentment that nothing will allevi-
ate, doesn't know where it's coming from, wants nothing
more than for it to go away. He imagines silencing each of
the children with his bare hands, strangling their playful
noises until the world is once again quiet around him, but
instead of comfort, it leaves him agitated.

This is what he wanted, isn't it? He wanted to feel
whole, and now he can't help but feel anything but. His
mind is overwhelmed by conflicting feelings. He feels torn
up inside. Until now even the unpleasant feelings were
welcome, but these are too real, too intense.

He considers, just for a moment, sampling someone new. Maybe a fresh engram injection will smooth out the rough edges, but even considering it fills him with a panic that he's never experienced before. It's torture. His brain is revolting against him, but he won't let it win.

Against everything his mind is telling him, he checks in with the conversations he's left dangling since he integrated with Grace. There are minds there, waiting for him. Offering themselves to him. Perhaps this is what he needs.

With Grace propping him up, integrating another mind could be even more satisfying. They could share in it together, and the new thoughts could ease the pain.

Yes. That is what he'll do.

It'll be good. For both of them. For *all* of them.

Just one more mind, and then he's done.

Every day, with every passing minute, Grace knits herself back together. She explores, wandering through Winter's mind like a terrible carnival attraction. A spook-house of memories. She watches him engineer his parents' death. Lives through his time in the shelters, where he learned to exploit his terrible gift to get what he desired, where he did what was necessary to survive.

She sees him exploring, tasting minds, inhabiting others' bodies like a spirit. She's shocked and horrified at what he's done, but she also feels the inert loneliness that's suffused Winter's every thought, his voiceless yearning to be normal. To be accepted.

To feel he's loved.

He's a monster, but he's also a victim. He didn't choose to be made the way he was.

He was created imperfect, and made horrible choices on

the back of that, which he will be judged for, but she's also able to conjure compassion for him, as she would for any broken animal.

And as she explores further, moving through the non-place she's trapped in, she finds something else: she isn't alone.

There are other thoughts—other people—trapped in the void around her. Mute presences bearing witness. She reaches out to one and is surprised when it touches back.

Winter selects the first supplicant who answers his return message. He goes to her, and she gives herself freely to him. In his haste to dilute the rage of emotions in his mind, he barely notices what she looks like, wants nothing more than to get her mind into his.

She was blonde, he notices afterwards, after her mind is seeping into his. Not that her body matters. He doesn't even bother to recycle it with Nandez when the integration is complete, and leaves it where it is. Someone will come across it eventually. The bother isn't worth the payment he'd get from harvesting it.

Still, fresh as her thoughts are, the thin gruel of her mind is barely enough to assuage the riot in his head. Grace's presence is too much for a single integration to quell.

No, he needs more. He'll keep the integrations up until his thoughts are once again quiet.

He believed Grace would be enough, but he should have known better. She was the One, yes, but she was only the beginning. She's plugged his holes, but now he needs to bury her completely, and tend the garden of thought her decomposition will nourish.

. . .

Grace feels the new presence immediately, feels the strange thoughts pass through her, the fresh feelings separated from the living mind like cream from milk, and knows he's started again.

He promised he'd stop hurting people.

She gave herself to him with the understanding she'd be the last. But of course he was lying. She knows him now. Knows him from the inside. He'll never stop.

She thought her destiny was to help Winter become whole, but she sees now. Sees with a newfound clarity: God doesn't want her to save Winter, He wants her to save the people Winter has trapped inside him, the host of souls wandering through the desert of Winter's mind.

She will be their shepherd, and with God's help, she will lead them to the promised land and free them from Winter's grasp.

If only she can figure out how, before Winter silences her for good.

WHILE SWADE GOES DOWN to scratch his carnal itch, we go back into Shelt's office to find Winter's doctor. I get Shelt to secure me a few more cycles on SecNet and step into my head to work up a series of queries with Connie. We end up with a routine that searches SecNet's personnel records for any Dr. Gartners who spent any time in one of the Union's relocation camps in the past ten years. It's a long shot, but it's all we have.

Shelt buys three search cycles and we use the first on the initial query. It returns a moment later with a grand total of zero results. Dead end. Could be Winter was lying or misremembers the name. Could be the doctor was using a different name officially, maybe a married name. Could be the only records are in old paperwork that never made it into SecNet.

Two tries left, and our best shot came up with nothing. I rejig the query to expand out to any doctors, named Gartner or not, who worked in the camps and interacted with children whose parents had died suddenly. That comes back with more results than I know what to do with. Tens of thousands. None of them involving anyone named Winter or Gartner. Strike two.

I'm stumped, until Vae suggests we expand the search once more to include all state-run facilities that housed orphan kids and employed someone named Gartner.

I don't see how an even broader search will get us anywhere, but I don't have any better ideas.

Shelt runs it and it comes back with a single answer: Dr. Beverly Gartner, a psychiatrist who worked at the Royal Ottawa Mental Health Centre for forty-five years. She retired in '56 and now lives in Perth, Ontario. A small town about an hour's drive outside Ottawa—and not much more than an hour away from here by hopper.

It's a long shot, but it's all we have. If we're going to learn anything about Winter, it'll be from her.

Vae and Shelt have things to do, so I go by myself, land in the one hopper pad in Perth, and hail a car to Dr. Gartner's house. Not wanting to show up completely unexpected at a seventy-eight-year-old woman's front door first thing in the morning, I call to let her know I'm on the way.

"Hello?" a woman answers, voice only.

"Good morning," I say. "Sorry to bother you this early, ma'am. My name is Finsbury Gage, are you Dr. Beverly Gartner?"

"Yes," she answers after a moment. I can hear the hesitation, a strange man calling her out of the blue. "And no bother, I'm an early riser. What can I do for you, Mr. Gage?"

"I'm hoping you can help me. I'm looking for someone who might have been a patient of yours."

"I'm afraid I can't talk about my patients, Mr. Gage. You understand, I'm sure."

"Of course, Doctor. I appreciate that, but this is a matter of life and death. I have a reasonable suspicion the man I'm looking for is dangerous. He's already killed two people that we know of, I'm trying to find him before he hurts anyone else."

"Are you with the police office?" she asks.

"Not anymore," I admit. "Retired, like you."

She's quiet, then asks, "What is his name?"

"We only know him as Winter," I say. "But he's gone digital. That's the name he's used since his transition. We don't know anything about him, only know your name because he mentioned you to an acquaintance of his. He said he's an orphan, that his parents died in a flood when he was young. He said a Dr. Gartner used to visit him at the refugee camp he grew up in, tried to help him."

"I only ever worked in the Royal," she clarifies. "I've never been to the camps."

"We assume he lied. Maybe even about his parents dying."

"I counseled many children over the years, Mr. Gage—"

"He'd be hard to forget. He claims he has no emotions, that he's suffered from a void in his head all his life..."

The doctor is silent. I can hear her breathing but she doesn't say anything.

"Dr. Gartner?" I ask.

"Why don't we talk about this in person," she finally says, and gives me her address. She remembers him, and I can tell by the sound of her voice it scares her.

"I'm already on the way. See you in ten."

When I arrive, she shows me into a small kitchen and pours me a fresh cup of coffee from a pot on the stove, an old percolator with the little clear glass bubble in the top.

She's small, not frail but getting there. Her hair is a pinkish white and hangs loose at her shoulders. She's wearing a thin white cardigan and well-creased brown slacks. It looks like she put on some lipstick and blush before I arrived.

I take a seat at the kitchen table while she remains standing, keeping the kitchen island between us. A small data stick lies on the counter in front of her.

"I've had many patients over my career who presented with an absence of emotion," she begins. "It's a common enough disorder called alexithymia, most often co-occurring with other disorders—autism, PTSD. It appears in about fifteen percent of the population and has been on the rise in the past decades."

"You know who I'm looking for," I say.

"Normally the condition doesn't imply the subject is dangerous," she continues, but steels her jaw, "but you say this person presents a clear and present threat to the public?"

"We think he killed someone two days ago."

"I really shouldn't be speaking to you without a warrant," she warns.

"I'll take anything you have."

A tremor works its way across her lips and she clutches reflexively at her chest, then says, "I'm not one for drama, Mr. Gage, or hyperbole, but I can tell you I've never met another person so empty as that boy. It would have been heartbreaking if he wasn't so evil."

"Evil?"

Her cheeks grow flushed. "I know what you must be

thinking, a subjective word hardly becoming of a doctor, but this isn't a clinical setting. Besides, I'm not sure how else to describe him. A more generous person might call him super-adjusted to reality, able to think only in goals and operation, completely unhindered by empathy or the needs of anyone but himself..."

"Sounds like evil to me," I say.

She nods and points to the data stick. "Alister Taft. I first met him when he was a toddler. His mother was a diplomat and his father high up in the civil service. They wanted the best and were referred to me. They suspected their son was autistic and brought him to the Royal for counseling. It only took a few sessions to uncover that Alister wasn't on the spectrum at all. Autism is a disorder referring to a variety of conditions—sub-average social skills, obsessive behaviors, communication difficulties—but Alister could communicate fine, as long as you didn't ask him what he was feeling, or ask him to identify if he was feeling anything at all. There would be rages or outbursts, but he couldn't explain them. He described them as though they happened to someone else. We settled on the diagnosis of alexithymia, and the brain scans showed a lack of cortical function all through the limbic system, but we couldn't attribute it to a trauma, and concluded it was simply the way he was born. I saw him over the next few years for regular ongoing assessments, and, again, this isn't clinical, but there was something missing in him, some spark that we all take for granted and don't even notice until we perceive its absence. We put him on a course of tailored neural balancers and his rages abated. He became more docile, or at least he appeared to. When he was eight his parents came to me, concerned. More than concerned—Alister was behaving strangely, even for him. They discovered he hadn't been taking his medication. Then found a burial ground of dead animals in the back garden. They were scared."

"What did you do?"

"Normally people with his condition aren't dangerous, but in this case...I'd gazed into that boy's eyes. They were empty, like a sea creature's. We made an appointment for the next day. They were dead before morning."

Winter killed his own parents. It's shocking but somehow not at all surprising. "What happened to him?"

Her eyes twitch. "It was ruled an accident—carbon monoxide poisoning. The family lived in a 100-year-old home that still had gas appliances, somehow there was a leak. Coincidentally at the same time the home safety systems malfunctioned and didn't sound an alarm."

"But Alister survived."

"His bedroom door was closed, his bed under an open window."

"Convenient."

She makes a noise in her throat. "I thought so too. But no one wanted to entertain the idea that an eight-year-old could somehow engineer a gas leak and undetectably tamper with a HomeNet setup. He played a wonderful victim, but I knew he was acting. There was no other family for him to live with, so he ended up in the system, but he didn't seem to mind. Almost as though he preferred it. I saw him from time to time over the years and the outbursts disappeared as he grew older. He was able to communicate, seemed to have adapted to his condition."

"Did he ever hurt anyone again?"

She shakes her head. "Nothing I ever heard of. I would have done something, had I suspected."

"Do you know what happened to him?"

"He discharged himself from the system at seventeen. I remember there was a trust fund."

"Is there anything else? Anything that could help me find him?"

"I'm sorry, Mr. Gage, that's all I can say. Any more and I'm afraid I'll need to insist on a warrant." She takes a hard look at the data stick on the counter. "Now if you'll excuse me, I need to prepare for an appointment. It was nice to have met you, I'll let you to show yourself out."

She turns and walks out of the kitchen, leaving the data stick lying on the counter. It's in my pocket when I pull her front door closed behind me.

WINTER'S IN HIS APARTMENT, seated in the single armchair overlooking Reszlieville, sorting through the correspondence in his head. Since he became famous, Winter's inbox is never empty. The notes and recordings and long, rambling virtcast messages flood in at all hours of the day.

There's always someone who wants something, to take a piece of him, or to make some small fleeting contact with an artist. He disregards most of the propositions he receives; he has no use for the lonely or star-struck souls who reach out, wanting something he could never provide. But since Grace joined him, he's begun to appreciate the notes more, to draw more from them than the potential for a new mind to integrate. He can now appreciate their desire to connect, understand more fully the drive to reach out and find kinship. The messages have come to be an unexpected source of solace—even joy.

Until today, when he reads two notes in quick succession.

The first is from someone named Shelt. Usually Winter consumes the notes quickly, scans them briefly and moves on, lingering only if the words or voice sparks something in him—but this one is different. Shelt asks about Grace. He seems to know she and Winter had a connection, and asks Winter to contact him.

His mind lurches, his heart races, and his hands grow moist. Something stirs in him he hasn't felt since Grace came to him: fear.

Someone knows about Grace, and if they know that, what else could they know about him?

Grace has had nothing but time. Time she fills wandering the endless halls of Winter's mind—her prison. She knows Winter inside and out now, knows what integrating with her has done to him. All his life, Winter knew he was different, and wanted nothing more than to be the same as everyone else, even though his "lack," as he calls it, was what made him who he was. It was almost like a superpower from those ratty comic books Amos and the other boys hid underneath their mattresses.

Winter never once in his life felt fear or hate or jealousy or self-doubt, and because of that, he never had those obstacles to overcome. But now that Grace has made him whole, he's as vulnerable as everyone else.

She feels Winter's sudden fear just as acutely as he does, but she's no stranger to the feeling. Life on the Preserves was many things—full of joy and toil and beauty—but it was never easy. The year she was eight the crops failed. A summer of torrential rain had rotted the wheat at the root, and she could see the worry in her father's usually stoic eyes. This had scared her more than the ghost stories her brother used to tell her, or having to venture alone into the damp cellar under their house for a bushel of potatoes. This was real. She learned death was always close by. Unseen. Waiting.

They had survived, but she never forgot the lesson. She learned to accept fear as part of life on God's Earth, to expect it—harness it. Fear could be debilitating, or it could be a motivator.

As Winter lets himself fall into his fear of discovery, of punishment for the many evils he's committed, she feels herself swell, feels her fingers and toes tingle. For the first time since she gave herself to Winter, she almost remembers what it's like to have a body—and she wants more.

The second note is from Nandez, and when she too asks about Grace, Winter nearly collapses. Worse, Nandez says Grace's brother has come to the city, looking for her, and even roped in some locals to help in the search.

His head buzzes with the implication and his extremities grow numb. All at once he understands: this is what it feels to be hunted.

He hates the feeling, the shrill anxiety, the loss of composure. Before, when he was in control of his mind, he could have shut these feelings down before they became overwhelming. But now he's at their whims, his head buffeted by the unrestrained emotion. He's dizzy. Bright suns dance in his eyes. He can't breathe, can't contain the sobs that erupt from his tight chest—

Amos is here! She knows this because Winter does, feels how scared it makes him—and she feels it too, but in a different way. She has no concern for herself, what worse could happen to her now? But Amos, he's come looking for her. She should have known he couldn't stay away, should have known he'd never let her simply disappear—

Winter composes himself, goes straight to RepNet, and requests a public profile of Amos Boldt. As he was born a grassr, the system doesn't have much on him. No rep to speak of, and the only listings show his recorded biokin movement since he's been in the city, but there's enough to see what he looks like—tall and lanky with piercing eyes and a face full of reddish hair—and where he's staying—a capsule hotel near the airport.

This man is a threat.

She feels the fear, the power of it, knows what Winter will do —Amos is in danger. She can't let anything happen to him. Can't let the terrible choice she made ruin her brother's life too.

The fear strengthens her, and rather than shrink from it she grabs hold and uses it to pull herself up.

It's been years since Winter's truly been threatened, not since that careless choice to wear his registered skyn out to hunt by the lake, and back then he had his rational mind to rely on. He didn't let the potential consequences of capture get in the way, but now, staring at the image of Amos Boldt's dark eyes, he feels paralyzed, like his body is no longer his to control, like he's slipping away—

—and then Grace once again has a body. Not her body, nothing like she remembers, but a body nonetheless.

She's seated in Winter's apartment, with a photo of her brother hovering in the air before her. Amos' face fills her with such overwhelming surprise and sadness that she can't help but cry at the sight of it. Dear brother, what have I done?

Beyond her brother's image lies the city that scared her so when she first arrived, and scares her even now, but Amos is here, somewhere, looking for her, and knowing he's out there gives her the strength to quell her trembling muscles. She takes a breath, in and out through her nose, the first breath she remembers taking for so long, and feels the air rush smoothly in and out of her lungs, feels the warmth as it passes over her upper lip.

This sudden emergence into the world is like a rebirth. She flexes, moving cautiously. Her body is foreign, more powerful than she ever remembers being. There's a strange tightness across her chest and an alien throbbing in her groin. She takes another cleansing breath, attempting to calm herself, stands, and stumbles forward. For a brief moment she pictures herself falling from the sky and plummeting to the street below, but she catches herself against the massive window, nose pressed to the cool glass, Amos' face still hovering in her vision, out above the city.

The vertigo is immediate and she pushes herself back, totters on her feet as she adjusts to the beautiful constraints of flesh and blood once more, and as she does she catches sight of her reflection in the glass—Winter staring back at her, his sharp features and ice-blue eyes taunting her. She's caught by the urge to flee, but steels herself. This is her reflection. She is Winter. Winter is her.

The weight of everything she's lost wells up inside her, and she wants to explode, to run to her mother and bury her face in her apron and cry into the smell of flour and onions, *but she knows she doesn't have the luxury of tears. She gave that all up when she foolishly thought she could save Winter from himself. What's gone is gone, but Amos is still here. She can find him, tell him what happened, and together they can go the law and tell them everything Winter has done, stop him from hurting anyone else.*

The cold is unyielding, relentless. He's adrift in his own mind, conscious but powerless, time and space bereft of meaning. Nothing exists but existence. It's his worst fears come true: he's lost himself to Grace.

Worse still, the flurry of emotions continues to torment him. He's wracked by terror and a mute, hollow rage. He screams but the sound rips from his voiceless mouth as a phantom pain in his throat. He's trapped in a prison of his own making.

This all started because of Grace. He should have known better, known she would be the ruin of him, but he was so caught up in her, in the desire to be one with her, that he couldn't see the potential for disaster. He should have been more cautious, should have put stronger precautions in place, but he wanted so desperately to be whole. If only he had known what that truly meant—

Those are thoughts for another time. Regrets are useless now. He needs to find his way back. He can only hope the swap isn't permanent, that there's still a chance to regain himself.

The trigger is obvious: the brother. Somehow Grace sensed his thoughts about Amos, and this charge gave her the power to rise up and take control. If she did it, he can do it. He can take control back.

Their minds are in flux, vying for dominance. Eventually she too will slip, and he'll have the opportunity to reassert himself, of that he's certain.

Hopefully he can endure the frozen torment long enough to act when the time comes.

Grace has spent enough time in Winter's mind to understand how to operate some of the technology he relies on. As reluctant as she is to dirty herself with its use, she has no other choice.

She quickly discovers Amos is staying at a hotel near the airport she flew into, and she's able to make it down the elevator and summon one of those cartoon-looking vehicles to take her there. She spent enough time in the city with Winter before her integration that whizzing along the busy streets in the belly of a bulbous vehicle precariously perched on a single wheel doesn't cause her to panic, and she's at least grateful for that. As impossible as it feels, this is normal. She's inside someone else's body, racing to find her brother before the owner can regain control, but the vehicle isn't going to fall over. Of that, and nothing else, she's certain.

She doesn't know what she'll say when she sees Amos, or if she'll be able to say anything at all. How will he react? Will he even believe it's truly her inside this stranger's body? There's nothing in his life that will have prepared him for it. She's had an eternity to come to terms with what she's done and still she sometimes hopes this is all a dream.

And even if he can, somehow, see through this stranger's face to his sister inside, how will she ever explain how she ended up here? The hubris of thinking she could somehow enact God's will by giving up her most precious gift—her immortal soul—to a monster in hopes it would save him.

What a silly girl she was. Even now the shame of it burns on her cheeks.

She can only talk to him, try make him understand why she did what she did. She made a mistake, but together they can make it right. With Amos' support, they can turn Winter in, bring him to justice for the pain he's caused. It doesn't matter what happens to her anymore, she was going to die anyway, and while her sacrifice won't have ended the way she envisioned, perhaps it won't be all in vain.

Winter slowly acclimatizes to his new surroundings. His lack of control is infuriating, but the desert of sensation he initially perceived isn't so bleak as he first believed. Thoughts wash over him, and images come unbidden as he intercepts flickers of Grace's consciousness. He wonders if this is what she felt, peeping at his life through a keyhole in his mind.

Though he only receives fragments, he's able to piece them together into a picture of what she's doing: the vertigo when she first takes over their body and tries to stand; the undulations in their stomach as the Sküte winds its way through traffic; the surge of remorse and satisfaction as she thinks about what she's done and what she's going to do next.

She's going to meet her brother, and together they'll turn Winter over to Standards.

The hate Winter feels for Grace's brother is absolute, it's his presence that caused this rift. If he'd stayed away they'd still be happy, Winter in control and Grace propping him up...

The intense rage he feels for Amos is only moderately less than the hate he feels for himself. He put himself in this position, with his irrational need to feel like everyone else. To be weak. To be helpless.

He gave Grace the opportunity to take over, and of course, she grabbed it. Winter doesn't blame her. She's acting on her emotions, and that's just what he wanted her for.

He doesn't blame her, but he can't let her remain in control. Once he regains dominance he'll flood his mind with new rithms, dilute her until she's just another drop of thought in the sea of his mind. He just needs one more chance.

Then he'll never let it happen again.

The pink-and-green vehicle drops Grace off in front of Amos' hotel and she runs up the sidewalk and to the lobby. It's small, clean, and well lit, but she can already feel the claustrophobia of the small space pressing in on her.

A squat robot trundles over the floor, cleaning as it goes. Three rectangular slabs of glass stand sentinel across the floor, halfway between the entrance and the bank of elevators on the back wall. There's no one to greet her, but a woman wearing a strange boxy hat and a shapely yellow dress materializes on one of the panes as she approaches.

"Good morning, Mr. Winter," the woman says with a wide smile that shows off her perfect teeth. *"Can I help you with accommodations?"*

"What?" Grace says with a voice she belatedly recognizes as Winter's. *"Oh—no. I'm looking for my bro—for a guest. Mr. Amos David Boldt. He's staying here, correct?"*

The artificial woman responds smoothly. "I'm afraid I can't divulge information about our guests."

"But he is staying here, right?"

"I'm afraid I can't divulge information about our guests," the woman responds in the exact same tone. "Can I assist you with anything else today?"

Grace feels her ire rising. "Can't you just tell me yes or no—"

"I'm sorry we couldn't be of more help," the image says. "Have a terrific day." It winks off.

"Hey—" Grace yells, but the image doesn't return. She wants to kick the glass but knows that'd be childish. What now?

She turns and leaves the hotel, not sure what she's supposed to do next. Outside everything is moving, there's too much to look at, too many competing noises, and she focuses her eyes downward taking one step at a time.

Ahead of her two men stand on the pavement. One of them is tall, more than six feet, and built like a farmhand, with broad shoulders and a tight waist, but skin like he's never seen a day's work in his life. His face is handsome, but etched with concern.

The other man is Amos.

"Winter—" He hears the boy say his name, and feels his chance to escape arrive. Grace falters, unsure of herself, wondering how her brother could know Winter's name. She's thinned out, her control hanging by strings. The shock of seeing her brother has made her vulnerable.

Now is his chance.

She feels her face scrunch up as she tries not to cry at the sight of him. She's never been happier to see anyone in her life.

"Mozzy..." *she says, hesitant, and the word coming from Winter's lips sounds like another language.*

Amos rushes forward and she opens her arms to hug him but he grabs her by the lapels of her vest instead. "How do you know that name?" *he yells. His voice is strained, but the hope is plain on his face.* "No one calls me that but—" *His eyes widen and he glances in disbelief at his friend before once more locking eyes with her.* "Grace?"

He sees. He knows she's in there. The relief is stunning, draining.

She's found him, found her brother. This is almost over—

And then it all falls apart as Winter once again takes control.

ONCE I GET BACK in the hopper I throw everything from
the data stick onto my tab and get Connie to scan it all and
give me a summary. It takes her a minute to compile it, and
the story she tells me about Alister Taft isn't that much
different than Dr. Gartner's. Running a rep search on him
shows a solid point eight-two rank, but no public activity
since he went digital in early '56. The transfer ID is
anonymized. But I already know who he became: Winter.

Now that I know his name, there's got to be some way to
find him.

I use another one of Shelt's hacked SecNet cycles to get
everything there is on Alister Taft. He's been careful.
There's no direct link between Alister and Winter, even in
SecNet. Alister's pre-transfer neural background checks all
came back green—with the notable assessment of a severe
cortical deficiency. But with no outstanding warrants or
debts they cleared him to a new identity and passed him off
to Second Skyn with a transfer hash and no ties back to the
person he had been.

If I were a cop I could force Second Skyn to ping

Winter's registered Cortex and lead me right to him, but I'm not, and I bet Second Skyn's data walls are sturdier than SecNet's. It'd likely take a competent hacker a few days to crack, and probably then require social hacking, or a little wetwork.

That's fine—I've got something better.

It doesn't take long to figure out exactly where Winter is hiding.

Alister is rich. Multi-multimillionaire rich. Numbered accounts and pass-through corporations rich. When he was seventeen he collected a trust fund, and through investments and real estate deals it took only five years to increase it by an order of magnitude.

From what I can see, he now owns properties all over the world. Several in Toronto and the surrounding area, a flat in Buenos Aires, a townhouse in Amsterdam, an entire floor of a Dubai moon-scraper. A hundred square kilometers of empty forest in Northern Quebec. He could be anywhere.

But he isn't.

I dismiss the out-of-town properties first. He's still here, still close to home.

He's got a house in Etobicoke, a massive condo on Hamilton Harbor, two multi-unit rental buildings, and another house in Port Union. But these aren't right. He's a creature of habit, probably been working out of the same place for a long time. Someplace high, with the world at his feet.

He's got a penthouse in one of the Playter Estates Towers on the very eastern edge of Reszlieville, overlooking the wooded valley on one side and the whole of modern creation on the other. That's where he'll be.

I consider not calling Standards at all and trying to get

to Winter myself, but once I'm about ten minutes away from the hopper pad nearest Winter's apartment, I figure that's stupid. Without the Service override, Winter's building has no reason to let me in, so I can't get to him myself anyway. Besides, if I call this in maybe it'll earn me some points with Galvan—he'll be pissed I got involved as it is.

I connect to the Standards AMP and have it relay a message for Agent Wiser and Detective Yellowbird.

"Hi guys, this is Finsbury. I'm calling with an anonymous tip. You'll find Winter in Penthouse 2 of the Playter Estates complex. Pre-reszo he was Alister Taft, the apartment is registered under his name. I'll give you ten minutes to get there and then I'm going up without you."

The AMP wants to keep talking, asking questions about Winter, but I drop the connection. It tries to ring back and I shut my tab down completely. Then the hopper starts dinging at me and the window darkens to show an incoming message. The AMP doesn't give up, and I ignore the insistent noise for another few minutes until the hopper lands and powers down.

The pad is only a half-block from Winter's building, close enough I have to crane my head back to see the tops of the three narrow buildings, and I let myself enjoy the moment. Winter is up there right now, and he has no idea his world's about to end.

Five minutes later I'm standing at the base of the middle building. The three structures are identical, rectangles shaved to long narrow points—like axe heads pointed at the sky. Wide at the base, the floors slowly narrow as they ascend, until the floors are surrounded by smooth black phovo on every side.

There's a series of long wooden planters outside, and I

perch on one and wait. It's still early morning. Low clouds
have massed on the horizon, and they're heading this way.
The valley behind Winter's complex runs north and south
along the river, and smells green and vibrant in the sunlight.
The air tastes of the river's slightly fishy tang.

I power my tab back up and find a bunch of important
alerts from the AMP, but nothing from Wiser or Yellowbird.
People come and go, in and out of the buildings, up and
down the sidewalk. Bots walk, fly, gallop, and roll by. Surely
none of them know who lives here, that a monster lurks
above them—

I throw my head back once more and try to see to the
penthouse, but the clouds are coming fast, throwing a mist
around the building's top floors. I figured I'd hear the sirens
by now, check the tab again. Nothing—

Where the hell is Standards? Or at least Yellowbird
should have called me back, right? The Service should have
been here by now.

The clouds thicken like a lid closing on the sky, and
suddenly I feel exposed, like Winter's up there watching
me, laughing as he prepares to make his escape. He probably has a dozen other names he can choose from, who
knows how many hidey-holes he can bolt to. If we lose him
now, we'll never see him again.

I gave Galvan enough time—I'm not letting Winter get
away. Before I get up from the planter I tuck the data stick
down in the loose dirt for safekeeping—or insurance. Never
can be too careful.

At the entrance, the building stops me and asks if I'm
visiting a resident.

Am I really doing this?

I cock my head and listen to the city's noise but still

don't hear sirens. My tab still doesn't ring. Well, if Galvan isn't interested in bringing Winter in, I'll do it for him.

I'm sure as hell not going to wait around with my thumb up my ass any more.

"Alister Taft," I tell the building.

It asks me to wait, and a moment later Winter buzzes me up.

How COULD things have gone so wrong?

Winter's made it back home, but his hands are still shaking. His mouth tastes like metal—perhaps he bit his tongue during the struggle, or perhaps this is the true taste of fear.

He hates feeling this way. Feeling anything at all.

Tonight, everything nearly came undone and he has no one to blame but himself. He wasn't prepared, and he acted out of irrational rage, a desire to punish Grace for her show of dominance. He wanted to hurt her, and nearly ended up losing everything in the process.

Amos is dead.

Trapped in Winter's head, surrounded by nothing, she feels colder than ever before. More alone. Amos only came here because of her, because she couldn't face her mother's grief, because her pride wouldn't allow her to leave this Earth without first performing some grand gesture to make her passing worthwhile.

Her arrogance led her here, and now others are suffering for her transgressions.

She made Winter mad, so Winter punished her. But he couldn't hurt her, so he took it out on her brother. She'd cry if she could, but she has no eyes, no tears to shed. The anguish has nowhere to go. She can feel it inside her, festering, curdling to rage.

Amos is dead, and it's all her fault.

Winter sheds his clothes, double bags them with the intention of dropping them in a recycler somewhere on the other side of the city, and orders the bot to scrub the apartment from top to bottom. He doesn't think he's tracked any of that boy's DNA back here, but he can't be too careful, not after the mistakes he's just made.

He was irrational, his actions driven by revenge. Grace had hurt him—the first person who'd ever managed to—and he couldn't help but respond in kind. The desire for retribution became all-encompassing, the intensity unlike anything he'd experienced before. It polluted his thoughts until he couldn't see anything else.

His plan was simple: contact Amos under the pretense of once again meeting his sister. After Grace spoke to him at his hotel, it was simple enough to make the boy believe his sister was reaching out for help, to lure him to a secluded spot in the valley in order to capture his mind.

But Winter didn't plan on integrating with him. No, Amos' stolen mind would act as a surety, a guarantee that Grace would remain docile. If she once again attempted to gain dominance, he'd take his vengeance on her helpless brother's soul.

He could drop the boy in a virtual world where his

every fear is made real, or simulate endless physical torture, or confine his thoughts to a virtual equivalent of solitary confinement, where he'd quickly go mad, then reset him and do it all over again. That would keep the girl in line long enough to bury her.

They met on one of the nature trails snaking through the valley. A remote location, away from the immediate eyes of SecNet. Amos was wary, but desperate to believe his sister needed his help, that much was clear.

Winter administered the sedative easily enough, and it was only a matter of waiting for it to take effect—but he didn't expect the ferocity of the boy's resistance.

Though no match for Winter even without the drugs sapping his strength, Amos fought, screaming all the while. He continued to resist even after Winter wrangled the transfer cap over his head and plunged the transfer spikes into the boy's nervous system.

Against all expectations, Amos struggled. Even blind and deaf and tiring from the paralytic, he managed to break free from Winter's grasp and dashed headlong from the path down into a steep wooded ravine.

There was no chance to retrieve the body, or even the capture gear. Amos' cries would surely have alerted some-one, even that early in the morning.

Winter had no choice. He fled. Scurried away from the scene with the sting of failure fresh on his lips and Grace's slowly dawning grief crying out from the depths of his mind.

Her anguish is hollow here, her anger futile. She's power-less...except...she isn't.

They're connected, two minds made one. While she

might not have any immediate control of her surroundings, she took control once, and that means she can do it again.

The trick will be in figuring out how, exactly, she's supposed to do that.

Last time it happened on its own. She didn't do anything —one second she was trapped in Winter's mind and the next she was in charge. She doesn't know how to make the switch happen. She doesn't have any tools, there are no levers to throw.

No, she only has one thing left: herself. Her emotions. Her desires.

Her belief.

He's scared of her, scared that he'll lose himself once and for all. This is why he went after Amos. He did it to guarantee he'd always be in control.

She should have seen it sooner—her emotions are his weakness. They're still too new, still too intense. He can't handle them yet.

That's how she's going to escape. She needs to stoke her emotions, make him irrational, make him unstable. Maybe he'll falter, and when he does she can once again find the crack that will let her free.

It's clear to him now: integrating with Grace was the worst decision he's ever made. She's brought him nothing but pain. Nothing but confusion and aggravation, the emotional support she provides not near recompense for the damage she's caused.

Once he's disposed of the evidence in Amos' death, he'll concentrate on burying her for good. He'll fill his mind so full of rithms she'll drown in the sea of thought.

He'll start tonight—hell, he'll start *now*. Why wait?

There's no shortage of willing minds longing for a call from Winter.

Once he's sure he's covered up his involvement in Amos' death, the hunt will begin anew.

He's already tingling with excitement, can barely contain his anticipation.

Back to the hunt—the only thing he's ever truly loved.

THE ELEVATOR TAKES me to the penthouse, opens onto a massive living space walled in by cloud. The apartment is quiet, lit only by diffuse sunlight streaming in through the mist. I take a few cautious steps across the polished concrete floor and my footsteps echo in the cavernous room. The place seems deserted, but someone let me up. Winter's here somewhere.

I creep in a bit further, on edge, waiting for someone to jump me. To my right is a metal spiral staircase extending up three stories, to the left an open kitchen that looks as though it's never been used. There's almost no furniture. Just a single chair in front of the window directly ahead of me and a huge piano near the kitchen, where a dining table might be.

It's spare. Industrial and functional with clean lines and nothing in it. It looks like the house Connie made me. The only difference is the view.

I'm living like a serial killer.

Shit. How fucked up am I?

I don't like it here. I should have waited for Galvan. I

have no weapon, no way to defend myself. If Winter were to come at me with a gun or a knife or even running a revved skyn...I should turn back now.

But I don't.

There's a shuffle to my left that sets my heart dashing. I spin, fists raised, but it's just a housebot emerging from its charging hutch. It's humanoid, vaguely female, with a smooth blank face. It notices me and glides to a stop, watching.

That's enough. I'm not playing this game anymore.

"Alister!" I call out, wondering if maybe Winter's hiding behind the bot's eyes. "Show yourself."

The bot doesn't respond, but an answer comes from behind and above.

"I don't like that name," offers a crystal voice. I spin again, and Winter's standing at the top of the spiral stair-case, hands on the railing. The sight of him sends an icicle of dread down my throat. I try to hide it.

He cocks his head with a reptilian twitch and regards me with inscrutable eyes. "Finsbury Gage. Widowed. Disgraced Service detective turned unlikely hero when you allegedly put an end to a rogue superintelligence—though questions remain and rumors abound." He's reading my dox off the link. "You were with the brother."

"His name was Amos," I say, keeping my voice loose. "You killed him."

His face shivers, as though he's suppressing a shock of pain. To cover, he runs a hand through his platinum hair, smoothing it back from his pale, angular face, then tugs at the bottom of the bright blue vest he's layered over a crisp white shirt and matching pants.

"He...resisted. I only wanted..." He strangles a sob and

his knees nearly give out, has to catch himself against the railing.

This isn't who I expected. Something's wrong with him.

"You wanted his mind," I push, trying to keep him off-balance. I need to keep him talking until Galvan shows. *Which should have been ten minutes ago.*

"No," Winter says, almost pleading. "I—" He cuts himself off, screws his face up, and clenches his jaw, fighting for control. When he speaks his voice is cold, more like I'd imagined. "How did you find me?"

"Dr. Gartner," I say. "I told her I was looking for a monster and your name came immediately to mind."

His eyes flare and he pushes himself back off the railing and curves down the spiral stairs, walking with precise, fragile steps, like he isn't used to the body he's wearing.

"I knew I should have quieted her," Winter says as he nears the bottom of the staircase. "But she was the only one who understood, the closest thing I'd ever had to a friend— I'll have to take her next. I can't have people knowing about me."

I drift back toward the kitchen as he reaches the ground. I don't want him too close.

"You don't get it, do you, Alister? Everyone's going to know about you soon enough."

"You shouldn't have come here," he replies, and I don't disagree. He begins to approach, head down, eyes menacing.

"I didn't come alone," I warn, backing up while feigning a confidence I don't remotely feel. "Standards is right behind me, will be here any second. You should give yourself up while you have the chance."

His lips quiver. "Give up? After all I've sacrificed? No, I've only just begun."

I steel myself, ready to react should Winter attack, but he only smiles as I hear the buzz of an electric switch and the puff of compressed gas—the bot. Before I can move a sharp pain spears the back of my thigh.

I grab at the pain and feel a dart jutting from my leg. I take hold and yank it out but it's too late. My leg goes numb and I stumble, try to catch myself, but there's nothing to grab onto and I collapse on the hard floor. The paralytic works its way over my chest and down my other leg, dulling my nerves. I try to drag myself toward the elevator, but after only a few seconds I'm completely unable to move. My body disappears and my head hits the floor with a thud that rattles my vision. I can still see and hear, but that's it.

"She's telling me to stop," Winter says from somewhere above me. "I can feel her, resisting me."

She—*Grace?*

The room swings as Winter grabs me up and slings me over his shoulder. My skyn must weigh 100 kilos, and he's tossing me around without any trouble. I'm at his mercy.

"I only wanted her to prop me up," Winter continues as he carries me over to the single chair in the middle of the room and sets me down, arranging me so I'm sitting up as though enjoying the view, "to be a scaffold toward my humanity, but instead she's taking over. I can't have that."

Then it's true. Grace is in there, fighting him. I want to respond, to somehow encourage her, but my lips don't work. My breathing is shallow, labored.

I can't help Grace. I can't even help myself. He's going to kill me. Or worse.

So, this is it.

With Deacon fouling my pattern I haven't dared back up my rithm—I end here. No doubt someone will bring me back, and it'll be the me just after the accident, and he'll get to live through losing Connie all over again. I'll be gone, but Finsbury will never die.

I wonder what he'll make of what's become of his lives.

At least Deacon will die with me, so there's that—

"I had hoped she would be the last," Winter says, "that she and I would balance each other out, I never anticipated I might be the one to fade. That can't that happen. I need to drown her out and since your mind is here, I'll add you as well. Fran," he calls off to the bot, "get me something to carry his head in."

"Yes, master," the bot says in a cool female voice and tiptoes away.

No. Not like this.

I've been avoiding and playing with death so long it's lost its power, but suddenly it becomes all too real. He's going to cut off my head, hack into my Cortex, and ingest me. Consume my mind like a psychic cannibal.

Adrenaline spikes in my brain but with my body on hiatus it has nowhere to go. I'm not restrained, if I could only get up—

I fight with everything I have to regain some control over my legs or my hands or even my fingers, just a finger, but the signals fizz off into nothing.

Galvan!

Winter walks out of view and when he returns a moment later he's holding a long curved sword, a katana, I think. He runs a sharpener along the edge, once, twice, with a slick scrape that rings in the open room. The noise cavitates through my mind, and Deacon's black tendrils slip in to fill the holes.

Oh no, not him too...

"I bought this sword with the intent of using it to sample my first target," he says, pulling the stone along the long blade again, then again, rhythmically. "But it always felt too showy. Too impractical. I'm glad to get the chance to use it at least once." My eyes bulge in panic as he continues. "I haven't taken a mind by force in years. Now, I ask for consent. There's far more to be gained from a willing participant. Everyone who's with me right now has agreed to be here. You'll be the first that hasn't come willingly—but I don't have time to convince you, I need to wash her out of my mind. I suspect I'll need many more before she's quiet."

Deacon's coming, I can feel him. The sharpening screech is hollowing out, my vision creeping toward nothing. But I don't know who's going to get here first, Deacon or Winter.

Winter puts down the stone, steps close so we're nearly face to face, and examines my neck. "You know, the neck is much denser than you'd expect. Sometimes multiple swings are required. That's why I decided on the eblade, it cuts so much smoother than steel. But the symbolism of using the sword to return to the hunt—it's fitting. I'll try to make it quick."

He steps back and raises the sword and I try once again to get up, maybe just move enough to make him miss, but I can't. My lips respond though, and I get out a noise, a grunt. It's not much, but it's something. A few more seconds, I just need a few more.

Winter pauses, offers a rueful smile. "The paralytic is wearing off. This is going to hurt."

"Waaait..." I slur, stalling. Wait for what? I have nothing.

Galvan, now's the time!

Standards doesn't come bursting through the doors. My shallow breathing roars in my ears.

This is how it ends.

Deacon's tendrils are pulling harder now, insistent. I can't stop him from taking over—which at this point is fine by me. Instead of resisting, I let go and slip into the black.

I'm going to die anyway, might as well be Deacon who gets his head cut off.

PART FOUR_

WINTER'S GRACE

WINTER BALANCES the long blade in his hands and visualizes the swing. One swift blow, tThrough the neck, below the thyroid cartilage of the larynx. That should avoid damage to the Cortex. The added flesh will be enough to protect the ports from damage while he travels.

Gage opens his mouth again, possibly to scream, and Winter flexes, wrists and shoulders coiled to snap the sword through through flesh and sinew and bone, but instead of a wordless howl Gage's face stiffens and shifts. His eyes narrow.

"Kill us, and Grace will own you forever," Gage says. His voice is different now, colder.

A quiver of shock trembles through Winter, vibrates down the blade before he can silence it. Gage is stalling, hoping for a miracle, but the Service isn't coming. There's no indication Winter is in any external danger at all. He should reset and take the swing, collect Gage's head and prepare to make his escape, but he can't, and Gage keeps talking. "She's taking over, isn't she? You've been there, locked-up inside your head. You know how it feels, is that how you want to end up?"

Winter wants to swing, to make the words stop, but he can't.

Gage knows. Somehow, *he knows*.

And then Winter understands. This isn't Gage. This is someone else.

Someone like Winter.

"Who are you?" Winter asks, the blade still poised to strike.

"I'm the guy living in Fin's head, just like Grace is living in yours, but she's way stronger than I am. I know she's fighting you, and I know you're losing. From what I can tell, you probably have twelve hours before she takes over— maybe a day if you're lucky. Then you'll be stuck riding shotgun in your own mind, just like I am."

"How could you know this?" Winter asks, trying to keep his emotions in check. He needs to stay calm, to keep Grace at bay.

"How do I know?" Gage says, and coughs through a raspy chuckle. "At first there's nothing, just thoughts hovering in the black, and you think maybe you're dead, but you're *thinking* about being dead, so how could you be? Soon you realize it's not death—it's far, far worse. I've been in here a long time, long enough I've even figured out how to move around a little, cobbled a world out of that nothing. Made myself a desert island. I've got a little hut, a tree. Sometimes a bird comes. And occasionally a thought or image filters through, like a message in a bottle, and gives me a glimpse of the life that should be mine. Day after day I stare at the sky, hoping for the chance to escape, plotting my next move, and those chances are more and more rare. I'm all alone in here. You want to end up like me?"

Winter lowers the sword.

"That won't happen," Winter says, "I have a plan. Integrate with enough rithms to drown her thoughts out for good. I had intended to add yours."

Gage shakes his head. "You don't want to do that."

Winter can see that for himself. He doesn't need the fragments of Gage's mind fighting in his head too. But still, he's curious. As unlikely the situation, this is the first person Winter's ever encountered who can understand his pain. "Why not?" Winter asks.

"I'll give you two very good reasons," Gage says. "First off, you don't want our fucked-up mind rattling around in your rithm. Wouldn't be good for any of us."

Winter nods. "And the second?"

Gage purses his lips in a grin, like he's won something. "It wouldn't do you any good anyway. You don't have the time and we both know it. You're barely holding her back as it is, I can see it in your face, the micro-burst of changing expression—you probably don't even notice. She's at the surface, waiting to bust through. The only chance you've got to keep your head is to restore from a back-up, wipe her out for good. And you need to do it now, like *right now*."

"Is that your plan?" Winter asks. "Would you wipe your mind to be free?"

"If it were only that easy," Gage says. "If I had a way out, I'd have taken it long ago. Fin and I, we're playing the long game here."

Winter considers this. *The Orchid facility.* A back-up had been his fail-safe plan from the start. If Grace grew too powerful, if something somehow went wrong, he could wipe her mind completely. It would mean losing the first joyous memories of their first time together, the swell of real emotion blossoming in his mind, but surely his continuing existence is worth that small sacrifice? "I have contingencies in place," Winter says.

"I knew you would," Gage says, and his eyes dart around in his head. "Probably got back-ups of back-ups squirreled away. Though none registered with Standards, am I right? You have something local? In the apartment, maybe?"

"No, nothing so vulnerable," Winter says, waving away the accusation he could be so careless. In some ways Gage is a kindred spirit, but Winter knows he's not saying these things out of compassion. He's trying to save his own life. Gage came here to kill Winter, after all. Or see him apprehended, which is the same thing. He couldn't exist in a cage. "But I do have options."

"Then why are you standing around here chatting with me?" Gage says. "Get to it."

"I have time yet," Winter answers. But he knows Gage is right, whether it's hours or days, Winter can't hold Grace back much longer. She's a master of the one weapon he's vulnerable to: feeling.

Winter raises the sword again. Holds it level with Gage's neck, elbows cocked to swing. Gage's eyes bug out.

"Wait," Gage snarls. "You don't have time for this."

"I have time enough," Winter says. He won't integrate Gage's rithm, but that doesn't mean he's any less intrigued by what's inside this strange creature's head. Studying a sample of another fractured rithm could provide valuable insight into his own condition.

Besides, he can't leave Gage here. Gage is a loose end. Winter made that mistake with Dr. Gartner, he won't make it again.

"I look forward to us becoming better acquainted in the

future, once I am myself again. I anticipate we will become friends, you and I."

"No—" Gage yells as he bunches his muscles, but this time Winter doesn't let his target's words stay the blow. He triggers the swing, snapping his arms in a powerful sweeping motion, intending to sever Gage's head, but the signal dies before it fires. The sword remains motionless, his muscles unresponsive.

Grace!

She holds the blade back, focusing her entire will on keeping Winter's arms from swinging. He's fighting her, but he has his whole body to worry about, all she's concerned with is keeping the sword from slicing that man's head off. She recognizes him— he was with Amos outside his hotel. She knows Winter's decided to erase her, if she can keep this man alive, tell him what Winter's planning, maybe he can help the police catch Winter first.

"*I won't let you kill him,*" he hears Grace say, her words bypassing his ears.

Gage is squinting, anticipating the blow, confused at the delay. Winter gathers his strength and tries to swing again and the blade shudders but doesn't move. It's as though he's blocked by some invisible barrier. After a moment of strain he steps back, frustrated and spent, and the blade clatters to the floor.

Grace won't let him kill Gage. Gage is right—she's too strong. He doesn't have much time, he needs to flee. "The *Orchid,*" he says instead, his mouth forming the words of their own insistence. *Grace again.*

Gage's face breaks into a grin. "Who's that now? Doesn't sound like you, Winter."

"Shut up!" Winter says, and this time it's him forming the words. He needs to run, get away from Gage before Grace can tell him anything more—

"Grace, tell me. What's 'the orchid?'" Gage says as Winter stumbles toward the elevator, concentrating on his lips, forcing them to stay closed.

"*Lake,*" Winter's traitorous lips squeak. "*Back-up. Cabin—* STOP!" he says, finally wresting control of his mouth from the devil inside him. The elevator door opens and he falls in and orders it to the garage. His pulse is pounding in his ears, his breath rasping. Has Grace doomed him?

He works through the steps, calming himself with rationality. He disabled the Second Skyn tracker in his Cortex long ago, it will take the authorities time to locate him—if they're even able to decipher Grace's warnings. The circumstances aren't ideal, but he should have time.

As the doors shut, Gage calls out, "Hey Winter, when Agent Wiser finds you, tell him Deacon says 'fuck you!'"

My senses come back to me slowly. There's noise, commotion, people talking. Is this it, am I inside Winter?

I get my eyes open and my head spins at the sight of Reszlieville from half a klick in the air.

I'm not dead. I'm still in the chair.

My hands spring to my neck, but obviously my head's still attached. I wouldn't be here if it wasn't.

I can move. I've still got my body. Galvan must have made it in time, somehow stopped Winter before he took my head.

Christ that was close.

Blood rushes to my cheeks. I can feel my skin burning with relief but I don't mind the sting. I'm happy to be feeling anything at all.

I take a deep breath and exhale slowly, lost in an unfocused stare at the never-ending bustle of the city below, my thoughts still hazy from the blackout, from the near-death experience.

It's over. We got him.

"Couldn't help yourself, could you?" Galvan says from

somewhere behind me. I turn to look over my shoulder and he's there, eyes shrouded, like he's been watching me, waiting for me to wake up. Yellowbird's here too, her face a blank slate, and that's enough to tell me exactly what she's thinking. I almost fucked up and got myself killed.

Again.

I'm sitting center stage in an active investigation. Standards agents are already collecting forensic data with their sniffers while a drone swarm roves about the apartment, recording the environment for later examination. The tactical officers are gone, but the ozone smell of gunfire remains. Winter's bot lies slumped against the piano, a spray of burned-out holes punched through its chest. There was a fight, and I was out for all of it.

But where's Winter? I don't see a body bag or any blood.

I move to get up and Galvan stops me. "Stay where you are. As far as I'm concerned, you're evidence."

"Yes, sir," I say, and sit back down. No point in arguing.

Galvan's face ripples through a fit of bewilderment at my uncharacteristic obedience. Whatever it was he was expecting me to say, I guess it wasn't that. There's no point in snarking back at him, we both know I messed up coming here, why make it worse?

"Are you okay, Fin?" Yellowbird says, her blank expression now drawn with concern.

"I'm good," I say, and give her a little smile. Everything in one piece.

She takes a step closer, pulls her tab to a point, and sets the end glowing like she wants to run an pattern scan. "You sure he didn't do anything to you, didn't get into your head at all? Let me check your rithm."

I can't tell if she's taking the piss or seriously concerned my personality might have been tampered with. I don't rise to a fight one time and everyone immediately thinks my mind's been hacked. Am I that much of an asshole?

Actually, I don't need anyone to answer that.

"Winter," I say, dodging her tab by looking around again. Maybe he's in a side room somewhere. "Where is he?"

"Why don't you tell us, Finsbury," Galvan says.

"What?" I don't understand. Yellowbird is shaking her head. "What do you mean? You didn't stop him?"

"We got here an hour ago, cleared the place top to bottom," Galvan says. "He wasn't here."

An hour? What time is it now? I check my inner clock and it tells me it's just now after two. It was closer to noon when Winter buzzed me up...

"He was—you stopped Winter from lopping my head off. Didn't you?"

Galvan's eyes widen but he shakes his head. "We followed your tip, used the override to breach the building. The bot was hostile and we had to put it down. Other than that, the only thing we found was you, sitting inert, exactly where you are now, without a scratch on you. So, Finsbury, why don't you fill us in."

Did something spook Winter? Or did he change his mind for some reason?

It doesn't make any sense.

I slump back in my chair. "He was about to take my head off. Why didn't he kill me?"

"Beats me," Galvan mutters. "Would have saved us some trouble."

"*Detective Wiser*," Yellowbird scolds.

Galvan waves the comment away, takes a moment to compose himself, then asks, "How'd you even get up here?"

I barely hear the question. My thoughts are racing.

Why didn't he finish me? He had plenty of time, was poised to swing the second before Deacon took over—

Deacon.

Jesus *fuck.* Of course, it has to be.

Deacon did something, somehow talked him out of killing me.

Killing *us*—

What the hell did he say?

"Mr. Gage—" Galvan repeats, his voice stern, and I cut him off.

"We have to find him," I say. "Now. He's planning on integrating as many rithms as he can. We have to stop him before he takes someone else's mind."

"Just settle down," Galvan says. "Standards isn't about to go running off chasing a whim—that's the difference between us: we have procedure. First we go through what happened here and understand what we're dealing with, then we decide what to do next."

"Is that what took you so long to get here, procedure? Procedure almost got me killed—"

I bite down on my runaway mouth. There's that old asshole rearing his head. At least Yellowbird will be relieved to know nothing's wrong with me—except what's been wrong with me this whole time.

Galvan's face widens in a satisfied smile. "Procedure keeps our heads attached," he says. "Make no mistake, this is on you. You almost got yourself killed and abetted in a suspect's escape in the process. We would have had him, if you only waited." I lower my head. Galvan's right. I chased Winter away, shouldn't have gone in on my own. "Don't worry though," Galvan continues, "we'll find him, soon enough. We know his name now. We flushed him out. There's nowhere for him to run."

"I have no excuse," I say, genuinely contrite. "I shouldn't have come up here. I got tired of waiting and buzzed up and Winter let me in. I was wrong. But don't let showing me up get in the way of finding him. He's been doing this a long time—you told me yourself: SecNet hadn't pinged on him in years. He won't be easy to find, and the longer you spend preparing to find him, the harder it'll be. We need to move. Now."

"We go when I say we go," Galvan says. "Not before."

We're wasting time. If Galvan isn't going to do anything, I will. I'll try to avoid any more reckless decisions, but I'm not just going to stand aside and let Winter escape while Galvan checks his playbook for his next move.

"Agent Wiser," I start, keeping calm, staying seated, "with respect, Standards and the Service need to be on this, top priority. I'm sure you know all about Alister Taft by now. We need teams to hit every one of his properties..." As I'm mid-sentence, a thought materializes in my head, a memory bubbling up from nowhere.

A memory that isn't mine.

Winter isn't planning on harvesting more rithms, not immediately anyway. He's going to restore himself instead. Put himself back the way he was before he started messing with his mind, and wipe all those psyphoned rithms he's captured in the process. Most of them will have backups somewhere, but Grace—it'll erase her forever.

"I've had enough of—" Galvan starts, but I don't let him finish.

"Wait—I just... Listen to me—Winter isn't on the hunt. He's going underground. He's planning on escaping into a new identity."

Galvan spits frustrated air through his teeth. "Two seconds ago you were sure he was poised for another spree, now you're saying the opposite. I've had enough of this, you're going to answer my questions, then you're going to go back into your head and stay there while the professionals do their work."

I look past Galvan to Yellowbird. It's clear she doesn't know what to think. She's been willing to give me the benefit of the doubt in the past, but even she has her limits. "Karin, I know what this sounds like, I do. I know this is my fault. But you have to listen to me. I know where he is." I don't know how I know, but I do.

Yellowbird shoots a quick look at Galvan before responding. "Why don't you slow down a little, tell us what happened here. Once we have all the facts we can decide how best to—"

"Karin," I plead, "I know it's hard, but you have to trust me."

"I don't know, Fin," Yellowbird says, hesitant. Even if she was inclined to believe me, this is Standards' show. I'm not sure there's much she can do anyway.

"Sixty seconds," I say. "Just give me one minute, and I'll tell you where he's heading."

"Agent Wiser?" Yellowbird says. She's going to let him decide.

Galvan huffs something between a growl and a sigh. "Sixty seconds, then you answer my questions."

"Have you mapped his properties?"

"Some," Galvan says. "The AMP is running the pass-through companies. It could take a while."

"Show me what you've got."

"Forty-five seconds," Galvan says as Yellowbird calls one of the lawbots over.

"Show us all the properties associated with Alister

Taft," she orders the bot, and it spits out a projection of the Earth, with red circles dotted around the globe.

"Restrict it to a thousand-kilometer radius, centered on our location," I say.

Yellowbird checks in with Galvan again and he shrugs. "Do it," she tells the bot.

The map reduces to a hemisphere that stretches west to Illinois, south to the Dixie Bloc, over to the Atlantic Ocean, and back up to the lower parts of Northern Ontario and Quebec. It's still a huge area encompassing most of the red dots. They represent properties in and around Reszlieville, even more than when I first ran the search. There are some in the surrounding area too. A bunch in New York. One in Chicago. And a huge one covering a massive plot of land in Northern Quebec, a few hundred miles north of Montréal. No roads. Completely off the grid.

That's where Winter would keep a backup.

I point to the big red area on the projection. "That's where he is."

"How do you know?" Galvan scoffs. "Asshole intuition?"

"I don't know," I say honestly. "I just do."

"You want me to send one of my agents on a two-thou-sand-mile round trip to the middle of nowhere on nothing but a hunch?" Galvan says.

"Winter had me paralyzed, was about to take my head off. He brought out a sword and everything..." How do I explain this without mentioning Deacon? "He might have hit me with an optical pulse that triggered my Cortex to shut down, I don't know for sure, but I recall fragments. Winter talking, saying he had a backup secured somewhere safe. I have an image in my head—trees, a cabin. That's where he's going."

Galvan squints at me, and at first I don't think he's going to buy it but he takes another look at the map. "That's a huge area. It'll take the drones a week to cover it all. Can you be more specific?"

I shake my head. "I can't, but that's where he's going. He's already got a huge head start. We need to leave now, and I'll figure out the rest on the way."

"Even if I was inclined to entertain these visions of yours, what in hell makes you think I'd bring you along?"

"Because whether you like it or not, I'm the only hope you have of finding him."

"Out of the question," Galvan says. "I'm not about to authorize a civilian to ride along on an active pursuit—"

"I'll take you," Yellowbird says.

Galvan swings around to face her, his mouth hanging open. "You will do no such thing," Galvan says. "This is Standards' investigation, and I'm the agent in charge."

"Alister Taft is the prime suspect in the murder of Amos Boldt. The last time I checked, investigating murder isn't part of Standards' mandate."

"For fuck's sake," Galvan sighs. "We have a killer on the loose and you want to chase your premonitions into the wilderness..." He stops and glares back and forth between Yellowbird and me, teeth clenched, jaw muscles bulging under his beard.

I sit quietly, waiting for him to make a decision, and at last he takes a breath and says, "Fine, but *I'm* taking you—I'm not letting you out of my sight again."

THE CHOICE IS SO simple as to be obvious. Winter should have seen it sooner—would have seen it sooner—if it weren't for Grace's incessant emotional barrage.

Weakening him. Corrupting him.

She's been bombarding him with feeling. Remembering the most fraught moments of her life, and by recalling them, forcing these emotions to well up in him as well, reducing his own thoughts to garbled, fervid noise.

Luckily the hopper knows the way, he only needs to remain seated while the vehicle takes him to the Orchid facility. The police will be in pursuit, but he's far enough ahead. Once there it's only a matter of strapping himself into the transfer pod, then he'll be rid of her and able to make his escape. Grace can throw what she likes at him, buffet him with the strongest emotions she has, but he can endure the fierce assault of feeling until then. He has no choice but to.

When Grace was five she found a baby bunny in the grass

behind the barn. She'd just come from cleaning the chickens and was going down to splash in the stream before she helped Mother prepare lunch for the field workers.

The bunny looked to be sleeping, sunning its downy body peacefully in the warm sun. Her heart swelled at the sight of it. Only seconds before she hadn't known the tiny animal existed, and now she was in love with it.

She dropped to a crouch and watched, waiting for the skittish creature to sense her presence and hop away, but it didn't. She crept closer, and still the bunny didn't move. Once she was close enough to touch it, she stretched out her hand, and moving as slowly and carefully as she ever had in her life, she stroked the bunny's soft fur. Still the rabbit didn't move.

Then she felt something sticky, and it wasn't until she pulled her hand away that she saw the bunny's insides spilled out onto the grass.

She was no stranger to death, even at five, but this was different. She'd never loved any of the chickens or the pigs that went to slaughter.

She got up and ran inside to scrub her fingers clean, but she didn't cry.

Father didn't like to see her cry.

He can't concentrate, can't sit still. Thoughts come unbidden, memories stirred by the emotions Grace is pummeling him with. Winter catches himself reliving the joyous first weeks after Grace joined him, when the world was reborn in his mind suddenly flush with emotion. The potential had been palpable, he'd nearly succeeded, thought he'd finally achieved his dream of humanity...

But Grace had ruined that too.

His stomach lurches as his mind whip-snaps from joy to a nauseating grief. For the loss of his dream. For the loss of his parents. For all the people he hurt. For the loss of everything he could have been if he had only been normal like everyone else—

NO!

He will not let her win. These are her feelings, not his. Even as he desperately feels the impending loss of his newfound humanity, he knows it's the correct path.

Once this is all over he'll never again suffer through regret or grief. He'll be pure, perfect in his own way, free from the irrational influence of emotion. Grace will no longer be able to hurt him.

And to think he was prepared to endure the suffering, to merely wash her out instead of incising her completely. What a sentimental fool he'd become.

Grace had always been curious—nosy, some folk might have said. She knew it wasn't always a good quality to have, but she couldn't help herself. She had to know. What was around the next bend in the path? What did it feel like to kiss a boy? What did Mother keep in that locked box in her closet?

Grace had just turned fifteen when she stumbled across that small wooden chest while looking for an extra blanket. It was all she could think about for weeks after. She'd sneak away whenever she could and retrieve it from Mother's hiding place, caress the worn and nicked edges, shake it to figure out what was inside. She even sniffed at the keyhole. It smelled like the library.

It wasn't until a year later that she found the key, loose in a drawer in the hall. She wouldn't have noticed it at all if she hadn't been hunting for something just like it for so long.

She waited five days, until she knew Mother would be off the farm for a few hours, and then she rescued the box from its hiding place, carefully inserted the key, and opened it.

Faded blue velvet lined the inside, and it was filled with stacks of yellowed paper. Letters, neatly printed out in black ink. There were dozens of them, tied in bundles with different colors of bright ribbon that looked as though they may have been recently replaced. Grace knew she shouldn't, that reading these letters was surely a betrayal, but she couldn't help herself.

She had to know.

They were from boys. Boys who weren't Father. She read them all, one by one, gently untying and retying the knots, and as she did the guilt faded, and she grew to love her mother more.

In reading those letters, she saw for the first time that Mother hadn't always been her mother. She'd been a little girl too. A girl with hopes and fantasies and fears. Just like her. It was the first day she realized her mother was just a person too.

She never told Mother what she'd done, but she never felt the guilt of it either, because she knew God had led her to those letters. They'd made Grace love her mother all the more, and how could that be a bad thing?

How odd that the source of Winter's newfound clarity was almost his next integration: that ex-cop—or, more specifically—whoever it is lurking inside him.

Deacon, he called himself, and how right Deacon was. Winter cramming his head with more and more fragile, needy, broken minds wasn't the answer. And as regretful in some ways as the prospect is—certainly the world will once again be a smaller place without Grace in his head—his only option is to regress, to restore his mind to a state before he integrated, back to when his emotions were his to control, and the only person in his mind was him.

In a strange way, it's comforting to Winter to know he isn't alone, that there are others like him, minds divided, struggling with themselves. And that it could be much, much worse. He still has dominance. He's still the one in control, unlike Grace, unlike that poor trapped bastard Deacon, passengers in their own heads.

He also knows that this empathy is Grace's doing, and will disappear once he's restored to his pre-Grace backup, but that's for the best. Empathy only gets in the way.

Emotion, he's realized, is, at best, a distraction.

At worst, it's treacherous.

Best to be without it completely, that way it can never betray you.

She was twelve when the tornado destroyed the barn. They heard it coming before they could see it, rumbling toward them like every clap of thunder she'd ever heard in her life all pealing at the same time.

They fled to the cellar while the sky darkened to yellow and rain came down in lashes. She and Mother and Amos had hunkered in the cellar as the storm raged above them and Father and the farmhands tried to prepare as best they could. It lasted no more than half an hour, but she was terrified the entire time. Father and the others joined them just as the funnel tore through the wheat, only just got the cellar door closed before a shriek she had nightmares about for years afterward sounded from the barn. Father got most of the animals free, but it was late May, and one of the mares had just birthed a foal and refused to leave her stall.

Father had to hold her back from the doors as the tornado slammed into the barn. She couldn't see what was happening, but the sounds were enough. The roaring wind tore through the wood. Glass smashed in the house above. The ground heaved when the barn collapsed.

Afterwards, Mother hugged her close until the winds died down and they dared to peek out into the devastation.

Winter squeezes his eyes shut, tries to ride out the undulating waves of emotion, but he's suddenly gripped by massive anxiety—what if he's caught?

What if he made a mistake somewhere and the police are closer than he believes?

What if they're waiting for him when he lands?

What if he restores but Grace is still, somehow, with him?

What if he's never free of her?

He opens his eyes and is reassured by the forest below. He's in no danger, and must keep telling himself that. His torment will soon be over.

The Orchid facility is completely safe, built to ensure the continuity of his mind. It's in the deep woods, accessible only by air, disconnected from the link, and doesn't appear on any official maps. His rithm backup is secured in a storage unit sealed in a hardened bunker drilled into the bedrock, impervious to wind, water, cold, or nuclear blast. Come the end of the world, he'll still survive.

The only drawback is the requirement that he make backups in person, but the flight isn't arduous, and the time spent worth the security of guaranteed existence.

There can be no one in immediate pursuit. There's no way anyone can track him here.

His fists clench. It's regrettable he won't be able to continue with the Winter identity, or enjoy the notoriety and associated rep perks, but Winter is exposed now, and if he should ever attempt to occupy the rep in public, SecNet will have the drones on him.

Damn her for forcing this on him. He's grown fond of his skyn, its striking features and sinewy measured movement, why should he have to give it up? Why should he have to abandon everything he's built, everything he's suffered for? He's abandoning a legacy that no one will ever know about. What a fucking waste—

—Multicolored spirals dance where her eyes should be. They form into trees, seen from above. They're in a car. Flying—

He shudders at the intrusion. Hammers his fist against the nav screen, fighting through the fog of anger, until the display spiderwebs and his knuckles are ragged.

He.

Won't.

Let.

Her.

In.

They found the mare dead in the field. The foal disappeared completely.

Grace stalked through the wreckage, gripped by an irrational anger stronger than she'd ever felt.

Why did this have to happen? That poor foal never had the chance to live, barely had the chance to know the world before it was ripped away.

And then, when she realized who she was mad at, when she realized that she could be mad at Him, her anger grew, flushed by the seeming injustice of the Lord.

How could He let this happen?

Emotions. Why did he covet them so completely? Emotions are an evolutionary holdover, nature's mechanism for adjusting the brain to its reality, shaping the world so the trials and betrayals and disappointments don't cause us to lie down and die. To make life feel as though it's worth the trouble of living.

They're arbitrary. Outmoded.

All this time he's been the next step in evolution, and he's been fighting to downgrade himself back to the limits of simple humanity.

He's moved past that now. He no longer needs emotions to adjust his brain to reality—like Dr. Gartner once said, he was born already superadjusted to it.

Let them hate him for what he is. Let them come for him, he'll outlast them all. He'll still be around when—

She gathers all her anger, the anger that she gave back to God when she surrendered herself to His hands and He returned to her as renewed faith—and lets it burn.

She feels Winter begin to crumble, feels his defenses fall.

Her toes come to her first, then vision returns as feeling creeps up her arms.

Winter is weakening.

She's doing it.

She's too strong.

He can't keep her out, but neither is he giving up.

There's still a chance...

He drops into his head and initiates a sleep period. They're still an hour from the Orchid, he'll shut them both down. Once they land they'll wake, and she'll be calm once again. Not for long, likely, but long enough. She won't have time to pollute his thoughts before he's able to dash into the facility and shut her up for good.

It's over.

He's won.

And already contemplating his next goal—a new hobby. A custom virt populated by the psyphoned minds of his followers, with Winter installed as their god.

That could be interesting.

GALVAN CALLS for a fresh hopper to the Playter Estates
complex and we ignore each other for the next three hours
as we fly through the increasingly turbulent clouds to
Montréal for a recharge.

Not that I'm complaining. I've kept to my head,
studying a virtual aerial view of Winter's vast property,
surveying hundreds of square kilometers of heavy forest and
lake-scraped Canadian Shield. There's nothing here. Not
that I can find, anyway.

The entire area is basically invisible to the link. There's
no drone traffic, barely any roads. Hundreds and hundreds
of kilometers of untouched wilderness. Even the satellite re-
creations aren't great, and the virt keeps me too high to
make out anything in the way of detail. I haven't seen a
house or a structure of any kind, no obvious destination
where Winter could be headed.

Who knows, he could have blasted a bunker into the
bedrock—or had the image of a vast compound scrubbed
from the link entirely.

I'm not going to find it at this rate, that's for sure.

My internal nav shows we're approaching the hopper depot in Montréal. Galvan's going to want a destination. No way is he going to let me lead him around by feel—I'll have to provide something more concrete than a hunch.

The thing is, I almost have it—I can feel it, a fuzzy picture in my head—but it refuses to resolve. I've been trying to retrieve it, circling over the virtual forest and hoping something will fall into place, but it remains just out of reach.

It's an image. Or a picture that represents a word. The answer is hovering there, three inches in front of my forehead like an itch I can't scratch—

This isn't working. I need a break.

I check back in with my body and stretch my neck out. The heavy clouds have finally burst and rain splashes the hopper's windscreens, turning the city below into an impressionist mosaic.

The hopper's a four-seater, and I'm sitting in the back while Agent Wiser runs the investigation from the cockpit—and not doing a bad job of it, all things considered. I was half listening to him work while I flew around the map in my head. He's got every Standards agent and cop he can find on the hunt, has them converging on Alister's properties. Has Winter's biokin flagged as a high-value alert on SecNet. If that pale skyn of his so much as glances at a camera, Galvan will know about it ten seconds later.

The Standards AMP is charting cases, sorting through unsolved mindjackings and skyn sprees, looking for correlations with everything they've learned about Winter's MO. So far the AMP believes it can attribute a number of individual high-casualty skyn sprees to Alister Taft as well. This guy isn't just a serial mindjacker, he's been wreaking havoc for years.

None of this will help. They won't find him. He's ahead of us, maybe already wiped his mind clean.

If only I could figure out where.

Galvan hasn't stopped working since we left the ground, and I'll give him this, he knows what he's doing.

He isn't an idiot. I know I look shady as hell. Mostly because I *am* shady as hell. The shit I did when I was Deacon—I know I'm not responsible for that, but I sure didn't object when Ankur covered it up for me. I collaborated with a rogue superintelligence. I'm harboring a hostile copy of myself in my head, and worse, I can't control him. I'm a rithm crime in action, and he's the head of Standards.

He doesn't know the details, but he's knows I'm hiding something. Plus, there's all the shit that went down between us that first time around. I'm the reason he's a quadruple amputee. No wonder he doesn't trust me.

I know he doesn't like me, and I don't blame him. I'm just not sure if he actively hates me or not. But unless he's changed completely from the man I half remember meeting that first day back at the station, he's a good man and a hell of a cop.

As big as it seems, Reszlieville is a small town. My crowd and his seem to have a habit of intersecting. We can't be at each other's throats every time we run into each other. If I'm going to venture back out into the world—and have any chance of staying here—I need to figure a way to mend our relationship.

He's kept the barrier down between the front and back compartments and I lean forward, poking my head into the cabin. "Sounds like you have everything under control up there."

He swivels his head toward me and regards me through

the blue wash of his lenzs, but doesn't say anything. He's listening to something only he can hear.

After a moment Galvan says, "Understood, good work. I want updates on the hour. Find yourself somewhere to observe and alert me the instant he shows."

"Standards did something right," I offer, "giving you command. You're better at this than I ever would have been."

I see him want to snap something back at me, and raise my hands in surrender. "I know you don't need my approval," I add. "Simply an observation. You're good at this. And I know this makes no sense to you, flying off to the middle of nowhere, but I've come to appreciate most things don't make much sense these days, so I've decided to go with it. I don't know what's in my head, or how it got there, but I can find him. He's ahead of us, I know it."

Galvan runs something around in his mouth, then swallows, and glances down at something flashing on a display.

"As it happens," he says after a moment, "I agree with you."

"Really?" I blurt, and from the way he rolls his eyes I must not have hidden my surprise well.

"Makes sense, tactically at least. If he truly has a secure rithm backup stashed away somewhere, I can't think of a better place than the middle of a link-dark forest, but it's a long-shot. Based on what we know about him, I wouldn't be surprised if he had five other contingency plans we know nothing about."

"I'm right," I say. "I just need time."

"I'm hope so—because if you can't find him with what-ever's rattling around in your rithm, with the terrain up there, we're going to be living out of tents for weeks while the search teams work. This time of year, the mosquitos are thick enough to climb."

"It's frustrating the hell out of me," I confess. "I've never felt anything like it."

"What happened, back at Winter's?" Galvan asks, but from his tone I can't tell if it's Galvan or Agent Wiser asking. Either way, I need to tell him something.

"He buzzed me up," I say. "Seemed to be fighting with himself, with someone inside him. When he took Grace's mind he was trying to use it as a vaccine or something. That's been his goal all along. All the minds he stole—he was born without emotions and he's been trying to fill the hole. He integrated with Grace but something went wrong and her rithm is becoming dominant."

Galvan nods. "We're seeing this more and more: polyneurals—multiple personalities sharing a single consciousness. Technically they're contrary to Standards, but for the most part they seem harmless."

"Winter isn't harmless," I say. "His bot hit me with a paralytic and he propped me up in that chair and told me he was going to wash Grace out of his head by flooding it with every rithm he could get ahold of, starting with mine."

"And then?" Galvan asks. This is what he really wants to know.

"Then, honestly, I don't remember."

"You claim you soft-locked?"

"I don't know," I say. Sure, I have a pretty good idea, but that's the truth.

Galvan narrows his eyes. "Okay, the stress of an impending beheading could trigger a pattern collapse. But your Cortex didn't immediately restart; instead it was inexplicably inert until it conveniently snapped back of its own accord a couple hours later. That isn't a plausible story."

"It's what happened," I say. No defense. Just fact. I'm not lying when I tell him I blacked out. I'm just not telling the whole truth.

"I'm sure it is. Even you wouldn't try to bluff something this hard. Which means you've got a kink in your rithm. Your conscious neural patterns aren't affected, so it's likely a matter of some sort of fragmentation in your core engrams." He gives me a hard look. "You may not even realize your personality is corrupted," he says. "But you'd know something was wrong. There'd be blackouts. Foreign thoughts. Spontaneous memories. Just as you've described."

Shit. I walked right into this.

I don't say anything. What's the point in denying it?

"I could order you in for a full rithm scan," he says, though he doesn't seem to take any pleasure in it. "If your pattern is corrupt you could be throwing personalities. You could be dangerous."

"I'm not dangerous."

"That other blackout, after you chased Winter, you know you hired a scrubber? Who do you think you're hiding from?"

"I never told you I blacked out."

"You didn't have to. Unless you're the one trying to keep something from Standards?"

"I have it under control," I say, trying to stay calm but my throat is suddenly tight. If he orders a personality scan I'm done for.

"Do you?" he asks with a laugh that's half astonished and half frustrated. "I'm not so sure. As of now I've only got you having an encrypted conversation with an unknown subject moments before you drop off the digital record completely. I can't prove you were responsible for hiring a scrubber, there's no ties to your rep or any known bank accounts or crypto records, but it seems like a hell of a coincidence, wouldn't you say?"

"I'm not dangerous," I say again. "I just want to help."

"And those fleshmiths at that warehouse, that you trying to help too?" Galvan takes a resigned breath. "I don't know what's going on in your head, Finsbury. I do believe you think you're doing the right thing. But at the same time, you can't help but be you: you're out here, chasing after short-term threats while ignoring the apocalypse on your heels. If you were truly good, you'd submit yourself to Standards and let us *help you,* before you have a split and we're forced to take you out. I've seen how this goes. It won't end well for you."

"It won't come to that," I say, my pulse racing. If they get into my head it won't take long for them figure out I'm harboring a fugitive. I'll end up in the stocks. Floating through an eternal monotony as a virtual ghost of myself. I'll put a bullet through my Cortex before I let that happen.

But then they'll just pull my backup and drop him in the stocks instead.

I'm breathing too fast, need to keep it together.

Galvan shifts around in his seat, gets serious. "That's the thing, you can't—"

"An orchid," I blurt. A word from out of nowhere.

And suddenly I remember—a cabin. On a lake. Winter said that to me in a conversation I've never had with him. I can picture it clearly: I'm still sitting in the chair, he's dropped his sword, and he looks like the autodoc just announced he has weeks to live.

Deacon had a chat with Winter and somehow talked him out of killing us.

On one hand, I'm relieved my head isn't in a jar, but on the other—someone other than me was in charge of my head. The thought that he's in here with me—that we're intertwined somehow, that he could be watching through my eyes right now—fills me with an unease I can't name.

I wonder if he knows I'm thinking about him. That I want him out.

I wonder if he knows I want nothing more than to erase him forever.

Deacon and I, in a way, we're like Winter and Grace. Winter's so scared of losing himself he's willing to revert to an earlier version—to end the person he is now—to rid himself of her.

Is that where I'm headed with this?

If I can't get Deacon out of my head, my only way out will be a restoration, and the only backup I have is the original capture right after the accident. Will I be able to let all this go, sacrifice everything I've experienced since I was last restored, and once again wake up fresh from death to do it all over again?

"What?" Galvan says, his eyes suddenly unsure I'm still me.

I'm there with him, but I'll have to worry about who I am later. Maybe Vae can help—as much as that thought unsettles me. But not until we have Winter.

"I've got him," I say.

"Where?" Galvan asks, spinning back around to the hopper cockpit. "Do you have coordinates?"

I hold up my finger. "Give me two minutes, and I will."

I jump back into my head, again looking down at the forested map, and get Connie to run a search for flowers in the names of lakes in the area Alister owns while I take another pass with the flyover, trying to spot it by air.

The search comes back empty, but she's has taken it upon herself to highlight a sweep of lakes to the west of my position in bright blue, and from this height they string together to make a picture—the rough shape of an orchid. A semicircle of water arcing around to join with a heart-shaped lake that narrows down to a long stem.

A long, skinny peninsula squiggles out from the top and into the heart-shaped lake, creating the orchid's stamen, and I know that's where Winter will be. At the tip of that peninsula.

I fly down as close as I'm able but can't make out anything special in the image. Doesn't matter, here's there.

The question is, how to get to him?

It would take hours to hike in from the nearest road. The entire area is forested and uneven, nowhere to land the hopper I can see.

I transfer the coordinates to Galvan and pop back into my body.

"Where are the emergency parachutes?" I ask, but Galvan ignores me, looking over the map.

"I guess it looks like an orchid," Galvan says, "but there's another lake just to the west there that looks like a duck's head, so I'm not sure what to think." He tries to zoom the map again but he can't get anything closer than I was seeing. "It is nicely protected. Virtually inaccessible. I suppose, if I was a psychopath reszo designing a bunker to house a backup of my mind, and money was no object? It'd work for me. Okay. Good a place as any."

"We can set the hopper to hover and use the emergency parachutes to drop in. Take him by surprise."

Galvan makes a noise in his throat. "And then what? Wait around for someone to come pick us up? No, I have a better idea." He puts on his Special Agent voice. "Get me a connection to the Sûreté," he tells the AMP, speaking the name of the Quebec Provincial Police in perfect

French. "Ask them if they have a floatplane we can borrow."

A floatplane. We make a fast run straight in over the lake, land, and swarm the peninsula. Then we can get back out again. We can even bring a couple SQ with us for backup.

"That *is* a better idea," I say.

Galvan shakes his head and buckles himself in as we descend through the rain and into Montréal to recharge.

Rain splatters the windows as we fly low over the sharp evergreen peaks, staying below the cloud line to maintain visibility on the smear of forest and deep black lakes below.

We're only minutes out from where I hope we'll find Winter. While I know he's going to be there, we're still all out here based on my faulty memory. Who knows what we're going to find or what he might have waiting for us.

We landed the hopper at a Sûreté du Quebec facility outside Montréal. The SQ has jurisdiction over the endless wilderness of the northern part of the province; they know the land, know how to get us in and out. When Galvan explained who we were hunting, and what he was capable of, they offered up use of an amphibious plane and even threw in some backup for good measure: Officers Bergeron and Siddique, one a forestry officer, the other a pilot. They suggested a tactical squad too, but Galvan decided a quiet approach was our best chance to take Winter by surprise. Figured anything big enough to carry a huge team would be heard long before it arrived and give him the chance to bolt.

He's probably right, though I tend to prefer having more guns to more time.

We hitched a ride in a SQ hopper to an outpost forty-five minutes north of the city, where we boarded a sleek white-and-blue aircraft waiting in an adjacent lake like an oversized kid's bathtub toy. Just wings, a massive floating fuselage, and two big propellers to keep it in the air. It's not much to look at, I wouldn't want to fly it into a war zone, but I had to admit it was a better option than the hot-drop out of the hopper that I'd suggested.

We'll be able to come in hard, land fast in the water, storm Winter's hideout and then still have the option to fly back out again when it's all done. Plus, I feel better having a couple more sets of eyes on our side.

The flight to the orchid lake takes an hour and change from the outpost, and we use the time to brief Bergeron and Siddique on Winter, and what we're likely to expect. He isn't going to just let us walk up on him. We're anticipating a fight.

We know he's responsible for planning and executing elaborate sprees. He could have anti-aircraft weapons. Bots stationed in the woods. Hardened auto-cannon bunkers. The place could be lousy with hostile-only mines.

Hopefully he doesn't have anything patrolling the water. An anti-craft aquabot could mess up our landing real quick, end this whole thing before it even gets started.

I flash back to my time in the Forces. This isn't the first bumpy airplane ride I've spent imagining all the ways I could die. I learned quickly to ignore these thoughts though. There's a fine line between prepared and scared. We won't know until we get there, so no use in worrying. We've got a plan, and that's the best we can do for now.

Twenty minutes later my head pulses sadly as it loses connection to the link. I usually keep the incoming din to a trickle, but still, I've gotten so used to having my head instantly wired to the global chatter. It's like part of me has just died—a sense I didn't know I relied on until it was gone.

Ugh. I'm a link addict.

I'm not the only one. The cabin gets quiet, just the whirr of the propeller, Bergeron clicking through her final gear check and Galvan's softly purring joints as he unconsciously flexes his fingers. We've still got radio for emergencies, but it's not the same. I stare out the window, watching the misty woods below.

I grew up in the country, spent my childhood roaming the thick forests around the small town I grew up in, but it's been years since I've been anywhere outside a city—and I'm suddenly dazzled by deja vu vertigo. A memory races across my thoughts like it just escaped across a demilitarized zone: I've been in the woods more recently than that. Or Deacon has, anyway.

Not heavy forest like this, but tall, sparse pine and cottonwood, with Colorado mountain peaks in the distance. He hiked for hours to a house on a hilltop, hunted the bots protecting it, dismantling them bullet by bullet as the world crawled by at a quarter speed. It's terrifying and exhilarating and my heart is urging me on, wishing I could be back there.

Then he murdered a crippled man trapped in a medpod. Burned his house down around him.

Darien Cole. He was rithmist. He betrayed Deacon, so Deacon killed him for it.

My head buzzes down my throat and into my stomach. *What else don't I remember?*

Another memory of the life I never lived, and another crime unpunished. More proof of the monster inside me.

I wish it had stayed buried.

The plane begins its descent and I shake off the sulk. It's go time. I can hate myself later.

We're coming in on a glide, engines on standby. The plan is to hit the water moving fast but as quietly as possible, try to get the advantage on him. He won't get much notice we're coming, but I don't think Winter's going to miss an airplane landing off his front porch. He'll be ready for us—which reminds me.

I lean over to Galvan. "I need a weapon."

Galvan gives me a pained look. "You're not going anywhere near that cabin. I'm not sure why I didn't leave you back with the SQ."

"I'm an asset—use me. I'm trained. And with all due respect I've been doing this a hell of a lot longer than anyone on this plane. Winter will be ready for you. You have no idea what's waiting for down there. It makes tactical sense to have another shooter on your side and you know it."

He shrugs, his mind made up. "I'm not authorizing civilian participation in an armed takedown. You'll stay in the plane with Siddique."

I notice Bergeron watching us, and she gives her partner a questioning look just as his mouth splits in excitement.

"Not to interrup' your spat, boys," Siddique calls out, his words thickened by his French accent. "But 'der she is."

We're above the orchid-shaped string of lakes, coming in fast and dark along what would be the flower's stem, and even in the murky twilight the cabin is easy to see: an A-frame with huge black solar windows overlooking the lake across a two-tiered deck.

Siddique asks something in French, concerned. I could toggle the translation routine, but between grade seven French class and Bergeron's frown, I get the drift. Somehow a serial killer built a summer house in their backyard and they knew nothing about it. And we're still relatively close to civilization here. There's a million square kilometers of rugged terrain stretching out north to the Hudson Strait, with some of the lowest population densities in the world. Who knows what else might be hiding up there?

I don't see any lights, but it doesn't matter. He's there, I know it. And he must know we're coming by now. Hopefully we're not too late to stop him from erasing Grace.

My stomach drops out as the descent increases, Siddique losing as much altitude as he can before he pulls up at the last second and lands with a slap on the lake's surface. We bounce once, and he drops all the flaps and pulls us in a hard left turn that slows us down and we come in to coast alongside the dock. The cabin's still dark. It's only a few hundred meters away from us, shrouded by rain, at the top of a set of wooden stairs. There's no movement. No sign of resistance. Nothing to indicate anyone is home. Nothing except the insistence in my head that he'll be in there.

God I hope I didn't drag us all out here for nothing.

The plane's starboard door slides open and Galvan and Bergeron exit first, hoods up against the weather. They hunch over their rifles configured to bull-pup and move carefully across the slippery dock to the stairs, watching for threats from above. They climb cautiously, checking each step.

I have absolutely no intention of staying behind with Siddique at the kid's table while Galvan and Bergeron breach the cabin. I know I said no more stupid mistakes, but this isn't one of them. Galvan's being hardheaded, not seeing sense. I may have my faults, but I'm a long way from some skittish civvy liable to get himself killed. I'm more help watching their backs than I am hanging with the ride.

I'll apologize afterwards.

Once they're about to reach the upper deck I jump out of the plane. Siddique makes a half-hearted attempt to stop me, but before he gets very far I'm already out of his reach and padding along the dock.

Galvan can't hear me coming through the splatter of raindrops and I'm nearly on them before he spins and catches sight of me creeping up on them. His face stretches in frustration, and he mouths an angry "NO" and jabs the muzzle of his rifle back toward the plane. I just smile and shake my head. Does he want to stand in the rain and have this argument or does he want to go find Winter?

He thinks about it for a long moment, but ultimately huffs in resignation, hands me the sidearm from his belt, twitches his head at me to fall in behind him, and turns back to see Bergeron watching us bickering in quiet disbelief. She gives him a *can we get on with this* look and Galvan nods, embarrassed on my behalf.

I have a lecture to look forward to when this is all over.

We get to the top of the stairs without incident. The deck is completely empty, rain pounding the wooden boards like some mad percussionist. The night is coming faster now, vision fading by the second, but we're almost inside.

I'm surprised we haven't encountered any resistance. This all seems too easy. Why isn't Winter throwing everything he has at us?

There's a door inset into the cabin wall, and we get on either side of it. Bergeron on one side, Galvan and me on the other. Bergeron does a silent countdown from four and tries the door, gently. I brace myself for a reaction of some kind. An explosion. Or for it to at least be locked, but it opens silently on hidden hinges.

Bergeron gives a questioning glance over her shoulder and Galvan moves ahead to take point, weapon ready.

I'm amazed I'm not more scared. Adrenaline's popping in the back of my throat but I'm enjoying it. *This is real.* I've been numbed by too many consequence-free deaths on the ice. Nothing like reality to make you feel alive.

Usually this is when I'd feel Deacon rising, his icy tendrils worming their way into my thoughts, but this time nothing comes.

He's leaving me alone for some reason. What's he up to?

Galvan breaches the cabin at full speed with Bergeron close behind, gunlights sweeping ahead of them into the darkness. I follow a moment later, and my heart thrumming in my ears, pounds even louder in the silence of the cabin. An instant later the room lights warm themselves on and show us a completely empty room.

Or *almost* empty.

There are no bots. No waiting gun encampments. Nothing that looks like it's going to hurt us.

Nothing but a simple medpod, anchored to the floor in the middle of the room. Winter's inside, lit by faint running lights, and he seems unconscious.

We're too late.

"He's already started the backup," I say as Galvan shoulders his weapon and hurries over to the pod, examines its exterior. There are no controls, no cables to pull, nothing to turn it off.

"I don't know how to stop it," Galvan says, searching again along the base of the pod.

"It has to be drawing power from somewhere," Bergeron suggests, spinning, looking the room over once more. "If we find the battery we can shut it down."

This place is empty. Likely the batteries are buried under the floor.

"We don't have time for that," I say, and rush to the pod, try to get a grip on the clear curved doors and pull them open, but I can't find any leverage. They're smooth plastic, with nothing to grab on to.

"Help me," I say, and lay my hands flat against the cool surface, try to use my weight to slide one of them open. Galvan joins me, and once Bergeron adds her strength we feel a mechanism slip and the door slides a few centimeters, just enough so we can shift around, get our hands between the doors, and yank.

The door motors engage and try to keep the doors closed, but we keep pulling and finally the pod gives up and opens them for us. I reach in and grab Winter by his bright blue tie and yank him free. He falls forward, breaking his connection to the pod, and hopefully interrupting whatever he had running.

He collapses to the floor without trying to catch himself, and his face slams into the concrete. His long braid of datastrips slaps the floor next to him. We stand over his inert body for along moment, just as frozen, waiting. For what I'm not exactly sure—to see who wakes up?

If anyone wakes up at all.

We might have interrupted the transfer at the wrong time, could have collapsed Winter's pattern and killed them all.

Nothing happens for what feels like forever, but then

Winter inhales sharply from the floor, and we all flinch. Galvan, with his mechanically accurate fluidity, gets his weapon back up faster than Bergeron. But not by much.

Winter moans, rolls onto his back and sees us over him, sees the guns staring him down. Blood streams from one of his nostrils as his face tenses in alarm—he's caught. And I don't think he's likely to give up without a fight.

"Standards," Galvan says, his gun never wavering from a spot directly between Winter's eyes. "You're under arrest."

The stress falls from Winter's face and he twinkles a satisfied smile, as if this is what he wanted all along. "Agent Wiser. I see your eyebrows have grown back. Or are those prosthetic as well?"

Confusion jiggles through Galvan's features, then something clicks. His aim wavers. "That was *you*, on the roof. You killed three innocent people that night." I can see Galvan fighting, he wants to pull the trigger. "You have the right to remain silent," he says instead. "You have the right to legal counsel. You have the right to the sanctity of your mind, excepting evidence of past-standard or otherwise unlawful alteration—and I'd say mindjacking yourself into a polyneural counts as both. Do you understand these rights as I've explained them to you?"

Winter draws the back of his hand across his nose, frowns at the sight of his blood.

"This is brutality," he says with a smirk. "You'll be hearing from my lawyer."

"You're lucky I haven't put a bullet through your Cortex," Galvan responds. "I'd have to file a longer report, but it would be worth it."

"My, my, Agent," Winter tuts from the floor. "Verbal threats are hardly the conduct I'd expect from the acting head of the Ministry of Standards. I'll add that to my complaint." He smiles and winks at me. "Besides, if you kill me then you'll never learn my secrets."

Shit—Winter talked to Deacon. I didn't consider what would happen after we caught him. He's going to have a hell of a story to tell Galvan. "You mean Grace," I say, trying to swing the conversation away from what he knows about me. "And the others you've got trapped in your head?"

Winter swings his smug gaze to me. "Oh, *do I*, Mr. Gage?" he says. "I wonder if Agent Wi—" His voice cuts out in a strangled garble and his eyes widen, momentarily terrified, then snap back to a fierce clarity.

"*Shoot me*," Winter says, but I can tell it isn't Winter. It's Grace.

"Are you Grace Boldt?" Galvan asks. He still hasn't lowered his weapon.

"*I don't know how much longer I can hold him*," Grace says though Winter's mouth. "*He needs to—*" Again his voice cuts off in an angry cry, and Winter rolls from his back and up to his knees. Galvan and Bergeron maintain their trigger discipline but shuffle two steps back, far enough to give them room to shoot should Winter try to rise any further.

"Don't move," Galvan orders, but Winter just sneers at him.

"You do not tell me what to do," Winter barks. "*I am in control here—*"

His face twists again, shudders, and Grace is back. "*He's too strong. You need to end this—*"

"What the hell is happening?" Bergeron cries.

"Hold your fire," Galvan says. "I don't want his Cortex damaged."

Because he doesn't want to hurt Grace, or because of what Winter knows about me?

"Get her out of me," Winter yells and clutches his head. "Get her out of me and I'll tell you everything."

"We'll figure out what's in your head after you're in custody," Galvan says, and swaps his rifle over to the stun setting. "Hands behind your back. Bergeron, get the binders on him."

We've got him. And only a matter of time before Galvan learns about Deacon. Winter and I are both headed for the stocks. Surprisingly, I'm not terribly bothered by the idea. At least I won't have to worry about being found out anymore.

Plus, we saved Grace, so at least something good came of all this. Though I'm not sure what "saved" means in this case, exactly, as she's still trapped in Winter's rithm. But at least some of her has survived. Maybe Standards will be able to separate them.

Winter, still on his knees, locks eyes with Galvan. He doesn't budge, doesn't blink. Galvan stares right back—until the moment passes and Winter's still staring, features frozen in place.

Galvan flicks his eyes at me and I just shrug. I have no idea.

The moments stretch and still Winter doesn't move, like someone paused his playback mid-stream.

Bergeron's still holding the binders, and Galvan motions for her to put them on. She nods, swallows, and creeps close, and just as she's about to grab his left wrist to snap the binder, Winter comes out of it.

His head lolls to the side as he blinks back to awareness, and Bergeron leaps back, startled. Out of the corner of my eye I see Galvan's finger slide down to the trigger. I shuffle another half-step backwards, just to be sure.

"*Don't shoot,*" Winter says, but instead of cool precision his voice is an exhausted drawl, like he just dragged himself out of a battlefield. It's Grace. "*I've got him...contained.*"

GRACE AND WINTER *return to consciousness at the same time. They struggle, vying for dominance, fighting without weapons. Without hands or feet or teeth. With only the power within themselves, the ferocity of their will to live.*

She knows she's stronger than Winter. She's felt around the edges of everything he is, can see exactly where he's vulnerable. Her intensity of emotion has weakened him, but he isn't broken.

As strong as she is, she doesn't think her emotions are enough to overrun him completely. She can't do it alone.

And then, she realizes, she doesn't have to.

She has an army at her back.

"Get her out of me!" Winter yells, and grabs his head. Squeezes as though he could remove Grace's tainted presence by force. They interrupted the transfer before it completed and he restored to the local backup, came out just as he went in—losing himself.

Grace will become dominant, it's simply a matter of time, and he'll do anything—*say anythi*ng—to stop that from happening.

At least, that's what he *wants* them to think. Today will end differently than Winter originally anticipated, but acceptably, all the same. "Get her out of me and I'll tell you everything."

"We'll figure out what's in your head after you're in custody," the Standards imbecile says, the smug prick. He has no idea the depth of Winter's foresight—

No keep that to yourself. He can't let Grace know what's about to come. That would ruin the surprise.

He only needs to resist for a few minutes more. He can do that.

Until now, Grace has been fighting Winter with the only ammunition she had—her thoughts. She hadn't considered the others in Winter's head with her. The lost souls all around. She can hear them, feel them calling to her like distant memories all returning at once.

She reaches out and accepts their touch, feels them flow into her, filling her, like tributaries feeding a raging river.

He's lost contact with his skyn, can't move, can't feel the rhythmic in and out of his breath. She's moving far quicker than he expected. His mistake was in not understanding how completely Grace would overtake him. How overwhelming the corrupting drive of emotion would be. He was powerless to it, which is why he knows now he'll never let it infect him again.

This was a fruitful avenue of investigation. He succeeded, became what he always wanted: to be human, to feel. And it wasn't until he'd achieved his goal that he understood he was already perfect the way he was born. A master of his emotions, not a slave to them.

And he will be again.

Any moment now.

He takes this last opportunity before his mind is subsumed completely into Grace to appreciate the trill of anticipation his fading mind gives him. He'll miss the shiver of spontaneous feelings—but then again, no he won't. He'll never feel regret or anything else again, not unless he chooses to.

This facet of his mind is about to cease, but he has contingencies.

This isn't the end of him.

Not by far.

Grace understands now. As the conscripted minds mingle with hers she becomes them too, remembers them, feels who they used to be—who they still are. They're each different and challenging and lovely, all of them, each rife with rot and beauty, each one unique. Each one the same.

And as they stream into her she feels her faith swell too. It grows until it becomes everything, encompasses every-thing, until the rainbow of voices concentrates into a single white point in her mind, a light of pure divinity —and then explodes.

The blast buffets her, but she remains. She feels it burn away Winter's thoughts—no, not burn—sterilize. He's still here, but inert, rendered harmless.

She did it.

Winter's reign is over.

"Don't shoot," she says, and the words fall out of her mouth like she's just run in from town with good news. "I've got him...contained."

"Am I speaking to Grace Boldt?" Galvan asks. He hasn't lowered his weapon, finger's locked on the trigger. He could take Winter's head off in a second. If this is a feint, Winter won't get far.

"I... I think so," Winter says. "Though I'm not sure exactly who I am anymore, with these other folks all in here with me."

That doesn't *sound* like Winter.

Could Grace have done it? Wrested control from Winter, stolen his body out from under him? For a brief second I find myself empathizing with him—he's now trapped in his mind while someone else is running around wearing his face—but only a second.

Winter deserves far worse than exile in his own head.

I can tell Bergeron doesn't know what to think. She's well-trained, obviously can handle herself, but dealing with lost hikers and survivalist nut-jobs haven't prepared her for a suspect whose mind is at war from within.

Even though I live this every day, I'm still right there with her. We've been chasing Winter for days now—he was ready to kill me—and when we finally track him down, ready to take him out, instead we find his latest victim has taken over *his* body.

What are we supposed to do with that?

Winter takes a few breaths, still up on her hands and knees, then looks at Galvan. "May I sit?"

Galvan purses his lips, then looks to Bergeron. "Stay ready," he says to her. She's obviously overflowing with questions, but keeps her focus on Winter. "Slowly," Galvan then says to Winter, and moves back, more time to react should Winter give him reason to, but his trigger finger slides back up to the guard.

"Thank you," Winter says, and very slowly lowers down off his knees to sit, twists around and stretches his legs out ahead of him. He takes a breath, then raises his head and considers the braid hanging from his skull for a moment before arranging it over his shoulder. Once he's settled he looks around the room and rests his gaze on me.

"I know you," he says. "Mr. Gage. You were in Winter's apartment, and with Amos. He was trying to find me..." His voice catches as he raises his hands to his face and shudders through a flurry of sobs. "I'm so sorry," he says as he struggles to compose herself. *"This is all my fault."*

If this is a ploy, it's a good one. Still, I wouldn't put it past him.

Galvan's resolve falters. He doesn't know how to handle this either. "I want to believe you, Ms. Boldt, but until we figure out what's going on, I need to take you into custody."

Winter doesn't resist. "Of course, that's best for everyone," he says, and his eyes lose focus. "I feel his thoughts. They're still in me. I've been part of him for so long...but I'm still not sure what he's capable of."

"Lean forward and cross your hands behind your back,"

Galvan says, and motions for Bergeron to put the binders on Winter.

Or should I call him Grace now?

No—*Wintergrace.*

Bergeron strides forward and secures Wintergrace's arms behind her. Once the binders ratchet closed around her wrists, Bergeron grabs her by the forearm and shifts weight to help her stand. But before she can get to her feet, Wintergrace flinches, throws herself out of Bergeron's grasp, as if reacting to something only she can see.

Bergeron drops her and springs away, reaching for her weapon, while Galvan has to decide if he should drop his dull black finger to the trigger and squeeze.

Winter hits the ground with a grunt. "*I'm okay,*" she says, hands outstretched. "It's still me—Grace Boldt. I just— I saw the oddest thing. A sentence appeared out in the room there and it scared the heavens out of me."

Galvan doesn't relax. "A sentence?" he asks, voice unwavering. He still hasn't decided if he's going to shoot.

"A question. *'Who am I?'*" She looks between us three, as if expecting us to have an answer.

And of course, Galvan does.

"It's a fail-safe," he says. "We interrupted Winter's backup, and now the system is requesting confirmation that his pattern is intact. If it doesn't get an answer, it'll assume the transfer was corrupted. Or someone interrupted the transfer and his backups are in danger of being seized."

"And do what?" Bergeron asks.

"The words are yellow now," Wintergrace observes from the floor.

"You're in his head," I say. "Can you look through his thoughts and get us an answer?"

She strains inward for a moment, then says, "I can sense

him, he's in here, but he's mad and doing his best to block me from seeing into his mind."

Okay, so now what? "Try Alister Michael Taft," I offer.

"Stop," Galvan orders, glaring at me. "Don't do a damn thing. He could have this place wired top to bottom if you get it wrong."

Good point. I take another look around the cabin. It's completely empty, just a roof over a poured concrete floor. Identical window and door setups on the front and the back. It's disposable. He probably has more of these, backups squirreled all around the world. We may never be able to catch him.

"Get to the woods. Out the back," Galvan says to Bergeron.

"Siddique needs to get the plane clear," I add. Winter might have the dock armed too.

"Tabarnak," Bergeron spits in an accent that's suddenly Francophone thick. She gets on her comm as Galvan and I stoop to haul Wintergrace up by her elbows and hustle her between us to the back door. Outside there's another wide deck and steps down to a path cut through the forest.

"These letters are looking awful angry," Wintergrace says before we're halfway across the back deck, and I barely hear her over the rain drumming on the wood. She's running for herself now, keeping up even with her hands behind her back. "But I'm not sure—"

"Forget the plane," Galvan yells to Siddique across the shared comm channel. "Get in the water."

"That lake can't be more than five degrees," Siddique objects.

"Better five than five hundred," Bergeron scolds, and we hear a muttered curse then a splash over the comm as we skid down the back steps and scramble into the woods, single file into the gloom, hoping we'll get far enough away before—

"The words are gone now," Wintergrace yells, and I get ready for the explosion, but nothing happens. "I don't think —" she continues.

Galvan quiets her with a yell and we keep running, tearing through the soaked forest, rain beating on our heads, noses filled with the smell of fresh pine, until Wintergrace slows again.

"It's not an explosive," Wintergrace says as she stops and faces back down the path. Galvan and Bergeron snap their gunlights on, keeping her in sight.

I'm starting to think she's right. Something should have happened by now.

"What then?" Galvan asks.

"His mind," she says, tapping her head. "It's all he has. He wouldn't risk destroying it."

"He must have more of these sites?" Galvan asks, and Wintergrace nods her head.

"He does, but he's cut off from them here—it's something else."

"It was a fail-safe of some sort," Galvan insists. "What are we missing?"

"What de 'ell is going on?" Siddique's chattering voice comes through Bergeron's comm. "*I'm freezing my ass off!*"

"Situation's changed," Galvan reports back. "We were wrong about the explosives. Get yourself back into the plane and dry off."

We hear sloshing and more muttered cursing before Siddique cuts the channel.

"He wouldn't abandon his mind," Wintergrace says, still trying to puzzle through an explanation. "The countdown was never for a self-destruct. He wouldn't give up. If there was a fault in the transfer he'd want to investigate what went wrong."

"A secondary backup?" I suggest. "Maybe when you didn't enter the passphrase, he initiated another restoration."

"And without a connection to the link—" Galvan starts.

"It'd have to be local," I finish.

"But there were no other pods in the cabin," Bergeron says.

"We don't know that," Galvan says, agitated. "We didn't search. We just ran. There could have been a basement, or an outbuilding somewhere..."

"Further up the path," Wintergrace says, hesitant, remembering someone else's memories. "Where he stores his flying car. He has additional bodies waiting there."

I notice movement out of the corner of my eye, spin and see a figure standing off in the trees, a weapon raised and pointed at Galvan. I leap and pull him out of the way just as a hole splinters in a tree behind where he'd been standing.

Wintergrace ducks and covers her ears as Bergeron returns fire, catches the figure dead between the eyes and bursts his Cortex with a flash of blue light.

"There'll be more," Wintergrace says from where she's crouched on the ground.

"How many?" Galvan asks.

"Three," Wintergrace answers. "They'll be working together to make sure one of them gets away."

"What are they planning?"

Wintergrace rises to her feet and looks up the path. "Escape, pure and simple. If he gets back in range of the link, he'll jump to a new body and that'll be it."

"Then we can't let him," I say, just as a low whine rises

above the patter of rain on the trees. Sounds like turbines spinning up.

"His flying car—" Wintergrace says, and Galvan's immediately running, his augmented legs churning through the mud. I take off behind him, leaving Bergeron and Wintergrace behind us, but I can't keep up with him, he's too fast.

We race up the path, and by the time I get to the building fifty meters ahead, Galvan's already burst through the wooden door and disappeared inside. It's pre-fab dura-concrete concealed by active camopaint, and nearly invisible in the rain. If I hadn't been looking for it, I might have run right past.

Before I can get through the door three shots blast from inside, *pop-pop-pop*. I swing through a moment later, weapon raised, but Galvan's already circling around the front of a four-seat hopper, head bent over his weapon sights, muzzle trained on the skyn in the pilot's seat.

The turbines are still spinning but the vehicle hasn't moved. I duck my head to glance inside the cabin. The passenger window is shattered and the skyn's slumped against the door, missing most of his head. He's not going anywhere.

Galvan still hasn't lowered his weapon. "I think you got him," I say as he pulls the hopper door open on the other side. Winter's second skyn spills out of the seat and lands on the floor.

"You can never be sure," Galvan says, as he nudges the skyn with his boot. "There's still one more somewhere."

"I don't think he's in here," I say. Other than the hopper and three empty medpods, the place is deserted.

Then Bergeron arrives, with Wintergrace close behind. "Everyone okay?" Bergeron asks.

"We're good," I say, then angle my head at Winter's skyn. "Him not so much."

Galvan leans in and disengages the hopper's turbines, but can't.

"The controls are locked to Winter's biokin," Galvan says over the hum of the engines. Doesn't matter. The batteries will wear down eventually.

Bergeron gets on the comm to update Siddique, and grows immediately alarmed when he doesn't answer. "We need to get back there," she says, concern etched on her face, and races out of the garage without waiting for us. We roll in behind her but barely get ten steps down the path before we hear the rippling back and forth of gunshots in the distance. Siddique's shooting at someone, and that someone is shooting right back.

"*Déguédine!*" Bergeron shouts as she puts on a burst of speed. We're almost back to the cabin when the whirr of the plane's engines spinning up drills through the splatter of water on the trees around us.

Winter's third skyn.

He's stealing the plane.

In the lake's echo chamber the buzzing engine noise seems to come from everywhere. We're still on the other side of the cabin. We'll never catch him.

"The plane was locked to Siddique's biokin," Bergeron says as we run, her voice furrowed in worry for her partner. "He must have unlocked it or..."

We get up the back steps to the rear of Winter's facility just in time to see the plane's running lights fading into the mist through the cabin's big triangular windows. The engines rev higher as it makes a left turn out toward the open water and disappears.

There's a pile of something lying on the dock. It could be Siddique, but I can't tell in the dark.

"*Siddique!*" Bergeron cries, pulls the cabin's rear door open, and sloshes muddy footprints over the bare concrete as she races toward her partner.

Galvan moves to follow her but I grab his arm.

"The hopper," I say, and tug him back the way we came. "Winter's in the plane, we have to stay on him."

He resists. "Officer Siddique is hurt," Galvan counters in his best Standards Agent voice. "We're duty bound to help a fellow officer." He tries to shake free of my grip but I tighten my hold on his arm.

"We're going to lose him. He gets away now and we'll never find him."

"The hopper's locked—" he starts, then looks past me to Wintergrace. "Can you get us access?"

She blinks, nods. "I think so, if I'm in it with you."

"Dammit," Galvan says, but turns and we once again head into the rain toward the garage.

It only takes thirty seconds to get back there, but we're already drenched, and running in wet clothes feels like moving in slow motion. The plane's engines are getting louder and fainter at the same time as the increased revving gets further away.

We get to the hopper and Wintergrace climbs into the back while I do my best to brush the shattered glass away and then drop into the passenger seat.

Galvan pulls Winter's skyn away from the pilot door and climbs in. "Get us in the sky," he says.

Wintergrace is puzzled for a moment but then seems to remember what she's supposed to do and says, "Go for takeoff."

The hopper's doors seal and the already-whirring

turbines engage, begin to kick up dust in the enclosed garage. Rain drenches the windscreen in a widening line as the roof slides apart. The hopper tilts slightly as it leaves contact with the ground, then lunges up into the sky.

There's a thump from the back and Wintergrace lets out a startled yelp, then clambers back into her seat and fumbles for the restraints.

"Now access manual flight controls," Galvan says, "and release them to me."

"*How?*" Wintergrace says as she finally clicks herself into the straps. We've stopped rising and are hovering about thirty feet up, just above the tree line. Rain lashes in at me through the broken window.

The SQ plane is ahead of us, barely visible in the downpour, already off the water and lifting into the sky. "Just say it!" Galvan orders.

"'Access manual flight control?'" Wintergrace says, flustered.

The hopper's dash reconfigures with the control panel and readouts, all locked in red. "That action requires verbal authentication," it demands.

"It's given," Wintergrace says. "Granted?"

The controls turn green and the flight stick swings down between Galvan's knees. He grabs the stick, leans it forward, then pushes the throttle as hard as it'll go.

We kick into motion, skim over the trees, shoot past the cabin, and see Bergeron racing across the dock toward Siddique. Winter's already above us and rising fast.

"We need to catch him," I yell over the roar of wind rushing in the cabin.

"What do you think I'm trying to do?" Galvan snaps back. "Hang on." He pulls back on the stick to gain altitude, and we start to rise after Winter. We're closing on him, but not fast enough.

Low tones sound and a warning flashes across the dash. Galvan is riding the engines to the hopper's safety limits, but this is a top-of-the-line unit. It'll go faster than this.

Just then Bergeron calls over the comm, panicked. "Siddique's not here, just some of his wet clothes—there's blood though, he could be hurt."

Shit. Winter took Siddique. One more reason we can't let that plane get away.

"Access safety protocols," I say, and a portion of the controls refigure to the safety panel. "Disable engine governors."

"That action is not recommended," the hopper chides.

"Do it," Wintergrace says from the back. "Authorized."

"Bypassing system safety protocols voids all warranties, and indemnifies SkyLift Inc. and its subsidiaries from legal recourse for any consequential injuries or damage. Please confirm."

"For heaven's sake," Wintergrace huffs. "Would you just do what you're told?"

The hopper status readouts return as the safeties disengage. The engine whine steps up an octave as Galvan demands even more from them, but we're gaining faster now. Hopefully we'll catch Winter before the engines burn themselves out.

We're closing, looks like we'll be able to intercept him, but what then?

Wintergrace is thinking the same thing I am. "How are we supposed to make him land once we catch up?" she asks.

"Get above him and use the hopper to force him down," I suggest.

Galvan laughs like he's clearing his throat. "Sometimes it's amazing to me they let you be a police officer," he says.

"Sure, that'll get Winter out of the sky, and the rest of us with him."

He has a point. "What's your plan then, Special Agent?"

Galvan doesn't respond for a minute as the hopper closes on the rising plane. We're nearly on him, and the long watery stem of the orchid is still below us. If we want to get Siddique down safely, we've got maybe a kilometer of water left to do it. Much further than that, the only place to land will be the trees. A high-speed landing into the forest will shred that plane and everything in it to ribbons.

"Give me your weapon," I say to Galvan. "I'll shoot out the engine. Winter will have no choice but to land."

Galvan looks at me, then at the plane's tail ahead of us. He knows as well as I do it's probably the best chance we've got, but still he hesitates, opens a short-range comm channel to the plane instead.

"There's nowhere to run, Alister," Galvan says. "We terminated your other skyns. Put the plane back down and maybe you make it out of this."

"That won't work," Wintergrace says. "He'll never give himself up."

The plane doesn't change course.

Galvan exhales, long and slow, then says, "Everyone buckle in." He swings the hopper to the right, putting the plane on our left, and forces even more power to the screaming engines. "Take the stick and hold it steady," he says to me, and the flight control on my side drops down. I grab it and hold it as still as I can while Galvan overrides the safeties and slides his door open. The hopper bucks to the left, the sudden wind resistance pulling us off course, and I fight to keep us steady. The drag from the open door is slowing us down, and the plane is pulling away once again.

It's a tough shot and getting tougher; if Galvan's going to take the engines out, he doesn't have much time left.

He gets his weapon out and levels it at the plane's engines, aiming to disable while still allowing Winter to make a crash landing. He steadies his aim and squeezes the trigger and misses. The plane keeps accelerating away from us.

He fires again and nothing, curses under his breath, wipes the water from his face and fires twice in quick succession. These shots hit high on the right wing but the plane doesn't slow. Another second and it'll be too far away. We'll have to close the door and race to catch up, and that won't give enough room for Winter to set down before the lake ends.

Galvan grits his teeth and squeezes the trigger again, then again and again and again. The first two bullets miss but we hit a pocket of turbulence on the second two and they go wild, tear holes in the plane's tail. The plane hitches then plummets, dropping far too quickly for Winter to control.

"No!" Galvan yells and yanks the hopper door shut. He retakes the controls from me and sets us into a steep dive, following the plane.

There's nothing we can do but watch the plane fall toward the water. It's able to glide somewhat, and Winter keeps the nose up, but it hits the water with a crunch, skips once, then tilts too far to the left and the wing catches the water and shears off, sending the plane cartwheeling. The nose slams into the black surface as the plane whirls into pieces.

It comes to rest missing a wing, half submerged and sinking. I'll be amazed if anyone survived that crash, and if they did they only have a few minutes before the craft sinks

completely. Galvan swoops us down and sets us in a hover
five meters above the surface of the lake. No one's moving
below. I haven't seen anyone swim free, but it's too dark out
here to see much of anything. Galvan snaps the landing
lights on, illuminating the wreckage through the streaming
rain.

"Does anyone see anything?" Galvan asks, scanning the
windows and the cameras, looking for signs of life below.

We can't see anything from up here. I slide my door
open and Galvan has time to say, "What the hell are you—"
before I slip out of the hopper and force my mouth to stay
closed as I hit the frigid water feet first.

I'm under for only a second, but the cold and black and
the rain and the hopper kicking up whitecaps are all immediately disorienting. I get my head above the water and look
back up, squinting through the frigid spray. Galvan's
leaning out of the hopper and he's yelling something I can't
hear above the turbines, so I just give him a wave and swim
over to the plane.

It's starting to list further now as it takes on water. I still
haven't seen anyone surface, which means I need to get in
there. I take a deep breath and I'm about to duck under and
find a way into the cockpit when there's a heavy splash
behind me. I twirl in the water, expecting to see Galvan's
face bobbing behind me, and find Wintergrace instead.
She's got her hands—binders still attached—churning water
in front of her.

What the hell does she think she's doing?

My first thought is she's been playing us. She's been
Winter this whole time and now she's taken this opportunity to finish me off. But I quickly dismiss the idea. What's
she going to do with her hands cuffed?

"We need to get that officer out of there," Wintergrace

sputters as she tries to keep her head above water. "You'll need help."

"Your hands are—" I say, then cut myself off. No time to argue. Instead I wave up to Galvan, cross my arms at the wrists, and point to Wintergrace. He can disable the binders from up there.

It's a risk, this could all be part of a ruse, but I don't get the sense Wintergrace is lying to us. Still, I don't have time to wait while Galvan makes up his mind. I get up close to the starboard window and peer through. The cockpit still has air, and the emergency lights show someone seated at the controls and someone else strapped into one of the rear seats, but I can't make out who's who, and neither of them are moving.

The plane is tilted over onto its port side. Opening this door would release the air trapped inside and that'll put a quick end to any rescue attempt. Winter's Cortex might survive a trip to the bottom of the lake until the divers show up to retrieve it, but Siddique won't. If I can get around to the underside though, I can get that door open and slide in like a moon pool on a submersible.

I check in with Wintergrace. Galvan still hasn't released her binders. She's taken hold of the side of the fuselage and is staring up at the hopper, waiting should Galvan decide to free her hands.

I don't have time to wait, I need to get into the plane now. I suck in a breath and duck my head under the churning waves, dive down and swim along the bobbing fuselage.

After the torrent above, underwater everything's eerily quiet. The hopper's landing lights offer some illumination, but not much, and the underside of the plane is in shadow. My skyn has pretty good night vision, and I'm able to find the emergency door release—a short handle in the side of the aircraft I need to pull out and down—but I can't get the right leverage to unlatch it.

My lungs are starting to burn with the effort when I sense someone beside me—Wintergrace. Galvan must have released her binders because she gets her hands alongside mine and we pull together. At first I don't think even the two of us will budge it, but the lever releases all at once and I'm able to pull the door's handle and slide it aside, opening the plane to the bottom of the lake.

I swim up into the cockpit and fill my straining lungs with air. Wintergrace pops up beside me a second later.

The interior lights are dimming, but there's enough to see by. Siddique is unconscious, strapped into one of the rear seats, wearing only his underwear and a bloodstained t-shirt. There's a dark hole in his lower abdomen. He must have stripped his wet clothes off when we told him the countdown was a false alarm, and didn't have time to change into anything else before Winter jumped him. He's breathing but his lips are blue. He needs medical attention immediately—if blood loss doesn't get him, the hypothermia will.

Winter's in the front seat, his skyn an off-the-shelf model that'd draw no attention. He could have slipped away into any town in the Union and no one would have known who or what he was. The restraints are still strapped across his chest, and he remains immobile as I inch closer. He waits until I'm right beside him, then his head raises and he coughs out a laugh.

"I have you now," he says, and laughs again, a clicking sound that contains no humor at all. I check Winter up and down, making sure he doesn't have a weapon, but he's unarmed, and not going anywhere. The nose of the plane has compressed down across his lap, trapping his legs. No way he's getting out of here without the Jaws of Life.

"Is this what you wanted?" Wintergrace asks from behind me. She's got Siddique free, ready to get him to the surface. "All the pain you caused, all the people you deceived. Was it worth it?"

Winter snaps his head around and sees his former skyn, no longer in his control. The smile falls from his face. "No—" he mutters. "Am I—?"

"Still in here with me?" Wintergrace finishes. "Yes. You're still here, we all are. But you have no power anymore. *You're* part of *me* now. That's what you wanted, wasn't it?"

"I didn't *want* any of it," Winter yells. "I was made this way—" he pounds his head with the side of his fist, "it wasn't up to me."

"I know you," Wintergrace counters. "I *am* you, and I know that's what you want to believe, but we both know the things you did were more than a compulsion. You *enjoyed* them. You *needed* them."

Winter coughs once more as the plane slips further below the waves. We need to get out of here. I scramble back and take Siddique from Wintergrace.

I know Wintergrace must be filled with questions, but I'm not going to stick around to chat. My fingers are numb and my feet well on their way. Even once we get to the surface we'll still be trapped in the middle of a frigid lake with an unconscious and injured man. We're not out of this yet, not even close.

"I'm getting out of here," I say to Wintergrace. "You coming?"

She looks between me and Winter, then says, "I'm right behind you."

I'm not about to argue, in ten seconds we're all gonna be at the bottom of the lake.

I grab Siddique under his arms and slip under the water, dragging him behind me, leaving Winter and Wintergrace inside. It only takes a few seconds to get clear of the wreckage and back to the rippling surface. I hold Siddique under my arms, tilt his head back to keep his airway open, and kick my legs to keep us afloat.

Siddique is bleeding, his warmth seeping from his stomach into the cold water. He's bleeding out and I can't do anything for him. It's all I can do to keep us afloat, the cold lake water is sapping my strength by the second.

A gurgle of air belches to the surface and the plane sinks faster. The fuselage slips below the waves and Galvan swings the hopper out of the way of the rising tail. There's still no sign of Wintergrace.

The aircraft is nearly gone, lost below the waves as I back paddle, trying to keep us out of the path of any potential debris that might snag us on the way down. Galvan hovers above us, keeping us in the landing lights. There's no way he can get the hopper close enough to the lake's surface for us to be able to climb in. With the rain and the spray the turbines kick up, he's risking another crash. I need to find my own way out.

We're floating in the middle of a narrow lake, but I can barely make out the shore. It's probably only a hundred and fifty meters away, but that's still a long swim dragging an unconscious man, and I'm already exhausted from the cold. I can feel my body succumbing to the shock. I don't know if I can make it, but I don't have much choice.

I take a few deep breaths and start backwards toward the lake's edge, pulling Siddique after me. I haven't gotten far when three objects break the surface in quick succession. For an instant I think it's Winter, that he's somehow freed himself and is coming to drag us down, but I realize they're life jackets and a plastic container of some kind. A survival kit, from the looks of it.

Then Wintergrace emerges, spluttering and coughing, a solemn look on her face.

"What happened?" I yell as she helps me get Siddique into one of the jackets and we start off toward shore, Galvan lighting the way.

"He finally got what he wanted," Wintergrace says as we drag Siddique behind us through the water. "A quiet mind."

WE SURVIVE THE NIGHT.

Galvan finds a narrow stretch of beach on the water's edge to squeeze the hopper onto, and we strip off our wet clothes, bundle up in blankets, and get Siddique back to Winter's cabin to stabilize him with the emergency gear from the survival package Wintergrace freed from the sinking plane. With the plane's radio at the bottom of the lake, and the hopper's long-range comm useless without a link connection, we're unable to call for help. We spend the night huddled in the cabin, but when Bergeron's scheduled check-in doesn't come through, the SQ sends the cavalry.

Dawn is just starting to warm in the sky as the misty lake in front of Winter's cabin becomes a busy runway, with two floatplanes and an old pontoon plane landing in quick succession. They come in hot, and when they see we're not in any danger, they immediately take over the scene. Galvan doesn't even pull rank, that's how tired he is.

They pack Siddique into one of the planes, turn it around, and fly for the nearest hospital, Bergeron with him. We offer our thanks for her help and while she's courteous with her goodbyes, I can tell she'd be happy to never to see us again. That leaves Galvan and me to answer the flurry of questions about what happened, and why a wanted mass murderer is sitting uncuffed between us.

Standards shows up next, and then Agent Wiser gets back to business. He directs them to search the premises, and they find an oProc server cube in a sealed crawl space under the cabin, presumably containing further backups of Winter's rithm, then he calls in divers to search the lake for his remaining skyn. They'll find him eventually. Not too soon, I hope. The thought of him trapped on the bottom of the lake—aware but helpless in the cold blackness—is the only bright spot in this whole ordeal. They should leave him down there forever. Let him suffer in complete emptiness, trapped in a rotting body with nothing but his tortured thoughts to keep him company until the battery reserves in his Cortex finally give out. I don't imagine Standards would go for that though.

I stay put for all of this, keep out of the way, sitting on the floor in damp underwear, wrapped in blankets next to Wintergrace.

She's been quiet since we returned, dutifully answering questions and submitting to a series of pattern scans, but otherwise keeping her thoughts to herself. Now that the excitement is all over, now that she's had time to think, I bet there's a lot on her mind.

It isn't until Galvan has everyone busy scouring the place for evidence that he comes back over to deal with us.

"We're almost done here," Galvan says. "We'll be heading out soon."

"What's going to happen to me?" Wintergrace asks, her striking elven skyn now in complete contrast to her composed demeanor.

Galvan tightens his lips. Technically she's a walking Standards violation, but a rare one—she's a stable polyneural. No longer just Winter, but an inseparable amalgam of Winter and Grace and who knows how many others, so who does that make her—the innocent grassr girl she was when Winter stole her mind, or the murderer who did all those terrible things leading up to that? She's the product of a crime, yes, and an affront to everything Human Standards is tasked with maintaining, but she's also a victim —they can't terminate her or throw her mind in a stock...can they?

"We have to take you in," Galvan says, but he seems conflicted about it. "For now at least, until the courts can figure out what to do with you."

"You can't," I object. "She isn't Winter, she hasn't done anything wrong. If anything, she helped us catch him."

Galvan throws up his hands, looks back at Wintergrace. "I don't necessarily disagree, but you're an unregistered pattern wearing the skyn of a serial killer—we have to bring you in. This will be all over the feeds, optics alone require it. You'll be at the center of a controversy that throws every-thing we believe about the inviolability of the human mind into question. I can't say what's going to happen, but I know it won't be quick or pretty."

I know he's right but that doesn't mean I have to like it. I open my mouth to argue but Wintergrace interrupts me before I can speak.

"I'm willing to do whatever's required," Wintergrace says. "And if that means I must be punished for my crimes, then I accept that as well."

"But they aren't your crimes," I say. This is all hitting a little too close to home. If Ankur hadn't orchestrated an alibi for all the things Deacon did, I'd be right where Grace is right now. "You didn't do anything wrong. You just ended up the big winner of a bunch of bad memories. They can't hold you responsible."

"In my heart I know that's true," Wintergrace says. "But I can remember everything he did, like it happened to me, like I was the one killing those people. If I can remember it, how am I not responsible?"

"You didn't ask for this," I say, defending her—and justifying my own actions in the process.

Wintergrace grows solemn. "Yes I did. I invited him in. In my hubris, I believed I could save him."

There's no point in arguing any more. Her mind's made up.

"You have to help her," I say to Galvan.

"I'll do what I can," Galvan promises, and helps Wintergrace to her feet. "The Standards rithmists will want to scan you, but now that polyneural rights are before the courts, I don't think they'll be able to shut you down or force you to open your mind for examination. I can already see your pattern is differentiated enough from Winter's that perhaps we'll be able to make an argument you're not *him*. Who knows, this is uncharted territory for everyone. But one thing's for sure—there'll be more like you before long."

"I knew the Lord had a purpose for me," Wintergrace says with a wan smile. "I would have preferred something more traditional, but who am I to question God's plans?"

"Time to go," Galvan says, and leads Wintergrace out of the cabin and down to the dock, where a float plane is waiting. I let them get in first and start to climb in but Galvan holds up his hand. "Sorry, I can't have you riding with a prisoner," he says, and I can tell he isn't at all sorry to be leaving me behind. "I've arranged for you to get a ride back to Montréal with the SQ. Someone should be leaving in the next few hours. You can find your own way home from there. See you around, Finsbury."

He pulls the door closed and motions for the pilot to head out. As I watch them pull into the lake and speed away across the water and up into the air, I can't help but think about how Winter and Grace ended up together, integrated as a single mind. Maybe hiding from Deacon isn't the right way to deal with him.

It hasn't worked so far, he's only getting stronger.

I can't run from him anymore. Maybe it's time to get some help, which means I need to let someone into my head.

Dammit.

CODA_

WINTER'S END

"WHAT IN GOOD Christ did you do to your rithm?" Vae says, studying the representation of my pattern she has up on her wall.

"I didn't know you were religious," I quip, trying to mask the tension I'm feeling in my gut. It took a couple of days after I got back to Toronto, but I finally gave in and called Vaelyn to ask for her help. I didn't tell her much, just that I was having problems with my head and didn't want to take them to Second Skyn. She wasn't as immediately testy this time, and told me to come by so she could have a look.

I already knew this, but seeing my mind all messed up on the screen makes it real in a way I didn't accept until just now. What should normally be a healthy sphere of light surrounded by a shifting aura of thought flickering like ball lightning, is instead a lopsided oval with bright concentrations above and one below—one me, and the other Deacon. The exterior of the pattern is spiky and ragged, with black filaments pulsing throughout. It's like seeing an MRI of the tumor that's killing you.

She laughs. "With fragmentation like this? I don't know

what the hell's keeping your pattern stable, but God's as good an answer as anything I got." She shakes her head at me and smiles like my shattered mind has somehow got her impressed. "You should be a gibbering mess on the floor right now, you know that? I've seen hardcore habitual shyfters with years of heavy use who have less decoherence than you do."

"I'm an overachiever," I say.

"No shit," she agrees. She points to the concentration of light at the bottom of the pattern. It's shifting and churning like a normal rithm would, if a bit misshapen. "This is you." Then she points to the second concentration, the one above. "This is—"

"I've been calling him Deacon," I tell her.

"You gave it a name?" she asks, more amused than ever.

"I have to call him something." I shrug.

"No, you don't," she says, but then continues. "This is another active rithm." She indicates the ovoid between us. "Two personalities sharing a core set of memories. You're a polyneural, but only in the loosest sense. Not so much conjoined as attempting to crowd each other out. What a mess."

"You said that—"

"It's a goddamn understatement," she adds. "Your pattern is unstable. Eventually it'll collapse and that'll be the end of both of you."

That's what I was afraid of. "Is there anything you can do?"

She shrugs. "I'm good at this, but shit. Why don't you just restore yourself? You must have a clean backup."

"One," I admit.

She sucks in a breath. "How much time would you lose?"

"All of it," I admit.

"You only have your initial reference point?" she asks, incredulous. "From when you first died? Shit, Finsbury, that's irresponsible in a startlingly badass way. You really are fucked, you know that?"

That's just what I wanted to hear. I move to get up. "Thanks anyway—"

"Whoa there," she says, her tone mollifying. "Sit your pretty ass back down. It might take me a bit, but ol' Vae will sort something out. I can likely whip up a shyft that'll keep that Deacon of yours suppressed while I try to finagle some way to separate you."

"What about integrating us?" I ask, not sure I want to hear the answer.

She looks at me out of the corner of her eye. "That what you really want?"

I shake my head. "But if there's no other option."

"Let's keep that as a last resort," she says. "In the mean-time, why don't you go downstairs and make yourself comfortable while I poke around in your mind for a while, see what I can see."

"Fine," I say, "but stay out of the private stuff."

"No promises," she says with a smirk and gets back to teasing my rithm apart.

I get up, keeping her cuff attached to my neck, and go downstairs to see what's in her fridge while she performs exploratory surgery on my mind.

It's not an ideal situation, but it's better than hiding. Better than putting myself back on ice.

Now that I'm back out in the world, I'd kinda like to stay a while.

I just hope being out here doesn't kill me.

Words and terms from the world of Lost Time.

AMP. *(Artificial Mind Pattern)* Advanced
neural code approximations running on
cortical processors. They are classified
as superintelligences but their use is
governed and their operating code
secured. Only licensed government
agencies and select corporations are
allowed to employ AMPs. The Ministry
of Human Standards is responsible for
monitoring and tracking down illicit use
whenever discovered.

BioSkyn. *An artificial, lab-grown body.
Components printed a layer of cells at a
time and then assembled and implanted
with an optical processing Cortex.*

Biosynth. *Someone who uses geneblocks*

to assemble unique, life forms—bacteria
capable of operating to order to create
atomically precise circuitry,
manufacture drugs, enhance the
immune system or replace biological
functions. Plants that grow directly into
furniture. Or wholly fabricated animals
for domestic or military uses.

Bit-head. Xero. Sudo. Derogatory slang for
a restored personality.

Bright. An extropian, far leftist, digital
human philosophy. Brights believe in a
creator of the Universe—or 'the
system'—and that humanity is one of a
billion billion probable physical
manifestations of rules that began to
play out at the moment of creation. God
didn't create us, but it allowed the
conditions for us to exist, like a scientist
fine-tuning an experiment, and
humanity its results.

Continuance of Personality Act. The
set of legal guarantees allowing for the
transfer of a consciousness from organic
to digital.

Cortex. Second Skyn's in-house neural
prosthetic. Now common slang for any
neural prosthetic.

Cortical Field. The composite image of a
scanned consciousness. Since
consciousness is stored holographically,
the stronger the field, the stronger the
fidelity to the original personality.

Cypher. *A rithm without an official restoration record from the Ministry of Human Standards.*

Digital Life Extension. *Extending a human consciousness past brain death as a psychorithm. The personality is captured, translated to a psychorithm and the resulting rithm loaded onto a prosthetic mind implanted in a bioSkyn. The Continuance of Personality Act provides digital humans with all the legal rights of a fully organic human, while Human Standards laws limit the extent to which digital humanity can augment its existence. DLE is fraught with political and social turbulence.*

Dwell. *A simple shyft that allows the user to speed up or slow down stored memory playback.*

Fate. *The rapidly growing corporation bringing immortality to the masses and hiring out low-cost knowledge work, all while reducing governmental expenditures around the globe.*

Fleshmith. *Someone who uses modified geneblocks and scaflabs to produce designer bodies and organs.*

Genitect. *Someone who architects and encodes custom geneblocks, the genetic code building blocks used to form the genomes of synthetic life forms.*

Headspace. *A digital human's customizable home running onboard their prosthetic brain.*

The Hereafter. *The brand-name of a virtual reflection of the real world, where digital humans can visit the living. It is the largest, and most populous, digital virt.*

Human Standards. *The legal baselines limiting human life extension, physical augmentation and neural enhancement.*

IMP. *(Intelligent Mediating Personality) Originally designed to assist with daily communication, the IMP's capabilities quickly expanded to become a full-fledged digital assistant that learns over time. Upgradable with personality sprites.*

The Link. *The worldwide stream of conversations, sensor data, cameras, feeds, virts, games, and everything else that arose from the internet.*

Lost Time. *The minutes or hours of memory between personality back-ups lost due to a pattern decoherence or Cortex damage.*

Lowboys. *A gang of low-rep petty criminals. Kids, mostly.*

Ministry of Human Standards. *The government agency tasked with enforcing Human Standard laws.*

Neurohertz. *(NHz or N) 1 N is the*

average speed of human neural
processing. Human Standards limit the
function of prosthetic brains to $1.15N$.

Past-Standard. The only Human
Standard criminal offense. Past-
Standard encompasses everything
related to genetic augmentation and
manipulation of a mind or body past
established human norms. Past-
Standard Offense and Psychorithm
Infractions often intersect, causing
friction between investigating
agencies.

Prodeo/Prodian. What digital-only
personalities against the restrictive
Human Standard laws call themselves:
Homo Prodeo. From the Latin "prodeo":
to go forward, and "pro Deo": 'before' and
'the supreme being.'

Psychorithm. The Conscious Algorithm.
The human brain's self-sustaining,
recursive algorithmic neural code
translated into digital.

Psychorithm Crime Unit. The Toronto
Police Services unit responsible for
investigating crimes by and against the
local Reszo population.

Psyphon. To extract a rithm from its
Cortex by force.

Recovered. A psychorithm is recovered
from a dying or unhealthy brain and
imprinted onto a cortical field.

ReJuv. *The genetic reset performed once a year through the intravenous injection of a gene-regulating cocktail.*

Rep. *The cumulative social reputation earned by a personality on the link. Also known as Social Faith.*

Restored. *Layering a recovered cortical field onto a prosthetic brain. Also a common identifier for a digital human.*

Reszo. *Slang for a restored personality.*

Revv. *A shyft that allows the user to bypass human-standard neural governors and run their rithm higher into the NHz range. The effects are limited only by the hardware.*

Rithmist. *Someone who hacks the psychorithm. From manipulating autonomous and emotional responses all the way to enhancing or creating new cognitive abilities.*

Second Skyn. *The global leader in digital life extension. In defiance of global courts, Second Skyn opened its first facility in a small South-East Asian country that had more pressing concerns than enforcing soon-to-be-outdated UN cloning laws. Once Personality Rights legislation was enacted, Second Skyn formally opened in Toronto, Stockholm, Seoul and Dubai, then expanded around the world as demand grew.*

Skyn. *Slang for bioSkyn.*

Scafe. *An illegally copied or hastily created skyn.*

SecNet. *The interconnected web of cameras, sensors, and databases that comprise the backbone of the North American Union's security and surveillance infrastructure.*

Shyft. *Slang for Neuroshyft. General consumer term for a neural state overlay. One-time-use code snippets legally sold to temporarily simulate drunkenness, enhance pleasure, dampen fear, or one of a thousand other emotional flavors. Much more powerful illegal versions also exist.*

StatUS. *Formerly a governmental organization, StatUS was spun off as a private company and is now responsible for providing and maintaining identification for all Union citizens and visitors.*

Veat. In vitro meat. *Meat products generated from cultured animal cells.*

ABOUT THE AUTHOR_

I'm a geek from way back. I grew up on Star Wars and Blade Runner and Green Lantern and Neuromancer and every other science fiction and fantasy book I could get my hands on.

I wanted to write for as long as I can remember. My first story was a Moonlighting fan fiction, though I didn't know that at the time. Back then I was just ripping off a TV show.

Thanks for reading. If it weren't for you, I wouldn't be able to keep doing this.

I'd love to hear from you. Email me at damien@damien-boyes.com, or come say "Hi" on Facebook, or sign up to my Reader Club for the occasional email treat.

Printed in Great Britain
by Amazon

38959802R00225